Praise for The Myth Adventure Series

"Asprin's major achievement as a writer—brisk pacing, wit, and a keen satirical eye. Breezy, pun-filled fantasy in the vein of Piers Anthony's *Xanth* series"—ALA *Booklist*

"A hilarious bit of froth and frolic. Asprin has a fine time with the story. So will the reader."—*Library Journal*

"Witty, humorous, a pleasant antidote to ponderous fantasy."—*Amazing*

"The novels by Asprin are loads of fun, extremely enjoyable humorous fantasy. We really like it."—*The Comic Buyers Guide*

"...an excellent, lighthearted fantasy series..."—*Epic Illustrated*

"An inspired series of magic and hilarity. It's a happy meeting of L. Sprague de Camp and the *Hitchhiker's Guide* trilogy."—*Burlington County Times*

"Humorous adventure fantasy at its rowdiest."—*Science Fiction Chronicle*

"Recommended."—*Fantasy Review*

"All the *Myth* books are hysterically funny."—*Analog*

"This is a fun read and series enthusiasts should enjoy it."—*Kliatt*

"Stuffed with Rowdy fun."—*Philadelphia Inquirer*

"Give yourself the pleasure of working through this series. But not all at once; you'll wear out your funny bone."—*Washington D. C. Times*

"If a reader is searching for sheer reading enjoyment, they need look no further than Robert Asprin."—*SF Digest*

"The Myth Adventure books are modern day classics. Again and again, Robert Asprin proves with effortless skill that he is one of the funniest writers alive today."—Nick Pollotta

CLASS
DIS-MYTHED

Robert Asprin &
Jody Lynn Nye

Meisha Merlin Publishing, Inc.
Atlanta, GA

Class Dis-Mythed

Published by Meisha Merlin Publishing, Inc.
PO Box 7
Decatur, GA 30031

Editing by Stephen Pagel
Copyediting and Proofreading by Easter Editing Services
Interior layout by Lynn Swetz
Cover art and interior illustrations by Phil Foglio
Cover design by Kevin Murphy

ISBN: Hard Cover 1-59222-091-6
ISBN: Soft Cover 1-59222-092-4

http://www.MeishaMerlin.com
First MM Publishing edition: September 2005

Printed in the United States of America
0 9 8 7 6 5 4 3 2 1

CLASS
DIS-MYTHED

Robert Asprin &
Jody Lynn Nye

Chapter One

"It's nice to be wanted."
J. JAMES

A high female voice ventured timidly, "Are you...Aahz?"

I looked up from a half-empty mug, and nearly spat out my mouthful of beer. Gazing down at me in the close confines of the Haggard Sheep Inn in the Bazaar on Deva were three Pervish females wearing trim, two-piece business suits and clutching briefcases tightly to their chests. My first impulse was to sidle away rapidly, keeping my back against the nearest wall. Next to dragons and Trolls, Pervect women are some of the most dangerous creatures in all the dimensions. I ought to know: I was a Pervect male. Our green, scaly skin covered impressively dense and strong muscles, and inside the skull between our batwing-shaped ears lay devious brains capable of following complex lines of analysis, always geared to our own advantage.

The females stared at me, yellow eyes watchful. I had long ago scoped out the exits in every public building within five miles' radius of our headquarters. The back door was fifteen steps behind me behind a curtain. Could I make it before they drew weapons or cast spells?

Guido, a Klahd and former associate with whom I was having a friendly drink, froze, then his hand inched toward the front of his suit coat where he concealed a miniature crossbow. His pinkish-tan skin paled to a buff color. He obviously shared my discomfort, but he wasn't going to let a business partner face a formidable foe alone.

"Who wants to know?" I growled at the three.

But the Pervish females weren't wearing expressions I associated with assassins or bill collectors. In fact, I realized that their suits were in fashionable pastels with short skirts and their satchels were color-coordinated to go with the outfits. At first I thought they must be lawyers. Then I realized how young they were. They weren't professionals. They were school girls.

As if to confirm my analysis, one of them giggled.

"You must be Aahz. You look just like your picture."

The others tittered. I eyed them.

"Where did you see my picture?" I asked.

"Your mother showed it to us," the tallest one replied.

"My *mother?*"

"Your mother?" Guido asked curiously, leaning closer. I waved him back.

"What do you want?" I demanded.

"Well, Aahz…mandius?" the tall one began in a tentative manner.

"Just Aahz," I interrupted tersely. I was aware that all the patrons within five tables, mostly red-skinned Deveels, the natives of this dimension, had stopped drinking and had leaned as close as they could, the better to hear our exchange.

"Aahz, then. We need—This is kind of embarrassing—"

"Then sit down and lower your voices," I advised, beginning to lose patience. I glared at the eavesdroppers, who suddenly remembered they had better things to do.

I gestured at the bench on the other side of the table. With uneasy and distasteful glances, as if they had just picked up on their surroundings, the three females slid onto it.

"Yeah?" I urged them.

They dithered.

"You ask him, Jinetta," said the smallest.

"No, it was Pologne's idea," the tallest said.

"It was not!" the middle one exclaimed.

My species is not easily embarrassed, so whatever was eating these three had to be pretty bad. From birth we Pervects are raised to know we're a superior race throughout the dimensions. Few types are capable of supporting both magik and technology, and Perv has both. We're stronger, faster and smarter than most other dimension travelers, or demons for short, so if that self-knowledge makes us a little arrogant, so be it. Of all the beings in the Bazaar, these three Pervects had come to consult one of their own.

I was becoming bored with the byplay. Cleared my throat meaningfully. The three stopped their bickering and turned to face me.

"Well, Aahz," the tall one began in a perky voice, interlacing her fingers on the table. "I just want you to know from the start that we're not beginners. We're all graduates of MIP."

I raised an eyebrow. The Magikal Institute of Perv was one of our finest seats of higher learning.

"Nice credentials, but so what?"

"Well—" the spokespervect glanced at her companions, "during our education, we took a lot of lab courses and had a couple of remote study opportunities, but really, none of our classes had much of a grounding in the real world."

"Stands to reason," I mused. "Professional academics, the kind who spend their whole lives in universities, don't have a lot of grounding in the real world. And they figure you're going to get plenty of practical experience once you get out. What's this got to do with me?"

"We need practical education," the most petite of the Pervects said. "Right away."

"We're looking for a course of intensive study," the tallest picked up the talking-stick again. "About six weeks. We consulted many, many people as to who the best possible tutor in any dimension would be to give us instruction, someone who would understand the really important issues of survival in the real world of magik. Only one name kept coming up again and again, including here in the Bazaar on Deva…"

I preened. I didn't realize that my name was still one to conjure with, so to speak. I eased back in my seat and rolled my mug around between my fingers.

"So you three sweet young things want me to teach you the ins and outs of practical magik?" I purred.

"No!" the three chorused. "We need you to help us find the Great Skeeve!"

"What?" I roared, slamming down my stein.

"Well, you're his partner, aren't you?" the tallest one asked in surprise, flicking the beer stains off her frilly blouse with little offhand magikal repulsion. "That's what the Merchants Association told us. They said that you'd be able to tell us where to find him. They said he's off-dimension, leaving no forwarding address, but as his closest associate, you're sure to know where he went."

"WHAT AM I, CHOPPED LIVER?" I bellowed.

The three regarded me blankly.

"I'm sure you're a magician of some skill," the medium-sized one said in placating tones that made my blood pressure blast through the roof.

'Get out of here!" I roared.

"But my Great Aunt Vergetta said that the Great Skeeve is the one we want," the tall one pleaded. "She said he was the best she ever met, the most effective magician in all the dimensions. Her club agreed with her. Lots of people said they've heard the same."

The others nodded earnestly.

I made myself calm down. I knew all about Skeeve's run-in with Vergetta and her Pervect Ten, a cabal of Pervish females with interlocking talents. I wasn't surprised Skeeve's reputation had gone so far. I had gone through a lot of blood, sweat, tears and expense to help spread that reputation around the dimensions. I also knew the true extent of his talents behind that reputation. Most of what Skeeve knew he had learned from me or the late magician Garkin, or picked up on the fly during one of our missions. He'd gotten by on native smarts, dumb luck, his own magikal ability and a little help from his friends. I wondered privately whether as a Klahd he could live long enough to really master the Arts Magikal. I wasn't going to subject him to humiliation from these three. Advanced degrees from MIP meant these three had gone through six years of the toughest professors and the best training in any dimension. Once they found out they were that far ahead of him, they'd tear him apart.

"Forget it." I hoisted my mug and drained it.

"Please!" the shortest one begged.

I slammed the empty stein on the table and planted my palms firmly on either side of it. "Can't you take 'no' for an answer? Get out of here before I rip your heads off!"

The Pervects weren't put off.

The medium-sized one leaned forward imploringly. "Please, just tell us where we can find him?"

"He's on sabbatical, and I'm not going to let you interrupt him on some whim. Go enroll in summer school."

"This is important!" the smallest one said.

"So are his studies," I snarled. "Forget it, I said."

"But we're willing to pay him," the tallest one said.

"He doesn't need it." I crossed my arms. I had recently gone to a lot of trouble to make sure Skeeve wasn't going to be disturbed for as long as he wanted to stay out of touch, and there was nothing these three fashion plates could say to change my mind.

"We really need his help," the tallest one pleaded. "We have GOT to learn how to survive—"

"Shh!" the other two shushed her.

"If you'd just let us talk to him," the smallest one said, fluttering her green-scaled eyelids. "Then he'd understand why we need his help."

"Sorry you wasted your time, ladies," I said. I turned my shoulder on them. The interview was over. I signalled for a refill. The bartender's potboy hustled over with a gallon jug, and slopped a quantity into our glasses. I took a casual swig.

"So, Guido, you try out that new Djinni restaurant yet?"

The Mob enforcer kept a weather eye on our visitors, but he gritted out a reply. "Too spicy for me. I like to keep the enamel on my teeth."

The Pervects drifted off the bench, but they didn't go far. They stood there in the middle of the grimy old pub like a fresh lick of paint on a garbage wagon, a neon sign to pickpockets and muggers that here were three easy victims. Anyone with half an eye could tell they needed some practical advice, but that wasn't my problem. Not really. But I did give a glare to the unsavory elements hanging around in the room to make sure they knew these females weren't to be picked on, even if they were as clueless as newborn kittens. With my luck they'd get creamed in the next bar fight, and I'd have to deal with locals who thought MAYBE Pervects weren't so tough after all.

They were still moaning. I didn't care. Skeeve's privacy wasn't going to be interrupted for a trio of coddled fashion plates.

"What are we going to do?" the tallest one wailed. "We won't be prepared! After my parents put me through MIP at a cost of 5,000 gold pieces a semester, I can't find a lousy tutor when it's a life-and-death matter? My parents would have paid *anything* to get the Great Skeeve!"

I pointedly hadn't been paying close attention to their conversation, but my keen hearing had picked up the words "thousand gold pieces." They had me from there on.

"You like Djinni food?" Guido asked me.

I held up a finger to put his question on hold.

"HOW much did MIP cost?" I asked the tall Pervect.

"*Five thousand*," the Pervect repeated, turning toward me. Her eyes were bright gold with unshed tears. "A semester. Plus books and equipment. Plus housing and activity tickets and my allowance—more than fifteen thousand a year!"

I couldn't see it, but I knew the little green-for-greed light had just gone off over my head.

"Sit down, ladies," I purred. "You know, maybe the Great Skeeve could make a little time to help you. If the price was right."

"Y'know, Aahz, the Boss said he don't want—"

"Give the ladies a chance, Guido," I interrupted smoothly, cutting off his protest. I didn't want to blow what suddenly had turned into a potential earner. My inner cash register was playing "We're In The Money" with a brass band and a full chorus. These were trust-fund babies or better. They perched on the bench, looking hopeful.

"Well, you know," I began, "the Great Skeeve don't work cheap. He is the best, and he expects fees according to his skills. And status."

The great-niece nodded. "Auntie Vergetta said we could expect that. How much would he want?"

"Well, the fees have to support our company's efforts," I said innocently, forestalling a squawk from Guido. "To carry on his efforts for the greater good. How about, say, five hundred a week?"

The three smiled with relief.

"Total?" the tallest one asked.

"Each."

"No way!" the middle one protested.

"Take it or leave!" I roared. "The Great Skeeve doesn't deal with pikers!"

"No, no!" the smallest one said. "How about three hundred each?"

I grinned. Now the dealing was going the way I liked it.

Chapter Two

"How would teaching get anyone in trouble?"
SOCRATES

"Skeeve, stop it!" Bunny ordered me, exasperation plain on her pretty face. "They're too pink!"

"Are you sure?" I asked. I stopped adding color and stood back to get a better look at my illusion spell.

"Yes, I'm sure! They're Klahds, not Imps!"

I peered at the image. It issued from Bunny's Perfectly Darling Assistant, or PDA, Bytina, a palm-sized clam-shell of brushed red metal, and had been blown up by me with a touch of magik to cover the surrounding walls, covering the peeling paint and worn woodwork of the old inn. Striking poses in a copse of fake hazel trees were several beings wearing elegant clothing that seemed out of both time and place. From what I could tell by the old-fashioned phrases they were spouting, the male wearing the cross-gartered hose was pledging eternal devotion to the young female with long braids and a dress so tightly bodiced that every breath drew my—attention. An older male in a long houppelande and a twisty turban, the female's father, was against the union. They were Klahds, members of my own race. Honesty forced me to admit they *were* more fuchsia than the usual Klahdish varegations of pale beige through dark brown. Reluctantly, I mentally unreeled some of the rainbow I'd fed into the picture. Bunny tapped her foot impatiently.

"How about now?" I inquired.

"Not yet."

"How about now?"

"No."

"How about now?"

"No."

"Now?"

"No."

"*Now?*"

"No! Yes," Bunny amended suddenly. Her shoulders relaxed. "Good. Now, make their heads smaller."

"Bunny, they look fine!" I argued. "You can see their expressions better this way."

She redoubled the exasperation and aimed it straight at me. I turned back to my handiwork and studied it. I had to admit she was right again. The people did have the aspect of lollipops on sticks. At the time I had thought it was advantageous, since the last time I'd been to a play the actors were so far away from me I could never tell who was emoting about what. Once I reduced the proportions to normal it seemed as though a crowd was standing in the room of the old inn with us. I liked the effect. I noticed that the backdrop they were standing in front of looked more unrealistic than ever.

"I could improve the scenery," I offered, raising my hands with my thumbs together to make a square. "Make it seem like a real forest."

"No, thanks," Bunny shot back.

"Oh, come on," I wheedled. "It'd be a lot better that way."

"No!" Bunny said. "What IS it about men, that they can't stop fiddling with controls for a single moment? I went for a ride with my uncle on that flying carpet he bought in the Bazaar, and he practically rebraided the fringe on one short little ride!"

I retired to the corner, chagrined.

"Well, if you don't need my help any more—" I began.

Bunny smiled sweetly at me. "I didn't need it to start with. But thank you for enlarging the picture. It does make it easier to watch."

She sashayed back to the cushy armchair in the center of the room, now surrounded by the play, already into its second act. She wasn't so hard to watch herself, being a very curvaceous woman the circumference of whose bosom was approximately two thirds of her height and with red hair that was clipped short to draw attention to the silky skin of her cheeks and neck. Don't misunderstand me—I wasn't interested in Bunny romantically. I had once underestimated her because of her looks. She had used them as camouflage to conceal a surprising intelligence, something that we in M.Y.T.H., Inc. came to appreciate more than her family and former associates in the Mob had. She was one of my best friends, someone whose judgment I trusted absolutely. It didn't hurt that she was fun to look at.

I'd been living back in the old inn for a few months, since leaving the other members of M.Y.T.H., Inc. behind in the headquarters we shared in the Bazaar on Deva. Bunny, our company accountant, had agreed to come along with me to act as my assistant and companion in my self-imposed exile on Klah. I had quit the company to study magik—really study, instead of faking it and learning a technique only when I needed it, sometimes almost too late to save our necks. Since the murder of my first master Garkin by an Imp assassin, my education had been taken over by Aahz. That period of my life consisted of one adventure after another, punctuated by emergencies, alarums, excursions, danger, lectures, financial crises, near forced marriages, and complicated political situations.

I had really enjoyed it. Then I had begun to think about my situation. I had been promoted far above my skill level. The time had not yet come when someone called me on it, but I kept waiting for that knock on the door, the one that would herald the coming of a dark, hooded cosmic being who would point a sepulcheral finger at me and proclaim, "You're a phony!" Then Ogres with moving carts would strip everything out of the offices, and I'd be evicted onto the street with my simple belongings wrapped in a handkerchief, while everyone I had ever met laughed at my humble retreat.

All right, maybe I didn't fear exposure, shame and dismissal. I'd been pretty straightforward with my friends and associates about my lack of experience and formal training and understanding of magik, and they had risen to the occasion, stepping in to help me when I couldn't do the job myself. They all had expertise in very different fields, had lived fascinating lives and handled situations I had never dreamed of facing. The person it bothered more than anyone else was me. I stepped away at the optimum time, to give myself a chance to catch up with my position in life, so that when I came back— if I came back—I'd be a worthy associate to my friends.

I had my mission: to turn myself into the wizard that matched the hype. The old inn that Aahz and I had 'inherited' from the madman Istvaan sat at the crossroads of several force lines which I could draw on for nearly limitless power. I had books and scrolls from numerous scholars on approaches to classical magik and access to practitioners in multiple dimensions. While I appreciated Bunny's sacrifice in sharing my exile, I wasn't a fool. I hoped she might become interested in my research, but she had her own life and interests. She was used to a lively existence in the midst of her Mob family (she was Don Bruce's niece) and in M.Y.T.H., Inc. I anticipated that she might become bored having to lie low in what was believed to be a derelict and maybe haunted building in the middle of nowhere in the middle of the woods of Klahd a place that would not attract attention to us. I made sure she knew I would transport her back to Deva or anywhere else whenever she wanted to go. I encouraged her to find entertainment, such as watching the magik pictures that Bytina brought in from the aether. Nor did I rule out visitors, though more for her sake than mine.

As if on cue, a knock came at the door.

"Quick, Skeeve," Bunny whispered, gesturing at Bytina.

I whisked a hand toward the tiny device. The crowd of declaiming actors vanished, and the room fell silent.

Mostly silent. My pet dragon, Gleep, had heard the rapping, and came hurtling into the room.

"Gleep!" he exclaimed.

"Shh!" I said.

I listened carefully. I could hear youthful-sounding female voices just outside the big main door.

"Girls," Bunny said. "I'll take care of it." She gestured at herself.

"See what you think of this illusion," I said. "I saw an illustration in a scroll, and I came up with a really scary variation."

Closing my eyes I superimposed the craggy, blue-tinged face of an ancient hag over Bunny's lovely features. She glanced in the mirror as she passed.

"Yuck."

I grinned, satisfied.

"Gleep!" my pet protested.

"You, too," I whispered. With another moment of concentration, Gleep became a terrible giant bug, a cross between a cockroach and a firefly. My pet gallumphed happily toward the door. I hope he wouldn't scare them too much. I would hate to be responsible for causing nightmares, when all I wanted was my privacy.

Then, the door swung open.

The last thing I had to worry about was that the three girls on the doorstep might be afraid of blue-skinned crones or flyiing cockroaches. They were Pervects.

They regarded Bunny with the disdain that natives of Perv had for most other races, completely unconcerned that live spiders swung from her lank tresses, or that her skin appeared to be peeling before their eyes. Aahz had once said that most Klahds looked alike to him.

The smallest one pointed a thumb over her shoulder. "They said in that little hovel down the road that the Great Skeeve lives here."

"Who wants to know?" Bunny shrilled in a voice like an elderly woman.

"We do," the tallest one replied. "This is Freezia and Pologne. I'm Jinetta. He knows my great-aunt, Vergetta. Can we see him?"

My ears perked up at the name of one of my recent acquaintances. I hurried to the door.

"Hi," I greeted them, holding out a hand to each one. "I'm Skeeve. What can I do for you?"

Pologne glared at me. "*You're* Skeeve?"

"That's me," I said.

My admission seemed to spark the expressions of horror that my illusion spells had not.

"This?" Freezia demanded of Jinetta. "*This* is the Great Skeeve your aunt was so impressed by? This skinny little Klahd? We've been had!"

"No, no, I really am Skeeve," I protested. I glanced past them to see if any of the locals were in sight. "Come on in."

I got the door closed behind them just in time to keep the argument from scaring every woodland creature for miles.

"You've got to be kidding!" Freezie shrieked.

"I told you he was a Klahd!" Jinetta said.

"Yeah, but he's a baby!" Pologne said. "We came all this way, wasting more time which we do NOT have, and what do we get? A kid! Barely out of swaddling clothes."

"A baby!" Freezia agreed.

"Er," I said, seeing the glee on Bunny's face. "I'm not a baby."

"Yeah, but you don't look like the guru of magik, either," Jinetta explained, sheepishly. "No offense."

"None taken," I replied. I blinked. "Guru of what?"

"Magik," Freezia snapped out. "We need a magik tutor. Now. Today."

"ME???!!!???"

Jinetta nodded. "My aunt assured me that you were the slickest operator she'd ever met, someone who can get a job done with no wasted effort. And your business manager gave us a big buildup, too."

"His *what?*" Bunny demanded.

"Business manager. Aahz. He said you were hot stuff. Just what we were hoping for."

"*Aahz* did?" I asked, now thoroughly puzzled. I knew Aahz's opinion of my skills. He'd told me enough times that if, magik were wind, I couldn't produce an audible *poot.*

"And Aahz told you I was the one you wanted?"

"Here," Jinetta said impatiently. She opened her buttermilk-yellow briefcase and rooted around with it. She came up with two rolls of parchment, one a long screed in ornate and difficult script asking me for a little favor, to help out her niece and her friends, signed by Vergetta. The other was a note scrawled by Aahz on the back of an old shopping list:

"Nice girls. They need some polishing up. Thought you could handle it. Aahz."

"Well," I breathed. I felt honored that my ex-partner had so much faith in me. Bunny had been trying to read the notes over my shoulder. I passed them to her.

"Well," I asked the three, clapping my hands together, "what do you need to learn? I, er, could get you started on some basic magik."

Pologna snorted and threw up her hands. "I told you he was strictly amateur hour!"

"We don't need *basics*," Jinetta said. "We're all graduates of MIP. *Summa cum laude.* We can give you credentials, if you need them."

"Oh." I felt very young and inept next to such well-educated Pervects. "Then what exactly do you need from me?"

"We'd like to intern with you for a few weeks, get a handle on practical uses of the arts. Your business manager said you'd welcome the chance to mentor a few worthy pupils. We all took degr—"

"How much?" Bunny interrupted.

We all looked at her in surprise.

"How much did you pay Aahz?" Bunny asked.

"Why?" Freezia countered, suddenly suspicious.

"Well, we need to know if you've signed up for basic instruction, or something more advanced. Let me see your receipts." Bunny held out an imperious hand.

"She's the bursar," I added when the three hesitated. I thought about it, and realized her wits were more in tune than mine. We both knew Aahz must have found a financial angle. It wasn't just altruism and belief in my skills that had prompted him to send me three apprentices. He'd dumped me into the drink a few times in the past with his passion for gold. Bunny was almost certainly right. There had to be some serious money involved.

The Pervects handed her small slips of parchment covered with Aahz's inimitable scrawl. Her face turned white, then red. She passed the slips to me. I gawked at the sum.

"Uh. Well, that's definitely the advanced course," I managed to choke out.

Bunny grabbed my arm and dragged me into the next room. "Give me the D-hopper," she said.

"What for?" I asked.

"I am going to march into that tent and give him a piece of my mind, since he seems to have lost his! What was he thinking? He knows you can't handle these girls!"

"Well, I don't know," I mused. "Aahz must think I can do it."

"That's the money talking. Look at me, Skeeve." I raised my eyes to hers. "This is just Aahz being greedy. What are you doing here? I mean, here, in this place."

"Well—studying."

"Because?" she prompted.

"Oh, I know, Bunny. I'm not the wizard everyone thinks I am, but Aahz must think I'm ready to tutor university students. Besides, he has put me under an obligation. I have to fulfill it. Those Pervects are counting on me. How bad could it be? We've got plenty of space for them to stay. They can each pick out a room. You'll enjoy the company—"

"You're talking yourself into it, aren't you?" Bunny could read a lot of my thoughts, and I always found it unnerving. "Skeeve, snap out of it! Aahz is flattering your ego. You don't know anything about teaching."

"I have to do it, don't I?" I countered. "Aahz made a contract in my name. I've got to live up to that. Otherwise, what happens to my reputation?"

She put her hands on her hips. "Will you put your sense of honor to the side just for the moment? It's not your reputation that's at stake here. Aahz made the deal without ever asking you if you would do it. You could say no. He knows what you're doing here. He'll just have to give those Pervects refunds."

We both stopped for a moment to reflect upon the mental image of Aahz forced to dig into his pockets and give money *back*. I almost laughed. It would almost be easier for me to learn advanced techniques and teach them to these young Pervects. It would sure take less time. No matter what Bunny said, I was stung by the challenge. I wondered if I could do it. If I couldn't, I'd soon find out. If I found I was in over my head, I could find a way to refund part of their tuition, and possibly find them a substitute teacher.

With a gesture of surrender, I returned to my new charges, who were waiting anxiously in the main room. Bunny stayed at my shoulder.

"Practical magik, huh?" I inquired.

"Yes," the girls said. "As soon as possible."

"What's the hurry?" Bunny wanted to know.

Jinetta hesitated. "Well, er, you know, no one wants to hire recent graduates who have no practical experience, right? I don't want to start out frying mimgrou ribs and asking 'do you want oil-soaked tubers with that?' I want a high-paying executive job. I want to get a jump on getting ahead of our fellow students."

"Me, too," put in Pologne. Freezia nodded eagerly.

"Me, too. And the key to big money is a reputation. And the key to that reputation is f—"

"Experience," Jinetta interrupted. "*Unpaid* experience. That's why we're looking for internships intstead of, er, entry level positions. So you don't pay us. Just teach us. Quickly."

That sounded reasonable to me. Having been on Perv once, I guessed it would be tough to jump into a good employment situation. Unlike Klah, everything seemed to move fast there.

"Okay," I said. "I'll do it."

"Thank you!" Pologne cried.

"It's a deal, then," Jinetta said, sticking out a hand. I hesitated for a moment, remembering Aahz's dislike for shaking hands with apprentices. But I was going to create my own style of teaching. I clasped her scaly fingers. The others grasped my hand in turn.

"Now what?" Freezia asked.

Chapter Three

"Nice effects."
S. SPIELBERG

What, indeed?

With three skeptical Pervish faces gazing at me, my mind went blank.

"Er," I began.

"Why don't the three of you pick out rooms to stay in?" Bunny said, distracting them from me for the moment. "This was once a coaching inn. You can each have a room of your own. The bathroom is a little on the primitive side, but there's always lots of hot water, and the insulation is good. Just remember to keep the curtains drawn. The locals think the place is haunted."

The three Pervects bustled upstairs eagerly, chattering nervously among themselves. I heard doors open and slam, accompanied by gales of wild giggles. Bunny caught my expression, and gave me an amused little smile.

"What are you going to do with them?"

"I think I'll take them to Massha," I replied. "She ought to have some ideas about how I can teach them, since she was my first and only apprentice. I might even see if she can take them off my hands."

Bunny shook her head doubtfully. "She's got a lot of responsibilities as Court Magician."

"All the better if she has three assistants to help her," I said brightly.

By the time they came jogging down again, I had my thoughts in place.

"Everything all right up there?" Bunny asked them. "We haven't really done anything to the place except clean it."

"Don't apologize," Freezia said, giving me a heart-stopping grin of brilliantly white four-inch fangs. "After our dormitories at MIP, these accommodations are almost palatial. They don't give students and apprentices a lot of consideration. I was jammed in the same size room with five other students. I had no idea it was going to be this nice. I can tell we're going to like it here with you."

"Er, thanks. Okay," I said, feeling a little guilty. "We're going to take a short trip to visit a friend of mine. It'll be a chance for you to get a good look at this dimension on the way."

"We've seen a good part of it," Pologne pointed out. "It's a dump. But, whatever you say."

I couldn't disagree with her about that. I'd always been fairly bored by my home dimension. My idea was to take these three into the kingdom of Possiltum, getting a little better idea of what they needed while we were on our journey. Massha had been no mere apprentice who started by sweeping my study and learning to light candles by concentrating on them. She had been an independent magician, working in the dimension of Jahk, who quit to come join me and my associates. I firmly believed I had learned more from her than she could possibly have gotten out of me. She'd specialized in practical magik.

I eyed the three females, mentally measuring the potential reaction of them on not only the local wildlife but my fellow Klahds. "You'll spook the neighbors if you go out like that. Can you ladies do a disguise spell?"

They beamed.

"Oh, sure!"

The room seemed to fill with flying sparks as the Pervects before me vanished. In their place, a gigantic green dragon curled around the walls of the room, cupping in its coils a sharp-toothed, gold-eyed mermaid with long flowing seaweed-colored locks and a tail full of green and blue scales, and a huge tree with sinisterly glowing green eyes. Gleep hissed. I frowned.

"Don't you like these?" the dragon asked in Jinetta's voice. "Not showy enough? How about these?"

The room swirled wildly again. I found myself facing three Trollish guards with white wherhide trews bound over their

thick purple-furred legs, wearing brass helmets with horns sticking out each side and carrying giant double-bitted axes.

"No!" I cried.

"No?" Freezia asked. "Okay. We'll try again."

Gargoyles, with fearsome smiles and stone tutus. I gawked.
"How's this?"

A volcano, a rainbow and a twinkling blue fairy.

"And this?"

Before I could stop them, the Pervects became unicorns,
Deveels, Ogres, towering robots with sparks sputtering from
the electrical contacts in their necks, winged Sphinxes, animate stone towers, undulating sea serpents, enormous spiny
red hedgehogs and, finally, a trio of pink elephants with floating ostrich plumes bound to their foreheads.

"No!" I shouted, waving my hands. "I mean, can you use a
disguise to pass *unnoticed?*"

The elephants lowered their trunks and stared at me out
of little wizened eyes.

"Why?" they asked, sounding hurt. "Aren't these good
illusions?"

"I think I'm beginning to see their problem," Bunny
observed, with an eyebrow lifted.

"They're terrific illusions," I assured them "but they're
inappropriate. We want to get to the palace without anyone
following us. We don't want to attract attention."

They looked at each other as if the notion had never
before passed through their minds.

"Well, then, let's just go as ourselves," Freezia said. She
made a pass with one huge round foot, and the three became
scaly green Pervects again. "Just like this. Come on." She made
for the door.

"No way," I said firmly, striding ahead of them to block it.

"Why not? We're not ashamed of our bodies," Pologne said,
planting her hands on her hips as she confronted me. "Is it our
clothes? Are these fashions too extreme for Klah? Two piece
suits? A classic is a classic."

"It's got nothing to do with you or your clothes," I said. "It's you. There's only ever been one Pervect to visit Klah, and he already frightens most Klahds out of their socks. Three would send whole villages running. Can you disguise yourselves as ordinary Klahds, like the people you saw on your way here?"

The three exchanged startled glances. "Of course we can," Jinetta said. "If you insist."

"I insist," I said.

They closed their eyes. When they opened them, I beheld the transformation. Before me were a hefty, slack-jawed man carrying a yoke of buckets who was the local village idiot, a sallow-faced man with a long nose I recognized as a tax collector, and a cow.

"Um, almost," I said. I perched a hip on the edge of the table and gestured to them to sit down. "Let's try again."

Using pictures conjured up by Bunny on her PDA, Bytina, I managed to point out images of Klahds who were not too limited, not too unpopular, and a bit more sentient than their first choices. Jinetta, Pologne and Freezia squabbled over who would wear what appearance, jumping from one image to another. They couldn't seem to make up their minds. I held my impatience for a few minutes.

"Look, you be that milkmaid," Freezia said. "She's taller than I am."

"Hey," I tried to interrupt.

"No, I'd rather be that burgher," Pologne said. "You be the milkmaid."

"Oh, she's so boring! Look at those wooden clogs!"

"Make up your minds, and let's go," I put in. They ignored me.

"That male in the tights showed some fashion," Jinetta said thoughtfully.

I pushed my way in between them and loomed over them. I pointed at each of my 'apprentices' in turn.

"Fine. Jinetta, you get to be the male in tights. Pologne, you're the burgher. Freezia, you get to be the lady in the blue veil. Chop, chop! Last one into her disguise is a rotten egg!" I clapped my hands.

Donning my own disguise, that of a cadaverous-faced master magician that served me better than my own fresh-faced boyish appearance, I swept toward the exit. I listened behind me as they fell into line. I expected some grumbling, but there was none. They accepted my authority without question. I didn't know whether to feel confident about that trust, or worried. Bunny held onto Gleep's collar as she waved me a cynical farewell from the doorway.

As we strode out onto the narrow, overhung path that served as a road through the thick of the forest, I dropped to the rear of the file and observed my new charges. I expected that there might be some kinks to work out as a cluster of inexperienced Pervects negotiated a new dimension, but I didn't quite anticipate the difficulties they would have in pretending to be something they weren't.

"Jinetta, stop swinging your hips like that," I ordered.

"Like what?" the tallest Pervect inquired, turning in a graceful circle to face me.

I waved a hand. "And don't swoop like that. The guy whose face you are wearing is going to find himself the object of a lot of jokes if we run into anyone who knows him."

Pologne tittered at her classmate's dressing down. I turned on her. "And as for you, never giggle like that again, not until we are inside Massha's house. You're supposed to be an old man. Grumble. Mutter to yourself."

She gawked at me. "What? As if I'm senile, or something?"

I groaned. "Yes, as if you're senile or something. You're an elderly man, with a lot of business interests and a son-in-law who's trying to cut him out of deals. Your wife has a bad temper, and your in-laws live with you. Mutter. Complain under your breath. A lot."

Pologne was appalled. "That *bites*. Let me be a girl, like Freezia."

"No," I said, folding my arms imperiously. "You're going to learn something out of this: how to make the best use of a disguise spell. I bet you never used your talents for anything more complicated than a Halloween costume. Right?"

"Well—yes." The medium-sized Pervect had the grace to hang her head.

The third Pervect, Freezia, minced along, feeling superior because she didn't have to do any acting to get along in her disguise. I was under no illusion (pun unintended) that I wouldn't have to find fault with her some time over the next six weeks, but it was all right with me if she got by this time. I had to admit she had captured the essence of the pretty girl in the blue gown fairly well. Anyone watching us make our way down the road might be a little surprised that the rich and spoiled Lady Melgarie Trumpmeier walking—make that striding—instead of riding her white pony or being conveyed in one of her father's expensive carriages, but the anomaly would give the locals something to talk about.

A party of five horsemen trotted into view. The path was too narrow for our parties to pass abreast. It would be less trouble to let them by, but with "Lady Melgarie" and me, a famous but mysterious magician, we couldn't give ground. The girls glanced back at me. I gestured to them to keep walking.

"One side!" the lead horseman demanded. A burly, black-bearded man on a gigantic destrier, he towered twice as tall as me, but I held myself upright.

"Who speaks so to Skeeve the Magnificent?" I replied, in sepulchural tones. Two of the horseman behind the leader cringed slightly at my name.

"Who dares to confront Lord Peshtigo of Sulameghorn?" the leader countered, drawing the sword that hung on his right hip. He might have heard of me, but he obviously had a reputation to protect.

I crossed my arms. "You impede our progress, my lord," I replied solemnly.

"You block our horses!"

"Surely mere animals do not take precedence over persons of quality," I admonished him as if he was a small child. "Turn aside, my lord. Give us room."

"We do not turn aside for anyone," Lord Peshtigo growled. "Move, or we run you down."

"I don't think you want to do that," I said, shaking my head. "The consequences may be more than you anticipate. Save yourselves the trouble."

"You are in our way! Move, or die!" Peshtigo bellowed.

"You want us to tear his head off?" Freezia asked, showing her teeth. She had completely forgotten about her disguise.

The horsemen gasped at her, then all of them drew their swords.

"Nay." Wearing my most bored expression, I made a pass with one hand. The sword flew out of Lord Peshtigo's hand. I kept the momentum going, so the gleaming blade twirled point over hilt, ending up with its length buried halfway into the mud at the edge of the road. It stuck there, quivering. His lordship's face turned scarlet then white.

When he spoke, his voice had gone up a few registers. "Lord—lord magician, I fear you have the advantage of me."

"I hope so," I said, allowing my hollowed cheekbones to lift in a wintry smile.

"I had no idea of your pow—I give you good day, gentlefolk," he said quickly, gesturing his fellows to make way for us. Not daring to demur, they all pulled their steeds off onto the muddy verge, where the horses' hooves promptly sank past their fetlocks. I nodded slightly and tilted my head toward the disguised Pervects to follow me. We made our way single-file past the snorting, white-eyed stallions.

As we passed, I threw up a hand. The sword flew up out of the mud and arrowed, point first, for Lord Peshtigo's scabbard. It clashed into place. The other men hastily sheathed their own weapons, just in case I was thinking of doing it for them.

"Good day, gentlemen," I said, in lugubrious tones.

"G-good day, Lord Magician!"

The moment we were past, they whipped up their horses and thudded off down the road.

"That was awesome!" Freezia exclaimed.

I waited until I was certain that the horsemen had really gone, then I turned to her, holding an air of nonchalance like a shield. "That seemed awesome to you, did it?"

She turned wondering eyes at me. "Oh, yes! I mean, you just used a little levitation spell, but wow! It really impressed them!"

"Did it ever occur to you," I began dangerously, "that I could have gotten us past them without using *any* magik?"

"Could you?" she asked. "Why didn't you, then?"

"Because," I said, "while I was beginning the negotiation of who held the higher rank they heard a lady of quality snarl and shriek out, 'You want us to tear his head off?' That changed the equation from a conversational volley to an open threat. Not only that, they're likely to tell that story in the towns up the road. Chances are now very good that Lady Melgarie's father is going to send an armed party out in search of the magician who kidnapped his daughter and threw a madness spell on her. We could have horsemen on our tails in an hour."

"Well, couldn't you deal with them, too?" Pologne asked. "You took care of these."

"That's because we had the element of surprise," I said, trying to keep my temper. "We won't have that next time."

"We could take off our disguises," Jinetta said. "That'd surprise them. And we can knock most of them out using magik. We play demon-volleyball. I can hit an opponent at over a hundred paces with a fireball."

I sighed. "And that would just increase the size of the mob after us. Look, you want practical instruction? Most Klahds are afraid of magik, power and anyone who doesn't look like them. The force lines around here are fairly weak, except for places like the inn, where several of them cross. You don't want to have to expend any magik on them if you can help it. Store up all the power you can when we get close to good lines of force, and be stingy with it in between. Use your head instead of your magik. Got that?"

"Yes, Skeeve," they chorused.

As I stumped down the road, I wondered why they didn't already know about being stingy, with magik or anything else. They were Pervects, after all.

Chapter Four

"Would you do a favor for an old friend?"
D. CORLEONE

"Skeeve!"

Massha flew forward to envelop me in a hug. When Massha hugs you, you know it. If I was to describe her as large, you'd know I was understating the situation by a factor of six or seven. Massha wasn't ashamed of being a well-rounded woman; far from it. She wore gaudy clothes and tons of jewelery which could not help but draw the eye to her shape. She also tended to dye her hair a vivid orange, and favored lipstick to match. Since becoming Lady Magician to the Court of Possiltum, Queen Hemlock presiding, and marrying the ex-general of its army, Massha had actually toned down the shock value, but the package was still an impressive one. She was one of my best and most trusted friends, so it didn't take her long to guess that I had something on my mind.

"So, what brings you out of your self-imposed exile, Hot Stuff?" she asked, directing me and my party to cushiony divans that took up most of the spare living space in her and Hugh Badaxe's cosy love nest. The cottage, occupying a corner of the courtyard in the center of the castle environs, actually had fewer square feet than the Court Magician's apartments itself, but with no shared walls to the rest of the castle it had the benefit of privacy. She pointed a finger at a drinks tray on a small table in the corner. The tray lifted itself into the air and settled on the fussily-carved wooden table at the center of the room. The stopper rose from the neck of the handsomely cut crystal bottle, which upended and poured amber liquid into five crystal glasses. Massha only let magik take it so far; she went over to pass the drinks around herself. "Bunny's okay?"

I accepted a glass. "She's fine. She wanted me to ask you when you were getting on the Crystal Ball Network."

Massha waved a hand. "I don't have time for remote entertainment, honey. We've got an invitational tournament coming up next month, and Hemlock wants me to put on a big show. You know," she added, waving a hand. Six miniature golden dragonets flew out of her fingertips carrying banners reading "Massha's Big Show!"

I chuckled.

"But aren't you going to introduce me to your friends?" She fluttered her lashes madly at the handsome young Klahd in gartered tights who struggled to keep his tunic from rising up to his waist in the thick velvet cushions.

"Save it, toots," Jinetta snapped, momentarily distracted from her hemline. "You're not my type."

Massha goggled then rose into the air, her face red with embarrassment. "I don't know where you came from, buddy, but around here you call me Lady Magician or ma'am!"

"It's not what you think," I said hastily, leaping up. "Girls, drop the disguises."

"Girls?" Massha echoed.

With a couple of whisks, the illusions faded, leaving three business-suited Pervects glaring at Massha.

"No wonder!" Massha said. Instantly, she went to a pair of cupboard doors in the wall and took out three huge steins and a gallon jug of liquor. "Let me offer you something more to your capacity, ladies. Here." She exchanged the delicate little crystal tumblers for more substantial servings of liquor.

"Thanks," Freezia said, raising the big glass to her lips. "Down the hatch!" She gulped her drink and held out the stein for more.

"So, what are you three doing in Possiltum?" Massha asked as she poured. The three Pervects glanced at one another uneasily.

"Uh, Massha," I said, "Can I see you alone for a moment?"

"Sure!" she said brightly, pulling me into her small kitchen. She beamed at the Pervects. "Excuse us a moment." She waved

a gadget I recognized as her 'cone of silence.' My three students could no longer hear us. They shot me worried glances,
so I just smiled reassuringly at them. Massha watched the
exchange curiously. "So, what's up, Big Guy? Who are they?"

"They're temporary apprentices." I explained how Aahz
had sent them to me. "They said they need some specialized
training. I, er, brought them here hoping you could help me
out. I'm pretty deep in my studies right now. I thought you
could give them a couple weeks' instruction in what you're
doing here. Practical stuff. They could help you with the fes-
tival," I concluded hopefully. "By then I'll have figured out
what I can do to help them. I really haven't got a clue how to
train them."

Massha shook her head. "Gee, that's too bad. I wish I could
help, but I can't. In fact, I was going to visit *you* in the next
couple of days. I have a pupil I wanted *you* to train."

"Me?" I squeaked.

"Yes!" Massha said, pleased. "And now that you have other
students, he'll have the benefit of working with others to help
him with his lessons. He's a nice kid. You'll like him. Bee!
C'mere, honey!" she shouted out the cottage's back door.

Beside the well in the courtyard, a stick with ears rose to
its feet. I realized at once it was a skinny young man, maybe
my age or a year or two older. He had a friendly freckled face
with big ears and a pop-jawed grin. When he saw me, the grin
widened but his eyes dropped shyly.

"Skeeve the Magnificent, this is Corporal Bee, late of Her
Majesty's army. He mustered out last week and came to see
me," Massha explained. "He wants to study magik." The young
man hesitated. I put out my hand and he shook it with a powerful grip that his slender frame belied. "All he needs to know
is how to get along in the big bad world. The army's been good
for Bee. He's had orienteering skills and survival skills hammered into him, and he has spatial relationships down pat, but
he's not great at self-direction and personal organization. He'd
get taken advantage of in a sophisticated scuffle."

"So could I," I muttered. But I got the point. I could help with that.

"Glad to meet you, sir," Bee stammered. "I heard a lot about you. Sergeant Swatter, I mean, Guido told me—you don't look the way he described you—"

"Oh." I laughed. "Is this more like it?"

I dropped my disguise spell. The boy let out a whistle of relief.

"Yes, sir! I mean, you were okay the other way, sir! I mean—" His face flushed scarlet, leaving the freckles in sharp relief.

"It's okay, honey," Massha said. "He won't bite you, whatever face he's got on."

"I can't say the same about my apprentices, though," I said thoughtfully.

"You've got other apprentices?" Bee asked enthusiastically.

"No, I mean, yes, wait a minute," I burst out. "Let's start over, from the beginning. How do you know Guido? I assume we're talking about the same Guido?"

"I guess so, sir," Bee replied. "The one I know's a very big man. Talked very tough. Knows everything about how to handle a crossbow, and about everything else, too. Swatter and his cousin Nunzio were great guys. We went through basic training together. He ended up as our sergeant."

"That sounds like our Guido," I said. "So, why do you want to study with me?"

Massha shoved him forward like a mother urging her little boy into the middle of the stage to make his speech on School Prize Day. Bee dithered a moment. I'd been there, done that, and bought the commemorative tunic, so I had a lot of sympathy for a youngster trying to ask for a favor. He seemed impressed to be in the presence of the Great Skeeve, no matter how embarrassed I felt about that, and nervous to have the Court Magician of Possiltum as a sponsor.

"Come on, honey, tell him."

"I was an apprentice magician at home, before I enlisted," Bee said. "Sergeant Guido promised me that, when I got out, he promised me he'd make sure Skeeve the Great would help me get trained up as a proper magician. Then I can go home and set up a practice in my town, sir. I don't need to be a great wizard, just good enough to help the folks out. Swatter was a great guy, sir, and he had a lot of respect for you. When I got out, I went to my CO to see if he knew where to find the sergeant, sir. He sent me to General Badaxe, who put me together with the Lady Magician, here."

Massha nodded.

Bee went on earnestly. "If I can study with you, sir, it would be an honor and a privilege. I won't be any trouble. I'm good at organization. I ran the whole supply depot under the sergeant, sir."

"I heard about that, corporal," I said. At the time, Guido had been giving me a full debriefing about his stint in the Possiltum army. The name Bee swam up out of a swarm of insect names. The fact that Guido had come to be called Swatter hadn't surprised me then, nor did the respect he had engendered among his troops.

I turned to Massha. "And you're not keeping him as your apprentice because—?"

"Two reasons, Big Shot," she said. "One, he asked for you. Guido made a promise to him. Two, I don't think I'd put him through the paces the way you would."

"But I've got so much studying of my own to do," I almost wailed. "You have a lot more experience of this type than I do."

"I don't agree. The fact that you're studying is the reason you're exactly the right person to help him. You learn the most about a subject when you're teaching it. That's what Hugh always says. But I won't leave you in the lurch. Friends don't do that to friends. I will help you with your trio if you take Bee on as a pupil. I'll come down and give a few lessons in gadget magik. I know I'm good at that. What do you say?"

Bee watched us eagerly. I gave in.

"Deal," I sighed. "All right, Bee, come and meet your new classmates. Massha, I'm going to hold you to your promise."

"I'm good for it, Hot Shot," she said. "You know that."

I stalked back to the old inn, wrapped in my own thoughts, almost cringing at the notion of what Bunny would say when she saw I had *four* apprentices in tow instead of three—or none at all. From the look in Jinetta's eye, the Pervects weren't too happy about another student joining what they assumed would be an exclusive teaching arrangement, and neither was I. We were all careful to keep our feelings from Corporal Bee, who was nattering along happily, unaware of the simmering thoughts just below the surface.

Bunny didn't meet me at the door, but Gleep did, galloping into the room and mowing me down so he could slurp my face with his long, pink tongue.

"Gleep!" he burbled happily.

"Stop that, Gleep," I said, pushing his face away from mine. His breath smelled like a week-dead skunk, and the stink clung almost as well as the odor from the Bazaar's famous Genuine Fake Doggie Doodle with Genuine Odor That Really Sticks to Your Hands. I scrambled to my feet. He surveyed the Pervects, having already tasted them, and leaped on Corporal Bee. To give the youth credit, he didn't blanch as my dragon pinned him against the wall and gave him a good sliming.

"Gleep!"

Apparently my dragon, whom I considered a very good judge of character, had decided my new pupil was all right with him.

"Just push him down," I advised Bee, who looked nervous, or nauseous. Gleep's breath could kill flies at ten paces. "Come on, Gleep! He's not used to dragons. Bunny?"

"In here, Skeeve!" she called. "Look who's here!"

I followed her voice into the main room, where Bunny was sitting in a cosy tete-a-tete with a being about seventeen times her bulk. The purple fur and odd-sized moon-shaped eyes were unmistakeable.

"Chumley!"

The Troll rose awkwardly to his feet and put out a hand. I ignored it and gave him a hearty hug. It had been months since I'd seen him.

"Oh, I say!" he muttered shyly. "Me mean, Crunch glad see you!"

I glanced back over my shoulder and saw that Bee and the Pervects had followed me into the room. Chumley, like most Trolls from the dimension of Trollia, tended to conceal his intelligence, lest the whole package overwhelm denizens of more insecure dimensions. He supplied hired muscle on a freelance basis under the *nom de guerre* of Big Crunch. Crunch, unlike Chumley, who was extremely well educated and possessed an erudite manner of speaking, expressed himself mainly in monosyllables. Around strangers, he maintained the subterfuge.

"Let me introduce you to my new apprentices," I said. "From left to right, that's Jinetta, Pologne, Freezia, and Bee."

Bunny looked startled for a moment then smiled. "See, Chumley, there's no problem. I told you."

"Good!" Chumley exclaimed, clapping his big hands together heartily. "See? Tolk!"

From the inglenook at the side of the big fireplace, an irregular brown-and-white shape unwound itself and trotted to Chumley's side. It rose to its hind feet and regarded me with large, chocolate-colored eyes. Tolk looked rather like a big hound with a slightly flattened face, jowls hanging down on either side of big black nose and long mouth. His paws had thick black nails, but fingers instead of pads. Chumley pointed at me.

"New teacher!" he boomed.

"Now, wait a minute, Chumley," I said.

He regarded me with a question in his big moonlike eyes. "Four, why not five?"

I didn't have a good answer for him. Tolk didn't wait for my approval. He trotted over to the Pervects and panted happily at them.

"I'm Tolk!" he yipped. "I'm from Canida! Nice to meet you, eh!"

"Jinetta," the tallest Pervect said, fending off a slurp from the newcomer's long pink tongue. "Give paw?"

"Hey, I'm better trained than that," Tolk barked. He grinned, showing teeth halfway as sharp as the Pervects', and shook hands all around. "Where you folks from?"

"Chumley?" I asked, as the five young people introduced themselves. "Who is he, and what's he doing here?"

"Sorry to descend on you without notice, old chap," Chumley murmured abashedly, keeping his voice down. "No time to explain, what? Tolk was in just such a hurry to find some decent training. I thought of you."

"Why? You have a lot more experience than I do." Trolls and their sister Trollops tended to have a lot of magikal talent, much more than Klahds possessed overall.

"Well, I don't practice much, as you know, preferring to depend upon sheer muscle. I consider it more reliable, what? I tend to leave the hocus-pocus to Little Sister. I wanted Tolk taught by someone who is in the field, so to speak."

I eyed him. "Then why didn't you go to Tananda? She's most definitely in the field, more than I am, lately. In fact, she might even be a better instructor for the Pervects."

"I wouldn't say this to anyone but a very close friend," Chumley confided, with a glance over my shoulder at the group, "but Tananda isn't much of a teacher. She is not at all interested in taking on a pupil. I might add that she is engaged upon a job, and does not want to confuse Tolk with moral issues."

"I see," I said. I did. Tananda, besides being a pretty good magician and a very dear friend, was also occasionally an assassin for hire. It was a facet of her talents I didn't want to know more about, and she had never forced me to examine the matter more closely.

Chumley continued, "I must add, Tananda feels that you are a better all around magician than she is, with the potential for greatness."

That was going too far. I scoffed. "She never said that."

Chumley favored me with an earnest expression. "I assure you, she did. I also feel that it is true. Tolk could not be in better hands."

"Forget it," I said, feeling foolish. "Find another tutor for him."

The big purple head wagged slowly from side to side. "I'm afraid I am committed. Tolk has invoked a debt I owe his family. I need to forward his education, and swiftly. He has a good deal of untrained talent, and it would be worthwhile to guide him forward."

I shook my head. "You can do it, Chumley. I can't. No."

Chumley fixed his big, irregular eyes full of hope on me. "Skeeve, have I ever asked anything of you before?"

The question stopped me cold. I gave it my best shot, searching back through my memory. Chumley had always been there for me and the rest of the M.Y.T.H., Inc. crew, but had never put us to the test on his own behalf.

"No, you haven't," I said. "Not a thing that I can recall. On balance, we owe you. I owe you plenty."

"Well, I wouldn't put it that way," Chumley said modestly. "I know I'm imposing, and I would be terribly grateful to have the matter taken care of. It's temporary, old chap. Five or six weeks, what?"

"All right," I sighed, hearing an echo in my head of my capitulation to Massha. "He's in."

Chumley slapped me on the back. The blow nearly flattened me. "Thank you, old shirt."

"Would you consider an application from someone to whom you don't owe a favor?"

Chapter Five

"This is getting out of control."
NOAH

The familiar high-pitched voice behind me practically shot me into the air. I think I turned all the way around before I landed.

"Markie!" I exclaimed.

It was. My one-time ward and would-be character assassin stood a couple of paces away. She still looked as cute and helpless as ever, with her adorable big blue eyes, her mop of golden hair, her tiny frame, all concealing a mind that could strike like a cobra's.

"Get out of here!" Bunny stormed. My assistant pointed to the door with a magenta fingernail. I recalled that she had borne the brunt of a good deal of Markie's Macchiavellian machinations. Markie didn't, as she once would have, let her pink rosebud of a lower lip tremble fetchingly. Instead, the genuine pathos on her face surprised me.

"Please hear me out."

"Wait a minute, Bunny," I said. "What are you doing here, Markie?"

"As I said, Skeeve," she said ruefully, "I've come to ask a favor."

"Forget it. Skeeve doesn't do favors for people like you," Bunny said, her eyes flashing. "He did you the only favor you deserve in not blowing your cover."

The Pervects, Bee and Tolk stared at the tiny child before them, but I wasn't about to enlighten them as to Markie's actions and subsequent unmasking.

"I thought you'd feel that way," Markie said, nodding in resignation. "I'm so sorry about my behavior when we last met, but it was a job I'd been hired for. You don't like what I do, but it's my profession, like being a Mob moll."

Bunny's face turned purple, and she started toward Markie with her nails out. I leaped to grab Bunny around the upper arms and hold her back.

"That was a low blow, Markie," I said.

Markie looked genuinely distressed. "I didn't mean it as one, Skeeve. I apologize again, Bunny. It's just a statement of fact, isn't it?"

"Not any more." I thought it best to intervene before Bunny took matters into her own claws—I mean, hands. Any moment my assistant could break loose from my grip. She worked out daily with weights, and was probably stronger than I was. "This is about you, not her. Why have you come?"

"It's not for me," Markie said, beckoning over her shoulder. "Come in here, Melvine."

A boy wandered into the room and favored us with a four-toothed grin.

"This big lug is my nephew, Melvine." Markie shoved him forward. He stood about one and a half times her size, but with his soft features, round tummy and nearly hairless head he looked like a big baby. For the first time I could really tell that Markie had to be much older than the five or six Klahdish years she looked. "You can see what he did to himself, and now he can't undo it. No Cupy ought to be that big. Even I am above average height for a doll in our dimension."

"It's not my fault," Melvine grumbled.

"Oh, yes?" his aunt asked, curling her tiny fists on her hips. "Whose fault, then? Name me another guy anywhere in Cupid who is anywhere close to your height. Name one. I'm waiting." Melvine remained silent. Markie appealed to me again. "You see? He needs help."

"Why me?" I asked.

The corner of Markie's mouth quirked up in a tiny grin. "It's your own fault, really. You taught me about good character and honest evaluation. While I was here I saw how your reputation came to be based on those traits. My big fool of a nephew doesn't know how to do anything small. He has no control. As you could probably figure, that makes him even more unpopular than an Elemental School graduate usually is. Melvine has been through about eight tutors, and he's intimidated most of them into approving of everything he does just to keep from having to deal with the aftermath. He's too bright and too powerful for his own good. I know he's screwing up." My other apprentices gawked to hear such words falling from the childish lips. "You kept one of the tightest ships running I have ever seen. Your friends were loyal to you no matter what happened. I admired your integrity. You told people the truth even when it hurt you, but you never tried to hurt anyone's feelings deliberately. My problem comes from my profession: sometimes I don't know when to stop. Melvine needs someone with your fundamental honesty, not to praise him or to clobber him too much. He only needs a steady hand for a few weeks. He ought to get a handle by then."

"That's right," the pupil said, turning big blue eyes just like his aunt's up to mine. "After that, I'm on my own, I swear."

I could feel Bunny's eyes burning a message into my brain—over her dead body would she let any relative of Markie's share the roof over her head—but the foolish, ashamed grin on the boy's face touched me. I'd been there myself. If it hadn't been for Aahz and Chumley, and even Bunny, I'd probably have gotten myself into some really stupid situations with no way out.

"This has nothing to do with our common history," I told Markie. Her eyes shone, and she practically climbed up me to hug me and give me a hearty peck on the cheek.

"You are one in a million," she said happily. She caught Bunny's fierce expression and jumped down from my chest. "All right. I'm out of here. Melvine can make his own way home at the end of the session. Can he stay here, or does he need to commute from Cupid?"

"No, there's plenty of room," I assured her absently. Bunny paused for a moment then nodded her head in resignation. "But this doesn't come free."

"I figured," Markie said, nodding knowingly. "I've got plenty. How much would you like?"

"Not money," I said. "I don't need your money, and I don't want to take it, knowing how you earned it. No offense."

"None taken," Markie sighed. "That's why I'm here. So, what *do* you want?"

I gestured at the other students. "I want you to come back as a guest lecturer one week. You, too, Chumley."

"Not good," Chumley said, pulling his big shaggy brow down towards his eyes. "Crunch better fighter than teacher."

I raised an eyebrow. "I'm sure you'll think of something to challenge them. They want practical instruction. Isn't that right, ladies?"

"Yes," Jinetta said cautiously.

"Good!" I clapped my palms together and rubbed them. "Then it's settled."

"Thanks again, Skeeve," Markie said, turning large, blond-fringed eyes up to me. "I owe you. I owe you, too, Bunny."

"I will collect," Bunny assured her. "My Family never forgets a favor."

"I expect it," Markie said.

She waved a hand, and the BAMF of displaced air momentarily deafened all of us.

"Crunch go, too," Chumley announced, looking pointedly at me. "Go home to Trollia. Bye."

He didn't want to be seen doing magik in front of the students. I drew power out of the force lines that crossed above and beneath the inn, and sent the big Troll away with another loud bang.

I decided to grab the male bovine by the horns. I drew a breath and turned to my circle of apprentices.

"Ladies, Tolk and Bee, this is Melvine," I said.

I realized it wasn't the bull I had to worry about, it was the cows. The Pervects looked furious.

"Was this some sort of scam to jack up the price your business partner was charging, telling us how reclusive you are?" Freezia demanded. "It looks like you're taking in found-lings right and left, without asking for a dime!"

"Now, just a minute," Tolk began, a little defensively. "Who are you calling a foundling?"

"You don't like us?" Melvine whined, his lower lip pouted out.

"You really expect us to associate with remedial students like these?" Pologne asked me.

"What's a dime?" Bee asked.

"My aunt must have been out of her mind," Jinetta said, throwing her hands up in disgust. "You're overcommitting your-self, and we need intensive tutoring. I'm beginning to wonder if you're equal to it. We haven't got much time, and you're making other arrangements—"

"HOLD IT!" I bellowed, raising my hands. That was it. I might have to come to terms with my conscience over whether or not it was a good idea to do Markie a favor, but it was MY conscience. "Quiet, all of you. ONE: I'm in charge here. I decide who I will teach. Not you. If you don't want to continue as part of a group, then feel free to go back and ask my pa—partner for a refund. TWO: you weren't ever going to have one-on-one tutoring. There were three of you to start with! THREE: you'll be able to help each other out. I can use your assistance, too. As college graduates you will be handy to have as teaching aides. You probably already did some of that at MIP. I'm guessing that the guys won't have had as extensive a formal education as you. You can help them over the bumps, in exchange for advanced tutoring. They might even have something that they can teach YOU."

"Well," Pologne began, dubiously.

"The situation is not negotiable," I said flatly. "I don't plan to go easy on you in my lessons, so maybe you ought to make friends with your classmates. Otherwise, you're all out of here. Get it?"

The Pervects all rocked back on their heels. Melvine stood in the middle of the room, sniveling quietly to himself. Tolk

dropped to all fours and trotted over to stand by him, a friendly and sympathetic look on his long face.

Bee broke the ice. He ambled over and offered a hand to each of the others in turn.

"Skeeve's right," the skinny soldier said. "I just got out of the army, and one of the most important things I learned is that you can't get by just on your own in a tough situation. How about it? Friends?"

"Temporarily," Freezia said, taking the hand gingerly.

"Good," I said, beaming. "Everybody go choose a room. Keep the curtains closed. Dinner's at sunset. Breakfast's at sunrise, local time, and we start classes first thing after that. Got it?"

All six pupils stopped arguing and gawked at me. Behind them, Gleep tipped me one huge, blue-eyed wink.

Chapter Six

"'Roughing it' is staying at a hotel that doesn't have room service."
K. CARSON

BAMF!

"...There yet? Are we there yet? Are we there yet? Are we there yet?" Tolk yelped, over and over.

"Shut UP!" Freezia snarled.

"But are we there yet?" the doglike creature asked. He turned his big brown eyes to me.

"Yup," I said. "We're there." I clutched the D-hopper close to my chest so none of them could read the settings, and stuffed it into my belt pouch.

The students looked around curiously. The landscape was nothing to write home about. I had always thought of Klah as the bleakest place in the universe, but since I'd started magik lessons, first with Garkin, then with Aahz, I'd come to realize I had been born in a fairly decent place.

Not like this.

We stood high on a hilltop overlooking a landscape consisting mainly of stone and clay. The hot wind whipped around us, flicking dust into our eyes and nostrils. Scrubby plants hugged the hillside in between rivers of pebbles. Clusters of depressed-looking moss-colored bushes studded with finger-long thorns huddled here and there, not brightening fields of windblown grass. A shallow stream ran downhill, the gurgle of peat-colored water doing nothing to lift the ambience. The sun hovered near the horizon, flinging pale orange rays upward in hopes of raising some cheer on the landscape. It didn't succeed.

"Welcome to Sear," I announced. "This is where we're going to have our first lesson."

"What a dump," Pologne said.

I wanted to offer some kind of sour rejoinder. I had hardly gotten any sleep the night before, getting everything set up. Her attitude dimmed a little of my excitement over this teaching assignment. My former pupil Massha had always been grateful for the time we had spent together, and I had come to appreciate how much she valued my instruction—when I hadn't ducked out on the responsibility. I took a moment to wonder why I had been so reluctant to teach her, and why I had jumped so readily at this job, with not one, but six students, all of different temperaments.

"What are we doing here?" Melvine asked in a whiny voice. The big baby was bundled neck to heels in a pale-gray garment that only *looked* like a romper. The bottoms of the feet had very solid, ridged soles, and I realized there were multiple openings for pockets. He wore a cute little cap on his nearly bald head. "I hate sleeping outside. Can't we go back to the inn?"

"No," I said. "I wanted to get out in the field. It'll be more of a challenge this way."

I'd told my students to get ready for camping outdoors, but gave no other details. The Pervects had dressed for the occasion in form-fitting t-shirt and short sets: Freezia in melon, Pologne in pale green, and Jinetta in what my fashion expert Bunny had defined for me as 'lemon sorbet.' Their talons, both finger and toe, had been freshly pedicured, and their polish matched their outfits. They also carried color-coordinated backpacks.

Bee, dressed in his Possiltum army uniform, leather skirt and breastplate over a long tunic, puffed up the hill behind us, hauling a huge pack that must have weighed about the same as he did.

"What's that?" I asked.

"Well, sir," Bee began, stopping to gulp for breath, "the army always taught us to be prepared. Sgt. Swatter also impressed it on me pretty persuasively. I don't want to end up without something I'm gonna need to fulfill any task you set me."

"This is intended to test your *magikal* solutions," Jinetta said with a sneer.

"With respect, ma'am, my magik is a lot more basic than I'd like it to be," Bee replied, his freckled cheeks red from exertion or embarrassment, or both. "I've got to find a physical answer sometimes. I just thought you oughtta know that, since you may end up counting on me one day."

"Thanks," the tallest Pervect said coldly, "but I doubt it."

"That's your first wrong answer of the day," I stated calmly. Jinetta looked shocked. "You're all going to work together. None of you succeed unless all of you do. That's one of the most practical things I ever learned, working with M.Y.T.H., Inc., and I'd be remiss if I didn't pass it along to you."

By contrast, Tolk had his possessions in a paper bag that had a rip down one side. The Pervects regarded him with the same distaste they would have given a stain on their immaculate outfits. Tolk took no notice as he gazed at his surroundings.

"Where are the trees?" he asked forlornly.

"Oh, I think there are some out there someplace," I said nonchalantly. "We'll find plenty of firewood for our camp tonight. If not, we can always burn dried animal dung."

"And smell up my outfit?" Freezia asked. "Not a chance. This is *haute couture*."

"If it's not hot *haute*," I said, "you might welcome the warmth when the sun goes down. You're here for lessons in practical survival, right? It doesn't get much more basic than Sear. Nothing fancy, but you can find what you need."

"But what are we doing here?" Melvine asked in his perpetual whine.

"Today's lesson is finding simple solutions to problems," I informed them. "You're going on a scavenger hunt. I came here last night and hid a bunch of items on the landscape. By the end of tomorrow I want all of the items assembled at land's end." I pointed downhill toward the silver sparkle of the distant sea that hugged this continent. "You'll find all the objects on this little shopping list. Oops!" I let go of the parchment, which I had conveniently torn into six pieces before we left Klah. The students leaped after them, jumping in front of one another, nearly racing up one another's backs to get at the swirling squares of paper. I groaned. They weren't thinking. They had all responded out of instinct, not intelligence.

"Hold it!" I said. The students all stopped and turned back to stare at me.

"What?" Pologne demanded. "They're going to get lost!"

"Not if you're smart. One of you, get all those pieces. Now!"

Tolk, quick as a wyvern, leaped into the air and snatched one with his mouth as the wind carried the fragment by. He jumped for another. The first one fluttered out of his mouth. Tolk snapped at the first one and lost the second. He turned this way and that, trying to decide which one to go for. One fluttered close. He leaped for it, but Freezia reached for it at the same time. They collided. Freezia jumped back with a shriek. Tolk landed on his back, and scrambled up.

"Gosh, I'm sorry!" he yelped. "Sorry sorry sorry!"

"Stop it!" she said, brushing hairs off her outfit. "I'm all right. Gack, you smell like dog!"

"That's good, right?" Tolk asked, puzzled.

The slip of parchment whirled up and away, untouched.

"I'll get 'em," Bee said, dumping his pack. A section of the list had settled for a moment in one of the thornbushes about a dozen yards from us. Bee pelted down the hill, just in time for a wisp of wind to flick it out of reach. He stretched out a hand, and the paper edged toward him. The next gust took it away. I realized he didn't have much of a command of basic magik. That'd have to be handled over the coming weeks.

Ignoring him, the three Pervects went into a poised huddle.

"What do you think, Jinetta?" Pologne asked, her finger to her lips. "Should we try Morton's Retrieval Spell?"

"This is too small a volume of matter for that," Freezia said severely. "The fragments might be crushed out of existence.

"I think Obadiah's Reassembly Spell is the best way," Jinetta said.

"Come on! Obadiah's is soo-oooo last week!" Pologne scoffed.

"Don't you think that's what Professor Maguffin would have suggested?"

The name seemed to stop the other two, and they adopted a respectful air.

"I don't know," Freezia said thoughtfully. "I never heard him say that Obadiah's was for outdoor use."

"But he didn't say it *wasn't*—"

Pologne raised her finger. "We could use Petronius's Beard Charm—"

"We'd get a backlash. Think of the third law of Sorcerodynamics!"

"Not the third law, the second!"

"That wouldn't address the ambient power sources," Freezia chided her friends.

"Obadiah's it is, then." Jinetta took out a small alembic and a bright red stick from her backpack. Pologne uncorked a small bottle and poured a few drops of thick liquid into the container. Jinetta stirred it with the stick, and the volume increased to fill the alembic. Scarlet steam started to pour out of the narrow spout. A thread of it shot upward, tilted and began to turn in a circle as if looking around, then headed off toward the nearest shred. A gust of wind caught the red smoke and wound it upward in a spiral. It tried to break loose from the wind, darting almost desperately at the invisible sides of the eddy, until it simply dissipated. The Pervects stared in dismay.

"It didn't work!" Pologne said. "What went wrong?"

"Oh, forget it!" Melvine grumbled impatiently, pushing them all aside. "I'll do it!" He clapped his hands and held them out.

The light whirlwind reconstituted and grew from a cute little dust-devil into an inverted cone thirty feet high. The wind picked up mightily, screaming around us like a hurricane. A gale picked up my hair and started to twist it into a tight spiral on top of my head. Markie had warned me about Melvine's success in Elemental School, and it appeared it had been well earned. I braced myself. The three Pervects clutched one another, hanging onto their bags and each other.

As the cyclone grew, it picked up every loose object on the ground. The closer to the source, the more powerful it was. Yelping, Tolk flew into the air and tumbled helplessly to Melvine's feet. Even Bee and his immense pack were dragged up the hillside, along with loose stones, dust, dry plants and a few small animals. Melvine flattened his hands, and the wind died away. The debris formed a raised ring about three feet high around us. A leg, a foot and an ear were all that showed where Tolk and Bee were half-buried by the dust.

Triumphantly, Melvine picked up the pieces of parchment.

"There!" he said, waving them at me in his pudgy little hand. "That wasn't so hard! What's next, Teach?"

"That was like drowning someone who only wanted a glass of water!" Jinetta snarled. She and the others dusted themselves off resentfully.

"Sour grapes," Melvine sneered back. "You don't know how to do anything with style."

"But it's exactly what I was going to say," I put in. "Melvine, look around you."

Tolk scratched his way out of the pile of dirt and shook himself vigorously. Bee stood up and brushed himself off. Both of them glared at Melvine.

The Cupy regarded me with a hurt stare. "What about it? Didn't I do what you asked?"

"And you ignored what I said about keeping it simple. How many lines of force do you see?"

He peered around. I knew what he was seeing, or rather not seeing. It was one of the reasons I had chosen Sear as a testing ground. The only other place I'd ever been that was almost as magik-bereft was Blut, but I had had a quick chat with Vilhelm, the vampire Dispatcher of Nightmares. He had suggested it would frighten the locals too much if I brought my off-dimension students there for a test. Since Blut didn't get many visitors, they might cause a riot. I agreed that it wasn't worth risking a lynching just for academic experimentation. On the other hand, the Sear natives were very friendly. I could feel them watching us now.

Melvine stared up at the sky then down at the ground, his pudgy face growing more and more distressed.

"Take a good long look," I said.

At last he gave up. "I don't see any."

"Tech-no-nothing," Pologne snorted. From her tastefully appointed backpack she produced a palm-sized orb that glowed the same green as her ensemble. "There's only one to speak of. It's over there, a long way, about fifteen miles."

"Right," I said. "Good call. I'm sure you've all had plenty of experience in storing magikal energy so you don't have to go looking for a line of force when you want to do magik. Right?"

"Uh, no," Jinetta said at last.

"Didn't think so," I said. "It's why your spell didn't work. Why not?"

"Well, there have always been plenty of lines of force when we need them! Perv is full of them."

"It's full of something," Melvine said nastily.

"I'll do the sarcasm here," I said, glaring down at the Cupy. "That was a pretty comprehensive spell. I'll bet you're mostly tapped out now, too. Where are you going to get more magikal energy?"

"From that force line," Melvine said with a sigh as if I was too dumb to live. He stared in the direction of the line Pologne had detected, and concentrated. In a moment, his face contorted. He had discovered something else, I had done the first time I'd visited Sear: something in the natural landscape absorbed magikal energy. Unless you were in line of sight to the lines of force, you couldn't tap into them. "I can hop back to Klah, or Cupid, and stoke up."

"No way," I said, firmly. "Anyone who bounces out for a single moment is off the course for good. You have to play this one out right here according to the rules, and Rule One is 'KISS.' It stands for 'keep it simple, stupid.' If you had just concentrated on the fragments of paper, you could have collected them with an easy attraction spell, or caused them to reconstruct into their original form, which would have been heavy enough to fall to the ground. Since you used up all your stored magik, we're going to have to go to the nearest source to get more. For those of you who aren't used to carrying your own around, it's a good practice to get into. I know that my best teacher," and here I was thinking of Aahz, "told me the smartest thing I could do for myself was to be prepared for an emergency. It's like taking a breath before you jump into a lake. Once you're under water, it's too late to think about air."

"Store energy inside ourselves?" Pologne asked. "You don't use a peripheral device?"

I shrugged. "I hate to rely on anything that can be taken away from me. I'm a rotten swordsman, so anything I wield could end up in the hands of an opponent. I feel the same way about magikal gadgets. That's just my opinion, but you're paying for it."

The Pervects looked anxious and hugged their backpacks. I grinned. Perv was one of the dimensions that made use of magik and technology almost equally. I'd seen for myself how the mix of available power sources made relying on nonmagikal means almost irresistible. In my view it left the users vulnerable.

"That's not fair," Melvine whined. "It's a long way to that line."

"Then stay here and get through the rest of this test without magik," I said pleasantly. "Anyone else up for a walk?"

"Wow, he sounds so serious!" Freezia whispered as I stumped down the hill at the head of the file.

"Yeah, Jinetta, it looks like your aunt was right about him!" Pologne added.

"Not bad," Jinetta said. "It doesn't sound as if he adheres to academic methods, but he seems to have a good grasp of how to present his subject matter."

I kept my chin up and tried to look as if I wasn't listening. I was glad I looked impressive, but inside I knew I was faking it. I hoped they wouldn't find that out before I figured out what I was doing. I didn't want to let them or Aahz down. Though I'd hate to admit it, I had taken the idea from one of the views Bunny liked to watch in her PDA, a dramatic contest called "Sink or Swim," in which the green-skinned master of ceremonies made his contestants go through difficult ordeals in order to get basics they would need to complete other tasks. Usually I tried to ignore the entertainments she viewed while I was working on my magikal research. I couldn't get excited over a game I wasn't watching in the flesh. Once in a while, though, I found myself listening to the absurd and often ridiculously dangerous things the announcer had his contestants attempt. The differences were that I was using this challenge to make a point, and that nobody would get hurt if they used even a little sense. In my opinion, the techniques I wanted them to learn were vital whether they became high-powered executives or the local wizards of ten-house hamlets.

The rising sun did nothing to add to the beauty of the countryside. What dew had condensed overnight evaporated swiftly. The temperature ascended with the white-hot orb, until Tolk was panting out every breath.

"Water water water water water!"

"If you didn't carry on talking, you wouldn't be getting dried out!" Pologne snarled. The Pervect seemed to have less patience with Tolk than either of her companions.

"Take it easy on him, ma'am," Bee said. "If you offered him a drink, he wouldn't keep sayin' it, would he? Here, fella." He offered the doglike being a bulging water skin. Tolk beamed at him. He squeezed the skin so a spray of water leaped up, and lapped at it with his long, pink tongue. His enthusiastic method of drinking sprayed us all with drops, which felt good in the increasing heat.

"Thanks thanks thanks," Tolk said. "That was great!"

"Don't mention it."

Bee slung the skin over his shoulder.

"Hey!" he cried.

The water container seemed to throw itself onto the ground. Bee bent to retrieve it, but it scooted away from his grasp. He hustled after it.

"Hey, come back here!"

I smiled quietly to myself. The fun was beginning.

The lanky soldier opened up his stride to follow the fleeing bag, but it kept just out of his reach.

"Hey, I've heard of running water, but this is ridiculous!" Melvine chortled.

"Offer to share!" I shouted after Bee. The young man spun and snapped to attention.

"What, sir?"

"I said—oh, never mind." Behind him, the water skin seemed to melt into the ground. Bee turned around and searched. The skin, and the hole into which it had fallen, had both disappeared.

Bee turned back to me, his earnest face puzzled. "Where'd it go, sir?"

"I'm afraid you were just hit by one of the local hazards, Bee," I said apologetically. "The locals really know how to make merchandise move. You can probably tell that water's pretty scarce here. Your water bottle represented a good deal of wealth to someone who lives on Sear. They prize shade and water above anything else."

"What locals?" Jinetta asked. "I don't see any signs of habitation."

"They live beneath the surface," I said, tapping the ground with my foot.

"They could be dangerous!" Freezia exclaimed. "They could overpower us! They could," she lowered her voice, looking around in fear, "kill us and eat us."

"I don't think so," I said reassuringly. "They're only about an inch high."

"What?" she shrieked.

"See," Melvine hooted. "You wet your pants for nothing."

"Shut up, you carnival prize!"

I marched onward. The students followed me, still sniping at one another. How was I going to get through six weeks of this?

I swatted at the back of my neck. A fly had been circling me for some time, evidently deciding where it would be best to plunge in its stinger. Gingerly I prodded the welt.

"Everybody with sensitive skin might use a little of their magik for pest repellent," I suggested. "This hurts a lot."

"I can fix it, Skeeve," Tolk said eagerly. He bounded over and touched the sore spot. The pain died away instantly.

"That's great, Tolk," I said. "I appreciate it. But don't forget to protect yourself."

He frowned and cocked his head to one side. "Not sure how how how."

"Picture a suit made of magikal force that fits your body closely but doesn't cut off your air supply," I said. "Don't use too much power."

"I don't think I can do that," Bee admitted. "I never tried anything like that before."

"What do you know how to do?" I asked.

"I only know a few spells," he admitted. "I'm not up there like these ladies," he indicated the Pervects, "who've had the benefit of advanced education."

The Pervects turned their noses up at him. Bee looked downtrodden.

"Well, we can build on what you have learned," I said encouragingly. "What are they?"

"Well, I can do Dispell," Bee began. A dust-devil spun in our direction. I recognized it as one of the Sear natives. It whisked up Pologne's leg, heading for her color-coordinated backpack.

"Aaagh!" she cried, batting at her tiny assailant. "Get it off me!"

"Bee, use it now!" I said.

Bee pointed at the miniature whirlwind. "Dispell!"

The gray cone died away, leaving a bright red node about the size of my thumbnail. The little creature dropped off Pologne's leg and promptly dug itself into the sand.

"Ugh!" she said, stomping on the place where the Sear disappeared. "Disgusting!"

"That's very useful," I told Bee. "It's a good defense as well as being able to undo mistakes you make. What's next?"

"Well. Datspell."

Melvine chortled. "Why am I not surprised? And what's that do? Put the spell you just took off back on?"

"Nossir," Bee said, hurt. "Well, it means I can disguise myself pretty good. Like this!"

Suddenly, the skinny frame of the former corporal was replaced by a familiar image. A male Klahd with a big, hulking frame, wide shoulders that tapered down to a surprisingly small waist, big hands that almost concealed the miniature crossbow in his hand. I felt a smile spread slowly on my face.

"That's Guido."

The image vanished, and Bee's narrow earnest face reappeared. "Yessir. Sergeant Swatter, we called him. I really admired him, sir."

"Stop calling me sir," I said. "Just Skeeve. Datspell's pretty good, too. What else can you do?"

"Well," Bee said, "just a few little things. But I practice them all the time. Spoo!" he exclaimed suddenly as we began the descent down a steep hill. He seemed to levitate over a rock in his path.

"That's pretty good," I said. "You know how to fly."

"Oh, no, s—I mean, Skeeve. That's just Cantrip. I learned that in the army. It helps a lot when you're on maneuvers over rough ground. A lot of the guys came in with sprained ankles and broken legs. Cantrip keeps me from falling over. 'Cept I gotta say 'spoo' to invoke it. It's 'oops' spelled backwards."

"How hokey!" Freezia exclaimed. Bee looked offended. I didn't blame him.

"Don't you use mnemonics in your magik?" I asked her innocently.

"Sure I do," she said. "But *spoo!*" She broke into giggles. "That's so silly!"

"If it works, then it's not silly. You'll see. Bee's going to teach us how to do it when we're back at the inn."

"Learn from a Klahd? Never!" Pologne declared.

I let the statement stand, and walked on in silence.

About four paces later, she spoke in a much smaller voice. "Of course, when I say Klahd, I don't mean *you*, Skeeve."

Chapter Seven

"Is it too late to try beads?"
G. A. CUSTER

It took almost two hours to walk over the rough dry terrain to where we could draw from the force line. The hike back was worse. The sun had risen higher in the sky, and the glare was blinding. I was hot, and my feet felt like they had been pounded between two large flat rocks.

By the time we were back in my target area everyone was in a bad mood, including me. Everything Melvine said came out as a whine. The three Pervects sniped at one another verbally, but united to belittle the others. Tolk growled if any of us got too close to him. Bee still spoke politely, but clipped his words off sharply.

"It's hot, and I'm tired," Melvine complained. "Let's go back to Klahd and do this tomorrow. I promise to be more economical. C'mon, Skeeve, what do you say?"

"Nope," I said. "This'll be fun. You'll see."

"Fun? This dimension is a drag!"

"Hey, you should go work for my cousin," Tolk sneered. "He's got the sullen-on-a-stick franchise for Lower Rangooza."

"Meanie!" Melvine sniveled.

"Grow up!" Pologne said. "I'm sick of both of you. It's like traveling with my little brothers."

"All right," I said, coming to a halt under the largest tree on the hill. "You've got a list of twelve things. Find them all, and get them down there," I pointed to the spit of land poking out into the glittering sea. "Go for it." I sat down against the tree trunk with my hands behind my head. I had a great view of the whole test area.

The challenge was a simple one. All of the items were brightly colored and in plain sight. The Sear natives had promised to keep from moving them until one of my students came within a couple of paces, and then they had to give a sporting chance, not dragging the item underground right away.

The other thing I had not told my class was that the natives had a very high body temperature. Freezia learned it the hard way when she spotted the first item, a bright blue cylinder. She and Bee noticed it at the same time. In spite of the Cantrip, Bee wasn't as fast on his feet as the graduate student. She dove for the cylinder, only to have it scoot from under her fingertips. Quickly, she brought the other hand smashing down, capturing the object. She plucked the tiny red Sear off the bottom of it.

"Ow!" she cried, dropping it. "They're hot!"

The little being, deprived of its shade, grabbed for the next nearest thing, Freezia's backpack. It started pulling at the strap with surprising strength. Freezia pulled back. Bee laughed at the sight of a full-grown Pervect having a tug-of-war with a creature a mere fraction of her size.

"What are you laughing at, you dolt?" she asked. "No, don't do that!"

The Sear, unable to take the backpack, crawled along the strap and wriggled inside. Freezia threw open the flap and began to excavate its contents, trying to find the intruder.

As her things began to hit the ground, more red dots came swarming up. They latched onto each item and began to drag them away. The Pervect suddenly looked up and saw her possessions disappearing.

"My compact!" Freezia shrieked, crawling after the nearest Sear. It was carrying a gold disk.

"Time!" I shouted. You don't have time! You already spent twenty minutes finding the first part!"

"I want it back! It's a Goochy San Channel!"

"You can get it later!"

She ignored me. The Sear vanished into a crack in the ground. She started picking away at the edge.

"Oh, my manicure!" she wailed as a chip of orange polish went flying. Furious, she pointed a broken fingernail at the earth. "Cavata!"

Stones and dirt began to scatter upward. She uncovered the gold disk, only to see it slip into another fissure. "No! You little thief!" The dirt flew faster. She disappeared behind the spray.

In the confusion, she had forgotten all about the cylinder. Bee picked it up and put it in his belt pouch, and went in search of the next item on the list.

With a full complement of magik under his belt, Melvine took to the air. With a pleased grin, he descended toward the spot where I had planted a folded yellow sheet. The look of alarm that crossed his face told me that the natives had appeared. They were going to beat him to it. Melvine whipped up a curlicue of wind and made it whisk around the circumference of the sheet to drive them back. I was glad to see him conserving energy.

Tolk found a bundle of bright green sticks. When he stooped to pick them up in his teeth, a native attached itself to his collar. When Tolk trotted away, his collar fell off. It started to bury itself in sand.

"Thass mine!" he exclaimed around his mouthful. He stood transfixed, staring at the swiftly disappearing neckwear. He opened his mouth to let go of the struts, then clapped his jaw shut.

"Uh-huh, you're no' go'a cash me gha' way," he said. He started digging furiously with his front paws, tossing hot sand in every direction. The collar surfaced briefly. Tolk tossed his head, and the neckpiece levitated.

But the natives had magik of their own, and they outnumbered him. He couldn't keep it in the air. He plunged forward to capture it in his paws, but it disappeared into the dirt.

"Da'!" he swore.

He trotted down to the headland and deposited his mouthful beside the cylinder Bee had already placed there. He saw me watching him, and shook his head furiously.

"My mother gave me that collar!"

I threw him a regretful shrug.

"Give that back!" I heard Melvine yell. I sprang up. The Cupy was halfway down the hill beyond a dry gully. He pointed a finger at a clump of dirt. The clump exploded upward. "No! Give it to me. Give it back!" Boom! He tracked his minute opponents to another clump, and blew that one up, too.

"Melvine! Don't waste energy!" I yelled. "You haven't got four hours to hike back to the force line!"

"They stole my blankie!" Melvine howled, his baby face screwing up in a knot. "I want it back!"

"Trade them for it!"

"I don't want to! I want my blankie!" He sat down heavily on the ground. "This isn't fun any more!"

By evening, only Jinetta of the three Pervects still had her backpack. The contents of Bee's field pack had been depleted considerably by the natives. Melvine kept patting his pockets to make sure none of his other possessions had gone missing. Every time we heard a rustle in the grass, all six of my students jumped.

When I called time, they staggered up the hill to where I was waiting. They looked tired and dejected.

"Let's get the camp set up for the night," I said. "I've got three tents here. The big one is for you ladies. The men and I will share the other two. When they're up, we'll make dinner."

"Stay in a tent?" Jinetta asked disdainfully. "Why not go back to the inn?"

"Because," I explained patiently, yet once again, "this is a test of your practical skills. You may never sleep outside again, but you're going to try it for one night."

"But it's inconvenient," Freezia said.

"Yes, it is," I said cheerfully. "Well, the tents won't put themselves up!"

"Sure they will," Melvine said. He aimed a thumb at the nearest bundle of canvas and string. The stiff arrangement of sheets animated, billowing out to the correct shape. Pleased with himself, Melvine relaxed his spell. The tent promptly collapsed.

"I'll help you," Corporal Bee said, starting toward the puzzled Cupy. "You forgot to put up the tent poles—"

I put a hand in his chest and pushed him back.

"Let him solve the problem," I said. "You can help me get the campfire going."

"Yes, sir, I mean, Skeeve."

"I know how to do it," Pologne said. "I reached the rank of Tracker in the Perv Scouts." She marched over to the next folded tent and started to take it apart. Melvine pretended not to care, but I could see him shooting furtive glances in her direction to see how she did it.

"What do we do about...?" Jinetta whispered in her friend's ear.

Pologne turned to me. "I don't suppose you have a shovel, do you?"

Jinetta immediately added two and two together.

"You're kidding," she exclaimed.

"Nope," I said. "No chamber pots out here. No flush toilets. Just the basics: you and a hole in the ground."

Freezia wore a meditative expression. "I suppose we could blink the you-know-what away."

"Don't waste power," I said firmly. "It won't kill you to use primitive means for one night."

"Yes," Pologne said. "I have done it."

"Me, too," Bee put in.

"Who cares about you?" Jinetta said, rolling her eyes.

In spite of the Pervects' disdain, Bee generously lent the camping equipment in his gigantic field pack for the others to use. Jinetta and Freezia disappeared over the ridge of the hill, and returned looking relieved but chagrined.

"That was *disgusting*," Jinetta was saying. "This had better help us a *lot*."

Fortunately, Jinetta's pack contained enough camp rations for all three Pervects. I had to grin at the expressions on the faces of the other three students as she ripped open a packet and dumped purple and brown lumps into a big dish.

"Are they dead?" Pologne asked, prodding the lumps disdainfully.

"No, just stunned," Jinetta assured her. As she spoke, the mess began to stir.

"It's alive!" Tolk barked.

"Of course it's alive, you silly canid," Freezia said. "Pervects don't eat dead food. Did you bring anything to put on them?"

"No," Jinetta sighed. "They were out of sweet and sour sauce at the camping store."

"Oh, Crom," Pologne said. "We have to eat them with *no sauce?*"

They divided up the dish and began to pick at their shares without enthusiasm.

Bee produced hard bacon and biscuit from the depths of his pack and set them simmering over the fire. I had a crock of stew that Bunny had cooked for us. I took the preservative spell off it and set it to heat up. Tolk tried bites of each. I thought it smelled pretty good, but he was unimpressed.

"No flavor," he said. "I mean, maybe it's nourishing, but bland!"

Melvine wouldn't eat anything at all. "I can't believe you didn't bring any mush for me," he said. "That's all right! First you try to drown me, and now you starve me! What's that?"

A fly the size of my fingertip zipped past the campfire. A few more circled around, and zoomed out of the light.

"Bugs!" he wailed. "I hate bugs!" He pointed a finger at them.

"Melvine, no!"

"Why," I asked again, as we sheltered underneath a rocky overhang with a huge dung fire going at the entrance to our makeshift cave, clutching our food to us in the tight quarters, "why didn't you just use a repelling spell? Why did you try to blow them up?"

"You have to admit, he succeeded," Tolk said, with a touch of humor. "He blew them up, all right."

Beyond the fire we could see and hear the giant stinging wasps buzzing furiously as they tried to get in at us. I strengthened the repellent spell I had placed on the cave mouth. I had conserved most of my power, knowing I would need it for many minor emergencies. Like this one.

"And our dinner burned because we had to get away from the killer bugs he created," Bee added.

"You're eating it anyway. The smell is making us sick," Pologne said. Again.

I shook my head. I knew that Pervects could eat anything, but these three had never been exposed to other kinds of food. They were very young.

"It's cold," Jinetta said. "How is it that it was so hot all day, and now it is freezing?" She huddled as near the fire as she dared, shivering in her thin clothes. I cast a light warming spell in the cave. Everyone relaxed visibly and finished their dinner without too many more complaints.

"Look," I said, after Bee had shown the rest of the group how to scrub the dishes out with sand in lieu of a handy water supply. "You didn't do too well today. You only managed to secure three items off the list. You forgot everything I told you, and you let your tempers get in the way of being effective in the field. It is not that hard to deal with the natives. I told you what is important to them. None of you exploited those traits at all. You've already found out that brute force doesn't get you anywhere. When you found yourself with two courses of action you could take, you usually fell back on the one that related to you personally, not to the mission at hand. I wanted you to operate in a practical and simple fashion, and all of you got fancy. You didn't have to."

"What has chasing red dots around the landscape got to do with anything practical and simple?" Pologne asked.

"Well, what do you think I meant you to learn in today's exercise?" I countered.

"I don't know."

"Not to waste power?"

"That's one of the lessons I hope you absorbed," I said.

"What else?"

"How to get ripped off by little monsters who sneak up when you're not looking?" Freezia asked.

"It's to teach you to make quick decisions," I said. "The *right* decisions. When you're faced with a dangerous situation, the last thing you can do is waste time, or I guarantee it *will* be the last thing you do."

"We'll be working in offices in six months," Jinetta said. "Making a slow and carefully considered decision is hardly going to prove fatal."

"You'll be at the top of your game if you can assess a situation coolly and take action before anyone else does," I countered. "Believe me, I've spent plenty of time in my office, talking to potential clients. The best solution is usually the one I hit on first. Let me tell you how well that's worked out for me: I don't need your tuition to get by. It's a lot of money, but it's *bupkis*," I used a term I'd heard Aahz use once— I assumed it was Pervish, "to what I saved from *my share* of M.Y.T.H., Inc.'s take, and I had a LOT of partners. I'm on hiatus for as long as I want to be, and if I felt like doing my research in the middle of the biggest city in the busiest dimension you could think of with room service, gold-plated doorknobs and hot-and-cold running entertainment, I could afford to do it. Sorry," I said to the others. "I don't like to brag about wealth, but if that's the only thing you understand, then I've got to do it. I *want* you to understand."

Looking thoughtful, they huddled together to go to sleep.

"So, what was it Skeeve said about the natives?" Tolk asked, in his friendly way, while the students were clearing up from breakfast. The flies had gone. Melvine looked relieved. As a means of atonement I made him take down all three tents. He was much better at striking them than erecting them.

"Too bad you weren't paying attention," Pologne said, holding up her research globe.

Melvine brightened. "You took notes!" He stuck out a hand, and the globe went flying to him.

"Give that back!"

"How does it work?" Melvine asked. He invoked the orb, and high-pitched babbling issued from it. "There."

My voice rang out tinnily. "...They prize shade and water above anything else."

"Trying to keep information for yourself?" Tolk asked suspiciously.

Pologne looked sulky. "I'm the only one who went to the trouble of taking notes. Why should you get the benefit of my work?"

"Teamwork," I said. "You'll get this done much faster if you work together."

None of them paid attention. They went off in six different directions, each with his or her eyes on the ground.

"Got one!" Tolk yelped.

He had spotted a long purple pole. Red spots began to bubble up out of the earth, preparing to drag it under. Tolk turned and lifted a leg over a piece of dry ground. The dots converged upon the area he had watered and began to burrow into it with a pleased noise. Happily, Tolk picked up the pole in his teeth and trotted down the hill toward the headland.

"Did you see what he just did?" Pologne asked Jinetta in horror.

"Well, I'm certainly not going to—you know."

"No," Pologne said thoughtfully. "But we have a canteen."

I leaned back against my tree and smiled.

Chapter Eight

"Where's the instruction manual?"
T. EDISON

By midmorning, all twelve of the objects lay on the spit of land overlooking the sea. The students looked at me expectantly. I gave them a smile of approval.

"Congratulations," I said. "You finished with over an hour to spare. Now, all you have to do is assemble this gizmo. It's pretty straightforward. The pieces slot together. Be careful. It opens outward under its own power."

"What's it do?" Melvine asked.

"You'll find out when you're done."

"All right," Jinetta said, tapping her hands together delicately. "Shall we try Obadiah's Assembly Spell?"

"Let's," Pologne agreed. The three Pervects put their hands together. A few of the parts twirled in place and began to slide toward one another, then drooped to a halt.

"Oh, I told you that was an indoor spell!" Freezia said. "There's too much interference out here. We have to find the right process. An *outdoor* process."

"Of course," Pologne said. She took out her small globe. "Let's see, there are enchantments for puzzle pieces, broken pieces, crazy paving—which one shall we use?"

I groaned. "You don't have to use a fixed process. Improvise. There are six of you. Come up with something new."

"But Professor Maguffin said—"

"Raspberries to Professor Maguffin," Melvine sneered. "I don't want to be here all day."

"We can do this without magik," Bee said. He started arranging things on the ground. "See, there's a triangular slot, and here's a peg that's the same shape."

"No, we can do it with magik," Jinetta insisted. "All we need to do is find the right spell. Freezia, what do you think?"

"I can't recall anything from Spellcrafting 501 that covered a situation like this."

"Maybe there wasn't one," Tolk said. "Look look look, let's just put the pieces together by hand."

"If you insist," Jinetta said, clearly distressed at having to think outside the box or, rather, classroom. "It still feels *wrong*."

"I found a flat tab and a flat slot," Melvine exclaimed. "Yeah!" He pushed them together, and they clicked satisfyingly.

"But what about this thing?" Pologne asked Bee, flapping the sheet. "It hasn't got pegs."

"No, but it's got symbols printed on it. See here? There's an arrow, and there's a circle. Look for parts marked the same way."

I began to understand why Guido had prized this shy country boy. He was a born organizer. With the Pervects balking all the way, he began to get the class working in the same direction.

It wasn't going to be easy or a one-man operation. I had scoured the Bazaar for a device that had to be levitated while it was being assembled. Until all the pieces were in place it couldn't be balanced on the single pole that supported it, and it could not be put together upside down. Once Bee figured that out he suggested politely that the more adept magicians use the last vestiges of power they were carrying to help support the incomplete device.

"I think this goes here," Melvine said, pushing the narrow blue fork into a slot. "It's a tight fit, but I can get it."

"Stop that," Jinetta ordered Melvine. "You're going to break that!"

"No, I'm not!" Melvine insisted. He pushed harder. The fork snapped. He glared at the Pervect. "See what you made me do?"

"What I made you do?" Jinetta echoed. "You did it."

"No, I didn't," Melvine said. "Didn't you see, Skeeve? She distracted me, and the piece broke!"

"You know who he reminds me of?" Pologne said to Freezia. "Carmellanga."

Freezia grinned. "Yes, I see. Here, Melvine, you can put this piece in for me."

She handed him a huge white spring. It packed substantial magikal power because it had to fling open the large yellow canvas. Melvine took it from her and ducked underneath the edge.

"Do you see a double-slot under here anywhere? Ugh! It's a tight fit. *Umph*—" he grunted.

Delicately, Freezia flicked her fingers.

The spring rebounded, sending the small Cupy hurtling end over end off the edge of the cliff. He landed in the sea about ten feet below us.

"Aagh! Salt water!" Melvine levitated out of the water and headed for the Pervects with blood in his eye. "Why did you do that?"

"Us?" Jinetta asked innocently, regarding the dripping Cupy. "Why do you think we did anything?"

"You," he turned angrily to me. "How come you didn't tell me this thing was dangerous?"

Pologne raised her recorder ball and invoked it.

My voice rattled out, "Be careful. It opens outward under its own power."

Melvine gave me a fierce look and flew about a hundred feet away from us to dry out and sulk. The Pervects shared a sly look among themselves.

"Uh, who is Carmellanga?" I asked.

"Oh, she was a girl in our sorority," Jinetta said casually. "Always blaming other people for the things she did herself. She was just careless, and she never liked to take responsibility."

"Lazy," Freezia added. "I never had patience with her. One day we just let her hoist herself on her own petard. The housemother caught her cheating on her thesis, and she had no one to blame but herself. Like you said, though, we don't have time to let nature take its course."

"That's it for me," Jinetta said apologetically as the large yellow sail sagged down onto her head. "I'm out of power."

"I've got a little more," Bee said. "Tell me what to do."

"Push the magik up under here," the tallest Pervect said, poking at the canvas from underneath. "Hurry! It's falling over. No, up. Up!"

"Where does this thing go?" Freezia demanded, holding a green box.

"Up under there," Tolk said, pointing with his nose to a spot inside the top of the sail. Both of his forepaws were occupied keeping the struts from collapsing.

"I see. I can't reach it!"

"I can," Melvine said. The box rose from Freezia's fingers, and just slotted into place before Melvine's hands dropped. "I'm tapped."

"That's the last piece," Pologne said with satisfaction. They all stepped back to admire their handiwork. "But what's it do?"

"It's a shade-caster," I said. "I told you that the natives are desperate for ways to get out of the sun. It's for them."

"Why should we give it to them when they stole all of our things?" Freezia asked with a toss of her head.

"Do you want your stuff back?" I asked. "Then trade this to them."

They looked skeptical until the red dots began surging up out of the ground under the shadow of the yellow sail. I invoked the activator, and the shadow spread out twice as far in every direction. More and more Sear natives popped up, cooing audibly as they enjoyed the opacity that shielded them from the pounding sunlight. Then I deactivated it.

The Sears let out a surprised squeak, retreating into the center, chasing the shrinking shadow. The yellow canvas umbrella collapsed until it was nothing but a palm-sized dot.

The red spots sank into the sandy soil. Soon, things began to pop up like bizarre mushrooms. Pologne's backpack was the first to reappear. Tolk's collar came up next, followed by an upheaval that revealed a heap of standard army issue items.

"Well, there's my axe and fire-starter kit," Bee exclaimed. He thought about it for a moment. "I was kind of fine without them, I guess."

Freezia's and Jinetta's packs returned very close to the supporting member, as if the Sears were hinting they would like the umbrella opened again.

"Not until I see MY stuff," Melvine said, folding his arms.

A flask, a yo-yo, a couple of books with lurid covers, a travel pillow, a box of candy popped up, as did a silky fragment of cloth. Melvine grabbed for them and began to stuff them in the concealed pockets of his overall. A pair of purple panties emerged next.

"Oops, that's mine, too," Melvine said, diving for it. His face scarlet, he put them away. I raised my eyebrows, but Melvine wouldn't meet my gaze. I made a mental note of it. Those panties looked suspiciously like one of Bunny's that I had frequently seen drying on our clothesline.

"Mission accomplished," I said. "Let's go home."

As soon as we returned to the inn, I took Melvine aside by the ear.

"Ow! Hey, what's your problem!"

"About those panties," I said in a low voice. "If those ARE yours, fine. But if they do belong to someone else, they had better be back where they belong in one second flat."

"You're accusing me of stealing?" Melvine whined defensively.

"I'm not accusing you of anything. I'm putting a hypothetical situation to you. And hypothetically, the next time anything belonging to anyone goes missing, you're out the door whether it's your fault or not."

"That's not fair! I'm telling my auntie on you!"

"So what?" I said. "I'll tell your auntie on YOU."

The rosy cheeks paled.

"Fine," he snarled, and vanished.

After a nice normal lunch and a relaxing bath, I set up some exercises in the courtyard for the students to practice basic levitation and traction spells. I had dropped back to Sear and brought one of the tiny red creatures with me to Klah. In exchange for a large supply of fresh water, the little creature agreed to run around the stableyard and dodge spells for the afternoon. I was monitoring the situation closely so it didn't get hurt by the clumsy maneuvers of my students, but I didn't have to worry. Most of them couldn't or wouldn't hit him. Only Tolk had made a successful attempt so far, clapping the Sear into an invisible cup of force. I had made the mistake of praising the simplicity of his spell. His smug scorn of the others had finally prompted me to send him out to take a walk on his own until he regained proportion. After Bee he was the weakest magikally.

I wondered how it was, watching Melvine and Jinetta having yet another argument about how much power to use for a simple levitation spell, that Aahz had never wanted to rip my head off for being an obstreperous pain. On the other hand, perhaps sometimes Aahz DID want to rip my head off. He had never done it. In retrospect, I admired his restraint. Melvine reminded me a lot of myself in the early days, when Garkin was trying to hammer the basics of candle-lighting and feather-levitation into me. I whined a lot, too, preferring to complain instead of putting in the grunt work. To complicate things, Melvine had tons more magikal potential than I ever did. He had already proved he was capable of misusing it. I was afraid he would get the others hurt or killed if he got careless at the wrong moment. I had to counteract his cockiness somehow. It didn't help that the Pervects put him on the defensive. They had their own insecurities.

"Don't overthink it," I cautioned Jinetta for about the millionth time, as we went over a practice exercise in the yard at the inn. "Just use a whisker of power. The process doesn't have to have a fancy name. Just do it."

The little Sear dashed up and back in front of Jinetta like a duck in a shooting gallery. The tall Pervect dithered until I thought I was going to go insane from frustration.

Her friends offered endless advice.

"How about a Haley's Capture Spell?" said Pologne.

"No! That's for non-physical images. Just work up a Sticky-Floor Charm," Freezia suggested.

"I keep *telling* you, that's an indoor spell."

"Quiet," I said. "You're confusing her. Let her work it out."

"But I can't," Jinetta said. "What if I get it wrong? What if when I throw it he runs out of reach?"

I groaned. "Just throw *something* at him. He won't even leave the yard. Your intent is to capture him. Improvise. Don't overdo it."

"But our professor said there's one ideal spell for every situation," Jinetta complained, also for about the millionth time.

"That's right," Freezia said. "He hammered it into us: 'one problem, one perfect solution.'"

I was starting to dislike their professor, and I'd never met him. "And what happens if the problem gets worse while you're trying to figure out what that perfect solution is?"

"Then I need to choose a different spell," Jinetta said. "Magik's not for wimps, you know. I can do it. I just haven't figured out the right one yet."

"There isn't just one right answer to any problem," I said. Inspiration dawned, and I could hardly keep myself from grinning. I threw up a hand, and the Sear stopped running back and forth. "I'll prove it. Class dismissed. See you at dinner."

Chapter Nine

"One man's feast is another man's toxic dump."
IRON CHEF

I rearranged seating at the broad, rough-hewn wooden rectangular dinner table, setting a seemingly random pattern of boy-girl-boy-girl all the way around along the big wooden benches. I wanted plenty of elbow room in between the students in case things got messy With the Pervects' help, Bunny served dinner. As before, the Pervects supplied all the food, though they prepared only their own courses. Bunny made the rest. Normally we shared cooking duties. She and I had agreed that for the duration I wouldn't have to cook, in order to maintain my high status as Lord High Professor, a position above such 'menial' tasks.

What I could only describe as 'mixed' aromas came from the kitchen as Bee and Tolk served the food: three bowls of noisome wriggling goo for the Pervects; Klahdish food for three of us; a bowl of pale gray, faintly moldy-smelling cereal for Melvine; and raw green meat for Tolk. Even after years of living with Aahz, it was hard to look at or smell Pervish food, but the others' preferred choices didn't look that much better to me. I'd tapped one of the massive kegs in the cellar, since beer was one of the few things we could all agree on, and floated two huge foaming pitchers to the table.

"Terrific!" I said cheerfully as I invited everyone to sit down. "Everything looks good. Thanks, Bunny."

"A pleasure, Skeeve," Bunny smiled. She shimmied onto the bench at the head of the table next to me.

"Smells terrific, ma'am," Bee said.

"Thank you!" The beam Bunny bestowed upon the skinny corporal made him blush out to his prominent ears. Hastily, he took his place.

"And now," I began as everyone picked up his or her cutlery, "before you eat, I want everyone to pick up his or her bowl, and hand it to the person on your left."

"What????" they demanded.

"Just do it," I said. "As your tutor in practical magik, I want you to take Tolk's food, and hand yours to Melvine." Trying not to grin wickedly, I politely handed my plate to Bunny, who passed her steaming bowl of broccabbage and brined meat to Tolk. I accepted a bowl of writhing purple goo. "Everyone got some? Now, eat up!"

"No way!" Melvine whined, pushing the struggling entrée as far away from him as he could. "I want my mush!"

"Not tonight," I said. "What you get tonight is in that bowl, and only in that bowl."

"No!" he howled, beginning to pound on the table with his fists. "I want my mush! I want my mush!"

"Melvine," I said ominously, "do you want me to go get your aunt?"

He looked up at me, his lower lip stuck out, tantrum forgotten. "No-ooo."

"Then try it," I said. "You might like it. You never know."

He wrinkled up his little pug nose. "It's *icky*!"

Privately, I agreed with him. I would rather eat my bowl than what was in it, but I had a plan for getting around the 'ugh' factor. I was happy to offer clues to the students to achieve the same end for themselves.

"If you can't stand it in that form, change it in some way. You know plenty of magik. Something in what you learned in Elemental School ought to work. Give it a try."

"Well—" The big baby poked at the creepy-crawlies with a spoon. "But they stink."

"True," I agreed. "Try deodorizing them. Or change the smell. Pour gravy on them. Freeze them. Cover them in cheese dip. I don't care. Just as long as, by the end of the meal, the contents of that dish are in your stomach."

"Ewwwwwwwww." Melvine might protest, but he was intelligent enough to know I meant business. He couldn't

outstubborn me as long as I held the ultimate trump card: Markie. He crouched down at eye level to the purple creatures to study them.

"You're not eating," I observed.

"Gimme a minute!"

I glanced at the Pervects. They didn't look any happier than Melvine. I knew Pervects could eat anything that didn't eat them first, but I guessed that the girls had lived such sheltered lives that they had never tried off-dimension food. The prospect was clearly bringing them to the extreme edge of nausea. I had to enjoy the look on Pologne's face as she picked unhappily at the bowl of mush.

"It's dead," she wailed. "It disintegrated!"

"That's the way it's supposed to look," I said. "Melvine doesn't have very many teeth, so he needs soft food."

Pologne took a spoonful, and promptly spewed it across the table. "Gack! It's like sand!"

"And this?" Jinetta asked, presenting what had been Bee's plate. "There's no smell at all! It might be made of plastic. That's not real food."

"Sure it is. Klahds eat it every day."

Jinetta looked horrified. "You guys are *sick*."

Tolk looked as though he agreed with her. His nose was almost flat against the table, as he stalked at the food he had received from Bunny. When he decided it wasn't looking, he lunged towards it.

"Grrrrrrr," he snarled at the chunk of meat. It didn't move. I was tempted to make it wiggle, just to make the contest more interesting. He shoved his sensitive black nose close. *Sniff sniff sniff sniff.*

"Hey!" he yelped, retreating. "It bit me!"

"It didn't bite you," I said. "It's just a sharp smell. It's cooked in vinegar."

"That's disgusting!"

Melvine paddled his food with his spoon. "No, THIS is disgusting!"

"Mine's worse," Freezia said.

"No, mine's worse!"

"Try it," I said, leveling a fork at them. "We're not leaving this table until you all eat your dinners. One way or another."

"*You're* not eating," Pologne said to me.

All the other students turned to stare.

Gulp. I knew that this acid test would come sooner or later. I was prepared for it—I hoped. I took a deep breath. With everyone's eyes on me, I swept my hands over the bowl in my best stage-magician style, and created an illusion of blinding light. Concealed by the glare, I sent one piece of the reeking, writhing Pervish food into a covered container in the kitchen and exchanged it for what the container held, which was cooked squirrel-rat meat dyed purple to look like Pervish food. Before the others' eyes could recover from the light, I stabbed the chunk with my fork and stuffed it into my mouth.

"See," I said, as I chewed. "Nothing to it." I swallowed hastily. "So, how was your day, Bunny?"

"Er, fine, Skeeve. Did you see anything interesting on Sear?"

"Not much," I admitted, 'enchanting' another piece of meat. "You've seen one arid desert landscape, you've seen them all."

Bunny pursed her lips in a little smile. "I only like sandy terrain when it's close to the ocean. Don't you, Tolk?"

She distracted the Terrier from his stalking of the corned beef. He was winning the contest, but just barely. "Grrrrr— Uh, yeah! I like to run in the waves. Good smells! Good smells! Yip!" He bit into a cluster of broccabbage, and it squirted butter all over his face. "It sprayed me! I must spray it back." He clambered up onto the bench, and prepared to raise his leg.

"No!" I burst out, levitating out of my chair and pulling him down. "It's good. Really. Just calm down. Look, you almost spilled the beer. Just sit down." I patted him on the head. The vegetable lay inert where he had dropped it. "See? It didn't mean any harm. Go on."

The canine shot several looks of distrust at the vegetables, but he returned to his seat. "Okay. You're the boss."

The Pervects snickered to themselves and shot meaningful glances at one another. Their expressions changed as they returned their attention to the food. Pologne looked like she might faint. Jinetta wore a skeptical expression. Freezia seemed so hopeless I thought she was going to give up and leave the table.

Bee had taken my instructions literally. After watching in astonishment that turned inevitably into horrified disgust at the attempted escape of his entree, he thwacked each bite of Pervish food firmly with the heavy end of his spoon. Then, with his eyes squeezed firmly shut, he gulped down the mouthful.

"How are you doing, Bee?" I asked.

"Okay, sir," he gasped out, cracking one eye. "Sometimes we got food as bad as this in mess, sir!"

"Carry on, then."

"Yes, sir!"

"I saw a prediction of bad weather in the crystal ball today," Bunny said, taking a delicate forkful of food. "It's supposed to hail tomorrow in the middle of the afternoon over most of western Klah."

"We'll work inside, then," I said. "Did you see anything else interesting?"

Tolk gulped the rest of his meal down in five bites, then gazed over his empty bowl at everyone in turn with big, sad, puppy-dog eyes. I didn't know if he was hoping for leftovers, or he had a bellyache from eating the strange food. No question about Melvine; he was in a full-scale sulk, peering down at the squirming objects in his bowl. He had only eaten one of them. I could tell that he was trying to figure out a way to persuade me not to make him eat the others. I calmly beamed another 'bite' from the kitchen and went on with my meal. Bunny and I went on with our conversation, doing our best to include our visitors.

"Oh, yes, I did see something fun, Skeeve! The semi-final of *Sink or Swim: Imper* was on the Crystal Ball Network last night," Bunny said gleefully. "Five full-grown Imps knocked on their fannies by one itty bitty female Gremlin. They were all disqualified at once. They should never underestimate girl power. Right, Freezia?" she asked, turning to the Pervect on my right.

The medium-sized student didn't reply.

"I'd have said, don't underestimate Gremlins," I chuckled, picking up the verbal ball and running with it. "I'm surprised she was visible for the crystal ball. Gremlins are hard to spot." I knew; I'd met a few in my time.

Bunny broke off a crust of bread. "Oh, well, they have magicians with several crystals focused on the site at the same time," she explained. "And a master magician coordinating the images to transmit to all of us viewers. She couldn't possibly keep out of sight of all of them at once. She goes on to the final contest with two or three others. The Deveel, the Gargoyle, and I think one other. It's so exciting! I wonder how they think of all the contests they have to go through!"

With the inevitable before them, the other students were finally letting themselves experiment. Freezia was trying out a sense-deadening spell so she didn't taste anything. She had to be careful not to bite her tongue or eat her own fingers. She bit the bowls off two spoons before she finally got the hang of eating, and was making steady if unhappy progress.

Pologne went the other way in terms of sensory input. She did a reanimation spell on the green meat. It jumped and writhed just like a genuine Pervish meal. She seemed to get some satisfaction out of chasing down and stabbing the chunks of meat, even if they were the wrong color and wrong texture. Jinetta threw an illusion on her food so it looked like and even smelled like the real thing. Pologne was still keeping her eye on me.

"I think *Sink or Swim* is kind of silly," I said. "I know crystal ball viewing is becoming more popular throughout the dimensions. I prefer seeing events in person."

"Well, we can't all get to where things are happening, Skeeve," Bunny said. "And if we did, there's no guarantee you would get a view as good as the magicians give us. Did you ever gaze while you were at college?" Bunny asked Jinetta.

The tallest Pervect froze. To cover her sudden discomfort, she speared some of her food. "Not much," she said shortly. She popped the wriggling mass into her mouth. "I did at home."

"Well, what did you like?"

"Er, nothing much." She stopped to spear a gooey pink organism that was probably a piece of corned beef in disguise.

"How about you, Tolk?"

"Not allowed on the couch," the doglike male said in some embarrassment. "I like to chew on the cushions, and Mama just didn't put up with it. I'm hoping to break the habit. I'm down to one throw pillow a day, but it's hard."

"That's tough," Bee said sympathetically. "I used to bite my nails as a kid. Papa cured it by painting iodine on 'em."

"Why would that help?" Jinetta asked. "Iodine's delicious. I like it on ice cream."

"Finished!" Melvine announced, pushing his empty bowl away. "How about that, Teach?"

I raised my eyebrows. The food was gone. I probed the dish with a mere thread of magikal energy, but it was really empty.

"Hey, wow, terrific, Melvine!" Tolk cheered, always ready to offer encouragement. "Way to go!"

"Impressive, Cupy," Pologne said grudgingly.

"Mmm," Freezia murmured, keeping her attention fastened on what she was doing.

"Well done, Melvine," I said, enchanting a new piece of food and impaling it on my fork. I even made it wiggle for effect.

"Thanks, Teach," the big baby said, leaning back with his hands interlaced behind his head. "Say, that was weird. But, you know, I'm still hungry. I could go for a big bowl of mush. How about it?"

"Maybe you oughtta eat the rest of your dinner first, Mel," Bee said unexpectedly.

The Cupy sat up suddenly. "Huh?"

"Well, I noticed something go whizzing by my nose a minute ago, and I'll swear it smelled like this," Bee said, holding out a stunned glob of goo. "In fact, a while before that, one of 'em landed flat in my plate."

"Why didn't you say something, Bee?" I asked, even though I could have quoted his answer almost word for word.

The sincere brown eyes met mine. "Soldiers in a unit don't rat on each other, sir. But one of these days Miss Bunny's probably gonna find pieces of rotting food stuck around this room. Not that they could smell much worse than they do fresh."

"Watch it, pal," Pologne said.

"I'm sorry, ma'am," Bee said, his cheeks reddening under their freckles. "You don't like my kind of food any more than I like yours, but a task's a task. I learned that on the farm before I learned it in the army."

"Why, you sanctimonious little prat," Melvine said, nastily. "I ate my whole meal all up. See?" He brandished the empty dish.

"Not by yourself, you didn't," Bee said. "I ate at least one bite of it."

"Tattletale!"

"Can you back up your accusation?" I asked Bee.

The rangy youth looked uneasy. "Yessir, I think so." He concentrated hard then pointed a finger upward. Unlike his previous weak attempts to channel magikal energy, this spell, or rather Dispell, packed some punch. Suddenly, we were caught in a rain of sticky globs as wriggling pieces of Pervish food fell out of the chandelier, off the ceiling, out of the gallery that ran around the upper level of the room. I brushed off a few of the crawlers, and bent the most disapproving eye I could on Melvine. The big baby cringed back into his chair.

"You said to use our imaginations," he offered feebly.

"I said to use your imagination to EAT the food, not hide it," I said. Using a wave of magik, I gathered up all the stray pieces and plopped them down in front of him. Melvine grimaced.

"Aw, come on, how can anyone eat this crap?"

"Aaggh!" Freezia cried, spitting out her mouthful of vegetables. "I tasted it! I tasted it! You—you idiot!" she shrieked at Bee, belaboring him with her spoon. "Your stupid spell took mine off, too! Ugh!" She reached for the pitcher of beer and downed it in three big gulps. She threw out her chin in defiance. "I'm done with this experiment, Skeeve. Fail me. I just can't stand it any more."

"You didn't fail at all, Freezia," I said. "You found a good solution to the problem I set. You don't have to finish the rest. See, Melvine, you can do it without cheating."

I put the forkful of food in my mouth.

"So, that was it?" Jinetta asked, her eyebrows rising as enlightenment dawned. "This is what you meant by finding more than one solution to the same problem?"

"Gah," I replied.

The Pervect frowned. "What? Forgive me, did I miss something?"

"Gaaa-aah," I repeated, with more conviction.

It was my own fault. I had been so intent on my lecture that it never occurred to me that Bee's Dispell not only got rid of Melvine's enchantment, and Freezia's, and Jinetta's, but mine, too. The swap spell had been interrupted, leaving me with a genuine piece of Pervect food on my fork. Which was now in my mouth, on its way to my stomach. It tasted worse than I had ever dreamed possible, a ragout of rotting hedgehog simmered lightly in skunk urine with a soupcon of Gleep's breath. To top it off, the creature felt as if it was *growing* as it went down my throat.

"Gaaa-uuuuh," I said.

Bunny gave me a funny look. "Skeeve, are you all right?"

"Igggaaaah," I stated a little more clearly, feeling my stomach rebel against the intruder, which seemed to have extended a pseudopod to explore my intestines. My abdomen contracted, pushing everything upward.

"Hoogh."

If I was lucky I might be able to run to the garbage heap outside the kitchen door before the morsel made its reappearance.

"Sguusme."

I sprang to my feet.

The next thing I knew, I was lying on my back, with the flickering flames of the dangling chandelier shooting around my vision like fireworks. The pain in my stomach was terrible. I thought my innards were ready to explode. I was about to die of Pervish cooking. I shut my eyes. *Not like this*, I prayed. *Not like this.*

"Clear!" Tolk's voice came. I opened my eyes in time to see the Canidian falling towards me, paws first. I goggled, and tried to roll away.

"Don't move!" Bunny commanded, grabbing my head. "You got a taste of your own medicine. Tolk's fixing it."

The canine landed on my belly with his weight on all four paws. I bent in the middle. The purple thing went flying out of my mouth. Pologne caught it neatly in one hand.

"A perfectly good *smushlik*, ruined," she said mournfully. "My mother would be heartbroken."

"Do you feel all right now?" Tolk asked, helping me to sit up.

"I—"

The truth was, I did feel better. I should have been bruised from having him leap on me, but I felt a sensation of well-being radiating from my stomach.

"What did you do?" I asked.

"Dogtor magik," Tolk said modestly. "I'm a healer. That's my talent."

"That's great," I said as the others helped me to my feet. "Thank you. That food, er, just went down the wrong way."

He peered at me. "You shouldn't eat anything else this evening. You've had enough solids," he advised. "Tea, maybe."

"I'll make him some." Bunny bustled away to fill the kettle.

The others were gathered around me, most of them looking worried. "Are you sure you're all right, sir?" Bee asked.

"Yeah," Freezia added. "I hope you're not going to drop dead. I don't look forward to trying to negotiate a refund out of your business manager."

"Thanks for your concern," I said dryly. "I'm fine. Tolk was right. I just—overate."

"More than the rest of us did," Jinetta said.

"It was to make a point. Did I get it across?" I asked.

"We don't have to be led from A to B," Pologne said. "Yes, we get it. There's no one single solution to a problem."

"That's right. You all handled it in different ways," I said. "Isn't it best to choose the most expedient and practical way of getting a job done?"

"Hold on," Freezia said, flinging up her hands. "Maybe you were right once. I'm still not going to concede Professor Maguffin's method is wrong."

"Nor am I," Jinetta added. Pologne nodded her agreement.

"Okay," I sighed. "I'm not here to shoot him down. I'm just telling you what has worked for me in the real world. That's why you came here, isn't it?"

"Well, yes," Jinetta admitted.

"That's fine," I said. "For now, we'll agree to disagree."

"Say, I'm hungry," Pologne announced suddenly. "Anyone up for a snack? I know where I can get the best iodine sundaes on Perv."

Chapter Ten

"It's gonna cost you."
ANY SURGEON, TECH REP OR AUTO MECHANIC

A vein popped out on Bee's forehead as he strained to concentrate.

"Lift the feather," I ordered. "Levitation is not that hard. If I could learn to do it, anyone can."

The next day I had decided to do something about the wide gap in expertise between the students. Melvine and the Pervects had had basic training before they finished cutting their teeth—well, before Melvine had, anyhow. I believed that the Pervects were born with all their teeth. Bee's instruction had come from his village hedge-wizard and whatever the Possiltum Army's library of scrolls had stashed in between nudie pinups and manuals on how to strip down and repair crossbows, plus what he'd picked up from Massha. I could tell, that except for his handful of homegrown spells, all his progress in magik could be attributed to the latter.

"Good try," Bunny said encouragingly. She sat polishing her nails on a down-stuffed cushion beneath a pavilion, and offering the occasional compliment to my apprentices. Gleep and Buttercup chased one another around the inn, offering a noisy distraction that I warned them all to ignore.

"Huh," Melvine grunted. He hovered in the trees, picking leaves off and tearing them to pieces without touching them. "What good is trying? Magik is about succeeding."

I glared at him. "Don't show off, Melvine. Couldn't you try to help?"

"Fine," he said. "Look, Klahd, just lift the feather. There's enough magik floating around here to raise the Titanic. Use some of it."

"But I don't know when I'm putting enough magik into it," Bee said.

"All right, let's add a wrinkle. We'll give you resistance to work against. It'll be good practical experience for both of you."

"It's not practical experience," Jinetta insisted. "These are just exercises. We used to do them all the time."

"Everything's practical. Bee, you push up on the feather. Jinetta, you push down."

"There's nothing to that," Jinetta said.

"Aha," I said, "but here's the catch: you can't push any harder than he does. He'll levitate it up to here," I held out a hand, "then you top it with your magik. Don't let him push it any farther. You can't let it go lower than the original level. If he lets it drop, that's his problem, but you can't push it down. See how much control *you* have."

Jinetta tittered. "That ought to be easy!"

But it wasn't, as I had reason to know. With endless power flowing into them, the girls were no more subtle than Melvine. They channeled whatever was in them. What they needed to learn was how to tighten the valve. The first time Jinetta pushed, the feather ended up embedded in a flagstone.

"Oops," she said.

"See what I mean?" I said. "Freezia, Pologne, I have an exercise for the two of you to work on while Jinetta helps Bee. I want you to work on storing up energy then releasing it—slowly!—until you get used to how much you can hold normally."

Pologne clicked her tongue.

"Why, when this place is full of lines of force? This is like Grand Perv Station!"

I eyed her sternly. "Assume that at any moment they could disappear, and then what?"

"Then Bee here wouldn't be able to lift his feather. Which he can't anyhow!"

"Hold on, someone's coming," Freezia announced. We all paused to listen. I couldn't hear anything, which wasn't surprising. Pervect hearing was a dozen times keener than Klahdish.

"How far away are they?"

Pologne consulted a gold pendulum. "About a mile," she said. "You Klahds make more noise than a dragon in heat."

"Gleep!" protested my pet. Buttercup added a nicker in defense of his friend.

"Sorry," the Pervect said, holding out her hand to Gleep. "You would almost think that they could understand me."

I was unwilling to reveal Gleep's secret to anyone who hadn't saved my life at least ten times. "Well, at least he knows the word 'dragon.' Drop what you're doing, people. Put on a Klahdish disguise. Something believable," I said, halting Freezia, who had promptly transformed herself into a cow.

"Ugh!" Freezia exclaimed. "You soft-skinned are uglier than ten miles of bad road. At least that creature has an attractive pattern!"

"Fashion later," I said. "Security *now.*"

Tolk came galloping back along the road. "A Klahd is coming this way!" he panted.

A mile might have been a long way for a Klahd to cover, but I wanted plenty of time to finish my arguments with my class before whoever was racing towards us emerged from the bushes. Tolk was having trouble focusing his disguise spell, so I transformed him into a large dog—no stretch of the imagination there—and Gleep into a goat. My pet caught a glimpse of himself in the trough and gave me a look of reproach. I shrugged. If we had been in the house I might have gotten away with making him a dog, too, but he had a tendency to forget what he was doing and eat anything that appealed to him. I could get away with explaining a *goat* eating a cartwheel or gnawing on an anvil. Buttercup's horn was easily erased, leaving him a robustly handsome horse, not an unusual beast to find on a Klahdish homestead.

In an instant, Bunny's red-headed beauty was swallowed up by the semblance of a toothless crone sheltered from the sun by a tattered gray cloth strung on a clothesline. The Pervects had assumed new disguises, having been coached by me and Bunny as to what represented beauty in our dimension. They appeared as three dainty lasses in the dress style worn by prosperous merchants—still in pastel shades, of course. Bee assumed Guido's hulking form. At first I was going to tell him to change back, then I realized he was thinking more clearly than I was. We had no idea whether the approaching being was hostile or not.

To diguise myself, I assumed my disgusting old man image, which was usually enough to remind casual visitors they needed to be elsewhere.

A Klahd came panting into the yard. My illusion made his red face go somewhat pale, but whatever was troubling him was enough to make him risk catching whatever disease or vermin I might be carrying. He fell almost at my feet.

"The Great Skeeve," he gasped. "Where is the Great Skeeve?"

"Who wishes to see my master?" I asked, in a creaky voice.

"He is summoned by Flink, the headman of Humulus," the man said after fetching several deep breaths. Bee came over to help the man to his feet. Tolk trotted over, took the man's wrist in his mouth shortly, then dropped it, giving me a nod. The man's pulse must have been all right. The other apprentices clustered around to listen. "I have been running for two days! There is a terrible monster destroying our village! It's attacking people, terrifying the livestock! The Great Skeeve must help us!"

He looked so distressed I felt sorry for him. Before I could open my mouth to offer my help, Bunny was beside me.

"*How* terrible?" she asked. "Is it really a monster, or are you exaggerating? What's your name, honey?"

"Norb," the man replied. "Time is of the essence, crone. I have to see the Great Skeeve!"

"In a moment," Bunny said silkily. "What is the threat, exactly? Are we talking about chewing furniture or tearing down buildings? The Great Skeeve doesn't deal with small-time vermin, you know."

Norb regarded her with distaste. "Woman, we are talking about burning buildings! It has a tail with a great spike! It roars fearsomely! The monster spits lightning bolts! Well, it doesn't spit them, exactly. It sort of sh—, er, well, it emits lightning!"

She and I exchanged a glance. "Well?" she demanded.

"Over to you," I said resignedly.

Bunny took Norb's arm and led him toward her pavilion. "Tell me, good sir, what kind of town is Humulus? Was it a thriving village before the monster invaded?"

Bee whispered to me. "What is she *doing*?"

"Business," I said shortly. "She's negotiating a fee for my services."

"She's what?" Bee demanded. He waved his arms, making him look even more like a scarecrow caught in a windstorm. "How come we aren't heading off to Humulus right now? Why aren't you dealing with the monster first? Aren't people more important than money?"

"Yes," Tolk asked, tilting his shaggy head. "What's going on? Why the delay?"

I looked around uneasily at my class. "This is not about money per se. This part has always been tough for me, too. This is another lesson that my mentors have been trying to hammer into my head for years. You all are going to have to learn that your time and trouble are worth something. Quite a lot, in fact when you're talking about magikal ability. Lots of people will take advantage of you if you don't set a value on your services. Believe me, I know what I'm talking about. 'The Great Skeeve' has a big reputation in these parts. I used to be the court magician in Possiltum, so my magik commands high fees, unless I do the work first. Long experience has taught me that it's almost impossible to get paid once you've already solved the problem. There is nothing as parsimonious as people who feel safe. If you're going to do this as a business, you've got to learn perspective. Think ahead, and remember you have to eat, too. Otherwise you end up doing everything for free, and people will waste your time because they don't have a high value that they associate with your services. The fact is, I'm not as good at negotiating as Bunny is, and I probably never will be. That's why she stopped me. I can't just offer my help for free."

The Pervects were nodding, but Bee looked mortified.

"Sir, permission to disagree, sir! I'll help anyone who ever needs me, whether I can ever do the big stuff or not! Sir!"

I shook my head. He'd learn the hard way, just as I had.

"It's your talent, Bee. I can't stop you doing what you want to do. But experience helps you prioritize. Money's one way of figuring out how important a matter is to someone else."

"When I'm a wizard I'll help everyone I can," Bee insisted. I sighed. Bee and I couldn't be more than a couple of years apart—in fact, I was younger than he was—but I suddenly felt old.

Melvine rolled his eyes. "*I* intend to make all the money I can."

I was upset with him, too. Money wasn't everything. It was nice to have—I wouldn't lie about that—but it would have surprised the young Skeeve who had started out life as an inept thief and even more inept magik-user that the most important thing in the world was one's friends and loved ones. He didn't seem to have compassion for anyone, not even himself. I lifted an eyebrow at him.

"I hope, Melvine, that you'll figure out one day that following that kind of philosophy too far at the other end of the spectrum will backfire on you, too. Let's look at it from the practical standpoint: if you're too greedy, you're going to miss out on jobs because clients will be afraid that you're more interested in the profit margin than in helping them."

"Huh," the Cupy said. I could tell I hadn't impressed him, but Bee looked a little more forgiving.

Bunny returned with the villager in tow.

"We've come to a suitable arrangement, lackey," she said. "It is time for you to summon the Great Skeeve!"

Now was the time for a fantastic effect, all the better for
Norb to report back to his headman. I'd picked up a little show-
manship from Aahz and Massha over the years, and it worked
really well in cases like this.

"Stand back!" I exclaimed, pushing back my sleeves. The
fanfare of a brass band blared around us, making everyone but
Bunny jump. The villager was wide-eyed with awe. I shook my
hands over my head. "Wugga wugga wugga! Balloo balloo
balloo! I call upon the master of magik, the big kahuna himself, commander of demons, conjuror deluxe, king of wizards
and wizard to kings—bring us the Great Skeeve!" I dropped
to my knees amid a forest of brilliant searchlight beams.

The 'disgusting old man' disappeared in a froth of multicol-
ored foam that bubbled up out of the earth. Angels blowing on
trumpets swooped down from the heavens and circled overhead. Cherubs followed, throwing bright blue glitter. I created a
final illusion, that of cloud-topped lightning descending from
the sky with my alter ego, the fearsome old magician, standing
upon it with his arms crossed. As "I" reached the ground, Norb
fell at my feet again, this time from awe.

"Could have used a few more fireworks," Pologne said critically from her vantage point on the sidelines.

"I think it was kinda over the top," Melvine added.

With one impressive forefinger, I signalled for my visitor
to rise.

He finally recovered enough to speak. "Why—why didn't
your manservant just go into the house to fetch you?" he asked.

All right, maybe I hadn't impressed him as much as I
had thought.

I lowered my eyebrows at him. "I was in a distant plane of
existence," I boomed, "not occupying a miserable hovel like
that. Why have I been disturbed from my studies?"

Norb gestured uneasily in the direction of Bunny's pavilion. "Well, you see, I just finished telling that old crone—"

I held up a hand. "Never mind! Your mind is an open book
to me! The Great Skeeve knows all! I will help your town.

Assistants!" I clapped my hands. "Make ready to depart! And," I called as an afterthought, "pack lightly!"

Norb guided us to the main northern road, and set as rapid a pace as he could. Since my new client couldn't give me or my 'apprentices' enough details to identify his 'monster,' I brought Gleep and Buttercup along as extra muscle. My pet dragon was as thrilled as Tolk was to go 'walkies' in the pleasant May weather, and spent many happy hours racing into the bushes beside the road, chasing the local wildlife and finding snacks. Gleep's taste in food was almost as dire as that of the Pervects, so I was happier when I could hear him but not see him slurping and chewing. Norb also seemed grateful that my very smelly 'goat' preferred to travel at a distance from him. He was very uneasy about my entourage. Bunny rode sidesaddle daintily on Buttercup's back. The war unicorn had never really gotten used to carrying civilians, but he adored Bunny. He blew out between his lips as Gleep disappeared again. I could tell he longed to romp with his friend, but his training held good and he remained on the road. I patted him on the nose.

"Are you sure you need all of these people, great wizard?" Norb kept asking me.

"They are my students and my servants," I intoned. "They accompany me to learn at my feet and to do those menial tasks such as preparing food."

Norb looked skeptical. "Well, I thought you could do that all by magik."

"Such tasks are beneath his attention," Bunny put in hastily.

Behind us, the Pervects burst into giggles over some private joke I couldn't overhear. Now clad in the illusion of fine travel gowns, they weren't at all pleased with having to spend days disguised as Klahds. When we stopped for food, which because of their prodigious appetites was often, I had to pretend I was conjuring elementals or summoning demons to aid me and protect us on our path to explain away why we had to brew cauldrons of 'protective potion.' We really didn't have anything to worry about. First, this was the main north-south trade route for this region, and was well patrolled by guardsmen in the service of the local ruler. Second, we were carrying few valuables to speak of. Third, those of us who weren't heavily armed packed a substantial magikal wallop. Fourth, and most importantly, anyone who got within ten yards of the Pervects' food was not going to cross the remaining distance, even if we had a string of naked dancing girls carrying baskets of diamonds. After one curious sniff, Norb put as much distance between himself and their cooking pot as he felt was safe. He kept pressing us to hurry. I calculated that it would take about two days to cover the distance on foot that he had run, but he had been traveling unencumbered and we, to put it briefly, were not.

In spite of my instructions, Bee had emerged from the inn with his whole field pack on. I had to admit that it didn't look oversized worn over the disguise of Guido's hulking build, but I could tell it was still Bee under there. Since he was more of a company clerk than a commando type, the weight was beginning to wear on him, though I think he would rather have undergone torture than admit it. He did manage to produce from its depths anything that anyone might even remotely need. I admired his preparedness, but it might have done the others some good if they had to improvise even once to make do. I couldn't criticize him again; he was trying so hard to live up to Massha's recommendation and my reputation. I did not feel worthy of such adulation.

Tolk carried a new cloth bag to replace the paper sack stolen by the Sear natives. A present from Bunny, it had once held half a bushel of garlic. Tolk loved it, and trotted along taking loving snorts from the stinking burlap. Melvine, resplendent in what Aahz would have called a 'Little Lord Fauntleroy' suit, swaggered onward hauling his belongings in a huge leather satchel that floated behind him like a balloon. Bunny, who ought to have known better, also claimed she was traveling light. For her, I suppose she was: two huge suitcases were slung over Buttercup's back like panniers. All she carried on her own person seemed to be a ragged sack. My illusion overlay what was an incredibly expensive designer silk bag Aahz and I had given her for her last birthday. Inside it was Bytina, her palm-sized Perfectly Darling Assistant, cosmetics, gum, a small amount of gold for our travel expenses, and the most powerful pocket calculator on Klah. Not that she needed it. What Bunny lacked in magikal ability was more than made up for by her facility with numbers. When she wasn't chatting with one or another of the apprentices, she was catching up via Bytina with one or another of her many correspondents in other dimensions.

I strode on in thoughtful silence, occasionally lowering my eyebrows as if deep in thought. In truth, I was. My conscience was barking at me, telling me I shouldn't be putting my innocent apprentices into harm's way. On the other hand, if I left them behind and the task took too long, I would feel I was cheating them out of several days' instruction. On the other hand, observing me in action wouldn't hurt, and they might even be able to help me. On yet another hand, I wondered if having them help might make the job harder than it ought to be. I decided that was enough hands. What would happen would happen, and I could only try to prepare my students to be flexible.

Norb accepted all of the strangeness of my entourage as befitting that of a notorious wizard. The one thing he couldn't tolerate was how slow we were moving.

"Hurry up!" he begged, not for the first time that day. "The road's good and the weather is fine. You could put a move on, wizard! Er, with respect, of course."

"If you're so impatient," Bunny said, also not for the first time that day, "why don't you trot ahead and see if there's a decent inn we can put up at for the night? We'll move much faster tomorrow if we get a good night's sleep."

"Old cro—madam, your witches' brew got us pitched out of the last one. I had to pay a substantial amount above and beyond the inn's fee not to have the tavernkeeper summon the local guards. Even the drunks were afraid of your potion's stench!"

"Actually, it was our—goat that made the smell," Bunny pointed out. Gleep seemed to have taken a fancy to Freezia's cooking. He had begun licking out their pot. Pervish cooking passing through a dragon's digestive system had unfortunate results, to say the least. Norb picked up on that with alacrity.

"Since you admit that it was your creature's fault that I was forced to waste the headman's money, then perhaps you shoulder the burden for tonight's lodging."

Bunny looked outraged. "You don't expect the Great Skeeve to pay for his own lodging? Not when he's going to save your town?"

Muttering something about "this had better be worth it," Norb trotted ahead into the woods, leaving us alone.

The moment he was gone, the Pervects went into elaborate gyrations and gestures. Their disguise spells dissipated, revealing their scaly green faces and four-inch-long fangs. Small animals and birds fled screaming into the trees.

"Whew!" Jinetta said, admiring herself in a pocket mirror. "My mother warned me if I made ugly faces I would freeze that way someday."

"How do you know it didn't?" Pologne asked cattily.

Jinetta pouted. "You don't have to be mean about it!"

"How are you going to defeat a monster that shoots lightning?" Bee asked when he was sure our guide was out of earshot.

"I don't know yet," I said honestly. From my studies I knew of a number that could have fit the description Norb gave us. Furry, big, lightning. There were giant furred spiders in the dimension of Phobia whose webs were crackling nets of lightning. That didn't sound exactly like the creature Norb was talking about—too many legs. There was a huge blue bunny on Vorpal that spat lightning. I shook my head. I knew too much and too little to help. The Pervects had been searching their information sources for furry lightning-shooting creatures, and had also come up with too many possibilities.

Mostly, I worried that my apprentices could be harmed or killed helping me with this mission. I had no intention of letting them get hurt, but I wanted them to try to rid this town of the menace. It would give them a sense of accomplishment.

Bunny was sympathetic. "I have faith in you."

"Maybe you were right," I moaned. "Maybe I've taken on more than I can handle."

"Don't give up now," Bunny said firmly. "You're just getting good at this."

"Thanks," I said glumly, but I appreciated the gesture.

"Here he comes again," Freezia announced.

"Put your disguises on again," I instructed the students.

Jinetta sighed as she assumed her Klahdish appearance. "I just hate not being me, you know."

"Think of it as a dreary necessity," I said severely. "You have no idea how much trouble we'd get into if they ever saw your normal face."

"The trouble with your Klahds is that you don't appreciate genuine beauty," Pologne said.

"Good news, wizard," Norb said, panting up to us. "I found an inn that hasn't gotten the news from the one we tried to stay in last night!"

Chapter Eleven

"Are these things supposed to act like that?"
S. KING

CRASH!

"We must be near Humulus," I said.

"The monster is still raging!" Norb shouted, pulling me along by the elbow. "Hurry, master wizard!"

"Either this is a very large town," Bunny murmured to me as we passed through the high wooden gates, "or this is one very slow monster. And the villagers haven't managed to overpower it?"

I shook my head. "I guess not. That's why they sent for a wizard. I don't know why it *stayed* here. That is the part that strikes me as strange."

The streets that unrolled before us as the portal slammed shut at our backs suggested the former. Humulus was, or had been, a thriving trading town. Nearly all the buildings on the roads I could see had three or four storeys with shops on the ground level, all deserted now, many of them with broken windows or balconies. I could hear more crashing and the shouting of hundreds of people not far away.

"That way," I pointed toward the loudest sounds of destruction.

FZZZAAAP! A tearing noise ripped through the air.

"What was that?" Melvine asked.

"Lightning!" I felt around for force lines. Luckily, there was a medium-sized blue-tinged line arching overhead. I latched onto it.

"Everybody fill up your tanks," I said. I noticed Melvine screwing up his face to protest. "No argument! Do it!"

I paused for a moment, to give my students time and to make sure my own reservoir of power was topped up as high as it would go. As soon as all of them had given me the nod, we shouldered our way into the town square.

The cobblestoned common was full of people, most of them flailing around with makeshift weapons: farm implements, brooms, ex-army spears and the like. The most action was coming from the far corner of the square, where a group of people was clearly trying to attack something in their midst, but definitely not wanting to be too close to it. I shouldered closer, followed by my retinue.

At first all we could see was a two-storey red brick building with terra-cotta gargoyles studding the wall just beneath the eaves. The side of the structure had been punched in, as if by a gigantic hand. While I watched, some of the bricks crumbled away, and a huge Klahdlike face, surrounded by a tawny-colored shaggy mane, appeared. The beast, which stood twice as high as a tall man, clawed at another piece of wall with a gigantic paw, dislodging more masonry that crunched down onto the crowd. The townspeople yelled and shifted away from the falling bricks.

The creature struggled for a moment then extracted itself from the broken building, pulling the rest of it down as it wrestled free. The shaggy head was followed by an immense, smooth-furred body with muscular haunches. The tail wasn't furry—it looked insectoid. Pale blue, jointed, translucent sections terminated in a stinger longer than my foot. I gulped.

"What is it?" Bunny gasped.

"It's a Manticore," I said. "They're native to the dimension Mantico. I've read about them, but never seen one before in the flesh. They're dangerous."

"No kidding," Melvine said scornfully.

I admit it was stating the obvious, as the Manticore bared a mouthful of long, white fangs. He snapped at the outstretched arm of a statue and bit it right off. He spat it at the crowd, who milled away from him, still shouting and brandishing their makeshift weapons. A few brave souls forced their way forward and threw rocks at the beast.

He staggered to his hind feet and roared. I had read that
Manticores were nonsentient, but my textbook was wrong.
This creature was wearing a uniform. Not much of one, ad-
mittedly: a polished gold-and-leather breastplate was tied to
his mighty furred chest. Strapped around his mid-section was
a wide belt from which hung several pouches and a gleaming
dagger. Another dagger was strapped to his right ankle.
Perched in the thick mane, in between the rounded ears, was
a dark blue, flat-topped cap with a brim. And in his right paw
was clenched a spherical container bound with leather straps.
When another shower of rocks flew at him out of the crowd,
he threw a massive arm around the container to protect it. I
raised my eyebrows.

"Did he steal that?" Bunny whispered to me. "Is that what
they're trying to get back?"

"I think it belongs to him," I said, in a low voice, heartened
by the sight. "If you ask me—"

"Here he is!" Norb grabbed my arm and dragged me toward a
huge bearded man standing behind a small army of crossbowmen
kneeling to fire. "Master Flink, here's the wizard!"

"Hold your fire!" Flink ordered. Norb hurried to whisper
in the big man's ear. The headman turned toward me. With a
few silver lines at the temples, Master Flink had hair and beard
as black as his beady little eyes.

"So, wizard, what do you think?" he demanded.

"I think," I intoned, "that you have a problem."

"Do you, now?" he exploded. "Well, you must be a sooth-
sayer as well as a wizard! As if anyone couldn't tell we have a
problem, dammit! Well, solve it! We'll pay you what Norb here
tells me you want. More! Just get this damned monster out of
my town!"

I inclined my head slightly, my expression grave. "As you
wish, Master Flink. I do not believe that this concern is so
serious that it merits more than my personal oversight. My
apprentices will handle this matter." I folded my arms into
my sleeves.

"Whatever you want," Flink growled. "Just get on with it! It was snoring away up to half an hour ago, but now it's up again, and look what it's done!"

"I assure you, the monster will be removed with as little additional damage as possible," I told Flink.

"Your apprentices will WHAT?" Melvine demanded. His shock was mirrored on the other five students' faces. The Pervects' jaws hung open. "You're kidding!"

I turned to them and lowered my voice. "No, I'm not kidding. You didn't like my exercises in the courtyard. You said they weren't practical enough. Well, here is a practical field exercise." I waved a hand in the direction of the Manticore. "Get a game plan together. Take him out of town. We'll deal with him there."

"Right," Jinetta said resolutely, assuming the leadership. The Pervects went into a huddle. She pulled her gazing crystal from her field pack and began to gesture over it. "Manticores, Manticores. Here's the entry in the *Encyclopedia Pervetica.*"

The other girls peered over her shoulder. Bee peered around the square, muttering numbers to himself. "Forty yards by forty-five. Nine direct routes in, not counting air." Tolk just gawked, his long pink tongue lolling in amazement.

"I see," Pologne said, glancing up. "This creature is an adolescent. You can tell because the whiskers are no longer ivory colored, but not yet fully golden."

"And one of them is bent," Freezia added, "indicating a defeat by a more powerful opponent, such as a dragon. I recall from one of Professor Simble's lectures that Manticore whiskers are one of the most flexible and tough fibers in all the dimensions."

"No, not a dragon," Pologne corrected her. "Only a magikal attack could have bent it! Dragons are unlikely to have cast a spell. They prefer to use brute firepower."

"Of course!" Freezia tittered. "I defer to your superior memory, Polly." She pulled out a notebook and made a note in it with an orange plume. "Physical attack. How long ago, do you think?"

"I couldn't say for certain," Pologne said thoughtfully.

"Master Flink, there he goes again!" one of the bowman shouted. The Manticore had pulled himself to his feet and was staggering across the square.

"Hold your fire!" the headman said. "The wizard's about to do something!"

"When?" demanded a fat man in a flour-spattered tunic and apron. I deduced at once that he was the town baker. "He's tearing up my granary!"

The Manticore had pushed aside the canopy that hung over the entrance to the white-plastered building, and appeared to be trying to crawl inside, to the detriment of the door frame.

"Well, wizard? Hurry! He'll destroy my entire shop!"

If you've never felt the eyes of a thousand people fixed on you all at once, let me tell you it's uncomfortable. I kept my face, wearing the guise of the venerable and formidable wizard, from showing any emotion, but underneath I was growing as impatient as the townspeople. Still, I waited. I was fairly certain no one was in any direct danger from this monster at the moment, and I thought my students had an important lesson to learn.

At last, one of them took action. Melvine tugged at my sleeve.

"Uh, Skeeve, how about we leave?" he suggested, in as suave a voice as he could muster. "This doesn't have to be our fight, does it?"

"Sure it does!" Tolk said, goggling. "Let's go get him! Let's go get him! Now-wow-wow-wow!"

"We made a contract, Melvine," Bee added.

"Strictly speaking, *Skeeve* made the contract," Melvine said, planting his hands on his chest. "I had no problem with the exercises you had us doing. My aunt exaggerated a lot about me needing to get close with big-time experiences. Look, if you don't mind, I'll just observe from over there. Maybe up that street on the left. Whaddaya say?" The Cupy began to back away.

"What are you afraid of?" I asked.

Melvine halted, mouth open in indignation. "I'm not say-ing I'm afraid! I mean, this THING, with those big claws, and all those teeth—!"

"Well, if he's not fully mature, he won't have all his rows of teeth," Pologne said, still engrossed in her reading matter.

"What does that mean?" Bee asked curiously.

Pologne dragged him closer so he could see into the crys-tal ball. "See the chart? His emotions mature at a perceptible rate. Depending on his age, he will understand certain abstract notions better than others."

"You're saying we should appeal to his better sense, eh?" Tolk asked, his tongue lolling. "Good idea!"

Some of the townsfolk began to remark among themselves about the novelty of a talking dog. I regretted not giving him human semblance before we started out, but that would have given people something else to talk about when he dropped to all fours to run.

Melvine began to edge toward the rear of the square. I grabbed him by the collar and tossed him back into the midst of the others.

In the meantime, the headman ordered the archers to let fly. The bolts peppered the Manticore, who brushed them off with a fearsome roar. Blood seeped out of the golden fur. The Manticore staggered blindly in the direction of the bowmen. The people in his way screamed and ran. The Manticore lurched toward the noises, stinging here and there with his tail, and swiping with one big paw, but was too slow to hit any of them. He was hampered by the fact that he continued to clutch the round container tightly to his chest. Growling in disappoint-ment, he dropped to all threes to crawl.

"Curse it, reload and prepare to fire!" Flink shouted.

The bowmen thrust the stirrups of their bows into the ground and yanked the strings back to the trigger, keeping one eye on the beast as they shoved fresh quarrels into the groove of their weapons. The Manticore snarled and kicked out at a haycart that unaccountably got in his way. The wagon tumbled end over end and crashed into the side of a building.

Some brave townsfolk mustered to throw more rocks at the monster. When he turned toward them, they fled to hide behind the archers, who were forming a trembling wedge behind me and my apprentices.

The Manticore stumbled over the shrubbery that surrounded a memorial garden in the middle of the square. With a huge splash, he fell flat in the pond.

The townsfolk broke into nervous laughter. The Manticore seemed to take this amiss. He rose up on three limbs, lashing his pale blue tail until his backside faced us. Then, he hoisted the tail high.

"Everybody down!" Flink yelled.

My limited knowledge of Manticores made me realize what threat lay in store. I hit the dirt. "Students! Down!"

The Pervects, distracted from their perusal of the crystal ball, looked at me aghast.

"In our good clothes?" Jinetta demanded, hands on hips.

By now the others had noticed the threat and thrown themselves to the ground. I reached out with a massive dollop of magik, just in time.

The Manticore's backside swiveled toward us, and the huge haunch muscles squeezed.

FZZZAPP!

I suddenly understood Norb's description of how the creature 'emitted lightning,' a fact unaccountably left out of the stuffy textbook I had been reading. A blue-white bolt erupted from the beast's nether parts and shot directly toward the young Pervect. I levitated Jinetta straight up into the air. The bolt missed her, blasting into a huge tree on the green. I reached for some more magik from the blue force line I could see overhead, but it was so thin I couldn't get more than a trickle out of it. I was left with less than half what my internal 'tank' could hold.

"I hope I'm not going to regret that later," I said.

"Well, thanks a million!" Jinetta said, insulted.

"That's not what I meant," I began. "Look out!"

"Aagh!" Melvine shrieked, diving for the cobblestones again.

The Manticore, once having hoisted his tail, was randomly blasting houses and buildings apart with lightning bolts. He turned once more to look directly at the cluster of people behind me, and a mean smile crossed his face.

"No!" shouted Flink.

The Manticore concentrated deeply, and the biggest lightning bolt yet shot out of his backside and hurtled into a white stone building at the end of the square. The face of it exploded, shooting fragments in every direction.

"The town hall!" Norb yelled.

"Do something, Master Skeeve!" Flink said in frustration. "Your assistants are no help!"

"I agree," I said mildly. I turned to the small cluster at my back. "Apprentices!"

"It looks like maybe it got hurt by those arrows," Tolk pointed out eagerly. "I can fix it. Maybe then it'll like us and stop causing trouble."

"That's one theory," Jinetta said. "It ought to understand the concept of gratitude."

"Hey, listen up!" I said to them in a low but urgent voice.

"I dunno," Bee said. "If, like you say, they're vulnerable between the eyes, I can probably hit it square if one of these fellows will give me his crossbow."

The Manticore seemed to revel in the dismayed groans of the assembly at the destruction of their town hall. He rose to his hind feet and staggered toward the building, pausing to take a swallow from the container en route. My apprentices didn't seem to see the action.

I cleared my throat. "Excuse me."

With the townsfolk in pursuit, the Manticore ambled unsteadily over to the smoking ruin and began to pick the statues and ornaments off its eaves one at a time, plinking them into the fountain.

"Can we appeal to its intelligence?" Pologne asked passionately.

Melvine blew a raspberry. "Do YOU speak Manticore?"

"Well, no."

I lost my patience.

"EXCUSE ME!" They all turned to stare at me. I glared back. "Before you try to appeal to his intelligence or sense of gratitude, hadn't you better stop him from destroying anything else first?"

"Huh?" they asked, almost in unison.

I stood back so they could get a good look at the ongoing destruction. The Manticore heaved a carved stone windowsill into the pond. The water splashed high into the air.

"Oh!" they exclaimed, as though surprised that he hadn't held still while they identified him as to genus, species and subspecies.

"Sorry, Skeeve," Tolk said, lowering his shaggy head. "We just kinda got caught up—"

"No time," I interrupted him. "Hurry up and get him out of town. Then we can handle him without anyone else getting hurt."

"No problem," Melvine said. "I can grab him with a whirlwind." He saw my concerned face and grinned. "It's okay, Teach. I've been refining it. Really."

His small face contorted, and he held out his hands. An eddy in the dust began to turn. It picked up bricks and stones in its wake as it started to trace a path toward the Manticore, who had discovered the curved blue roof tiles. He was picking them off one at a time and eating them as if they were cookies.

The tornado grew very slowly, seeming to sneak up on the monster, skirting behind trees and buildings whenever he turned his head. I admired Melvine's tactics. They might even work, as long as the creature didn't notice. The tip of the wind touched the beast's toe.

"Huh?" the Manticore said.

WHOOSH! Before he could move, the tiny windstorm snaked up his body and enveloped him. The bemused face, the last to be absorbed, whipped helplessly around in circles.

"Yeeeaaaah!" Melvine carolled, dancing around. "I'm the Cupy! I'm the Cupy!"

"Move it out of here!" I shouted.

He gave me a sheepish glance. "Oh, yeah."

The Cupy tilted his head, and the whirlwind started to weave down the street toward the gate. Respectfully, the townsfolk moved aside. I admired Melvine's control. He *had* been practicing. Markie was right. All the kid needed was a little direction.

The crowd followed, chanting and brandishing its homemade weapons.

"Yay! Death to the monster! Death to the monster! Death to the monster!"

The Manticore wasn't going without a fight. Little jets of lightning zipped out of the maelstrom, leaving tiny black burns where they hit. The Klahds jumped back, some of them yelping in pain.

"Melvine," I said as the tornado started to drift off true. "Melvine, watch it. You're getting too close to that—"

CRASH!

"—lamp post."

I looked down. Beads of moisture dotted the Cupy's brow.

"I can't hold him! I'm losing power!"

"Why is your spell failing?" Jinetta asked critically. "Didn't you invoke all the correct parameters?"

"There are no correct parameters, sister," Melvine snarled. "YOU try holding onto it! My magik is fading! This worked fine in my practice sessions with rats!"

"Rats!" Freezia sneered.

"Obviously there's something you missed," Jinetta said.

"Not me! It's not my fault!"

"There is something!" Pologne exclaimed, lifting her eyes from the crystal ball. "Manticore lightning drains force lines!"

I groaned. My text really had missed out on all the important facts about Manticores.

Melvine blew a raspberry. "No wonder! See! I didn't blow it! How come YOU didn't tell me that, with all your research?"

Jinetta shrieked in outrage. "Me? How much do you think I can read in five minutes?"

I rolled my eyes. "Stop arguing! Bee, Tolk, help Melvine."

"With respect, Master Skeeve, I don't know how to make a tornado," Bee said.

"Me neither," Tolk barked.

"You don't have to," I said, watching desperately as the wind stuttered. Pretty soon it was going to fade to a summer breeze, and we'd be back to where we started. "Picture a big pair of hands. Each of you make one and put it on one side of the tornado. Steady it, and help Melvine push it out of town. That's all you need to do. Ladies, stand by. If all we have to work on is what power we're packing, then we have to use it where it counts. Remember Sear! And don't let your disguise spells drop!"

"Yes, Master Skeeve," they chorused.

Bee and Tolk put up one hand apiece, and concentrated. The spell was rough and unsteady, but they started to move the sputtering whirlwind.

Two of them managed to get the Manticore partway out of the gate before the whirlwind collapsed. The Manticore dropped to the ground, his fur in knots. He shook himself mightily, then checked to see that his container was all right. It was. The Manticore roared angrily. With a look that presaged revenge, he started to crawl back into the center of town.

The people of Humulus scattered widely as soon as the tornado had faded. I was relieved to have them out of my way. If he was angry before, the Manticore was out of his mind with fury now. He plunged his free hand through the nearest shop window and came out with an entire table, which he used to beat down the rest of the street lamps within reach. Without the whirlwind, Bee and Tolk strained to push the

Manticore towards the gate. They were losing the contest. I had to get the rest of the apprentices engaged on the task.

I reached for a force line, any force line. Unfortunately, Jinetta had been right: the local lines were depleted by the Manticore's lightning spell.

"Ladies, I'm going to need your help *right now*," I said.

"But we haven't finished studying the Manticore yet!" Jinetta complained.

"You haven't really studied this one at all," I pointed out. "You're only reading books about the species. Put the crystal ball away. What can you see about this one that will help us get it out of town? Use those analytical minds Pervects are so proud of."

"Uhhh" The three girls fixed their gaze on the beast.

"He's very angry," Freczia said.

"That's not interfering with his effectiveness," I said. "Believe me. But, stop and think about it: why do you think he's been here five days?"

"He's lost?" Jinetta suggested.

"Look at the jar in his arm," I said. "He's doing everything he can to keep us from hitting it. When he runs into an obstruction, his first concern is for its safety."

"It's a baby!" Freezia squealed. "He's saving his baby!"

"Er, no," I said as the Manticore raised the container over his head and squeezed a long stream of green fluid into his maw. "I'd say that it's liquor. He's drunk."

"That's awful!" Pologne said. "Abusing alcohol to the point of incoherence! I've never heard of such a thing."

"And how does that help?" Melvine asked.

"Use your imagination," I snapped. I had wanted them to save the town by themselves, but they really *didn't* have a clue. Like it or not, I had to lead again. "He'll go where his jug does. Jinetta and Pologne, take over for Bee and Tolk. Bee, you're the best at orienteering. We passed a gum-gorse tree a few miles outside of town. Go and locate it for me. When you find it, stay on the road as close to it as you can."

"Yes, sir!" The ex-corporal took off running. I turned to the Pervects.

"Freezia, have you got a good retrieval spell?"

"It depends on what you want to use it for," the petite Pervect said, matching my businesslike tone. "Is the object animal, vegetable or mineral? Is it bigger than a breadbox, or small enough for angels to dance on its head?"

"It's that bottle!" I said, out of patience. "Get it out of his grasp and fly it out of here." The Manticore shot another bolt of lightning out of his bottom. "Now would be a good time."

"Oh, hurry, Freezy," Jinetta gasped. "That blast weakened my spell!"

"Well, I'll try!" Freezia said. "My goodness, he has a tight grip! I—I can't do both spells at once!"

"Neither can I!" Pologne wailed.

Shades of green were beginning to show through my apprentices' peaches-and-cream complexions. In a minute, the townsfolk were going to have three Pervects in their midst. Having been involved in riots with Aahz on Klah once before, I wanted to avoid the possibility. I threw what little power I had left into the disguise spells.

"You're under wraps," I said. "Keep trying to get that bottle!"

"I'll distract him! C'mon, Gleep! Hey, critter!" Tolk and my dragon galloped straight for the Manticore.

Surprised by the two creatures advancing on him, the Manticore stopped spraying the surrounding buildings with lightning. Tolk, looking very small beside the beast, started worrying at one of his big, shaggy feet. Gleep burned the other foot with his tiny spear of flame. The Manticore roared in surprise. His tail lanced down over his head. Yelping, Tolk dodged the spike. Gleep saw the whole thing as a game, and started jumping around, yodelling every time the raging Manticore missed him.

"Gleep! Gleep! Gleep!"

"Now!" I bellowed.

Freezia jerked at nothing with both hands. The round container lunged out of the Manticore's grip.

She pushed, and it sped out of the gate into the woods.

"Hey!" the beast roared. He dropped to all fours and began running after the jug.

"Buttercup, stay with Bunny!"

We started running after the Manticore.

Within a few hundred yards the mob had fallen behind. I was relieved. My magik was just about depleted. I let the disguise spells fall away. What power I had left might serve to light a candle, no more.

Freezia kept the bottle just out of the Manticore's grip, teasing him one way or another, but not letting him run faster than we could keep up. The beast never noticed us, being completely focused on getting the booze back. The young Pervect played him like a fish on a line, reeling in the jug then yanking it back out again.

"This road is so rough," Freezia gasped. "I'm afraid of losing control. Oh, I hate having no magik!"

"I can put the Cantrip on you," Tolk said. "I think I learned it well enough from Bee."

"Klahd magik!" Pologne snorted.

"I think that's a good idea," I said. "I'd take him up on it, if I were you."

"Oh, just as long as she doesn't start wearing tasteless clothes," the Pervect said, rolling her eyes.

It took a lot of concentration to cast an unfamiliar enchantment on the run, but Tolk did manage to bespell Bee's spell.

"Rrrrrrr!CANTRIP!"

We all felt the results. The Pervects may have been scornful of the magik and the magician, but it seemed that we were running on air, all the stones and ruts cleared out of our way.

"I'm proud of you, Tolk," I panted. "Good work!"

"Thanks, Skeeve!" Tolk barked, racing around us in a circle. "I did good. I did good. I did good."

"That's much better," Pologne said, reluctantly.

"I've got a flight coupon," Jinetta said, digging in her backpack as we ran. "I can zip ahead and see where Bee is."

"Oh, good idea!" Freezia praised her.

"Thank you!" she beamed. From her bag she fished out a slip of blue paper and blinked at it. "Nothing is happening! I know this ticket isn't outdated!"

"It's the strain on the force line," Pologne said. "It's nothing more than a thread! Those tickets need a lot of magik to work!"

"Oh, I *hate* this!" Jinetta said. "I feel so helpless!"

"You're not helpless," I said. "Not as long as you can think."

Fine words, I chided myself, as we chased a drunken Manticore five times our size down the road. I wondered if my students thought I sounded as supercilious as I felt.

A slight figure in the distance stepped out of the bushes and waved its hands over its head.

"There's Bee," I said. "Everybody get ready. Freezia, send the bottle after him."

I waved back to Bee, pointing into the woods. He beckoned to us and stepped off the road to the right.

The gum-gorse was one of the nastiest pieces of nature that it had ever been my misfortune to run into. Its fragrant, blue-green bark was said to be good to eat, but it was defended from predators by a thick layer of viscous goo and studded with long, red spines that not only hurt going into one's skin, but worse coming out because of their minute, backward-facing barbs. When I'd been an inept junior thief, I once tried to get away from someone I had robbed by climbing up into one. My victim had laughed at seeing me stuck there among the thorns, and left me, saying it was a harsher punishment than he had planned to give me. I had only been freed by a kindly passerby who knew the tree's secret.

This specimen almost waved its branches as if to say, "Come and get me, sucker."

I ran up beside the tree and clapped my hands togther. "Throw it here, Freezia!"

The young Pervect flicked her fingers, and the bottle came hurtling towards me. It smacked into my arms. It was bigger than I thought, about the size of a medicine ball.

"Oof! Hey, big guy!" I shouted, waving it at the Manticore. "Do you want this?"

"Roooooaaarr!" the beast gargled. He lumbered in my direction.

I looked around.

"Bee! Go long!"

The ex-soldier dashed out a little way and held out his hands. Using a touch of magik to offset the weight, I heaved the container to him. Bee turned around and threw it to Freezia, who nearly let it drop in surprise. The Manticore peered from one to the other, trying to follow the flight path of the beloved jug. He started to gallumph toward Freezia. She saw him coming, and called out.

"Catch, Jinetta!" The tall Pervect leaped into the air, intercepting the ball like a pro.

"Oh! Oh! To me!" Tolk yelped. Jinetta slung it to him underhand. It rolled past him, and he galloped after it, his tongue flying. Gleep beat him to it, and the two of them fought over it, each tugging the strap in opposite directions. Gleep won the tug-of-war, and dashed around through the trees with the Manticore in pursuit. As he passed me for the second time, I reached under his chin and yanked the bottle away.

"Gleep!" my pet protested.

"Sorry, but you're not helping!" I said. I tossed the container in a high lob toward Bee. The ex-corporal dove for it, snagging it out from under the beast's nose, and tossing it to Pologne.

The Manticore roared in frustration. The bottle bounded around him too fast for his addled wits. He staggered toward one of us, then another, then another. His legs seemed to be getting tangled up underneath him. The insectlike tail lashed, stabbing over his head. We ducked under cover of branches and into bushes to avoid the deadly sting. With the container in my arms, I dodged towards a heartwood tree just ahead of the Manticore. The sting missed me. The tree took a direct hit. It let out a low moaning sound, and red sap dribbled down the trunk. The Manticore edged around the tree, his claws reaching avidly for the bottle. Hastily, I heaved it all the way across the circle. The Manticore turned to follow.

I felt for the force line. It was refilling; the Manticore hadn't thrown a lightning bolt in several minutes. Pologne reached out to snag the bottle and cocked her arm back to toss it.

"Don't throw it!" I called. "Can you levitate?"

"I think so!" she called back, her Klahd-disguised face wrinkled pensively. "Where?"

"Over the gum-gorse—right NOW!"

The middle-sized Pervect looked doubtful, but she crouched and sprang, just ahead of the Manticore's leap to retrieve his property. Pologne hovered above the tree.

"What do I do now?"

"Taunt him!" I yelled. "Pretend he's your little brother!"

The look of doubt became even more pronounced, but she reached inside herself for her inner big sister. "Hey, Manticore!" she said. "I've got your whateveritis! You can't have it back! Nyah nyah nyah!"

"Don't touch the thorns!" I warned her. "Everyone else, spread out! Don't let him past you!"

"How?" Tolk asked.

I didn't have to worry. The Manticore cared for nothing but getting his jug back. His tail slashing, he stalked around the gum-gorse tree, measuring his chances of leaping up at Pologne. As I had assumed, the branches were too thick. The beast started to climb up the trunk.

"Yeowch! Yeowch! Yeeee—uhhh?"

Within two steps, the accretion of viscous sap was enough to cement the Manticore's limbs to the trunk. With total bemusement on his Klahdlike face, the Manticore tried to pull a forepaw loose. It wouldn't come. Neither would the other. He yanked at one back leg then the other. No luck. With a fearsome snarl, he swung his tail around for a killing stab. The stinger plunged deep into the bark—and held fast. The growl died away to a puzzled whine.

"It worked!" Melvine exclaimed. "Wow. You got that right, Teach."

"Thanks," I said drily.

The Pervect continued to float around the treetop, spewing her version of invective. "You're ugly! And Mother doesn't love you! And I don't like it when you blink my cosmetics out just when I'm about to put them on—"

"Pologne!" I called. "You can stop now!"

"Oh," she said, clearly disappointed. "I was just hitting my stride. Are you sure I should not abuse it a while longer?"

"No," I said. "Come down. I want to talk to it."

Chapter Twelve

"I think we've forgotten something."
ALAMO COMMEMORATION COMMITTEE

The Manticore heaved wildly, trying to pull each limb loose. He was not going anywhere. The sticky gum had merged with his fur, creating a thick felt that could have been used for roofing. He couldn't launch lightning bolts at us now, even if he wanted. The scorpionlike tail had been wound halfway around the bole of the tree. Truthfully, the Manticore looked pretty pathetic. Dribbles of blood oozed out of the long fur from where the thorns had pierced the skin. His eyes rolled with fear as we converged upon him. Gleep flattened himself on his belly, and snarled. The Manticore cringed back even farther.

"Now, we kill it?" Melvine asked, advancing on the creature with a bloodthirsty gleam in his eyes.

"Nope," I said, stiffarming the Cupy several feet from our captive. "We just talk to him."

"What? What fun is that?"

I turned to the Pervects. "Can any of you speak Manticore?"

"Well," Freezia said, raising a forefinger. "I did a course in comparative languages. But he hasn't said anything yet for me to compare it to!"

"Let's see if we can get him to say something."

I had not spent several years in the Bazaar at Deva for nothing. Most of the Deveel vendors there knew several languages, the better to cheat—I mean, *deal*—with buyers from numerous dimensions, and none of them would ever let a sale slip by for ANY reason. The usual means of communicating with newcomers was a spell or an amulet of translation. I felt the force line. It was plumping up nicely. I scoured my memory for the spell that I had learned from a friendly merchant named Bellma—for a price, of course. Nothing was free in the Bazaar, but it was often worth the cost.

The magikal force had resurged sufficiently for me to include all of my apprentices within the range of the spell. It didn't have a physical manifestation, but I felt as though we were now linked by tubes that led from our mouths to everyone else's ears.

"Who are you?" I asked the Manticore.

The beast jerked back—as far as he could, covered with glue—and gazed at me. "You speak my language!"

"Uh, sort of. I'm Skeeve. These are my students."

"I am Evad, ensign of the Royal Manticorean Navy. You must be a powerful general to have captured me," the Manticore said. "I bow to you." He couldn't do that much, either, but I appreciated the effort.

"Actually, I'm a magician," I said. "What were you doing tearing up that town? You wrecked most of the place."

The Manticore showed his fangs. "They were not intelligent. I asked them where I was, and no one could tell me! I tried to insist that they send for a translator, and they kept hitting me with things. That was rude! I got impatient."

I raised an eyebrow. "So you got drunk and smashed the place up? What's your commanding officer going to think of that?"

For the first time the creature actually looked ashamed of himself. His big, shaggy head drooped. "Not much. I have only five days left on my leave, and I'm wasting it in this stupid backwater! No offense."

"None taken," I replied with a smile. "It's nothing I haven't thought myself from time to time. This dimension is called Klah, though not by the people who live here. They've got pretty particular ideas about keeping your hands off other people's houses, by the way. You'll have to make up for the damage you did."

The Manticore moaned. "My head hurts!"

I turned to Tolk. "Can you do something for him?"

"Sure-sure-sure!" the Canidian said. "Happy to try. Never had a Manticorean for a patient before, eh? Hold still."

"You are being very kind to a stranger, especially one who tried to kill you," the Manticorean said as Tolk leaped up on his back and climbed up to perch on his shoulder. Tolk laid his paws on the other's shaggy mane.

"Would you rather we killed *you*?" I asked.

Evad thought about it. "I might save face that way," he said. "I will go back now in disgrace. An officer in the Royal Manticorean Navy, getting lost in the wrong dimension like a first-year student! Ah, that is better. But, alas, I am sober now! Thank you, brown-and-white being."

"Tolk's the name," the Canidian said cheerfully, leaping down. "You're good as new."

"More likely I will die attached to this fierce plant!" the Manticore said dramatically.

"Not really," I said. "The sap runs when it gets warm. All we have to do is heat it, and you'll slide right off. No problem, apart from the thorns."

"I will bear the pain," Evad said bravely. "I do it for the honor of our Queen."

"Hey, Gleep." I put out a hand, and my pet ran to me. "Can you warm the sap just a little bit? Not enough to set it on fire."

"Gleep!" my dragon replied happily. He dashed to the side of the tree and exhaled. A flame tickled out from his throat, and the brown goo began to bubble. The Manticore writhed and tried to pull his feet up out of reach.

"What are you doing, O wizard?" Evad wailed. "Would you burn me at the stake?"

"Gleep?" my pet turned large, puzzled blue eyes up toward the Manticore.

Jinetta put up a timid hand. "May we try? That is one spell we use frequently, to heat bathwater in our dorms. It would be nice to put it to use in a real-world setting."

"Go right ahead." I took the time to ponder Evad's pride problem.

The Pervects gathered around the tree and concentrated. The gluey resin changed from opaque to translucent and began to swell slightly. I had an idea even before the Manticore slid to the ground with a *bang!*

"Too bad," Melvine said. "A Manticore head would have looked pretty impressive over my mantlepiece."

"You are a fierce opponent, Klahd," the Manticore said as the rest of the goo dripped off him in sheets.

"Thanks, but I'm not a Klahd. I'm a Cupy."

The Manticore made a courtly bow. "I am corrected. I am afraid you all look alike to me."

"Well, you better remember in the future," Melvine said, his baby face fierce. "We're tougher than we look."

"Stop threatening him, Melvine," I said. "Hitting a fellow when he's down is small-minded."

"That's not what my aunt does," Melvine interrupted me. "She—"

"And Markie put your education in my hands," I interrupted back, as the Pervects moved in, ears pricked with curiosity. "Does that tell you anything?"

"Ei, do what she says, not what she does?" Melvine ventured.

"Let's start there." I turned to the Manticore.

"What can I do, O Skeeve," Evad asked miserably. "I am an honorable male, but on an ensign's pay I don't have the funds to make up for the trouble I caused, nor do I have the time to work off the amount. I have no valuables except my insigne."

"Well," Bee suggested, "you wouldn't be the first ensign to have to hock his uniform to pay his way out of trouble. It happened a fair amount in the Possiltum army. You can redeem it later."

"I couldn't," Evad said, horrified. "It belongs to the Queen!"

"I have an idea," I said. "That venom of yours: does it kill or wound?"

"It depends upon what I mean it to do," Evad said, his big face puzzled. "Most of the time it will only make the flesh swell up and become painful. Those people I struck will recover, unless I pierced them in a vital area. I will apologize to them. I am ashamed to have used brute force on civilians."

"No, that's not what I mean," I said. "I'm more interested in the venom itself. So, you can produce it in different strengths, or are they different fluids?"

The Manticore looked as though he was getting another headache. "I do not know, O Skeeve. I have never really thought about it. Why?"

"I'm doing comprehensive magikal studies," I explained. "Could you, er, give me a sample of each kind? I would like to study them. I'd like to do some experiments to see if there is any difference, and if either is good for other magikal purposes. I'd pay you for them. A fair price."

Evad looked suspicious.

"I could do that," he said. "But such a small amount will not discharge my debt to the people of that village."

"Oh, I think it will," I said airily. "Here's my offer: I'd be willing to pay you the going rate for Manticore venom on Klah."

"There is no Manticore venom on Klah, so far as I know," Bee said. "I would have heard about a weapon like that when I was in the army."

"That would make it pretty valuable, wouldn't it?" I asked innocently. Evad perked up as he began to catch my drift.

"O Skeeve, if you would do that, I would be your servant for life!"

"Let's not go that far," I said hastily. "What about the deal?"

"Yes! I agree! Shall we drink on it?" Evad asked congenially. "Where is my bottle?"

"Maybe we should just shake hands," I suggested.

We hiked back into Humulus, Evad walking among us with his shaggy head bowed to show contrition.

"I don't get it," Melvine kept saying. "I mean, that thing is as big as a house, and you make friends with it? You had it where you wanted it, and you let it go? What if he suddenly goes crazy on us?" He glanced over his shoulder at the huge Manticore shuffling along in our wake.

"I think," Jinetta said tentatively, "that it is very impressive that Skeeve turned an enemy into an ally."

"Yeah, by paying him off!"

"No, by meeting mutual needs!" Tolk said, his pink tongue flapping happily as he ran beside us on all fours. "Wow, that's so cool! Skeeve, you're brilliant!"

"How did you think of doing that?" Pologne asked.

"It's something we did a lot when I was with M.Y.T.H., Inc.," I explained. "A win-win deal leaves everyone happy."

"Why bother with a win-win? You had a savage killer at your mercy. He was helpless! You could have gotten much more out of him than you did."

"Look," I explained. "I don't need more than a couple of vials' worth of venom right now. If I do, I know where to find him. I don't want a slave. He needs the money. Everyone gets what they want, right?"

"Not exactly," Freezia said, looking ahead. I peered into the distance.

Neither my sight nor my hearing was as keen as the Pervects', but within a few steps I could make out the citizens of Humulus huddled together just inside their village gate. They were chanting.

"Kill the monster! Kill the monster! Kill the monster!"

We hiked closer, and I could see the villagers' faces change from anger to astonishment, and slide right over into fear. They hoisted their weapons still further, and their voices became more shrill.

"Kill the monsters! Kill the monsters! Kill the monsters!"

"Master Skeeve," Bee said, "I think we forgot one *little* thing."

"We did," I groaned. "No one remembered to put their disguise spells back on, did they?"

A quick glance around revealed the awful truth.

"No, sir," Bee confirmed.

"Nor I," said Jinetta.

"Or us," the other two Pervects chimed in.

"How about we run away, right now?" Melvine asked as the villagers began to move towards us.

"Bowmen!" Flink's voice rose above the others. "Prepare to fire!"

"No!" Bunny shrieked. She thrust aside a couple of big men and sent them staggering. Her disguise had dropped, revealing the beauty beneath the hag. Two larger men jumped in and grabbed her arms. It cost a dozen or more of them bites, gouges and bruises to subdue Buttercup, but they captured him, too. "Skeeve! Run for it!"

"I don't think we're going to get the chance," I said hastily. "Let's take it on the offensive. Everyone remember their levitation spells? Grab arrows first. Next, whatever other weapons they point at you. After that, we may have to raise a few people's consciousnesses. Let's go."

I squared my shoulders and marched forward. It took the others a moment to catch on, but Bee double-timed it to parade at my shoulder. Tolk trotted up, showing his teeth ferociously. Gleep led the way, lashing his tail and spewing out a stream of fire nearly two feet long, not bad for a baby dragon. The Pervects minced along behind, their dainty steps out of context—to my fellow Klahds—with the green scaly faces and long teeth. I meant to play on that disparity. But first, I had to disarm our employers before they killed someone.

"Fire!" shrieked Flink.

The first flight of arrows came winging at us. I waved an imperious hand, not so impressive since I was now ordinary Skeeve, all blond hair, blue eyes and lanky build, but with a full tank of magik to draw upon it was no trouble to send the bolts flying on over our heads. They thudded into the road behind us, raising a cloud of dust.

"Is that all you've got?" I shouted.

A few brave souls hoisted homemade spears and prepared to throw.

"Ladies?" I said.

"Oh, let me!" Pologne piped up.

"No, you got to taunt the Manticore," Jinetta said. "It's my turn!"

"*Someone* do it," I gritted as the villagers let fly.

Jinetta sashayed out from our ranks and held out her hands. The makeshift spears halted in mid-air and began to whirl, describing complicated patterns.

"I was in marching band in secondary school," she explained to me cheerfully over her shoulder. The spears fell into her outstretched palms, and she sent them flying again. "I was the best baton twirler in Sangafroid! I still remember the fight song! 'Fight on for dear Sangafroid! Kill the other team! Rip their heads off/ For dear old Sangafroid!'" she warbled. She caught the spears deftly in each hand and did a back flip, landing on one knee. "Ta-daaaa!"

"Brava!" I called, breaking into applause. My apprentices and Evad joined in.

The villagers didn't. They broke into a run, heading back towards the gate. Jinetta looked disappointed.

"Freezia, you were very good at the retrieval spell," I said. "Can you find the catch that holds up that portcullis and release it?"

"Oh, yes, Master Skeeve!" the petite Pervect exclaimed. She went through a series of complicated gestures then pulled one hand back as if yanking a lever.

The big gate came crashing down, just as the villagers reached it. The first ones there slammed into it, and the following waves of people piled into them. I strolled up to Flink, who was at the back of the group with his archers. I leaned forward and smiled.

"Hi."

He jumped about three feet backwards, stumbling into the beleaguered bowmen. Then, recovering his dignity, he pulled down his tunic and thrust out his chin. "You have us trapped, wizard, but we will fight for our lives against your cohort of monsters."

"Monsters?" I asked innocently. "Do you see any monsters?" I glanced back at my students and let out a deep laugh. "Are you fooled by my illusion? I cast these semblances upon my apprentices to strike terror into the Manticore and force him to surrender! Behold!"

I whisked my hand, and all of the students assumed their disguises. I became the imperious Skeeve the Great once again and Gleep turned back into a goat. The villagers relaxed.

Flink swallowed. "You must admit their appearance was very convincing, er, wizard."

"Of course they are," I said calmly. "I am the best."

"You mean, this gorgeous girl is really a hideous hag?" asked one of the men holding Bunny. He thrust her away. "Eeeyuch!"

"You're no prize yourself," Bunny said, tossing her hair in annoyance. "Master Skeeve, is everything okie-dokie?"

"It certainly is," I said. "Behold! We have captured the Manticore!" I waved him forward. "Evad!"

The Manticore shuffled up to us, his cap in his hands. "Me sorry," he said, in the Klahdish I'd taught him on the way up the road. Close, but no Norelco shaver.

"Captured?" Flink roared. "Why didn't you kill it?"

Behind him, the townsfolk began to chant again. "Kill the monster! Kill the monster!"

Evad looked alarmed.

"That was not in our contract," I said coldly. "Norb brought us here to rid your town of the intruder. He didn't say anything about killing."

"I would have thought that was implied, wizard!"

"Magik is a very specific study, Master Flink. I do not deal in inference. If I was that unclear in my spells, I'd have had my guts ripped out by demons a long time ago."

"Then, kill it!" Flink ordered.

I crossed my arms.

"That would require a renegotiation of our agreement, Master Flink," I said, "involving substantially higher fees regarding magikal wear and tear, disposal of the body, that kind of thing."

Flink looked dismayed. I pressed my advantage.

"Wouldn't you be happier if I said that this Manticore here was prepared to make amends for the destruction he caused?"

Evad came forward, his big paws clasped together contritely.

"Why—" Flink thought about it. "I suppose so."

"He stabbed my husband!" a woman cried out.

"And my nephew!" boomed a stout man, bringing forward a boy wearing bloodstained coveralls.

"He hurt a lot of people, not just buildings," Flink pointed out.

"Well, we can fix that, too, at no extra charge," I said agreeably. "Tolk!"

"Yessir!" the Canidian said, trotting forward.

I pointed to the wounded townsfolk. "Heal!"

Chapter Thirteen

"We're not in this for the money."
W. GATES

In spite of having to maintain our disguises the walk home was much more relaxed than the outward journey. My students laughed and congratulated one another, recapping the whole mission to Humulus and their own successes.

"You were brilliant, Jinetta!" Pologne exclaimed. "I have never heard the fight song rendered with more spirit!"

Jinetta preened with pleasure. "I wish Coach could have been here to see it. But you, Pologne! Your hovering was picture perfect. We could have been back in the lab!"

"That was some pretty flying," Bee said wistfully. "I wish I could do that."

"Oh, you will," Jinetta assured him. "It just takes practice. I'll spot you."

"We all will," Freezia promised. "That was amazing! To think all the magik we learned in school actually has a use in the real world! I thought all the 'power-in, power-out' nonsense was just academic. And, oh, I was never so grateful to see a force line in my life!"

"Me, too," Melvine grunted. "You don't really appreciate them when they're gone. On Sear it didn't seem like such a big deal, but here—"

"You were fabulous," Jinetta told him enthusiastically. "I'm sure none of us could have held on to that big lummox for so long with a diminishing power ratio! And with all those people yelling, too—it was so distracting!"

"Don't forget Bee's calculations," Tolk said. "Wow-wow-wow! We rebuilt that whole town hall in an hour!"

"That was nothing," Bee said modestly. "I read in an old scroll that items that had been bonded for any time had a sympathetic cohesion that could be rejoined by magik. I wouldn't have believed you could have put it together again like a jigsaw puzzle, until Melvine here showed us."

The Cupy waved a hand. "Easy! With all of you and Evad there to steady the stone blocks, I had no problem raising the walls. Nice redecoration, there, by the way, Freezia. When you were done I couldn't see a single crack in the plaster, and the frescoes looked like new."

"Thank you," the petite Pervect said, beaming. "A Magikal Arts major doesn't seem to have turned out to be the useless piece of parchment my parents were afraid it would."

"And how about Pologne's illusion when Skeeve sent the Manticore home?" Bee asked. "Those flames were so real I could almost smell them."

"Oh, it was just a little of this, and a little of that," Pologne said, blushing green.

"We are the best," Tolk exclaimed. "Hey, you know, we oughta have a name! Like—Skeeve's Students! Then we could have matching tunics, and school colors, and everything!"

"Ehhh," Jinetta said. "I don't know about the rest, but I like the idea of a name. Skeeve's Students is a little too pedestrian, and it sounds sort of grade-schoolish. We're here for advanced studies. No offense, Tolk."

"None taken! I'm not very good at names. I bet you are! What do you think?"

"I don't know. Someone throw out some ideas."

"Well," Bee began. The others turned toward him eagerly. "You know Master Skeeve and my sergeant, Swatter, were partners in M.Y.T.H., Inc. What if we called ourselves something related to that."

"Oooh," Pologne squealed. "My parents would be so impressed. I know they've heard of M.Y.T.H., Inc."

"They're famous for magik," Tolk said. "But you Pervects have a lot of amazing machines. So, we're both magikal and technological. Can we do something with that?"

"That's a great idea, Tolk," Freezia exclaimed. "How about it, Jinny?"

The tallest Pervect knitted her scaly brows together. "I know! How about Myth-ka-Technic University? That combines both disciplines along with ancient spirituality!"

"Oh, that's good," Pologne said. "It sounds—advanced."

"Terrific, Miss Jinetta," Bee said. "I like it."

"Not bad," Melvine agreed. "You're good with words."

"Well, thank you!" Jinetta beamed.

"Now, about those tunics," Tolk said.

I listened, letting them jabber on happily, heaping praise on one another and accepting compliments. I was pleased with the way things had turned out. Mostly. I had taken Bunny aside while Tolk was repairing jabbed thighs and gouged shoulders to ask her for our bag of gold. Facing her was almost worse than facing a drunken Manticore. Even after the two extra days we spent in Humulus offering our assistance repairing the town hall as a gesture of good will, she was still angry about it.

"I cannot believe that you paid out our entire travel budget on two tubes of poison!"

"Manticore venom," I corrected her, but my ears were burning. Bunny was the only one who wasn't ecstatically happy about the outcome of our adventure. Gleep trotted alongside her, laying his long neck against her knee, and rolling big blue eyes up at her.

She ignored him, stalking along with crossed arms. "I don't care. You gave away a whole bag of gold because you felt sorry for that sting-tailed oaf! He's the one who got drunk. You didn't put that bottle into his paws. You're not responsible for his problem."

"No," I said with a sigh. She was right. I was being soft. Part of me knew it was counterproductive, but part of me was glad. Evad had been so grateful for my 'deal' that I didn't even think ahead to the fearsome task of having to explain to Bunny why I needed our entire traveling budget so the Manticore could pay off his debts. The reward we had been paid by the head-man did cover the amount I had given Evad, plus a little left over. Bunny was not appeased. Still, I thought it had been a great learning experience for my pupils.

"Look, Bunny," I said persuasively, "think of it as an invest-ment. What if you had a potion that changed its effect when you wanted it to? Studying this phenomenon could get us a big profit one day. Think of the applications for non-magicians!"

In spite of herself, she let the corner of her mouth quirk up in a half-smile. "You're just trying to dance your way out of trouble. Skeeve, it's your money. I wouldn't be a very good accountant if I didn't tell you when you were wasting it."

"You're the best," I said sincerely. "Who knows? This really could be the beginning of an important magikal break-through. An exclusive!"

"Right up until the time that the Deveels figure out what you did and undercut your deal with the people on Mantico," she pointed out.

I grinned back. "So it's a limited exclusive. But we made a profit, didn't we?"

"My uncle wouldn't consider it a very good return, and neither would Aahz."

"If I'd continued on in magik the way I started out, only caring what I could make from it, you wouldn't still be here, would you?"

Bunny shook her head. "I wouldn't give you the time of day. All right, Skeeve, it's your money."

"It's ours," I declared. "We all earned it."

"Gleep!" my pet crowed, happy that we had made up.

"You were terrific, too," I told him. He jumped up to slime me with his long tongue. "Ugh, Gleep!"

"Gleep," he declared, and trotted off into the woods to find something to eat. Bunny and I grinned as he disappeared into the undergrowth.

"...It's decided, then," Jinetta was saying as we dropped back into the group. "Tomorrow we'll work on Cantrip. Once we're good at that, I wouldn't mind learning Tolk's anti-head-ache remedy."

"It's easy! It's easy!" the Canidian promised enthusiastically.

Even the old inn seemed to wear a halo of contentment. I wasn't even bothered by the wave of stale air that blew out in my face when I unspelled the main door.

"Come with me," I invited the students. "I have a surprise for you."

Murmuring with curiosity, they followed. I gestured for them to gather around the scarred and stained dining table.

"I assigned you a hard task. You not only rose to the occasion, but you threw in your own flourishes that made it more than a success. You worked together, and you played off each other's strengths. I'm proud of your progress, and I'm proud of you. So, let me add to the festivities a little." I produced the bag of money that Bunny had collected from Headman Flink. "Here's our reward. We get half, since I'm teaching you and Bunny is my support staff. But the rest should rightly be divided between all of you."

I dumped the shining stream of silver out onto the table top. The coins bounced and jingled and rolled around the wooden table top. When the last one vibrated to a ringing halt, I could have heard a fly cough in the big room. I looked up at my students. To my amazement, all of them were staring at me with expressions ranging from dismay to horror.

"What's the matter?" I asked.

"We can't accept this, Master Skeeve," Tolk said.

"We don't deserve it," Bee added. "If it wasn't for you, we'd have fallen on our faces a bunch of times."

"But you didn't," I assured him. "All you needed was a little confidence. I did very little. It was your efforts. Take it."

"No!" they protested in unison, the Pervects loudest of all.

"Why not?" Bunny asked. She sorted the money into neat piles, a large one for us and small ones for each of them. "You earned it."

"We can't accept any money from you," Jinetta said, almost desperately. I was puzzled: a Pervect refusing to take money?

"It's apprentice wages," I said calmly. "Less than I'd accept for such a task, even at your level of experience. If you were my partners, you'd be entitled to equal shares. You did a good job. You should participate in the reward."

"No," Melvine said, crossing his little arms. "We won't accept it. Not a copper piece. Not a wooden nickel."

"Are you sure?" I asked.

"We can't," Pologne insisted, her yellow eyes large with alarm. "Really. All we want from you is an education. Nothing else. And we'll have to ask you to take that as our final word."

They nodded in unison. I shrugged.

They seemed to be more in accord than they had been at any time before, appearing to have achieved a mutual understanding on the long walk home.

"Well, if that's what you want," I said, "but I promise you would still get the same education from me whether you accept this reward or not."

"No!" Tolk said. "You can't force us to take it."

"Force you?" Freezia snorted. "You wanted to take it. I could see it in your eyes."

"That's not true," the Canidian howled. "How about you? Perverts are greedy. Everyone knows it. Why don't you just take your shares? You know you want to."

"You liar," Jinetta said. "And that's Pervect!"

"In your dreams! Eating food that smells like garbage. That's perverted!"

"Yeah, you're such hypocrites," Melvine sneered. "Slurping down purple worms then it's 'oh, dear, look at that bug! It might crawl on me!'"

"You should talk, Mr. Fearless," Bee said. "What was with you when we first got to Humulus? You're the most powerful of us after Master Skeeve, and you kept bawling like, well, a baby!"

"I had Manticore nightmares as a kid, okay?" Melvine snarled.

"Back off him," Pologne said, her voice rising to a shriek. "Where were you when we were working on containing that beast? Running away yourself?"

Bee's face went pale under its freckles. "With respect, ma'am, I was following Master Skeeve's orders."

"You mean, because you couldn't do magik, right? Spellfree freak!"

I opened my mouth to say that Aahz had been without his magik for a few years, that he was no less formidable without it, but that wouldn't have made Pologne respect him or Bee any more than she did.

"You were sure buddying up with him before," Freezia said scornfully.

"How dare you suggest I'd make friends with a Klahd?"

"Hey," I protested.

In the blink of an eye, the good mood had been shattered. I didn't know how I had managed to ruin it, but the camaraderie had evaporated the moment I had emptied those coins out on the table. Distrust ran wild throughout the class, even between the Pervects.

"What is going on here?" Bunny asked. "Ten minutes ago you were friends. What happened."

They all turned to us, as if caught in the act.

"Oh, nothing," Pologne said, too brightly.

"Look at the time!" Jinetta said hastily. "Dinner soon! We'll go out and get supplies. I hope they still have some fresh *sgarnwalds* in the market at this hour, don't you, Freezia?"

"Let me pitch in," Melvine insisted, digging in his pocket for coins.

"And me, too," Tolk said. Bee opened his threadbare belt pouch and produced a couple of coppers, which he placed in Jinetta's palm.

"It's only right," Freezia explained to me and Bunny. "Whenever I stay with friends I always buy groceries. I almost never eat up their food. And we know what you like, too. It'll be good. I promise. Bye!"

Before I could reply, the three Pervects disappeared.

"Something is up," Bunny said. She turned to the three male students. "What is going on?"

"Nothing," Melvine said hastily. "Boy, I could sure use a nap." He vanished, the displaced air BAMFing behind him.

"Gotta go walk myself," Tolk added. He scampered out of the door.

"I, uh," Bee began then turned and quick-marched after the Canidian without finishing his sentence.

Bunny, Gleep and I were left alone in the big room.

"*Something* strange is going on here," Bunny said.

"I think they're just tired," I replied. "Don't be so suspicious."

Bunny narrowed an eye. "You're too trusting. Tolk was right: Pervects never turn down free money. That's more than strange."

I sighed. "They're not all the same as Aahz. I found that out when I was on Perv. Maybe there is some code among MIP students not to take gifts from their teacher. Probably one of Professor Maguffin's rules. They're always quoting him."

"I don't know," Bunny said, tapping her foot on the floor impatiently. "I'm going to keep my eye on them. All of them."

"Gleep!" Gleep announced.

"Yes," I agreed, patting my pet on the head. "Me, too."

If I had thought the dinner at which I made them switch main courses was awkward, this one deserved a medal for going above and beyond the call of gut-twisting, in more ways than one. Almost as if they wanted to taunt the others, the Pervects, who sat together at one end of the big table, made a point of serving their food in small bites, making sure to give everyone a good look at each slimy, purple pseudopod dripping off the spoon. As promised, the food they brought back for the rest of us was fine, even delicious, though it was harder to enjoy with the nauseating whiff of Pervish cooking overwhelming us.

Melvine sat sniveling to himself during the entire meal. "Nobody likes me. I wring myself dry for them, and they make fun of me! I'm going to run away and go home."

I thought he was expressing the unspoken sentiments of the whole group fairly well.

"You're all selling yourselves and each other short," I said. "You just proved what I've been trying to tell you all along: the best thing you can do is learn to work together. You find one another's strengths and supplement them. That's true whether you're trying to survive in a wilderness situation or in a high-powered company. My associates and I couldn't be beaten because no one could drive a wedge between us. When you're busy cutting each other's throats, then it's easier for someone to sneak up on YOU."

"That's too simple," Tolk said. He remained civil to Bunny and me, though he growled whenever the others glanced his way.

"It's more complicated than it sounds," I said. "There are a lot of factors beyond a person's talents you have to take into consideration. Climate. Uh, personal phobias." That got a wince out of Melvine. I regretted hurting his feelings, but it was a valid statement. "Experience. Inclination. Willingness. You can be the greatest magician in the world, but if you won't get out there and try, you might as well have no magik at all."

"Hmmph," Pologne snorted.

"Look," I said. "We've all been through a lot in the last few days. I don't know about you, but I need a break. Everyone just enjoy themselves this evening. We'll start on some more exercises in the morning. All right?"

"Yes, sir," Bee muttered, not raising his eyes from his plate.

The others murmured their assent. I threw an exasperated glance at Bunny, who shook her head.

After the dishes were washed, I retreated to my study and hoped they'd take advantage of my absence to argue it all out and make peace. I set up an experiment with a couple of strange metallic elements I'd come across in a Bazaar trick shop, but I couldn't concentrate on it. I found I was straining to listen to what was going on in the rest of the inn. Except for the music and voices from Bunny's PDA in the next room, I heard nothing but furtive footsteps on the upper floor.

One tentative set tiptoed down the stairs, coming toward my study.

"Hey, Freezia, do you want to watch *Sink or Swim* with me?" Bunny called out.

"Uh, no, thanks, Bunny," the dainty Pervect said, almost in a gasp. I heard her feet patter back up the stairs to her room. I heard the murmur of hasty conversation above, then silence. No cheerful conversation, no joshing, no mutual admiration society. The rooms on the upper floor might as well have been vacant, except for the almost-visible waves of distrust that radiated out of them.

I pushed aside my experiment and sank my head into my hands.

What had I done wrong? I pored over the memory of the day over and over again, but I could recall nothing that seemed even remotely like criticism or an insult. I'd lived with a Pervect for years, so I thought I knew their thresholds of intolerance, which in Aahz's case mainly had to do with me being stupid. If I did something wrong out of innocence, he was pretty good about it; if I did something inane, he would flatten me for knowing better and not thinking. I *had* thought about the gesture of sharing the reward, all the way back from Humulus. Was I too late? Should I have divided up the spoils sooner? Had I been too cheap? Were they looking for a larger percentage of the take? They certainly had earned it. Now they were adamantly against taking any money at all.

I had run into a situation like this on Perv, when I had inadvertantly offended a friend named Edvik by offering him cash as a tip in thanks for services rendered instead of as a gift between equals. It took some fancy talking to straighten things out, the results of which got me into so much trouble that I had been ejected from the dimension permanently as *persona non grata*.

That was it, I told myself. I might be their teacher, but courtesy needed to extend in both directions. I promised that I would be more careful about my students' pride in the future.

Chapter Fourteen

"Is anybody happy?"
G. BUSH

"It's like this," Bee explained for the eighth time as he pointed out the obstacle course he had designed in the inn's courtyard out of chairs, fire irons, a few pots, heaps of books and stones. "You concentrate on walking a perfectly smooth road, and when you've got it in your head, you think 'Can't trip.' Get it? 'Cantrip.'" He grinned at her. "You can't trip. But you say 'spoo.'"

"I get it," Jinetta said, studying her nails. She picked a fragment of scale off her cuticle then polished her fingertips against her blouse. "In fact, I got it the first time you said it, over a week ago, and every time since then. This is beginner stuff."

Bee reddened. "It came in awful handy in Humulus, Tolk said."

"I'm sure to a Canidian it looks very impressive."

"Look, how about you try it yourself?" Bee asked, very politely. I gave him points for keeping his temper. Jinetta was doing her best to provoke him into an outburst. "I'll help you all I can."

"Well, that's a fly-leg's worth of meat at a banquet," Jinetta observed.

"I didn't know Pervects ate flies," Bee said, but he kept his voice low. Jinetta snarled. One point to Bee.

Tolk wasn't faring much better with Pologne. She hadn't wanted to work with him, but she declared she wasn't going to work with Melvine. Tolk wasn't thrilled with the pairing, either. I ordered them to cooperate or go home.

"How do I know she's any good at teaching?" he asked.

"How do I know you could possibly understand anything I taught?" she countered.

After sitting and staring at one another for half an hour, Tolk started demonstrating a healing technique. Out of sheer boredom Pologne began to listen to him, but she nitpicked at everything he said.

"Don't you mean *close* the wound?" she asked. "'Seal' the wound sounds like you're just covering it over."

"I went through an eight-year apprenticeship to learn this," Tolk growled. "Words aren't as important as deeds."

"Professor Maguffin would wash your mouth out with soup for saying something like that," Pologne spat.

"Soup? I love soup!"

"Weirdo!"

"Pervert!"

I left them alone, hoping that they would eventually gain some kind of understanding, but I doubted it. They had frozen up, and nothing I did seemed to make an impression.

Melvine and Freezia had gotten into mutual snits over his whirlwind spell, and were shrieking at each other from opposite ends of the courtyard. That had started over technique. It seemed that one of Melvine's gestures was an obscenity on Perv. I didn't know that there *was* a symbol for sex with multiple small animals.

I was fed up with all of them. I had sat up all night trying to figure out a way to break the ice again, and now I was too tired to do anything but supervise. Once in a while I made the rounds, offering encouragement and breaking up petty arguments, but I spent most of the time in the shade on the sidelines, sipping a glass of wine. On purpose, I had not brought the bottle outside with me. It was too tempting to get soused out of sheer frustration. I'd hinted that I'd like to know what had changed the group from teammates into bitter rivals in the matter of seconds, but they all pretended they had no idea what I was talking about.

"Cantrip!" Jinetta shouted as she hopped up onto Bee's obstacle course for the fourth time. I felt the magik in the overhead force line surge slightly. Everyone turned her way as she sauntered seemingly over thin air. Her body stretched and contracted as her feet touched down lightly, but her head stayed at the same level. "Voila!"

"Hey, pretty good," Bee said grudgingly.

"It was very good," Jinetta insisted. "It only took me four tries." She glanced at me. "All right, my turn." She went to pick up her buttermilk-colored briefcase.

"Something useful," Bee said, looking over her shoulder. "Not like how to change the color of my nails."

Jinetta glared at him. "This IS useful, you hayseed. It's really easy." She opened her snap case and began to dig through it. "You only need a piece of paper big enough to wrap around your hand." She pulled out a spiral-bound notebook.

A loud jingle attracted all of us. I glanced down as Jinetta removed the pad and stared down at a leather bag underneath.

"I smell money," Tolk exclaimed. He trotted over to sniff as Jinetta opened the bag and poured the contents into her hand. I recognized them at the same time as everyone else.

"Those are from Humulus," Melvine said.

"No!" Jinetta protested. "It couldn't be."

"It is," Tolk insisted, sticking his wet black nose right into her palm. "It's got the same scent as the money we got from Master Flink."

The tall Pervect looked outraged.

"Who put this in my bag?"

"Well, since it locks by magik," Bee said, "I'm gonna have to assume it was you."

"You, Jinetta?" Freezia looked aghast. So did Pologne.

"You must have made a separate deal with Skeeve for pay," Tolk said. "Behind our backs!"

I sprang up.

"Hold it right there," I said, advancing on them.

"Just didn't want to be seen accepting money in front of us, huh?" Melvine smirked. "So much for keeping it a teacher-student relationship."

"Melvine!" I warned.

The Cupy looked up at me in horror. "It wasn't me, Teach. I swear. I didn't do it. Ask Long Tall Sally, here. Looks like she did."

"How dare you?" Jinetta gasped, reaching for him, nails out. He threw up a wall of fire, and she recoiled. "I did NOT put it in here. I didn't touch that money! Someone else must have sneaked it into my briefcase!"

"Yeah, sure."

Jinetta whipped a knuckle-sized globe out of her bag. "Take that back, Cupy!"

Melvine fanned out his fingers. "You make me, Pervert!"

Bunny started to get up from her spot on the grass. I waved a hand to keep her from getting into the line of fire. Gleep automatically moved to protect her.

"Don't you threaten my friend!" Freezia shrieked, pointing a finger already beginning to generate sparks. Melvine cringed behind his wall of flame.

"Maybe she *stole* the money!" Tolk said, his brown eyes wide.

"You idiot! Her father owns the biggest carriage company on Perv," Pologne snapped.

"Who are you calling an idiot?" Bee asked. "You Pervects think you're so smart."

"We *are* smart, Klahd!"

I thrust myself in between them, feeling my eyebrows crisping from Melvine's spell. I dampened it with a heavy blanket of magik. "Stop it! I did not pay Jinetta anything. I didn't pay any of you anything. You turned me down, remember? Remember?"

Reluctantly, the six of them muttered, "Yes."

"Good," I said, firmly. "Now, go back to your exercise. You're making good progress. Keep it up."

"Will you swear to that?" Melvine asked.

I spun to face him. "Swear I didn't pay any of you or make a secret deal for compensation? Yes. I swear it."

His baby face seemed to crumple with disappointment. "Well, those coins are from Humulus, aren't they?"

"Bunny," I called. "Would you mind checking the strong-box and see if any of our reward money is missing?"

Bunny rose, and Gleep trotted after her, with a backward glance to make sure I didn't need him. No one moved while she was gone. When she returned, her face was grave. "Fifteen coins are missing," she reported.

I held the bag out to her. "Here they are. I'll have to come up with a better magik lock that only you and I can open."

Bunny took the money from me, and shot a distasteful look around at the apprentices. I knew what she was think-ing. She was still convinced that there was something fishy going on.

"I don't like this," I told them. "Playing little jokes on one another is one thing, but I won't put up with outright crime. Someone stole that money from our strongbox."

"Someone set me up," Jinetta insisted furiously.

"I don't know that," I said. "Either someone set you up, or you want me to believe that someone did. I even bet it's point-less for me to do a trace spell. I'm sure whoever put the money here covered his or her tracks. But I'll tell you here and now that if I catch anyone doing anything dishonest like that again, you're out of here. Got that?"

"Yes, Skeeve," they chorused glumly.

"All right," I said. "Back to work."

No one moved. Their eyes darted from face to face, prob-ably trying to figure out, as I was, who had sneaked the bag into Jinetta's briefcase, or if she had done it herself.

"Come on," I said sarcastically. "Are you waiting for an engraved invitation?"

"Hey, hey, hey, are you an audience or an illumination?" a hearty woman's voice asked. "Why so silent?"

Massha floated into the courtyard. She appeared to be carried on the shoulders of four young and good-looking courtiers dressed in Queen Hemlock's personal livery, until she sailed on beyond their grasp and settled to the ground on the toes of a pair of pointy orange silk slippers.

"Massha!" I went to greet her, and received one of her patent bone-crushing hugs. Bunny came over, too, and gave as good as she got.

"What's the silent treatment for?" she asked, looking at the group, who were now intently studying their feet.

"A misunderstanding," I said, passing it over casually. "Welcome! Do you want to freshen up before you start your lecture?"

"No way, Hot Shot! It was a relaxing jaunt. Wasn't it, boys?"

"Yes, Lady Magician," they chorused.

Massha elbowed me. "I'm trying to get them to sing it in harmony, but Marco there in the left back corner is tone deaf. So, how's it been going? I see Bee's still standing." The young corporal blushed crimson and kicked the dirt. Massha grinned.

I grinned back. "Let's all have a drink, and we'll give you the short version."

Chapter Fifteen

"Oops."
LAST WORDS OF ANY BOMB DISPOSAL EXPERT

"Well, you're still in one piece," Massha said, setting down her empty mug on the little table beside the heap of cushions that her attendants laid out for her to lounge upon in Bunny's sitting room. Gleep was curled next to her feet, his long neck resting contentedly along a spare lump of cushion. "So that's what really happened! A troubador from the town came to Possiltum and sang a song about the Great Skeeve defeating a beast by turning its lightning back on it."

"Not exactly," I said modestly, toying with my wine glass. "I just appealed to its self-interest."

"Most powerful force in the universe, after love," she agreed. "Hemlock was impressed. She'll laugh herself silly when she hears the real story." She surveyed my students, who sat around the cosy room on chairs or the floor. "And you all sound like you're making Master Skeeve proud. Old Massha was his first student, and look where she ended up? Happily ever after!"

"Thanks for the plug," I said. "I really can't take credit for where you've gotten. That was all you. I think you're doing a better job than I ever did."

"Don't sell yourself short, Superstar! You brought out the best in me."

"I thought Hugh did that," I said innocently. Massha blushed as bright as her lipstick. I turned to my class to give her a moment to recover. "All right, individual exercises are over for the day. At the beginning I promised you guest lecturers. This will make a welcome change of pace. I think we could all use one. The Lady Magician of Possiltum has come all the way from the royal court to demonstrate something in which she has more expertise than anyone I have ever met, including most Deveels: gadget magik."

"You bet. Quintin!" she called, clapping her hands. One of the muscular, liveried courtiers ran in and knelt at her feet, presenting an enormous bag that clanked as it moved. She chuckled. "Don't you just love it when they hustle?"

"Adorable," Bunny agreed, waggling a couple of fingers at the page. "Hi-ya." She winked at him. The page blushed to the roots of his long pale hair.

Massha whipped out a heavy silk cloth and left it floating in the air while she sorted through the clunking collection and laid several items out. "Here are a few of my favorites, stuff that's gotten me out of a couple of nasty situations, and a few that are just plain useful."

"Oh, come on, I've been playing with things like those since I was two," Pologne complained, flipping a couple of pieces over with her talon. "There's a wince whistle. Makes the noise from barking dogs rebound on them. And that's a stuff-sack, for getting more things into your purse."

Massha shrugged. "This is gonna be old hat for a few of you, honey, but I just love toys. Oh, here's a good one!"

She drew out a heavily jeweled gold wand. "This one's good for changing ambience. Short range, but this room's a good size. No verbal invocation, just point and shoot." She stuck a finger in her ear and aimed the wand at the ceiling.

A loud report momentarily deafened us, followed by whistles and toots. Over our heads, flower-shaped gouts of fire erupted, filling the ceiling then drifting down over us. Where the cooling sparks passed, the room shifted before our eyes. The whitewash warmed to a honey color. Framed pictures shimmered into being, along with lamps, vases, occasional tables and knicknacks, and finally a fringed rug of complicated pattern spread itself on the floor.

"I like it," Bunny said with an approving nod. "That makes the room much more cosy now. Skeeve and I just haven't really taken the time to redecorate."

"Freaky!" Melvine hooted. "Instead of looking like a dreary old pub, now it looks like my granny's house!"

"I think it's nice," Bunny said, sounding hurt.

"Yeah, right," the Cupy said. He picked up the wand. "How do you make it do something about five hundred years more modern?"

"Turn the dial," Massha said, pointing to a ring near the base of the wand.

Melvine shot the wand toward the crystal lamp in the middle of the ceiling. BANG! Within moments, the walls were stark white again. Tapestry upholstery had changed to russet or stone-colored leather, and the wooden tables had become chrome frames with glass tops. All of the fussy ornaments had vanished, and the pictures on the walls turned to abstracts. Massha's freeform cushions assumed geometric shapes. "Much better. The other stuff made me gag."

"Oh, geometrics are so downmarket," Jinetta said.

"Hey, you don't know a thing about design," Melvine shot back.

"And you do?"

"What do you think?" Massha asked Bunny. "It's your house."

"I like this, too. My tastes are pretty eclectic. You can leave it like this. If I get bored with it, I'll redecorate. What else have you got there?"

Massha spread her hands generously. "Take a look, kids. Try them on for size, but don't invoke anything until you check with the proprietor first. A lot of these gizmos look alike! I don't want any accidents, and I'm sure Skeeve doesn't want the place brought down on his head."

Bee picked up a gaudy ring with a blue stone and fiddled with it. "What's this one do, ma'am?"

Alarmed, Massha plucked it out of his fingers. "Don't point that at yourself, Honeybunch. Joke ring. It fills the mouth of the person you're facing with soap suds. I think it started out as a punishment device for smart-mouthed kids. Be careful.

Just because it looks pretty doesn't mean you can laugh off the results. See?" She picked up a ring with a glittering opal in the bezel. "Watch this. I got this one for saving a merchant from an Ogre he had cheated."

She turned it toward the open window and pressed inward with her fingers. A bolt of blue-white lightning shot out of the window.

"Ho-hum, another lightning ring," Freezia yawned. "I got one for my twelfth birthday. You got taken by the merchant, too, lady. You should have negotiated better. Those cost about three gold pieces brand new. Five with the decoder wheel."

Massha looked crestfallen. I was furious.

"That's enough," I said. "I shouldn't have to tell you that the Lady Magician deserves respect from you whether or not you're impressed."

I raised my eyebrows meaningfully.

They took the threat. Jinetta reached for a bangle bracelet studded with rubies and began to examine it closely.

"Make music," Massha suggested. "Touch the jewels."

Jinetta tried one tentatively then broke into a wide grin at the tinkly sound. She began to play a tune with her fingernails. Freezia and Pologne looked over a cloisonné vase with a long neck, laughing when a snake jumped out of it. Massha showed them how to reload it.

"I left that one in the queen's boudoir last week. She just howled. I think she wants to plant it on visiting ambassadors."

"What about this?" Tolk asked, offering her a long purple plume.

"It writes romance stories," Massha said. "Dunk it in hot water if you want it to get really steamy."

"Ooh," Freezia cooed, reaching for it. "I adore love stories."

"You would," Melvine sneered. "I bet you've read all of Loebis Nasus's novels."

Freezia eyed him. "How in Perv would you know about her?"

"I don't," Melvine said hastily. "Never read a single word."

"Uh-huh," Freezia said skeptically. "How about this belt, Massha?" She dangled a gaudy strip of gold leather studded with rutilated quartzes.

The Lady Magician of Possiltum settled back on her cushions with a hearty laugh. "There's a story attached to this one, kiddies! That belonged to a wizard named Polik who used it to make himself look thinner than he really was. Trouble is, it's only an illusion, and no one told the doors to believe it. He got stuck in Hemlock's privy during a state banquet, and traded it off to me in exchange for keeping silent about having to extract him."

Bunny howled with laughter. "That little blue powder room behind her throne?"

"That's the one!"

"What do *you* do with it?" Pologne asked pointedly.

"Trade goods," Massha shrugged, refusing to take offense. "If I find someone who's got a treasure they don't need, we swap. It's fun. Listen, I had an idea to make this interesting. I won't tell you any more about my hoard. You take an item and figure out what it does without killing yourself or your fellow classmates here. How about it? Skeeve wanted you to try out what it's like to be working magicians. We have to do this with mystery items all the time, especially in the Bazaar at Deva. Of course, about 90% of the stuff you can buy there are fakes or toys. It's a contest. Whoever identifies the most items gets a prize. Bunny can keep score."

"I'm on it!" my assistant declared, reaching for a pencil and a pad of paper.

Pologne grinned, showing what had to have been a few hundred gold pieces' worth of orthodontia in her mouthful of gleaming white, four-inch-long fangs. "That sounds like fun."

"It can be," Massha smiled back. Her teeth were nowhere as impressive, but the feral expression more than made up for it. "Go on, give it a try!" She spilled the baubles out on the floating cloth.

Bee goggled at the array of treasures. Gingerly, he picked up a skinny silver wand. Carefully pointing it away from all of us, he invoked it. Nothing happened. He shook it and listened to it. Still nothing. Tolk gave an excited bark and immediately ran his shiny wet nose up its length.

"Cures poison," he said at once.

"How do you know that?" Bee asked.

"Unicornium," Tolk said, grinning. "Only element in the universe that can counteract poisons. Besides, it smells like Buttercup out there."

Bee put the wand to his nose. "I guess it kinda smells like a horse. It's kinda hard to tell past the dragon smell. No offense, Gleep."

"Gleep!" my pet said, the friendly expression in his wide blue eyes asserting that no offense was taken.

"If it gets rid of poison, you ought to use it on that food of yours," Jinetta sneered.

"Just because I don't eat live vermin?" Bee countered.

"At least I know my food is fresh!"

Bee almost retorted then, seeing my pointed glare, reached for another gadget, an egg-shaped chunk of glass.

"Whoops!" Freezia exclaimed as she invoked a silver medallion and vanished from our sight.

"Invisibility amulet," Pologne said immediately.

"Nope," Massha said. "Give her a chance."

In a moment, Freezia reappeared. "Dressing room," she said, tossing the disk back onto the cushion. "I was in a kind of enclosure with hooks on the wall."

"You went invisible all of a sudden," Bee said. The glass egg in his hands lit up. He gave it a speculative glance. "You were gone for hours." The egg turned black. "Lie detector," he said quickly, forestalling the others.

"Good guess," Massha praised him.

The contest got going into high gear. All of my students reached for items from Massha's bag of toys, the females oohing and aahing over the jewelry. The males seemed to go for the less-adorned gadgets. Massha had generously brought dozens of pieces. Each student played with an object for a while, turning it over looking for clues as to its function without actually invoking it, but sometimes they couldn't help it. A few of the magik items went off by themselves. At one point everyone in the room had purple fingernails, orange lipstick and screaming scarlet rouge, thanks to a powder puff that exuded a cloud of dust. The plain walls had become festooned with pairs of shoes, flowers, racks of knives and crossbows, and a huge poster of four long-haired males holding musical instruments with a signature in the corner that said, "Love is all you need forever." I was fascinated with the rest; I had never appreciated the range of her collection of swag. Massha always forestalled a student from using dangerous items, but let them have free range with the harmless stuff.

"Some of these things you just invoke," Massha warned them. "Others are triggered by controls. A few have got safety catches. Be careful. Those are the most dangerous."

Of the six, Bee was the most cautious. He had seen a few of her treasures before, and identified them instantly, earning him points right off the bat. Since then he had fallen behind his companions, who could do more advanced magik-sniffing than he could. In Tolk's case, the sniffing was literal. His sensitive nose picked out obscure compounds and alloys that smelled all alike to me under a mask of Massha's powerful cologne. The Canidian was also capable of making shrewd guesses that turned out frequently to be correct. Melvine was good at figuring out some pretty obscure things like joke toys.

The Pervects could reel off IDs for every mass-produced trinket, from the Bazaar to some upscale manufactories in the far reaches of distant dimensions, and fought to be the first to call out its name. Once they exhausted those pieces, they were left almost as clueless as Bee. With regard to jewelry custommade for Massha, almost everyone had to cry uncle.

"What's this?" Melvine asked crankily, holding up a platinum-banded ring with a moss green, egg-shaped bezel.

Massha's full cheeks turned scarlet. "That was a special present to me from my sweetie, Hugh, on our first anniversary."

"But you haven't been married for a year yet," I said.

"Not since we *married,*" Massha said, settling back with a satisfied air. "Since we—"

"Too much information!" I protested.

She chuckled warmly. "It's a real humdinger: an incendiary grenade. That's my Hugh, always thinking in terms of mass destruction. Once a general, always a general."

"Very nice," Bunny said. "Hugh has good taste. That's the kind of gift my uncle would give."

Melvine began looking it over for controls. "How does it work?"

I flipped it out of his hands with a dollop of magik and put it back among the other items. "It doesn't. Try something else. So far, you've got nine points. Jinetta's ahead of you by three."

Six pairs of hands sifted through the clanking collection on the silk mat. Pologne got tangled up in a braided cord that tied her wrists together and bound every finger to the corresponding digit on the other hand.

"It's got me!" she shrieked. "Who invoked that on me?"

"Trollish finger trap," I laughed, dispelling it for her. "It works by itself. It's a practical joke. Deveel school children leave them in each other's lunch bags."

"Hmmph," she snorted.

"Look at this one," Jinetta said, homing in on a burning-red jewel. "Massha, should this gem be glowing?"

"No!" Massha said in alarm, grabbing it from her. "Oh, no, it's the grenade! It's armed! It's going to explode!"

"When?" I demanded.

"About fifteen seconds."

"I'll throw it into the pond," Bee announced, pale but composed. He took the ring from Massha and made for the door.

The ring flew out of his hands back toward the center of the room.

"No, we have to destroy it here and now!" Pologne insisted. "Burn it—no, it's going to burn. Freeze it!" She pulled the crystal ball out of her backpack and started scrying for information. "I know the right spell's in here somewhere."

"We have to smash it!" Melvine yelled, pointing his hands at the ring. It started to spiral around in the air. "I'll crush it on the fireplace! Let me get some momentum up."

"No," Freezia exclaimed. "That will bring the inn down on our heads. Smother it with something!"

"There's no time for that!" Tolk grabbed it out of mid-air in his mouth and deposited it in Massha's hand. "Can you turn it off?" he asked.

Massha fumbled fruitlessly with the controls. "No. The failsafe's been engaged."

"We're going to die!" Melvine whimpered.

"No, we aren't," I said. "Everyone calm down. Massha, let me have it."

In panic, Jinetta grabbed Massha's wrist to look at the ring. The gem was as bright as an ember now. "There must be something we can do!"

"Everyone *duck*!" I barked out. I levitated the ring out of Massha's palm and sent it flying straight up the chimney. "What's the range?"

"About five thousand yards," Massha said.

Talk about overkill! I nodded grimly and flew out the window. SQUAWK!

A flock of blue-and-white ducks flying overhead scattered outward as I shot up and over the roof of the inn.

"Sorry!" I called. They quacked indignantly among themselves as they reformed into a vee heading north.

I scanned the sky above me for the glowing dot of red light. There it was! I pushed hard at the face of the earth with enough magikal force to send me soaring upward. I hoped no one was traveling the road below, but this close to twilight they might not notice the man-sized shadow heading towards the clouds.

I had no trouble following the ring through the overcast sky. The ruby-red light was just a pinpoint. I flew towards it, hoping I was maintaining a safe distance. How far was five thousand yards? Keeping a hefty pad of magik around the ring, I shoved it higher and higher. How much longer did I have? The red light disappeared into the clouds. I made ready to follow it.

BOOM!

A red globe bloomed within the cloud overhead. The sound rang in my ears. Dizzy, I lost control of my flying spell. My stomach headed for my mouth as I dropped like a stone. A wave of heat knocked me down a few hundred feet farther. In a moment I retrieved my wits and retreated hastily toward the ground. Success. The ring had detonated where it couldn't possibly hurt anyone.

While I descended, the cloud gave off another tremendous *BOOM*. With a roar, heavy waves of water began gushing down on me. The grenade had triggered the load of moisture in the cloud and caused it to start raining.

"Thanks," I grumbled at the sky. "That's what I get for being heroic."

Chapter Sixteen

"Confession is good for the soul."
T. BECKETT

I descended as swiftly as I could to get under the shelter of the forest crown. In my mind I ran over the sequence of events. There was no way that explosion could have been triggered by accident. That grenade ring had a full-scale failsafe on it, not to mention a couple of safety catches to prevent it going off if Massha caught the bezel on something. I was reluctant to come to the obvious conclusion: that someone had set it off on purpose.

But why? If the inn had blown up, we would *all* have been killed.

Not necessarily, I reasoned, as I landed on the side of the road. At least four of my students were proficient at instantaneous transfer between one dimension and another. In the confusion while we were trying to get rid of the bomb, the guilty party could just have BAMFed out, leaving the rest of us to be blown to smithereens.

But who?

I didn't look forward to figuring that one out.

When I arrived back at the inn, shivering and soaking wet, I was greeted as the returning hero.

"You are amazing, Master Skeeve!" Jinetta exclaimed, gathering me up into a bone-crunching hug. "You saved us!"

"I was so frightened," Freezia admitted, hugging me in her turn and passing me along to Pologne. Bee merely stood to attention, his freckled face pale. Tolk ambled over and stuck his nose into my palm.

Melvine wasn't completely over his sulk, but he came forward and flicked his fingers at me. My clothes and hair dried instantly. "It's an Elemental School desert spell," he said. No apology, no gratitude, but I got the message.

"Thanks," I said. It did feel good to be dry again.

Massha enveloped me in folds of translucent orange silk.

"I'm sorry, Cupcake! I never dreamed the ring could go off like that."

"It didn't," I said shortly. I turned to my students. "Which one of you set that off? Maybe you thought it would be funny to have us running in circles."

"No, sir," Bee said, fervently.

"Did you do it?"

"No! No way, sir."

"I saw Pologne handling it last," Tolk said. "If you could get some of the pieces I could sniff them and tell you for sure."

"Tattletale!" Pologne snarled. "That's a lie."

"What about you, dogface? You had your nose in everything. It could have been you!" Freezia snapped.

"Me? How-how-how dare you?"

"Hold it. HOLD IT!" I shouted over the sudden pandemonium. "The only person I want to hear from right now is the one who set off the ring. I don't care if you thought it was a joke. I don't care if it was an accident. Just tell me."

Silence. The students all eyed one another with open distrust.

"All right," I said, shrugging my shoulders. "That's it, then. I've had enough. Lady Massha, thanks for coming. Do you want to take Bee back to Possiltum with you? I'm sure he can catch a wagon or something else going toward his home town."

"Sure, if that's what you want, boss-man."

"Thank you very much." I turned to the assembled student body. "The rest of you are on your own."

"What?!?" the students asked in outraged six-part harmony.

"It's over," I said simply. "Girls, I'll reimburse you the remainder of your tuition. Tolk, I will make it up to Chumley somehow. Same for you, Melvine. I'll explain to Markie if she wants to drop by. I'd appreciate it if everybody was out of here by sunset. I'm sorry to say it, but I can't teach any of you any longer. Somebody is playing dangerous games."

Jinetta's eyes went wide with panic. "You can't do that!"

"I certainly can," I said. "Someone just put us all in danger, and he or she won't admit it."

"Oh, please," she begged. "Don't send us away. We need you."

"That's right," Tolk said. "Come on, Skeeve. One little explosion."

"Little?" Bunny squeaked indignantly. "That could have taken out half the Bazaar."

"Master Skeeve, I wish you'd reconsider," Bee said. "I've learned more in a week and a half from you than from anyone I have ever known, except for Sergeant Swatter, of course. I don't know about my fellow students, but I bet we all feel the same."

The others nodded vigorously.

"I'm not responsible for your feelings," I said. "I just discovered that one of you is capable of playing a nasty trick on the rest, me included, and I have no intention of giving you a second chance at it."

"I didn't do it!" Melvine sniveled. "Aunt Markie will kill me if you send me home!"

"Skeeve, we *really* need your help. Don't send us away now," Freezia pleaded, twining her arms around one of mine and looking up at me with big, beseeching eyes. The effect of Pervish orbs of green-veined yellow was more frightening than wistful, but the emotion behind them was clear. "What about the rest of us? One of us might be a joker, but the other five are all very sincere students, and we are really enjoying our lessons. Honestly." My resolve wavered.

"Well—"

Pologne attached herself to my other arm. "I know we've been touchy. I mean, I know I have. I'll keep my temper better. You're right: we have so much to learn from each other. Please, be fair."

I sighed. She'd just hit me right where I live. I wanted to be fair, and punishing five for the sins of one was not. "All right. I'll give the bomber one chance. I'll be in my study until dinner. If he or she comes around and tells me the truth, I'll reconsider. No guarantees."

"We understand," Jinetta said, her head bowed. The group filed out of the room.

Massha clicked her tongue. "Well, my lesson sure went off with a bang. Don't worry, Skeeve," she added as I frowned. She held up her Cone of Silence amulet. "No one can hear past this."

"Thanks," I sighed, and slumped into a chair. "I'm sorry about the ring. I know you treasured it because it came from Hugh."

"I'll get over it," she said. "I've still got the man. Trinkets don't matter. He'll find me something else just as deadly."

"Why didn't you just send them all home?" Bunny asked, standing over me with her arms folded across her chest. "I told you something was up."

"This *could* just be an accident," I said. "Someone thought he or she would be funny, and it blew up—literally—in their face."

"Or it could be an attempt to kill someone in the group," Bunny said, eying me. "You're too trusting, especially when you're the most likely target."

"Me?"

"Well, who else? *They're* all too young to have made enemies. But you're the Great Skeeve! It's not like this is the first time a rival magician has decided to try and take out the opposition."

"Why me? I'm not even in the lineup right now. I'm out of the picture."

Bunny eyed me. "Just the perfect time to take a stab at you, if you'll pardon the expression. I told you this morning I was worried. I think you ought to go to Uncle Bruce and ask for a couple of his men to watch your back. I know Guido and Nunzio would jump at the chance to help you out. They miss working with you. Both of them have said you're the best boss they ever had. In fact, they'd do it out of friendship, no contract involved."

"No!" I said, jumping up. "I won't impose on friends. They have another job to do. Bunny, I appreciate your concern, but I don't need outside bodyguards. I've got Gleep."

My pet raised his head from where it rested on his stubby forearms.

"Gleep!" he announced, looking as brave as a baby dragon could.

"I've got you," I continued, "and my own wits."

"And me," Massha added. "There's no way old Massha's going to let you twist in the wind."

"Thank you, Massha, I appreciate it, but go ahead and go home. Fortunately, you only had one exploding ring. If this was a serious assassination attempt, the perpetrator would have had his or her own bomb. This looks more like a prank or a crime of opportunity. I can try and draw whoever it is out into the open."

"Assassination is not really your field, Hot Stuff," Massha reminded me.

"I'll call Tananda," Bunny said, pulling Bytina out of her purse. The little red PDA snapped open at once, and images danced off her palm-sized crystal mirror. "That IS her field."

I clapped the little device shut. "No, don't. I can handle this. Let's see if he tries again."

"Or she," Bunny said.

"Whoever it is," I agreed. "Now, if you'll excuse me," I squared my shoulders, "I've got to go set a trap."

I sat in my office with my back to the door. I was trying out the Manticore's stunning serum on a housefly I had caught in a glass bottle. It hadn't moved for at least five minutes by my candle. The process had taken less than a pinpoint's worth of venom. This could be a great tool—or a weapon.

Footsteps approached, brushing along the flagstone floor in the corridor. My door creaked open slowly. I didn't turn around.

"Skeeve?" a quiet voice said. "Can I talk to you for a minute?"

"Pass the potatoes, please," I said.

Silently, Jinetta picked up the earthenware dish and handed it down the table to me.

"Thank you."

"Don't mention it," the tallest Pervect mumbled, dropping her eyes to her bowl.

Bunny sat at the head of the table, cutting her meat into very small pieces as if she was looking for hidden explosive devices. No one spoke except to ask for food.

I wasn't much of a conversationalist myself. Nothing I had done that day had turned out the way I planned it. The spell-sharing exercise had turned out to be a disaster. Someone had broken into the strongbox in an effort to frame one of the students for theft, and I still had no idea why. Massha's long-awaited demonstration had been derailed by either an attempt at assassination or a foolish mishap. I had sent my regrets back to Hugh, apologizing for the destruction of his anniversary gift to Massha and offering to replace it at my own expense. I knew that it was an inadequate gesture, but what could I do? Massha herself had forgiven me, but I had not forgiven myself. It had happened right under my nose. At the moment I was leaning toward deliberate sabotage. Replaying the events in my mind, I could see a pattern where no one had made a serious attempt to get rid of the ring-bomb. In fact, it looked to my mind's eye as though at least three of them had made efforts to keep the device from leaving the room.

My trap to catch the student who had set it off had failed spectacularly. Or, rather, it had worked too well. I didn't get one confession from the attempted bomber: I got five. They all confessed, everyone except Bee.

One by one, as dusk came on, they crept into my study. With shamed faces and the utmost sincerity they all apologized for having made a stupid mistake and being too ashamed to admit it. Melvine's confession had been particularly impassioned, which surprised me, in light of the fact that he had never taken the blame for a single thing he had ever done, but his statement was almost word for word what the others said.

"Look," the Cupy said, giving me a sheepish, sideways grin, "the ring was just sitting there. You know I can't keep from fiddling with things. I wanted to see what it looked like with the spell armed, so I invoked it. The bezel started glowing. Then I got curious about what the other buttons did. I played with them a little. One of them turned out to be the failsafe. I knew as soon as I touched it that was the wrong thing. I couldn't get it to turn off. I didn't know what to do. I couldn't disarm it. I couldn't throw Massha's ring out the door without admitting what I had done. I should have said something right away. Instead, I just left it on the cloth with the other jewelry. I'm sorry. Don't tell the others. I feel like an idiot already."

I was puzzled. Why would five of them own up to causing a near-fatal accident when four of them, and maybe all five, had to be lying? Why did they want to stay with me so badly? For that was what they wanted, without exception.

The last to talk with me, Jinetta, had hung back at the door. "You'll keep us on, now that you know what—who the joker was. Right?" She had given me a meaningful glance then slipped off into the dim hallway. Her confession had sounded as sincere as the others, all of which I now doubted.

Bunny and I now really suspected Bee, who was looking mournful. As soon as the meal was finished, he sprang up.

"I'll do the dishes, Miss Bunny," he volunteered.

The others listlessly took on the other chores. Pologne went for the broom and pan. Freezia cleaned the table. Even Melvine pushed the benches back under the edges of the table.

I cleared my throat.

"I've, uh, decided," I began. The students whirled to face me. "I've decided you can stay. I've had a talk with the, er, perpetrator."

"Hurray!" Melvine whooped, sailing into the air and zooming around the ceiling like a flannel-clad bumblebee.

"Hold the happiness," I said. "This is provisionary. I will go on with the lessons if, and only if, there are no more near-death experiences and no more thefts. I want the six of you to start getting along again the way you did in Humulus. Is that clear?"

"Yes, Skeeve!" they chorused. Even Bee cheered up.

Bunny's eyebrows rose to frame the question that she did not ask out loud: why?

I hated to admit the truth even to myself: I didn't want to fail. I had taken on this class. I saw their misbehavior as a failure on my part to express my wishes and make them stick. I would have to be very clear from that moment on to let them know everything I wanted from them. On the other hand, I could hear in my head the voice of my mother, who had been a teacher, and a good one, all her adult life.

"And if they stick beans up their noses, will you feel responsible because you didn't tell them not to?"

I didn't know. I might. But I had to try. The students, and my own self-esteem, were counting on me.

Chapter Seventeen

"Tag, you're it!"
B. V. RICHTOFFEN

"Aaaarroroooorrraaaaagghh!"

A huge, purple form came rushing into the courtyard where I was teaching advanced levitation. It bore down upon the cluster of students who were holding themselves above the ground and a variety of objects at different levels around them. Bee immediately lost focus and fell heavily to the flagstones. Melvine took off for the top of the trees. Tolk let out a whimper of pleasure and started swimming through the air toward the being.

The Pervects screamed then, seemingly caught in mid-shriek, raised their hands as if they were calling the spirits of the dead. The purple form was hoisted into the air.

"Oh, I say!" it exclaimed.

Chumley. I chuckled. "Let him down, girls! It's my friend Big Crunch."

"He is?" Jinetta asked. "Oh! Of course it is. I am so sorry, Mr. Troll. Permit me."

"I'll do it," Pologne snapped out.

"If you want," the tallest Pervect said.

The Troll was lowered gently to the ground. I was reasonably pleased. That exchange had even passed for civility.

The preceding week had tried my patience in more ways than one. I had gained no more insight on who was responsible for the explosion. Bee was still my major suspect, which I based on the absence of a confession and the fact he was the only one of the six who might ever have had close experience with ordnance weapons. General observation would have made him the last person I should ever have considered. He continued to be polite, hard-working and cooperative.

So had the others. In fact, each one was determined to show me that he or she was THE most cooperative, willing and hard-working pupil who had ever lived anywhere in the universe. Unfortunately that cooperation still didn't extend to one another. The distrust had taken firm hold, and refused to be detached. Even the Pervects were beginning to keep one another at arm's length. It distracted me from being able to concentrate. My lesson plan began to look like a dance chart, making sure none of them spent too much time with any of the others.

Instead, they all made efforts to spend as much time as possible with Bunny or me. Each clamored for private instruction and practical training from me. I ran through all the ideas I could glean from my own experiences, and not a few I stole from the shows on the Crystal Network, like having them extract a fragile glass bubble, intact, from a nest of horned weaselsnakes without getting bitten. As usual, each tackled the tasks in different ways. The Pervects still tended to go for the academic approach, but I was pleased to see that more frequently than ever they put aside the books and tried to analyze the situation in the real world. Bee looked at everything from a logistics and supply point of view. I thought his solution was the most elegant of all, setting out the weaselsnakes' favorite prey at a distance from the nest, and retrieving the bubble at his leisure. Tolk tried to make everything his friend, disastrous in the experiment with shield-hornets, but very successful in getting the local townsfolk to lend him enough ingredients to make a pan of scones. Melvine whined and complained a lot, but away from the distraction of others he buckled down. He really was as smart as Markie thought he was. His easy command of magikal force had made him lazy. Once he stopped blasting everything full force, he became more effective. The surgical precision with which he whisked the glass ball out of the snake nest was a beautiful sight to behold. I wished the others had been there to see it, or even evinced the most remote interest in hearing my recitation of Melvine's success.

They were scrupulously polite at meals, and each vied to take over Bunny's chores. It had escalated to the point where the Pervects had fought over cleaning the windows and ended up making new curtains for all of the inn's many casements. Melvine had made it a matter of honor to seal up every crack in the old building's walls, to the point where the inn was now virtually airtight. When the front door slammed, all of our ears popped. Tolk weeded the garden and 'healed' all the plants of black spot and wilt. The vegetables grew visibly larger after that. Bee inventoried everything not indicated as private property in the neatest handwriting I had ever seen. For the first time, I knew that Isstvan had left me nineteen and a third kegs of beer, four hundred and fifty-three bottles of indifferent wine and eight bottles of wine so good it should be saved for coronations, and three well-hidden casks of hard spirits. I was glad I hadn't known about all of that in my dipsomaniac phase. Bunny enjoyed the leisure to an extent, but told me privately she was getting bored having nothing to do. She spent more and more time each day communicating with her friends through Bytina.

The practical jokes had gone on in a minor way. I was sorry I hadn't given them my mother's lectures on beans up their noses, because each time I had forbidden a certain behavior, they came up with something else that didn't violate any of the previous rules. One night someone had short-sheeted all of the students' beds. Whoever the troublemaker was had learned to include everybody in the prank, including him or herself. When I forbade apple-pie beds, then everybody's clean clothes turned up tied in wet knots. That morning's exercises had been conducted in pajamas and bathrobes. At no time were my or Bunny's things disturbed, and nothing else of ours went missing. I suppose I could have put the annoyances down to the usual social interaction between young people, but I couldn't, not after the exploding ring incident.

The cold war also, I was glad to note, did not extend to guests. Tolk galloped up to the Troll and romped in a circle at his feet.

"Chumley, Chumley, Chumley, how are you? I'm so glad to see you! Where have you been? You smell like vanilla!"

"Crunch busy. Tolk good?"

"Oh, I get it!" the Canidian replied, wheeling on his rear legs and dashing the other way. "I'm fine. Skeeve's fun. Everything is exciting. I'm learning so much!"

"Good." Chumley lumbered up to me. He was maintaining his identity as the enforcement-Troll, Big Crunch. I had dropped in on him on Trollia to make the arrangements out of the hearing of my students so that Chumley could communicate his intentions to me in words of more than one syllable. Only Tolk was in the know about Chumley's alter ego. "All ready."

"Great! Everybody lower what you're doing, and come over here," I called. The Pervects descended daintily to the ground, setting the objects they had been levitating with equal delicacy. Melvine bounced his items off the wall and into the basket from which they had come, and floated over to survey Chumley at eye level.

"How's it going?" he said, though his voice squeaked. "I wasn't scared by you, no sir!"

I grinned to myself. He'd shot up eight yards when the Troll had come charging out of the woods. I covered my amusement with a loud *a-HEM!* Everybody gave me their attention.

"I want all of you to welcome this week's guest lecturer," I said. "Big Crunch is well known for his skills at protecting clients or a client's interests. He has guarded kings, business tycoons and leading entertainers. He's safeguarded everything from castles down to mud huts, and designed alarm systems that have foiled some of the best thieves in the guild. He's been a bouncer at some of the finest establishments throughout the dimensions." Chumley nodded modestly at this recitation of his accomplishments. "One of the most valuable lessons I have ever learned from him was how not to underestimate an opponent. It's easy to make judgements based on looks alone. A poisonous snake doesn't look like much more than a piece of angry clothesline, but the bite can kill. Naturally, Crunch isn't much for lecturing," I stopped to clear my throat. Chumley himself was an exceedingly literate gentleman. "His instruction will be a practical exercise. We have a whole building and the surrounding forest at our disposal. Gleep and I will keep a lookout for any approaching parties of Klahds so you won't be observed. Your object for today is not to be caught and, if possible, catch Big Crunch. If Crunch catches you, you have to come back here and stay in Bunny's sitting room until lunch time. If you catch him, the game's over. That's all. Got it?"

"Sounds lame," Melvine said.

Chumley reached out with a massive purple paw and patted the Cupy so hard he bounced off the ground. "Little man easy to catch."

"Oh, yeah, hairball?" Melvine sneered. "We'll see about that."

I pulled a whistle out of my belt pouch. "Everybody ready? At the signal, hide!"

PHWEET!

By the time I put the whistle back in the pouch, not an apprentice was to be seen in the courtyard. Melvine had vanished with a loud displacement of air. The Pervects split up and flew off in three different directions. Bee took off running in a zig-zag pattern. Tolk simply galloped into the trees. Chumley tipped me a wink of his big, moon-shaped eyes.

"Wish me luck," he said.

A book open on my chest, I lounged in the comfortable crook of a tree limb that overhung the north end of the road that led past the inn. I'd been there for over an hour. During that time I had seen most of my students creeping by, trying to skirt the central area of the woods where loud crashing noises seemed to indicate that Chumley was stomping around, seeking his prey. I knew better than to make an assumption like that, but I enjoyed seeing the intent looks on the faces of my students.

When I was a boy, my friends and I used to play "Demon In the Dark," where one person was chosen as the Demon, hunting down all the others and 'killing' them. Your heart pounds in your chest when you think you hear someone sneaking up behind you. It was hard not to shout out when the Demon grabbed you and hauled you away to wherever the holding area was, usually someone's cellar or a stall in a handy stable. We would always laugh hysterically when it was all over, as much out of relief from the tension as from the fact that it was a lot of fun. My students didn't seem to see the fun in playing the game with a real life Demon, or dimension traveler, as I now understood the philological origin of the word. All of them looked deadly serious, even frightened, as they tried to keep away from Chumley. He was making it easy on them, crashing around like a charging bull. From where I sat I could see a couple of the trees he had pushed down across the road, just shouldering his way through the undergrowth.

Suddenly, silence fell. I grinned. Chumley's secret weapon had just gone into play. I wondered if any of them would remember what I had said. The biggest mistake they all made was assuming that just because Chumley had come charging in like an avalanche, that meant he couldn't move any other way. I was almost ashamed of them, after the detailed introduction I'd given him.

A wild yell from the depths of the forest told me that he had just captured a student. I couldn't tell who it was by the shrill screech of surprise. I knew I could just go back to the inn and see who was sulking in the sitting room with Bunny. Oops, there went Tolk, galloping on all fours over the pathway. So it hadn't been him. I settled down to read a few pages.

I looked up at the sound of rustling grass. Not far from my coign of vantage, Pologne sat on a large rock painting her nails. I sighed. It was a good illusion, but I could tell easily that it WAS an illusion. The image wasn't making any noise. That wasn't going to fool Chumley. I glanced around for the real Pervect.

Moving twigs on the other side of the clearing gave her away. She had dug herself in behind a hollow tree, hoping to surprise Chumley. I imagined she hoped to capture him single-handedly. I had no idea how she thought she'd accomplish that, without the physical strength to subdue him or even a rope to tie him up. I imagined that at least a few of the others, most likely Bee among them, had similar intentions, and were laying traps instead of merely trying to avoid detection and capture.

Melvine came flitting through, just ahead of the crashing noises. He saw Pologne sitting on the rock. I could see an evil grin spread on his face. He doubled back into the woods and came out with a handful of red tree-buds. He flicked one at the back of the Pervect's head. She never blinked. The acorn clattered to the forest floor. The evil grin grew wider.

It had been dry that day. Melvine had no trouble kicking up a miniature whirlwind that raised enough dust to fill the clearing. Too late, Pologne saw that something was up. The dust collected itself and surrounded her like a cloud. She started coughing uncontrollably. Feeling blindly around the ground, she located a rock and heaved it in Melvine's general direction. He bobbed out of reach.

"Nyah NYAH nyah!" he taunted. The minicyclone whisked across the forest floor and went up the leg of Pologne's shorts.

"You little monster!" she shrieked, dancing around. She batted at her pants until the little wind dropped out again and skittered away. Magnificent in her fury, she stalked toward Melvine and pointed a hand at him.

Too late. A purple-furred hand, a dozen times the size of her own, snaked out of the underbrush at her back, and clapped over her mouth. The other appeared and dragged her into the bushes.

Melvine looked astonished for a moment, then gleeful. He flitted off into the woods again, no doubt to see if he could get any other fellow students snagged, at no risk to himself.

When we broke for lunch, the sour expression Tolk shot at the Cupy suggested to me that Melvine had had one more success. At the far end of the table, Melvine was bragging to Bunny how he lured Tolk into his own leaf-covered pit, from which Chumley had hauled him out.

"Isn't he being unfair, Master Skeeve?" Tolk demanded, slamming a paw down on the edge of his plate of green meat.

"Yes and no," I said, swiftly fielding the cold gobbets of flesh with a small net of magik. I put them back on his plate. I'd had plenty of time to think about it while guarding the road. "On the one hand, Melvine's not being a team player, but that should come as no surprise to you. He hasn't shown a lot of loyalty to the group."

"Hey!" Melvine protested.

"On the other hand, his behavior is fair because in the field you are going to have outside distractions. Pologne, you forgot you had an objective out there. Melvine exploited your temper by picking on you. You fell for it and forgot to be vigilant. That's not his fault."

"I should have ignored him pitching acorns at me?" she asked, her yellow eyes molten gold with anger.

"Probably." I shrugged. "It was childish of him, but your reaction didn't do you any credit."

"I suppose that kind of thing never happened to *you*."

"Wrong," I said coolly. "It happens to me all the time. Any of my friends will tell you that I have gotten distracted often, but I try not to let it jeopardize my mission. Or I try to turn the situation around and make a winner out of my mistake. Most of the time you can, if you try. Don't make the assumption that I'm trying to pass myself off as perfect. That's not why you came to me, is it? You came because you want to know what's effective. Let me tell you, nothing teaches you faster than making mistakes. Freezia, you and Bee got tagged because you didn't hear Crunch sneaking up behind you. You knew he could move silently, because he arrived here without having alerted everybody else for miles around.

He just made noise when he got here. And did I mention his skills at surveillance?"

"Yes," they all chorused peevishly. I nodded. My point had been made.

"He didn't catch me," Jinetta said.

"Root cellar," Chumley announced. "Not have time before lunch."

"Oh!" The Pervect's eyes flew wide open.

"Or me," Melvine added.

"Got you once," Chumley said. "Left. Yes?" he asked Bunny.

"Yes. Melvine broke jail," Bunny said. "I think you caught him first, didn't you, Big Crunch?"

"Yes."

"Cheater!" Pologne sneered at him.

"Whiner!" Melvine gibed back.

"Stop it!" I said. "Let's start over this afternoon. Everyone's out of jail again. This time, keep your mind on your task. Give Crunch something to worry about."

Thus challenged, the six students stalked out of the inn like gunfighters heading for a showdown. Chumley stayed at the table long enough to finish one more cup of tea, dabbed at his lips with a napkin, then rose.

"Better go see what they've thought up, what?" he asked cheerily.

The twilit sitting room smelled strongly of wet Troll. Chumley sat in front of the fire wringing his fur out into a bucket while my six pupils sat looking as smug as cats fed an exclusive diet of canary.

"Four times?" I asked one more time to make sure I'd heard it correctly.

"Yes," the Troll said. I couldn't tell if he was speaking as Big Crunch, or as Chumley himself being terse.

"They threw you in the pond *four times?*"

"Not say again!"

I turned to the class. "I'm impressed. How did you do it?"

The three Pervects glanced at one another. Finally, Jinetta spoke.

"Well, you said to give Crunch something to worry about. Freezia here realized that none of us could take him on by ourselves."

"So. You decided to work together?"

"Was that against the rules?" Tolk asked, his big brown eyes sad.

"Not at all!" I said. Inwardly, I was pleased. Whatever it took to get them cooperating again. Chumley's pride would heal. "Let's hear the details."

"Well, he caught Pologne again," Jinetta began. "But before he could get her back to the inn, we devised a little trap."

"Little!" Chumley exclaimed.

"Bee really designed it," Freezia said.

"It wasn't much," Bee said modestly. "Just a deadfall attached to a rope sling with a sled made out of branches that catapulted its load into the pond. Very simple, really. Tolk tied all the knots."

"I almost fell in the water with him," Pologne said excitedly. "After that, I came up with *another* surprise. It was easy after the first one, because all I had to do was dig a shallow pit and cover it with leaves so it looked like a trap. Then we draped a tarpaulin in between a couple of rocks on the bank and covered them with dirt and roots so it looked like the path continued around that way. And he fell right in!"

By now, Chumley's head was hanging in shame.

"Then, we levitated him over—" Melvine began. I held up a hand to halt his narrative.

"I understand," I laughed. "We don't have to relive every one of the splashes." Melvine looked disappointed. I turned to Chumley. "Big Crunch, I think your seminar has been a huge success."

"More than huge," Chumley mumbled. "They did good job."

"Top marks," I said. "Everybody, take the evening off. You've earned it."

Tolk dashed to the door then back to Bee. "I'm taking a walk! Come with me!"

The young soldier scrambled up from his bench. "Why not? Permission to go walkies, sir?"

"Granted," I said. "Have fun."

"How about you?" Tolk asked the Pervects.

"That's very nice of you," Pologne said, "but I'm just dying to have a hot bath."

"Okay okay okay! Tomorrow?"

"Maybe. Thanks."

Freezia approached Pologne almost shyly. "I noticed your manicure got snagged while you were stringing up those nets. I'm going to do my nails. Would you like to use my buffer?"

"Oh, yes!" Pologne exclaimed, clearly grateful for the détente.

"Then we can try on each other's clothes," Jinetta said. "I think you'd look lovely in my new twinset, Freezia. I know it'll be a little long on you, but that's the style this season, you know."

"That is so nice of you, Jinetta!" Freezia beamed. "I love that sweater set." They bustled toward the stairs. The exchange didn't have the warm friendliness that they had arrived with some weeks before, but it was less tinged with fear and distrust than some of their earlier exchanges.

"I thought they'd never leave," Melvine said. He stumped out of the room.

Chumley let out a low whistle. "That's a formidable lot you have there, old scout. Particularly when they do put their minds to it to work together."

"Yes, it is," I said. "It's a shame they'll never see each other again when they leave."

"The girls will," Bunny said. "But I've noticed they really shine when they add their talents to the guys'."

I shook my head. "I may suggest they join forces, but they have to go their own ways. It's a shame, if you ask me. They could put their mark on the world."

Chumley eyed me with amusement. "Someone to assume the mantle of M.Y.T.H., Inc., perhaps?"

I grinned back. "Don't give ME any ideas, Chumley. I'm still trying to make up my mind what I want to do when I grow up."

Late that evening, I went to look out at the stars. I had been enjoying the company, but the wide open night sky reminded me I occasionally craved solitude. Sometimes I liked it when it was just me and the universe.

A hard-scaled head came and thrust itself underneath my palm. I grinned and scratched behind Gleep's ears. Just me, the universe and my dragon.

Gleep's head twisted around, and he let out a low growl in his throat. A moment later I heard scratchy footsteps.

"Uh, Skeeve, can I talk to you?"

I relaxed. "Sure, Bee. What is it?"

"Well, sir," the figure moved closer. Bee's homely face, blue in the faint starlight, looked concerned. "I notice you've been watching me pretty closely, and I think you must be disappointed. I wonder if you think I ought to stay or not. I don't think I'm living up to your expectations."

"I don't have any expectations," I said, surprised. Then I stopped. That wasn't quite true. "Yes, I have been watching you."

"Permission to ask why, sir?"

I decided to lay my cards on the table. "Massha's ring. I have been thinking you blew it up."

"Why, sir? You said that the perpetrator apologized to you, and that the matter was settled."

"Not exactly," I said. "*All five* of the other students came forward and said they had set it off. You were the only one who didn't."

"But I didn't blow up the ring, sir," Bee said, sounding puzzled. "Why would I confess if I didn't do it?"

I was taken aback. Why indeed? Why had the others been so quick to assume responsibility? I had to think about that. I believed Bee's protestation of innocence. I felt ashamed of myself for my assumption.

"You're right," I said. "I wouldn't expect you to take the blame for something you didn't do. I'm sorry if I gave you the impression I suspected you. No, you're doing fine. I don't want you to leave, unless you're unhappy."

"Oh, no, sir," Bee said. "This is the best thing that ever happened to me since I was born, except for meeting Sergeant Swatter and Nunzio."

"Everything's okay," I assured him. "You're doing fine. I'm proud of the progress you're making."

Bee stood up straighter, if such a thing was possible. "Thank you, sir!"

He spun on his heel and marched back into the inn.

I stayed out for a while longer with Gleep and the stars.

Chapter Eighteen

"I don't want to talk about it."
G. GARBO

"You're pinned to the wall," Markie taunted Pologne. The Pervect clung to the wall behind her, quailing from the tiny figure at her feet. Markie advanced on her, hands curled into claws. "You have no options left. I'm coming for you, and I'm packing serious magikal heat. What are you going to do?"

"Do I have my purse?" Pologne asked.

Markie dropped out of her threatening pose, which, when a being stands less than three feet tall and has a head full of soft golden curls, was not threatening in any traditional sense.

"If you normally carry your purse everywhere, then, yes, you have your purse."

"Good," Pologne said. She reached into the capacious handbag, whipped out a shiny silver four-foot-long gun and leveled it. I pulled Bunny down to the floor. The rest of my students hit the dirt. Markie walked up to the Pervect and knocked the barrel toward the ceiling. She aimed a finger at the Pervect's nose.

"Never, and I mean *never*, point that at anyone you don't plan to shoot. And never whip out a weapon like that unless you are planning to use it."

"Oh, but I would," Pologne said. But she sounded doubtful. She caressed the barrel. Studded with blue gemstones, it looked like it was made of solid platinum. Since I never carry anything larger than a pocket knife, I had no idea what the bulges and protrusions meant. I guessed that neither did Pologne.

Markie seemed to have the same impression. She planted her tiny hands on her hips. "Have you ever shot that thing?"

Pologne looked horrified.

"No, it would mess up the finish. Isn't it pretty? Daddy gave it to me as a graduation present."

Markie sighed. "Then leave it at home. Hasn't Skeeve ever told you that hesitation just hands a weapon to your enemy?"

"Well, he has, but we don't have any enemies!"

Markie raised an eyebrow. "The universe is full of danger, sweet pea. What happens when you move into your first sixth-floor walkup, and a drunken jerk who lives on four staggers over to you in the laundry room?"

"Why, I would never be in any place like that!"

"All right," Markie said. "That's good."

"That is?"

"Yes. You wouldn't be in a situation like that because you have planned ahead. You would have checked out the entrances and exits, and kept your eye on the door, right?"

"No," Pologne said. "I mean, I wouldn't live in a sixth-floor walkup because no elevator means it's a dump. Right?"

Markie groaned. "Think of it in more general terms. You can apply those rules to any situation. You already know what you think of as an acceptable scenario. Let's dissect the state of mind which led you not to be in that apartment in the first place. You want a place to live. You assess where you need to be, what geographical points you need to be near. Add in your personal level of risk, balance that against your cash in hand, tolerance of noise and other nuisances, and so on. That will kick out a list of things you can avoid while still leaving the field open for the greatest number of viable choices, including some you might not have considered at the outset. When you leave out the undesirable factors, only your personal prejudices and preconceived notions would prevent you from seeing all the possibilities."

"Ah," Jinetta said. "When you break down the analysis in those terms, we understand it."

Markie whistled. "Finally! Do you see? The idea is not to leave yourself without options in *any* situation. Choosing an apartment is a scenario you can take at your own pace. Now, let's move up to one where you don't have as much time to make a decision. That's what I was trying to get you to do. Assess the situation with a cool head, and move quickly in response. You know the old saying, 'he who hesitates is lost'?" The students nodded. "That statement is true most of the time. It only means life and death once in a while. It can be simpler than that. If there is, say, only one item of value to be had, or one opportunity to be taken, and you have a rival for either, then allowing your rival to move first is essentially letting him or her choose the battleground. Make the first approach, and you will win. Most of the time."

"Like when there's only one slice of pizza left," Melvine said flippantly.

Markie looked impatient at her nephew's interruption, but she nodded. "Define a contest on *your* terms. I assume most of you, like Pologne, have some kind of protection, magikal or otherwise?"

"Of course!" Tolk exclaimed.

"Keep it as a last resort. Magik and weapons are limited options. Your brain is your most valuable and reusable commodity. Don't waste your resources or your allies. You might need them later."

"Allies?" Freezia asked. "Skeeve is always hammering away about allies. He doesn't much say how to do it on your own."

"That's because it's a lot harder to get by on your own," Markie said. "I work alone. I get paid top dollar for my services because I deal in a difficult field with considerable expertise, entirely as a solo act. It would be a lot easier if I had allies, but in my job they are not only hard to find, but a liability."

"Just what IS it you do?" Jinetta asked, curiously. "Kill people?"

"Hardly ever. Never mind what I *do*; I'm telling you how I *think*. If I'm echoing anything Skeeve says, then maybe you should listen to both of us. Otherwise, what are you wasting my time for?"

"I hope we're not wasting your time, Miss Markie," Bee said politely. "I see a thread running through the lessons. But when I go home, I'm gonna be working by myself as a village magician. I've got to know the best choices to make, because I'm gonna have to make 'em without help."

"Take the big picture. 'What is going to help me live to a ripe, old, healthy, stinking rich age?' Try not to tell me you're not thinking in that direction, because everyone except saints do, and saints are a very small proportion of the population, in my experience. You want the best possible outcome for the long run. Then refine it all the way down to the small picture, to that action you need to take at that moment in order to get to the big picture. Sound hard?"

"Yes, ma'am."

"It gets easier and faster to make those decisions after a while, once you've refined your priorities. And just because you choose those priorities doesn't mean you can't change them." She glanced up at me, almost shyly. "I have."

"But how do you practice making quick decisions?" Jinetta asked.

Markie grinned. "I thought you would never ask."

"Come on!" Markie cried, beckoning with both tiny hands. "Don't stand there taking turns like a lot of well-mannered movie ninjas! Jump in! There's only one of a kind! Get them before I can! Kettle! Flower pot! Face powder! Poker!"

It was on my lips to ask what a 'movie ninja' was, when I had to duck or get beaned by the fireplace poker flying through the air toward the waiting hands of Pologne. Tolk leaped up to snag it in his teeth. Bee forestalled him by diving to the floor underneath it.

"Dispell!" he shouted.

The poker dropped toward his waiting hands.

With a wicked grin, I twitched the poker away.

"Ha-HA!" I chortled.

"No fair!" Bee said, but he was grinning, too.

"Too late!" Markie cried, having secured both the flower pot and the kettle in spite of the others' best efforts. She planted her small form in front of them. "Now, get the item when I call your name. Freezia, basket! Tolk, wood! Bee, pen! Melvine, armchair!"

Tolk galloped to snag a piece of wood off the pile beside the huge fireplace. Bee pointed at the pen on the little table near the front door. His face ran with sweat. The quill wobbled into the air and started to crawl towards him. Freezia simply ran over and snatched it out of the air. She stuck her tongue out at the young soldier. Bee never hesitated, but ran to tug the chair down out of Melvine's hands. The Cupy guy swung in the air like a grumpy piñata.

"You jerk, that's mine!"

"It's yours if you can hang onto it."

"Mine!" Markie sang out. While they were arguing, she snagged it with a thread of magik. It joined the growing pile of household goods behind her.

Just as quickly, I reached for the kettle, sitting forgotten on the floor. It caught Markie's leg. She went flying.

"Opportunity!" I shouted.

Jinetta's eyes went wide. "Everybody! Now!"

The class rushed toward the heap of possessions. Things started to leap around as a few of the apprentices employed levitation, gusts of wind and ropes of power to yank them toward one student or another. Pologne had armloads of items piled into the basket. Bee and Jinetta glared at each other over a teddy bear. I got into the fray with the rest of them. I grabbed the flower pot and tucked it under my arm while I air-lifted the armchair, a box of candy, ten books and a cushion.

"Gonna do some reading?" Tolk grinned at me as he seized the cushion in his teeth. "Rrrrr-rr!"

"Gimme that!"

"No way!"

While we engaged in a tug of war, someone relieved me of the candy and the flower pot. I let go of the cushion to fly a footstool, a retort and a stuffed beniguana to me. Freezia charged me to take the beniguana. I managed to juggle the booty in the air while keeping her at bay. Melvine got into a war of the weather with his aunt. The two of them turned into whirlwinds that careened around the room, vacuuming up items. The rest of us just tried to stay out of their way.

The younger Cupy was by far the more aggressive. He kept trying to back his aunt into corners. Markie outmaneuvered him, the tip of her miniature tornado flicking past him just when he thought she was trapped.

"Aarrgh!" he grunted, backing up several feet. "It's clobbering time!"

The Cupy doll skated insouciantly around the room, sucking up a hatstand here, a pail there. She deposited them with the others then settled in front of the heap to guard it. Melvine's tornado seemed to gather itself in a coil like a snake, and drove straight past her, heading for the stash.

"No!" Markie's voice called, from the center of the driving winds. "Don't cross the streams!"

Too late! Melvine's contrail intersected with his aunt's. The tornadoes spiraled around one another in a braid that staggered blindly around the room. In the confusion, the face powder was knocked open, blinding all of us.

In the white-out, or rather, pink-out that followed, I grabbed for items that hit me as they went by. Books, rolls of tapestry, a beer mug. I'd hold onto them, and just as quickly they would be whisked away.

When the dust, or dusting powder, settled, I found myself in the corner, wiping my eyes. Melvine lay on the floor, sneezing uncontrollably. Pologne hung from the chandelier by her heels. Tolk lay upside down in the empty scuttle. Freezia and Bee seemed to be intertwined under the big table. Jinetta was nowhere to be seen.

Scuffing noises came from the door of my study. Jinetta crawled back into the room, her couture outfit all askew.

"I'm all right," the tallest Pervect announced, rising to pat down her clothes and dust off face powder which rose in clouds from her garments. "Ker-CHEW!" she sneezed. "Goodness, I don't know what hit me!"

"I think it was me," Melvine groaned. He rolled to his side and stood up. "You've got hard ribs!"

"Now," Markie called to us from the top of a heap consisting of every piece of movable property in the room, "wasn't that fun?"

"Fun?" Freezia groaned. "Get off me, you Klahd."

"Sorry, ma'am," Bee said. He scrambled up and offered her a hand.

"Okay, everyone take five," Markie said. She climbed down from the pile of furniture, marched over and stuck the pen into my tunic front. "Nice job."

"Lunch in a few minutes, if you all would like to wash up," Bunny said, coming into the main room from the kitchen. Savory smells, and a few not so savory, followed in her wake.

"I know I would," I said cheerily. "Class dismissed!"

"Well, that was the waste of a morning," Pologne whispered to Freezia as they headed toward the steps. "The last part was kind of fun, but useless." Pologne giggled her agreement. They glanced back at me to see if I had heard. I pretended not. I was disappointed. I hoped that Markie's seminar would make them think. By the thoughtful look on her face, Markie had heard them, too. I hurried to assure her I thought the morning was worthwhile.

"That was really amazing," I said. "I had never broken down the whys and wherefores of making the first move—and the last move. I do a lot more on instinct than I realized. You've given me a lot to think about."

"You were terrific, too," Markie said, whisking the remaining powder out of the upholstery and back into the round box. "I'm impressed with how much you've improved since I saw you. I like how you economize on power expenditure. That's some sophisticated manipulation of magikal force there."

I shook my head. "It's nothing compared with what you did. You're good. You played them like fish. Your control far outstrips anything I can do. Remember, I never saw you use your magik on purpose before. All the spells you cast while you were staying with us looked like accidents caused by a little girl with the power of an insane dragon."

"Gleep!" Gleep protested.

"Sorry, Gleep. I didn't mean all dragons are insane." I reached over to pat him on the head. One of the pieces of firewood was still lying on the floor. I slung it across the room for him. Cheerfully, he rose and trotted over to retrieve it.

"I know what it must have been like for all of you," Markie said ruefully. "But seriously, Skeeve, I had no idea you would progress this fast. At this rate there are no limits to what you can achieve. When you hit the big time, remember, I knew you when."

"Thanks," I laughed. "IF I hit the big time, I'll remember all the little people who made it possible."

"Was that a short joke?" Markie asked, narrowing one eye at me playfully.

"Better than the nonstop mutual admiration society you two were forming," Bunny said, breaking in impatiently. She turned to Markie. "Will you stay for lunch?"

It was a peace offering. I held my breath.

"I'd love to," Markie replied warmly. "May I have something to drink? That was a lot of work."

"It was exciting," Bunny replied. "Almost like one of the games I scry in my PDA."

"You're a crystal fan?" Markie asked.

I knew they'd found a bond.

"I'll get some wine," I said, and hurried down to the cellar.

When I returned with two sloshing pitchers, it was clear that I had been the main subject of conversation.

"Skeeve, Bunny told me all about what happened a couple weeks ago," Markie said, her tiny face serious. "I agree with her. I think the so-called 'gag' with that grenade was meant to take you out."

"I don't agree," I said. "What good would it do anyone?"

"A notch in someone's belt is a good enough reason. Take it from me. I know all the excuses people give for hiring me. You're temporarily out of the picture. Who wants you out permanently?"

"No one!" I protested then hesitated. I was sure I had tied up all of my loose ends when I took my sabbatical. Bunny had assured me her uncle was only disappointed, not angry, that I had stepped away from protecting his business interests. There had been a lot of people I had tangled with in the past, but most of them understood that it was business, not personal. I'd done my best to make sure I parted with everyone else on civil if not cordial terms. I shook my head.

"Well, maybe it isn't you who is the target, but these apprentices are all kids. What value is there in seeing one of them out of the picture? Which one of them is worth killing innocents as collateral damage? You know, if you hadn't gotten rid of that bomb and it detonated unobserved, it would have destroyed not only the inn but half the forest. Have you really checked out these students? Do you really know who they are?"

"They were all brought to me by people I trust," I said, surprised.

"Maybe it's your ex-partner," Melvine said, popping into the room. He sauntered over and helped himself to wine. "It wouldn't be the first time someone's ex-partner took him out, for money or just to take care of unfinished business. At least, that's what I see in the Magik Lantern pictures."

Markie blinked out of existence and reappeared on the other side of the room beside her nephew. She slapped him soundly upside the head.

"Hey!" he whined. She shook a finger at him.

"You watch who you are speaking to in that disrespectful fashion. This is Skeeve, whom I trust a lot more than I trust you. He built a magikal business with contacts you just wouldn't believe. He was trusted by Don Bruce with his most precious operations, and by plenty of others who had plenty to lose."

"Yeah, but he isn't doing it any more," Melvine said.

"I'm just on vacation," I gritted out, saying something even I wasn't sure was true. Yet.

"Oh. Well, that isn't what it sounds like when you and Miss Bunny talk."

"That's it," Markie breathed in a very quiet voice that sounded like the first quiet rumblings of an approaching earthquake. I was once again reminded that she, too, had been at Elemental School. "I'm taking you back to Cupid to learn a little respect. You have been *eavesdropping* on him?"

"I—er—" Melvine looked very guilty and frightened.

I stepped in. "It's not that big a deal, Markie," I said soothingly.

The little round face hardened. "Forgive me for contradicting you, Skeeve. You were good to me when I didn't deserve it, and you gave me respect even when I did not earn it. I admire that, as I told you. I was hoping Melvine could pick up a few lessons in decency as well as control. I am saying that this young imbecile is showing that he's forgotten even that amount of training in basic manners, and he needs remedial classes to correct that failure."

Now the younger Cupy was sweating. Perhaps Markie was right, but it sounded as though the punishment she was threatening far outstripped what I saw as a minor infraction.

"Come on, Markie. It's not as though this place is soundproofed. Anyone could have overheard us if they tried. The Pervects' hearing is so sensitive, I bet they wouldn't have to come all the way downstairs to hear us talking."

"See?" Melvine said. "He doesn't deny it."

Markie gave me and Bunny a very pained smile. "Will you excuse us, please?"

She and Melvine vanished.

When they reappeared, Melvine looked chastened. He came up to me with his head bowed.

"Sir, I would like to apologize. I knew eavesdropping was wrong. I won't do it again."

His respectful tones almost knocked me off my feet. I eyed him to make sure it wasn't sarcasm, but I couldn't detect a trace of it. Markie was one tough disciplinarian.

"Thanks, Melvine," I replied. I glanced at Markie, a question on my face.

"Just using a little family leverage," Markie said, her eyes still flashing with anger. "Git!" she snapped.

Melvine got. He vanished out of the room in a BAMF.

I whistled. "That wasn't necessary, but it *was* impressive."

"If you don't keep the fear of Crom in him he will relapse," Markie said tonelessly. "That's been his problem all along. He gets comfortable, he gets confident, then he gets cocky. He'll listen better from now on."

"I'm not an experienced teacher, but I think he really is doing well. You would be surprised how much work he's really putting in."

"I would," Markie said with a sigh. "I'm sorry you had to see that. My guess is that he started listening in on your conversations at night to find out what the lesson is for the next day."

"Oh," I said, subdued. "Bunny and I never really talked much about that."

"Have you got a room for me?" Markie asked.

"Why?"

"Because I'm staying. Your big bodyguards aren't here any more, and you need backup. I may not have their presence, but I pack my own punch."

"That's a good idea," Bunny said.

I have to admit I stared. Bunny grimaced.

"Don't seem so surprised. I may not have been crazy about Markie before, but even if I wasn't—coming around, I'm not going to let my dislike jeopardize your life. What if she's right?"

"No, thanks," I said firmly. "Either I'm the target—and as you point out, that won't be the first time—or I'm not. I'll handle the next attempt when it comes. Face it, Markie, Melvine won't learn if you're here watching him. He'll just do what you want, or what he thinks you want. Go on. You can drop in and visit again, if you want. Any time."

"You'd better believe I will," Markie said. "You be careful, all right? I can get messages sent through a crystal ball. Bunny can find me if you need me."

"I won't need you," I assured her. "Come on, let's eat."

I gave the students the afternoon off. Now that I was aware of potential threats, I felt fairly confident I could handle them, but I wasn't a fool. I set up little traps of magikal interference, so I would know if anyone made another attempt on my life or Bunny's.

Taking Markie's advice a little further, I investigated the students' backgrounds. I was kicking myself for not having done it before. I ought to know the risks of trusting people to be what they seemed on the surface, but I couldn't help it. Now I had to backtrack and take care of the thing I should have done first.

Ironically enough, Melvine, the biggest troublemaker, was the only one whose provenance was absolutely without reproach. Markie felt she owed me an apology and a debt. I had kept her secret for some time now. It was leverage that she couldn't take away from me, unless she went out of business. She would not be the one to land me with a fake nephew to finish the job she had failed at all those years ago.

I believed that Chumley thought he knew Tolk had no secret agenda or unsavory connections. If he had, Chumley would never have brought him to me. But what if there was some dark past the seemingly amiable Canidian had concealed from his benefactor? I left a message for Chumley with his mother, asking where he'd met Tolk and how long they'd known each other. Then I dimension-hopped to Deva and the Bazaar.

"Youse don't have to worry about Bee," Guido told me when I dropped in on him to ask about his former noncom. "He's a good kid."

"Is this him?" I asked, presenting an ethereal image that Bytina had taken of the class. It had also occurred to me that someone calling himself Corporal Bee had presented himself to Massha, claiming he knew Guido and asking for help.

"It sure is," the big enforcer said, sitting back in his chair. "He's fleshed out a little since I saw him last!"

"He has?" I asked, taking back the picture. Bee was so skinny that I could probably blow him down with a hefty sneeze.

"Yeah. Used to be about half that wideness. Hey, Nunzio, look here. It's Bee. He's studyin' magik with Skeeve. How's he doin'?"

"He's learned a few things," I said. "He's intelligent and he works hard. I've never known anyone who was a better organizer, except perhaps Bunny."

"Somethin's worryin' you, boss," Guido said shrewdly.

I told him and Nunzio about the grenade ring and the missing money. "Bee looks like the most likely one to know how to operate an explosive device, but I can't believe he would endanger all of us for a joke. And, after what you've said, I know I'm wrong to suspect him. So I have to keep my eyes on all of them."

"You're smart to be on guard. But that ain't what's really botherin' you, is it?"

How well he knew me. "They're always complaining. If they don't like my lessons, why are they so desperate to stay?"

"Have you ever tried finding an honest magik teacher?" Guido countered my question with a question. "I bet there ain't no more of them then there is honest used-wagon salesmen. A whole lotta them just want a caboodle of apprentices to follow 'em around and say how wonderful they are. Some of 'em are downright phonies who don't know any more about magik than I do. You're not like that. If I had any talent I'd be proud to sign on wit' you, if you were fillin' a class. I'm glad

Bee's got the chance to learn from you a little. They're gettin' more than they would anywhere else. You know kids; they grouse about anything. It's just natural. I wouldn't take it personal if I was you."

I felt a little better. That left only the Pervects.

Aahz wasn't in the office. I left a note for him, and dropped in on Vergetta and the rest of the Pervect Ten on Wuh.

"So, Skeeve the Great!" Vergetta exclaimed, coming over to give me a hug. The elderly Pervect, clad in one of her favorite flowered dresses. "Look, Caitlin, it's Skeeve!"

The very young Pervect turned away briefly from her computer screen to give me a grin that showed three missing top teeth.

"The others are out doing sales calls, except Niki, who's knee-deep in machinery, as usual. That girl, always with the mechanics instead of good old magik." Vergetta threw her arm around my shoulder and marched me to the end of the long table in the huge stone chamber. "I know you didn't come here just to see our smiling faces, bubbeleh. What can I do for you?"

I wasn't sure where to begin. "You know, your niece has been taking lessons from me for the last few weeks."

Vergetta nodded as she poured tea into a tall glass and pushed it towards me. "Yes, Jinetta. A good girl, smart but not too imaginative. Take some sugar, it'll make you strong. And how is she doing?"

"Er, pretty well, really."

"Good! She and her friends—you know they're just fresh out of school, right?—were so interested in finding someone who knew what they were doing to give them some pointers. I don't know what's the hurry, but they kept saying it's so hard to get a good job unless you have practical experience. I didn't have the time to teach her the ropes, and she wouldn't listen to a relative anyway, so that's how come she ends up on your doorstep. Not that there's anything wrong with them! Her friends are all right. They're so interested in boys and makeup until recently. Now they all want to be the heads of major corporations. Girls today!"

I waited until the spate of conversation slowed and jumped in. "Listen, Vergetta, what did you tell them I could do for them?"

The old Pervect grinned. "Can you grow them some common sense? No? I didn't think so. I see you," she pointed a gnarled fingernail at me, "as the antidote to those teachers of theirs. Especially that Mr. Magoo-whatever. He knew nothing but what he read in books, but they worshiped him like a god. I thought that, if anyone could, you'd show them there was something more past the end of their noses. If you succeed in teaching them *that*, you're a hero."

"I'm trying," I said. "Sometimes I think I'm getting through, and sometimes I don't."

"Fifty-fifty isn't bad odds. Well, Skeeve, nice of you to stop by. I have to get an order out to Skloon. Now, don't be a stranger. You should stop by when you have time to take a tour of Wuh. It's shaping up so well, you won't know the place."

I returned to Klah to find a note from Chumley waiting for me. Tolk had been a member of the Alpha Males, Omega Males club where Chumley volunteered as a mentor once a month. Now I had *no* suspects, and I was none the wiser as to who was causing all the trouble among my students.

And trouble there was. In my remonstrations with the students not to do stupid things, once again I had forgotten to tell them not to swap cosmetics for bird excrement. The Pervects came screaming down the stairs with white goo hardening on their faces, complaining that SOMEONE had tampered with their very expensive cosmetics. Tolk was upset because his shampoo, Gee Your Fur Smells Edible, which did smell like used food, had overwhelmed him with green bubbles, staining his fur. Melvine and Bee hadn't been left out, joining the circle of protesters. My eyes watered when they got close enough. They smelled of skunk.

"It was in the soap, sir," Bee said, weakly. "It didn't start reeking until I rubbed it on myself."

"Who did this?" I demanded.

"He did!"

"She did!"

"He did!"

"She did!"

They all pointed at each other. I glared at them. They glared back. Exasperated, I threw up my hands.

"Forget it," I said, turning away. "Go to bed."

"But, Skeeve!" Jinetta said. "You're supposed to handle these things."

"I'm just in charge of magik instruction," I said. "Nothing else. Read my contract."

"But we don't have a contract with you!"

I looked back over my shoulder. "Exactly."

I stalked into my room and locked the door. The expected grumbling about my being an unfit teacher and uncaring individual arose then escalated into some pretty creative name calling. In about twenty minutes, they all ran out of things to say and stalked off. Relieved, I pulled my blanket up and went to sleep.

BANG!

I sat bolt upright in bed. Where had that noise come from? I craned my head to listen in the dark.

I heard night birds in the distance squawking and fluttering away from the disturbing sound. It probably had originated in or near the inn.

With a flicker of thought, I lit the candle on my nightstand and got up to investigate.

"What was that?"

I held up the candle. Bunny fluttered out of her room, wearing the briefest and sheerest of nightgowns. It did nothing to conceal her considerable charms or her toned biceps. In one hand she held a well-sharpened hand axe.

"Nothing, I hope," I said. "I'm going out to look."

"Be careful!" she said.

The Pervects tiptoed down the stairs. "What happened? We heard a crash!"

Well, they weren't responsible for this disturbance.

"I don't know," I said. "Stay here with Bunny."

The night was clear, with a brilliant half-moon hanging about a third of the way across the sky. I circled the inn a couple of times. Nothing looked out of the ordinary. I went into the stable to check on Gleep and Buttercup.

The war unicorn nickered to me from his stall.

"Hey, boy," I called softly as I came over to rub his nose. "Did that disturb you?"

Buttercup nudged me to the side of his stall with his big head. I ducked under his horn and investigated the enclosure. A few mice squeaked and ran out of the straw bedding. Nothing out of the ordinary was to be found. I checked on his food supply, and forked some more hay into his manger.

"Gleep!" my pet dragon announced sleepily from the middle of the floor. I could see his snaky neck illuminated by the moonlight pouring in the open half-door.

"Is everything all right out here?" I asked. No one knew the secret we shared: that Gleep was intelligent and could speak. "Did you hear that noise?"

"Noise nothing," Gleep said, opening his big blue eyes wide. "Skeeve okay?"

"I'm fine," I assured him, scratching just behind his ears.

"Go bed. Nothing hurt. Gleep love Skeeve."

"I love you, too, Gleep."

Gleep had very keen senses. If he wasn't alarmed by the noise, I shouldn't be, either. I petted him again and went back inside.

Just in case, I put a few more 'feelers' around the door, window and fireplace flue in my room. Better to be safe than sorry.

Chapter Nineteen

"You think you've got family problems!"
L. LUCIANO

I was in my room brooding when a knock came at the door.

"Skeeve?"

"Can it wait, Bunny?" I asked, recognizing her voice. "I'd kind of like to be alone for a while."

"We've got a visitor," came the reply. "It's my uncle. He'd like to say hello."

That was different. Aside from liking him as a person, I was well aware that her uncle was not someone you would ever want to ignore or offend.

"On the way," I called, and started for the door.

Even if I hadn't been forewarned, there was no mistaking the short, heavyset figure sitting at the dining room table. If nothing else, his trademark lavender suit was a dead giveaway.

"Don Bruce!" I said as I approached, then hesitated. As long as we had known each other, I wasn't sure what a properly respectful greeting should be.

I needn't have worried.

"Skeeve!" he crowed, popping to his feet and sweeping me into a massive hug. "How's the old pizano? How's the retirement goin'?"

"Okay, I guess," I said. "How are things with you?"

I had hoped to keep things light, but Don Bruce hadn't gotten where he was by missing things.

"Just 'okay'?" he asked, cocking his head and peering at me. "This wouldn't have anything to do with these students that Bunny's been tellin' me about, would it?"

I shot a dark glance at Bunny. While Don Bruce had been nice enough about my retiring, he had also made no secret of the fact that he wanted me back working for the Mob. As such,

I wasn't wild about the fact that Bunny had let him know that I was working again, even if it was just as a teacher.

"Well, yes," I admitted. "This teaching thing is turning out to be harder than I thought."

"The kids givin' you grief?" he asked sympathetically. "Grab some wine and tell me about it."

To my surprise, I found myself pouring out my disappointment with how the class was going. Particularly, how unhappy I was with my own inability to control the bickering and backbiting among the students. I had never really chatted with Don Bruce before other than in a business context, and it was nice to unload my worries on someone who wasn't directly involved in the proceedings. He listened intently, nodding and making occasional sympathetic noises, until I finally wound down.

"I think maybe I can give you a little hand with that," he said when I was done. "Would it be okay with you if I had a word or two with these hotshot students of yours?"

That caught me flat footed.

"Um, sure, Don Bruce," I said. "If you think you can spare the time, that is."

Again, he noticed my hesitation.

"Whatzamatter?" he growled. "Don't you think I'm up to it?"

"No! It's not that at all," I said hastily. "It's just that these kids are kinda mouthy and, well, I'm not sure they'll react to you with the level of respect you're due and are used to."

Don Bruce threw back his head and laughed.

"You hear that, Bunny?" he said. "You wonder why I love this guy? I want to give him a hand and all he worries about is that my feelings might get hurt."

He leveled a pair of hard eyes on me, all trace of laughter gone.

"Just get 'em down here," he said. "Let me worry about how respectful they are."

I looked at Bunny and shrugged.

"Roust the students," I said. "Tell them we have a surprise guest lecturer."

By the time the class was assembled around the table, Don Bruce and I were standing against the wall, conversing in low tones. I was asking him about what he thought would be an appropriate introduction, while he kept insisting that I keep my comments to a bare minimum and let him handle the rest. That sounded vaguely ominous to me, but I had little choice but to go along with him.

As I turned to the group, my heart sank. The three Pervects had their heads together, giggling as they shot glances at Don Bruce, and Melvine was leaning back with his arms crossed with an "impress me" expression on his face, and Tolk was chewing at an itch on his foot. In fact, the only one who looked remotely attentive was Bee, who was watching Don Bruce with a thoughtful, puzzled expression.

"All right, class," I said, raising my voice, "I apologize for the short notice, but I didn't know this speaker would be available until he dropped in for a visit. This is Bunny's uncle, a successful businessman here on Klah, and he's offered to share his insights with us on operating in the real world."

I nodded to Don Bruce and stepped back, mentally crossing my fingers.

He stepped up to the table and took a drink of wine before starting.

There was a titter of laughter from the Pervects.

"Yes, ladies?" he asked, looking directly at them. "Was there something you wanted to ask before I started?"

"I was just wondering where you got your outfit," Jinetta said with a grin.

"Yes," Pologne added. "Do you always dress like this, or is this special for our class?"

This set the three of them to giggling again.

"I dress this way because I want to," Don Bruce said calmly after the giggles had subsided. "When you reach a given level in the real world, you get to do that. In my mind, it's better than dressing to blend with or imitate any given group, or to rebel against an established norm."

"Exactly what line of magik are you in?" Melvine asked, a note of skeptical challenge in his voice.

"I don't dabble in it myself," came the response. "When necessary, I hire it done."

"Then why should we listen—" Melvine began then seemed to think better of it. "Then exactly what kind of business are you in?"

"You might say I head a little family business," Don Bruce said with a tight smile. "Actually, it's not so little. More like what you would call a mob."

There was a moment's silence as the class exchanged glances.

"Excuse me," Melvine said, his tone cautious. "Are we talking about organized crime here?"

"Maybe that's what it's called from the outside," the Don said. "When you see it close up, like from the inside, it ain't really all that organized."

"Um, sir?" Bee said, holding up a cautious hand. "Would your name by any chance be Don Bruce?"

"Guilty as charged," the Don said with a nod, then he winked at me. "That's something you won't hear me say very often."

My students were murmuring back and forth, their tone and manner noticeably more subdued.

"Now then," Don Bruce said, returning his attention to the class, "I believe you were about to ask why you should listen to me. Before I answer that, let me ask all of you a question. Why did you all want to study under Skeeve here?"

That took everyone aback. For a moment, no one spoke. Then they all tried to talk at once.

"My aunt told me—"

"Well, I heard—"

"Everyone knows—"

Don Bruce silenced them all with a wave of his hand.

"Let's start at the top," he said. "Mostly, each of you wants to increase his or her value on the job market. Right?"

There was a round of nods from the class.

"To my thinking," he continued, "what that actually breaks down to is the acquisition and use of power."

The nods were slower, and Bee raised his hand.

"Um, not to disagree, sir," he said, "but I just want to help people. I thought that studying under Skeeve would help me to do that better."

"Good answer," the Don nodded. "Very admirable. But you don't see many weak or poor people helping others, no matter how nice they may be as people. To help others, you have to be in a position to be able to help, and that gets back to what I was saying, acquiring and using power. See what I mean?"

"I—I think so," Bee said hesitantly.

"Now, this all gets back to why you should listen to me," Don Bruce said. "I may not be a magician but, as a business-man, one thing I have to know is how to acquire and use power. The problem with young folks like you, with the pos-sible exception of the young gentleman here and the furry guy sitting next to him, is that you wouldn't know power if it bit you on the leg."

He turned his attention back to Bee.

"I couldn't help but notice that you seemed to recognize me or my name. Can I ask if I'm right?"

"Yes, sir," Bee said. "I was in the army with Swatter—Guido—and he often mentioned you with the greatest respect. Just like he mentioned Skeeve."

"The army, eh?" the Don smiled. "I thought you showed more sense than normally comes out of a book. For the record, I have the highest regard for Guido. I only wish he was here to help me make my next point."

"Um, if I may, sir. If it will help—"

Bee closed his eyes in concentration, and suddenly Guido was sitting there in his place.

"Hey! That's pretty good," Don Bruce said then turned to me. "What is that? Some kind of transfer spell?"

"It's just a disguise spell," I said. "It's actually still Bee sitting there."

"Well, it'll do for the moment." He went back to addressing the class.

"Now, my question to you is this: Look at Guido here, then look at me. Then tell me which of us you would least like to have angry with you."

It really wasn't much of a choice.

"Guido," Melvine said. "No offense, sir, but he's a lot bigger."

The rest of the class nodded their agreement.

"Uh huh," the Don said. "Guido is not only big, he's one of the best, if not *the* best, at what he does—which is to say, controlled violence.

"Thank you—Bee, is it? The point is made."

There was a shimmering in the air, and Bee was back.

"Now, you all made the obvious, expected choice. Unfortunately, you're all wrong."

He smiled at the frowns around him.

"Guido is big and strong, and I'd never disrespect him," he said. "The truth of the matter, though, is that I have over a hundred like him working for me. All of them specialists in controlled violence. If Guido gets mad at you, you have to deal with Guido. If I get mad at you, you can have the whole pack of 'em down on your neck. Are you starting to see what I mean about power?"

The class was murmuring back and forth again, but they were also watching Don Bruce with a new level of respect.

"The key word in what I was saying," the Don continued, "is *control*. Guido doesn't walk around randomly pounding on people. He knows how much power he has and the repercussions if he misuses it. He's not a bully looking for a chance to show off. He's effective and only uses as much power as is necessary for the situation. Technically, I have more power at my disposal than Guido has. That means I have to be that much more careful about how and when I use it."

He leaned back and smiled.

"All of that brings us back to why you're studying under Skeeve. Now, if I understand it right, most of you were recommended to him or heard about his reputation. I'm willing to bet that you were all a little disappointed when you actually met him because he isn't flashier or more impressive. That's because most of you are still young and tend to look at the surface, just like you were more afraid of Guido than of me."

All of a sudden, he wasn't smiling.

"Well, I'm not young and impressionable. I've been around for a long time and earned my position against some tough competition in conditions where, if you make a mistake, you don't get a bad grade or expelled from class, you get dead. Based on long, hard experience, I'll tell you here and now that your teacher, Skeeve, is one of the most powerful men I've ever dealt with. What's more, I don't think there's anyone that I admire and respect more."

He looked at me and gave a slow nod with his head in salute.

Startled as I was by his declaration, the only thing I could do was return his nod with equal dignity.

He turned his attention back to the class.

"You might want to hear a little of how he built that reputation. Since he's not likely to tell you himself, let me fill you in on few of the highlights.

"When I first met Skeeve, he was the Court Magical for Possiltum. At that time, he had just backed off the largest, best-led army this dimension had ever seen. What's more, he did it with only a Troll, a Trollop, a Pervect, an Imp, a Gargoyle, a salamander, and an Archer to help him."

"Gleep was there, too," I said.

"I stand corrected. And a baby dragon. Even so, that's fairly impressive odds by anybody's books. As I was saying, when I met him, he was standing in for the king, who had taken it on the lam to get out of a marriage. If Skeeve had wanted to, he could have stayed and run the kingdom from then on. Instead, he straightened the mess out and moved to the Bazaar at Deva, where the Chamber of Commerce hired him for their Magician in Residence.

"On the side, he and a few of his friends challenged the two champion teams on Jahk to the Big Game and beat them out of their own trophy. Then there was the time that his partner, Aahz, was in jail in the dimension Blut—that's the one with vampires and werewolves—and Skeeve had to bust him out and prove his innocence."

That one got a reaction from the class. I had told them I would be sending them to Blut on a field exercise, but I had deliberately neglected to mention to them how I happened to be familiar with the place.

"One bit you ladies might find interesting was the time that Aahz resigned from M.Y.T.H., Inc. and Skeeve here went to Perv all by himself to convince him to come back. I'm still gathering information as to exactly how he pulled that one off and came back intact."

The three Pervects were eyeing me now with thoughtful expressions. I was glad Don Bruce had either failed to find out or chosen to omit mentioning how that little escapade got me deported from Perv as an undesirable.

"Now, you might think that all that would be enough to build a reputation for anyone. Well, it might, but in Skeeve's case, it's only the tip of the iceberg. Where his real reputation comes from is that he's a true gentleman.

"I said at the beginning that I was telling you all this because he won't. That ain't his style. He don't brag or bluster or swagger. What's more, he don't throw his weight around unless it's absolutely necessary. He don't have to. His track record speaks for itself. More important, Skeeve genuinely likes people. He's polite and respectful to everybody including his enemies, whether they're strong enough to hurt him or not. If you don't believe me, ask around.

"You've all met Massha? Well, when they first met, they were opposite sides of a caper—specifically, that Big Game on Jahk I was telling you about. Afterward, not only did he accept her as an apprentice, he set her up to replace him as the Court Magician at Possiltum. And my niece, Bunny. She had it in her head that she wanted to be a mob Moll, so I sent her to Skeeve as a bit of a test for both of them. As it turns out, he won't let her be a floozie. Instead, she ends up using all the financial training she got at school to straighten out the kingdom's books for Possiltum, and now she's got a rep of her own as a financier and negotiator. As a matter of fact, there's at least one bank in Perv that's been trying to hire her away from Skeeve for years, but she won't budge."

This was the first I had heard about it. I glanced at Bunny, but she was smiling at the class and nodding.

"*That's* the kind of reputation Skeeve has. Everybody respects him. He earns the kind of loyalty from his friends and associates that money can't buy."

He looked around one more time and rose to his feet.

"Well, I've been ranting here for a long while, and I'll be on my way. Just one last thing, though. Remember when I said I was more powerful that Guido? Well I'll tell you here and now that your teacher, Skeeve, is more powerful than I am. Of everyone I've met or worked with, he's at the top of my list to turn the Mob over to when I retire. Think about that the next time you want to mouth off about how your professors or friends know more than he does."

With that, he waved at Bunny and me and left.

It was a quiet, thoughtful group that drifted off back to their rooms.

After Don Bruce left, the dirty tricks and practical jokes seemed to tail off for good. The students listened more closely to what I had to say. Not as Melvine had after Markie left, but in a more thoughtful manner. What Don Bruce had said to them may have been profoundly embarrassing to me, but it seemed to touch my six students deeply. I was grateful.

"Okay, guys," I said, winding up the D-hopper, "this is your final examination. I'm sending you on a field mission, to infiltrate a party of strangers and retrieve an object for me. I want you to go to Limbo, a dimension I've had some experience in. It's a very *interesting* place. Your object is to visit the Woof Writers." They're a couple of Werewolves I know who live outside the main city. I want you to bring back one of their books. I wouldn't have suggested going there before, because the people in Limbo are very nervous about dimensional travelers. Most of them are vampires."

Bee clutched his throat. "Vampires! Are you sure we have to, sir?"

"Don't worry," I chuckled. "They are a LOT more frightened of you than you could be of them. They don't do a lot of magik because there are few force lines in Limbo."

"Oh, not another underprivileged dimension," Melvine groaned.

I paid no attention. "Keep your disguises up all the time, and you should have no trouble at all. If you need help, look up Vilhelm. He's the Dispatcher of Nightmares in the city of Blut. I've written out the address. Are you ready?"

"Yes!"

"Good. Who's going to be mission commander?"

Modestly, Jinetta stepped forward. "They've selected me, Skeeve."

"All right." I handed her the D-hopper. "It's set to take you to Limbo. Move the dial back to here to return. You've got," I peered out the window at the midmorning sun, "eight hours until sunset here. Go!"

BAMF!

Suddenly, they were gone. I tried to shove aside my feelings of worry. They weren't greenhorns any longer. Bunny stood behind me with her arms crossed.

"Are you sure this is a good idea, Skeeve?"

"I am," I replied. "Well, almost sure. I set the whole thing up with Drachir and Idnew. They've got an encounter group staying with them who pretend to be Klahds and play elaborate live role-play games that echo what they think a Klahd lifestyle is like. They dress up in flowered and striped clothing and paint their faces pink or brown. Drachir thought it would be very funny to have a real Klahd drop into their midst. Bee's second best spell is Datspell, so he should be able to keep up a vampire disguise on unless he wants to drop it. They were also eager to meet Tolk. I think they believe Canidians to be long-lost cousins of Werewolves. Vilhelm will be monitoring the group from the time they appeared in Limbo. It's all as safe as I can make it."

"How safe is that? Aahz nearly got killed there. So did you!"

"I am aware of that," I said. "But I know a lot more about the dimension now, and I have a few friends there. It's not as if I am sending them into the unknown, or making them walk a tightrope across burning coals. They have all day to do what ought to take them as little as an hour, maybe two if they fall for one of Drachir or Idnew's rituals. They said they had some really funny ones dreamed up for the Klahths, which is what the wanna-be Klahds call themselves, but Idnew assured me they're harmless. Disgusting, but harmless."

"Things can still go wrong," Bunny warned me.

I sighed. "I know it, but I can't always be there to hold their hands. Tomorrow they go home, and they'll be on their own from then on. At least tonight we can have a round-table critique session on where they thought they were weak. That will give them something to think about in weeks to come. In the meantime, I can spend the day worrying."

"I've got a better idea," Bunny said, pointing in the direction of the kitchen. "I've been doing all the chores for six weeks. You can clean up while your students aren't here to see it."

I grinned ruefully. "I deserved that." I went off to find the broom.

BAMF!

At the telltale noise, I dropped my dishcloth and went running into the main room of the inn. Bunny followed me. My students, somewhat disheveled and red-eyed, stood leaning on one another. Melvine was clinging to Freezia's back. Jinetta held onto the D-hopper as if it was her lifeline. They were smiling. That was a good sign. They were singing. That was also a good sign.

"What do you do with a drunken vampire? What do you do with a drunken vampire? Fill his glass with week-old ketchup, ear-lie in the morning!"

"Ow, ow, owwww!"

I raised my eyebrows. I'd heard the song before. The verses contained plenty of salty language, most of which I never thought would pass the lips of the genteely raised graduate students, but here they were belting it out in three part harmony with a Canidian howl for counterpoint.

"What do you do with a drunken satyr? What do you do with a drunken satyr?" Freezia began then paused.

"I dunno!" Pologne said, a trifle unsteadily. "What comes after that? I've forgotten the words."

"Shing it again!" Melvine's voice quavered. He lost his grip and slid off Freezia to the floor.

"What do you do—hiya, Skeeve! Hiya, Bunny," Jinetta said, grinning at us with every tooth showing.

"Teach! Howya doin'?" Melvine shouted. He was dressed in a plaid kilt with a flowered shirt the sleeves of which were rolled up to let his hands stick out. He waved his arms to get his balance and sat up. "We're back!" He fell down again. "Uggghh. I don't feel so well."

"Here's the book!" Bee said, thrusting a blue leather-bound volume into my arms. He wore a pie-eyed expression, not as far gone as Melvine but still well on his way to ethanol poisoning. He had a suspicious-looking mark on his neck. I peered closer. He backed away.

"Line of duty, sir," he explained. "One of the hostiles—er, wasn't really hostile, sir. She was kinda friendly, really."

"No questions asked," I assured him. "So, you were successful! Congratulations!"

"Yes, sir," Bee barked out. "We arrived at approximately ten in the evening Limbo local time, sir! Observed some local native inhabitant residents of the dimension and created disguise spells appropriate to blend in with them. Proceeded along road according to instructions, following turns indicated on the map carried by Mission Commander Jinetta! Isn't that right, ma'am?"

"Why, yes!" Jinetta said. "You're telling it very well. Go on."

"Ma'am! We proceeded to the domicile inhabited by the Woof Writers, sir! Except it was also inhabited by fifteen other people, wearing really strange clothing…"

"They said it was Klahth clobber," Melvine said. "I didn't see any clobber. They told me to look closely, then they clobbered me. It was a joke, get it? I mean, aren't these the most awesome threads you have ever seen?"

"Identified ourselves as 'friends of Skeeve' to Subject One, Drachir, Woof Writer. They have impressive teeth, sir."

"I know," I said.

"We joined the gathering. At approximately +80 minutes into mission, Subject Two, Idnew, issued refreshments. They were unfamiliar, but we felt required to partake in order not to appear out of place. Sausage pizza, salad and cannoli, according to Freezia's interpretation."

"I looked it up," the smallest Pervect giggled then hiccuped.

"The additional people, who identified themselves as Klahths— I can give you a full list of their names if you want, sir!"

"No, thanks," I said.

"They ate the food with some difficulty. Thanks to your training, sir, we were able to consume the offered rations. I thought they tasted okay, sir."

"Horrible!" Jinetta shuddered. "Crunchy leaves!"

"Then they started daring each other to take a drink. Then they dared us. The beverage tasted like plain old whiskey to me, sir. It was no trouble to drink it, sir. It was pretty smooth."

"Hundred-year-old, single malt Dragoncroft," Melvine said with a reminiscent smile on his face. "Can you believe it? They were chugging it down like rotgut. 'Course, some people don't know how to hold their liquor anyhow." He glared at the Pervects.

"Tasted pretty good for non-Pervect liquor," Jinetta admitted. "Then they brought out the red stuff."

"Blood?" I asked, blanching.

"Er, no. They called it bug juice. I have to tell you, Skeeve, at home I never drink bugs, but this was very nice! I must start trying off-dimension food."

"Me, too," Freezia put in.

"Not of animal origin," Tolk assured me. "Plant. Fruit, really. Fermented. I made sure it was safe before I let anyone drink it."

"I dunno why you said it was dangerous," Pologne said. The veins in her own orbs were bulging slightly. "Those are some of the nicest people I've ever met!"

"They started a sing-along. Jinetta taught them our school fight song."

"She charmed them," Freezia insisted. "They were nervous about strangers, but Jinetta made them feel as though they have known us all their lives. Tolk did, too. They never suspected we weren't Limboans."

"Aooooo!" Tolk said, his nose raised toward the ceiling. "Aaa—cough cough! Boy, that's going to take some practice!"

"What is?"

The Canidian trotted in a circle around me. "The Woof Writers made me an honorary Werewolf. It was intense! All I have to do is to learn to howl properly. They said I'm awful but I could learn!"

"They didn't mean you were really awful," Jinetta said. "They were just joking. Very helpful."

"Until we asked for the object of our mission," Bee reminded her.

"Oh, yeah—"

"What was the problem?"

"Well, sir, it took a while for me to be able to ask about the book. I got kind of interested in my surroundings—"

"In that GIRL," Tolk teased him.

"Er, yeah," Bee said, blushing. "She was, uh, a friendly neutral. I think maybe I had too much to drink, sir."

Jinetta raised a finger. "I remembered about it. Idnew said she couldn't remember where she had put it. Drachir said we'd all hunt for it. It turned out we had been using it as a tray for the chips and dip. Well, as soon as I moved the food off of it, the Klahths grabbed it. I tried to get it back, but they started playing keep-away with it. Just like little children," she fumed. "So, I levitated it back to me. I'm afraid it frightened them."

"Such a natural little action," Freezia said, "and they all stampeded to the far end of the room!"

"I remembered that you said they don't do magik, so I laughed." She essayed a high chuckle. "Then I said it was a party trick. You do party tricks at parties, don't you?"

"Drachir backed us up," Tolk said. "What a guy! What a guy!"

"He didn't want a riot starting in his own house," I said drily.

"So they all wanted to see it again," Jinetta continued. "They took back the book. I got very angry and stamped my foot. I went after the Klahth who had it. I'm afraid I threw some people around." She hiccuped. "I guess I'm stronger than I thought."

"One of them went right through the window," Pologne added.

"Then it got kinda complicated," Bee said.

"A brawl," Melvine explained. "A real brawl. It was great. I kept the bottles and things from hitting the girls."

"But *you* saved the day," Jinetta said, putting her arms around Bee. "We couldn't get near the person with our book, and time was running out. Then Bee thrust out his hands, and the book came FLYING back to us—with the Klahth still attached to it! I didn't know he could do anything like that. He hasn't been able to in all these weeks!"

"I didn't know he could, either," I said in surprise.

"I've been practicing, sir," Bee said, his face red. "Late at night, out in the stables. I didn't want you to be disappointed in me, sir. Your dragon thought it was kind of fun to watch me. Last night I even levitated him. That was why the Klahth was no problem."

I was speechless. So that was the source of the mysterious banging. Bee must have dropped a heavy object. I glanced at Gleep. My dragon gave me an infinitely innocent blue-eyed gaze then winked one eye at me.

"I'm proud of you, Bee, especially for showing such initiative on your own. I'm proud of all of you!"

"We've prepared a feast in your honor," Bunny said. "Come on in. We've been waiting for you."

The Pervects looked pale. "Maybe just a few *skyrerth* on toast," Freezia said. "I don't think I could face much else."

"Me, either," Bee said.

They looked a little peaked at first, but the smell of good food revived their appetites. When we had all pushed our bowls away, I got up to make a speech. I'd been thinking all day about what to say, but I tossed all of my mental notes aside at the sight of the six of them talking and laughing together, the way they had when we returned from their first successful job.

"First of all," I said, raising my wine glass, "here's to the first, and probably only, Myth-a-Technic University graduating class. You've all done better than I ever thought you could, especially with me as your teacher. I've only had one apprentice before, and I think she owes a lot more of her success to what she *thinks* she got out of me than what she really *did*. I believe you're the same. I have offered you the wisdom of my friends and colleagues, because that's what enabled me to get along in life. I couldn't make you take it or use it, but you have. And, I feel, you will use it to achieve great things in life. For that you deserve congratulations."

"Yes," Melvine said, raising his own glass, "we do."

"Hear, hear!" Pologne said, waving her glass.

Bunny let out a shrill whistle of approbation.

"Second, you came to me as individuals, but you have acted not only as individuals but as a cooperative team, and that was one of the keys to your success. You had someone to watch your back, and someone to accomplish the parts of the task that you couldn't. You can see from that interaction a little of what made me so happy with my friends in M.Y.T.H., Inc. I believe you can't beat a team. So, in your future endeavors, remember to 1) make friends, and 2) delegate."

Down both sides of the table, I noticed odd looks being exchanged between Tolk, Melvine and the Pervects. Jinetta raised an eyebrow and nodded slowly at Melvine. Bee kept his eyes locked on me, a contented smile on his narrow, freckled face.

"So, when you leave here tomorrow morning, I just want to tell you that I learned as much or more from having you here as you did from me. Thanks for an amazing experience."

I sat down to tumultuous applause. Jinetta rose and cleared her throat.

"I think I speak for everyone when I say thank you for all the trouble you've gone through for us, Skeeve and Bunny. Skeeve, you're a great teacher. Believe me. You gave us exactly what we needed, and made us take some necessary reality checks. You don't know how much it meant to all of us. I know I've enjoyed being here."

"Me, too!" Freezia said. "It was worth every penny. More."

Tolk stood up. "Thanks a million! To Skeeve. Wow wow wow!"

The others raised their glasses. "Wow wow wow!" they chorused.

Bunny smiled at them. "I'll be sorry to see you go," she said. "It's been nice to have company. Come back and visit us some time." She started to rise and picked up her bowl.

"We'd be honored," Bee said. "Oh, don't get up, ma'am. I'll do the dishes."

"We *all* will," Jinetta said.

"Like I said," Bunny said to me, as the self-appointed cleanup committee hustled around us, "I'm going to miss them."

In no time at all, the dining room was swept, wiped, and scrubbed. All of the dishes went back onto the shelves, and the leftovers were scraped into Gleep's bowl. My pet stuck his nose into it with a whiffle of pleasure.

"If that's all we can do," Jinetta said, "then we're going to go up. Is that all right?"

"Of course," I said, smiling. "You're graduates now."

Gravely, the students each shook my hand.

As they were heading for the stairs, Jinetta threw her arm over Bee's shoulders. "Come with me, kid. We need to talk."

Chapter Twenty

"Who thinks up this stuff?"
E. KNIEVEL

I sat at my study table, ostensibly comparing the power capacity of two hunks of magikal crystal from Herkymer. It had been about a week since my students had left. The old inn was quiet again—too quiet. Bunny had taken a few days off to take Buttercup to a unicorn show, leaving me and Gleep to our own devices. Gleep, usually the most ebullient of pets, was depressed at the absence of his best friend, and sat at my feet emitting mournful sighs and the occasional whiff of stench. We were both grateful when they returned earlier this afternoon, Buttercup proudly showing off his medallion for Best War Animal. He and Gleep had charged off into the woods to play. Bunny entertained herself quietly in her sitting room. Having been by myself for several days I was ready to hear all about her trip, but she had forestalled me with an upraised hand.

"Now, don't pay any attention to me, Skeeve," she chirped brightly. "Don't stop your research just because I came home. I brought back a stack of new magazines to read. Just pretend I'm still not here."

After the enforced silence, that was impossible. I found myself glancing up at any little noise, just to have a distraction from the silence. It surprised me how much I missed the class. Or, maybe, I was more sociable than I thought I was. Living like a hermit was not my natural habit and, as soon as I felt more like a master magician than a faker, I'd be back in the thick of things in a blink.

A trill of birdsong brought my attention away from the blue chunk. I had to stop that. Mastering complex magik required concentration, and the best concentration was found in silence. It was one of the reasons that old Garkin had his cottage way out in the woods—that and the penury that often accompanies sincere magikal study. I was enough of a realist to know I was more than fortunate being able to take a sabbatical with a full strongbox. I wouldn't have to scratch, as my old master had, to buy thurifers and censers and candles and all of the paraphernalia that magicians surrounded themselves to assist in their studies. Most of it was unnecessary window dressing, to impress a client. Consecrated salt? I had a barrelful. Rare incense? You name it, I had it. Still another percentage of items only served as another focus for concentration, such as gazing crystals and magik mirrors. The remainder was genuinely useful for certain kinds of magik, storing power or focusing it in some way that might not come naturally to a practitioner, or for use by a non-magician. I had a crate full of such gizmos. Each of them had been fun for a while, but I had put them aside in search of processes I could evoke rather than invoke.

For a moment I was ashamed of the remarkable plenty I enjoyed. Maybe, when I decided to rejoin civilization, I'd endow a scholarship to help poor magicians get a start in their studies. If they couldn't make it after learning the basics, they were on their own.

The bird sang again, its voice echoing in the emptiness. Maybe I should take up bull-wrestling, or foster a houseful of banshees, just to raise the sound level a little. Or maybe I should start a game show.

In the study next door, Bunny had hooked into the Crystal Network again. Voices and music made me strain to hear. In the midst of it all I heard a BAMF!

"Tananda! You made it!"

"Hey, Bunny! I brought popcorn. When's it get started?"

"Soon! Let me pour you some wine."

"Hi, Bunny," a little voice said. I recognized it as belonging to Markie.

I heard a clunk as the wine carafe rang against something solid. Tananda's voice rang, too, with outrage. "What is SHE doing here?"

I stood up, wondering if I should charge out there and get between them. I didn't have to worry. Markie could take care of herself.

"She's—not so bad, Tanda," Bunny said slowly. "She was ready to jump in and help Skeeve out a few weeks ago. It turned out he didn't need her, but I thought it was pretty nice of her to offer."

"Well—that's different from the way she was before."

"She's trying to be different. I'm trying to—accept it."

"I brought some wine," Markie added eagerly. "It's just a little 'thank you' for letting my nephew stay on here. You can't believe the difference it made in him. I'm sure you will like it. Chateau Cupido, extra sec, from my aunt's vineyard."

"I'm not saying that would make everything all right," Tanda said, but her voice started losing that constricted quality.

"No," Markie replied. "I'm not asking for that. Just give me a chance."

"Well, sit down, I suppose. Do you do any crystal-gazing?" Tanda asked.

"When I get a chance. You mean you're a fan, too?"

"Do chocolate bunnies get their ears bitten off? You bet!"

Bunny became positively expansive. "I love it. It's really opened up the world to me, you know? And I've gotten to know so many other people through the ether. Oh, look. It's about to start!"

"Did you see the first three episodes?" Tanda asked.

"Oh, yes!" Bunny said. "Everyone at the unicorn show was a big fan. We spent *hours* watching!"

I moaned to myself. Crystal-gazing fans. Now they were going to talk about one of their programs until the trivia bled out of my ears.

"Where's Skeeve?" Markie asked.

"Studying," Bunny said. I heard the glug of liquid. "He'll come out later."

Guiltily, I bent over my table to try to make her easy assurance ring true. The three of them laughed and chattered. I peered at my crystals. The pink one held more energy than the blue one, but didn't retain it as long. Would it be possible to transfer power from the pink one to the blue one? Treating the crystal as if it was a force line, I drew on the pink power. It began to fill my inner 'battery.' So far so good. Now, I tried transferring it to the blue crystal. It grew hot. I dropped it on the table and began to rethink my approach. Pernadairy's Treatise on Magikal Crystals listed eighteen different means of releasing power from natural prisms, and only the three messiest made any reference to heat.

A series of crackles, pops and snaps erupted in the next room while Tanda and Bunny sought the connection in the ether they wanted.

Bytina, the little red PDA, was almost as good as a real crystal ball, but being a philosophical device more than a magikal one, she had odd problems of her own. The way she used power tended to build up a static-like charge that attracted nuisance emissions, insubstantial images, which infiltrated the house and appeared suddenly out of closets or other unexpected places. I saw a Troll carrying a sword pop up out of my clothing trunk one day. I nearly blasted my own wardrobe apart until I realized it was just an advertisement for a collectible weapons dealer. Tanda had showed me how to deal with commercial interruptions so I could dispell them for Bunny, but since Tanda was here, she could banish them herself.

A sepulcheral voice boomed throughout the inn. "THIS is *Sink or Swim: Perv.*"

Peppy theme music started playing, resonating in my crystals. The blue one started glowing, making the skin on my hands lose its normal hue. I got interested in the phenomenon and stopped listening. *Sink or Swim* like all the remotely-viewed contests only held my interest in a marginal way. I found it hard to work up enthusiasm without being there. *SOS* was no sillier than any other game.

At the beginning of each show the relentlessly cheerful announcer, Schlein, arrived in a puff of smoke. He would

recap the previous day's exploits and explain the concept anew
for the audience. The rules were arbitrary but ironclad. Only
amateur magicians could enter, meaning that they could never
in their lives have accepted pay for performing a spell. Schlein
always followed that rule up with "It's not too late to go back in
time and return that quarter to your Grandpa, kids!" Which was
met by hysterical laughter by the studio audience. No weapons
except those allowed in the rule book, which Schliney always
showed was empty. (Earning another big laugh from the viewers.) In fact, the contestants had to go into this contest practically naked. Pretty tough for a contest where the prize was
survival itself. Some of the tasks the contestants were set were
so dangerous no one but a complete fool would even consider
undertaking them. It was stupid. I had no stake in it. No interest. I forced myself to concentrate on what I was doing.

The music ended and a deep, friendly voice spoke.

"This is *Sink or Swim*! And now, the host with the most, the
one, the only—heeeere's Schleiny!"

BAMF!

I didn't have to see it to know that Schlein, a handsome
male from Sittacom, had emerged from his puff of theatrical
smoke. He had a habit of rubbing his hands together like a
predatory insect which, apart from the green skin and anten-
nae, he did not otherwise resemble. As spotlights swung to
and fro over his head, he began his traditional introduction.

"Welcome to *Sink or Swim*! This is Day Four of the brand
new series set here on Perv. Our original sixteen teams have
already been pared down to eight. Following is a holographic
representation of some of the highlights of the last few days."

Exciting music with a catchy, rapid beat rang out.

"Yes, indeed, you had to be there! Now, you know the
rules of *Sink or Swim*, but we're going to recap them for you
now. Amateur magicians only. Entrants can never have accepted money for doing magik under any circumstances. It's
not too late to go back in time and return that quarter to your
Grandpa, kids!"

Hilarious laughter from the studio audience and the three women watching from the sitting room.

Schlein continued. "That restriction is enforced by an oath administered by our Spectre team with dire consequences visited upon anyone who is lying to try to get in. We don't mess around here, folks! All the contestants are split up into teams of one to eight players. Each team must fulfill any task assigned to it. No weapons except those listed in the rulebook. Uh-huh," he added gleefully as the audience laughed again at what I knew was an empty book. "That's right, folks. Mechanical or physical objects are not allowed. You have to use your wits!"

Well, that was a weapon most of the viewing public wasn't going to be able to wield.

At that moment the blue crystal emitted a shower of sparks. I tried to get it to do that again. When I next found myself paying attention, Schlein was several paragraphs farther in his introduction.

"...Magikal interference with the performance of others is not only allowed, it's expected! Once you're out of a round, you may not use magik on anyone else remaining in play, or your whole team will be disqualified. Failure of any team to complete a task will put it on the Wheel of Misfortune, where one team will be eliminated after the end of each day by a spin of that day's most successful group. Once all teams but one have been eliminated, the members of that team will be pitted against one another in a life and death struggle for the Grand Prize—a commission to work for the famous Mistress Montestruc!"

I didn't have to glance into the room to see the silhouette that appeared in Bytina's expanded image. When I had sat with Bunny to watch *Sink or Swim: Zurik*, I'd gotten the impression of plenty of long, red hair piled up on the head of a formidably statuesque female form. Because the rest of the figure was in shadow, I had no idea Mistress Montestruc's race. All that was visible was a glimmer that could have been satin or a glistening hide. Bunny cooed at the glimpses of huge, glittering gemstones around Mistress Montestruc's neck, waist and wrists.

Schlein went on with his spiel. I could have recited it with him. "This fabulously wealthy and reclusive heiress has business interests across the dimensions. Who knows? You may end up president of a shipping company, operator of a casino, or running errands for the lady herself in her fantastic villa in the exclusive dimension of Nola! All this to one lucky contestant at the end. And now—will our teams *Sink or Swim?*" In my mind I could see Schlein wave his hands. "Sink or Swim: Perv," etched themselves in huge green letters on the air then dissolved.

"Here's what happened yesterday!"

More dramatic music, over which Schlein offered peppy narration. I had noticed that no matter which game or contest Bunny viewed, the commentators were all relentlessly cheerful, remarkably stupid, and endlessly talkative.

"The All-Pervects really got into it with the Dragonettes. Where they had lost ground with the Volcano Challenge, the All-Pervects really surged back into the lead with the eating contest. At the gun the four Trolls and a dragon team had consumed nine whales, and the All-Pervects, nine and a half! What a mouthful that was!

"Next, the Sorcerer's Apprentices, who won the Free Pass Challenge on the Acid Trapeze the day before yesterday, got to sit out the Wheel of Misfortune with the rest of yesterday's winners. The Dragonettes, the Gargoyle Girls, Sid's Slashers, Garonamus, the Bald Guy with Muscles, and the Sharkbait teams all had to spin to see who goes home! What suspense! What terror! What a surprise when Sid's Slashers drew the unlucky straw!"

A trumpet blew a scale of descending notes, indicating disappointment. Tananda and Bunny added their sighs.

"Well, we're happy they were here. The rest of the teams are still raring to go!"

Fanfare!

"Since we're past the halfway point in *Sink or Swim: Perv,*" Schliney went on suavely, "we invite our on-the-spot odds-maker to give us his insight into how the contest is going. Will you all welcome—The Geek!"

My ears perked up at the familiar name. I had known the Geek for a long time. He was a Deveel, well known around the Bazaar. The last time I'd seen him, coincidentally, was about the same time I had seen Markie. He had foisted her off on me to try and destroy my reputation in the Bazaar. To say there was no love lost between us was to make the relationship sound warmer than it was.

"Geek, welcome."

"Schlein, always happy to be here."

Yes, that was the Geek, all right. He sounded oily enough to grease a castle drawbridge with his tongue. Not a bad notion, now that I thought about it. I wondered how I could engineer that happy accident, and whether I could sell tickets. I knew plenty of people who would buy one.

Temper, temper, I chided myself.

"Geek, you've been watching the action since Day One. Give us your feedback, and let us hear your predictions for the outcome of this most thrilling contest."

"Well, Schlein, we've lost a few contenders. I gave good odds that the Battling Bugbears would have made it through to the final round, but when the Imperators tripped them up on the obstacle course, all bets were off. Then the Imperators got their own clocks cleaned by Sid's Slashers—my odds-on favorites—who just lost the Wheel of Misfortune challenge. Then there was the problem that the Gargoyle Girls had against the always-dangerous Second Lieutenants with Compasses, but eventually won out. As for the others, I told you from the beginning the odds in their favor were too long to bet on."

"I'll *bet* you did!" Schlein retorted perkily. "So, as we go into the next round, tell me the odds on the remaining teams. What's your angle on today's contest?"

"Well, Schlein, the Ogre-wrestling contest has always been a favorite of mine..."

Chapter Twenty-One

"Did I forget to mention that?"
B. ELZEBUB

Before I knew I had even gotten up, I found myself on the threshold of Bunny's dimly lit sitting room. Tananda sprang up from the squashy chair in the corner near the fireplace and folded herself around me like a very tight-fitting straitjacket.

"Hey, Tiger, how are you doing?" She kissed me thoroughly, which is just a Trollop's way of saying hello.

"Mmmph mppphhffpp!" I replied, in no real hurry to extricate myself. She was a wonderful kisser. Too bad I had come to think of her more as a sister than a potential love interest.

"Is that all you can say to me?" Tananda asked with a wink.

"Hi, Skeeve," Markie said shyly.

"Couldn't stand eavesdropping any longer?" Bunny asked.

"I heard the Geek talking," I said, trying not to sound sheepish. I felt my way through the illusion that Bytina spread across the room to find myself a place to sit. "I guess I was curious. His angles are usually bent in some way."

"I don't see how," Bunny said, frowning. "These are games of skill, not chance. You can't deal a volcano off the bottom of the deck."

"I understand where you're coming from," Tananda acknowledged. "The Geek's only as honest as the facts that can be checked."

We all gazed at the image.

The Geek looked about the same as when I had last saw him, but his race lived a very long time compared with Klahds. Schlein looked dapper and sincere in a white collar and blue-flowered tie. Between the red Deveel and the green Sittacomedian, a huge chart appeared.

"Here are my picks in reverse order. At twenty-five to two against, Sharkbait! Next up the list, I give the Gargoyle Girls twelve to one. The Bald Guy with Muscles, our only surviving one-man team, is at nine to one. The Shock Jahks comes in at five to two. The Dragonettes are at three to one. I give Garonamus three to one. The All-Pervects are at even odds."

Schlein interrupted him. "But the real surprise is how well the Sorceror's Apprentices are doing. You've got them at six to one to win today's matchup!"

"That's right, Schlein," the Geek said suavely. "This under-dog of a team—no offense to the Canidian in the ranks!—has survived every one of their tasks, even the dangerous Crocodile Cage Match. Frankly, I'm amazed. You'd think any team that had a Klahd in it would be his-tory from the get-go. But no. He's not holding them back too much. So, they're a team to watch. But the All-Pervects are still my number one pick."

"Do you hear that? His number one pick!" Schlein an-nounced to the audience. It responded with roars of approval. "Yes, Perv has reason to be proud of its Perverts!"

"Booooo!" the crowd roared.

"I mean Per*vects*, of course! The All-Pervects are the top of the chart!"

More cheering. Schlein wiped his brow.

"A Klahd on a team?" I asked. "I'm amazed he hasn't been toasted by now."

The others shot me an impatient look. I shut up.

Images of the teams popped into view next to their names on the chart, then each picture spread out around the room, increasing to life size so they were easier to see. The All-Pervects were fierce, four males and two females in cover-alls that made them look like they meant business. The Bald Guy with Muscles wore black trousers and a skimpy shirt without sleeves. He snarled at the magician capturing him in crystal. For a moment, the image shook. I chuckled. He had psyched out the magician. I bet he was a tough competitor.

The laugh died away in my throat as I turned to the next bubble. The Sorcerer's Apprentices looked strangely familiar. I gawked at the faces of three Pervects in matching pastel jumpsuits, one Cupy in a flannel sleeper, the Canidian in question, and one Klahd. One freckled, red-headed Klahd: Bee, formerly of Her Majesty's Army of Possiltum. My blood seemed to freeze in my body.

"What are THEY doing in there?" I exclaimed.

"Oh, Skeeve," Bunny squealed, clutching my arm, "I forgot to tell you when I got home. The Myth-ka-technic University group entered *Sink or Swim*! See? They named themselves after you."

"They did?" I thought about it. Sorcerer's Apprentices. I might have liked Skeeve's Sages or The Spellbinders better, but Sorcerer's Apprentices wasn't bad. "I guess they did." A horrible realization came to me. "Is this why they asked me to teach them? For a GAME?"

"I guess so," Bunny said. "Aren't you happy this is why they needed you, and not some nasty reason?"

"For *material gain?*"

"And why is this suddenly a problem?" she asked. "Isn't that why *you* wanted to learn magik in the first place?"

"I—" Honesty compelled me to stop and admit that to myself. My own motives had not been pure. I'd thought only of magik as an adjunct tool to help me in my first profession, theft. "But *why* didn't they mention it?"

Tanda cuddled in on my left side. "I guess, Tiger, that they didn't want you to know. They might have been embarrassed." I frowned. This from a woman who was scarcely ever embarrassed about anything. "You might have said no. You know what you just said. Maybe other teachers would have had scruples against helping amateurs crib for a contest for pure monetary gains."

Garkin would have, I realized. He kept trying to tell me to study magik for myself, but I'd been young and stupid, like these kids were. No, they hadn't been stupid—I had. There were so many questions I had not asked.

"Did Chumley know about this?" I demanded.

"I—" Tanda's green cheeks deepened to the color of spinach. "Yes, he did. He told me, but he'd been 'sworn to secrecy, what?'" she added, in an imitation of her brother's cultured speech pattern. "And he asked me to keep it mum. Believe me, I thought about letting you know, but I couldn't see the harm in it. After all, it's not like they were dragging you in there with them."

"But they are!" I exclaimed. "I mean, what if something happens to them? I'll be responsible for giving them a false sense of security."

"You did nothing of the kind," Markie assured me. "I was here. I saw how you encouraged them to get into the game and try. Even my horrid nephew prospered, and I thought he was a forlorn hope."

"So YOU knew, too."

Markie nodded. "Frankly, I was hoping that spending time with you would make him realize he didn't want to enter the contest, but you cannot tell kids anything. You are selling yourself short, Skeeve. I think you've given him and the others a chance at surviving it honestly. I wanted you to give him the confidence not to have a tantrum and get distracted. That would be the worst thing he could do."

"It could be far worse," I said severely. "Have you seen some of these contests? He could get killed! All of them could! What about Bee? I can't believe Massha would hand me a green youngster and expect me to turn him into a killer contestant!"

"Ooh, look, there he is!" Bunny said suddenly, picking up Bytina to increase the level of sound.

At the side of the arena, a perky Sittacomedian stood with my former students. She was interviewing Bee.

"...Surprised to see someone from Klah in the competition," she was saying. "Tell me, how did you come to join us here on *Sink or Swim?*"

"Well, I was just learning some extra magik—Ooof!" He stopped as Jinetta edged into the picture and nudged him hard in the ribs with her elbows. "I met these folks on Klah, and well, we all get along pretty well. I never heard of the contest before. They liked me enough that, when they left Klah, they convinced me to come with them. They said it would be fun."

"And is it?" the winsome reporter asked with a huge smile toward the crystal ball.

Bee nodded vigorously. "Oh, yes, ma'am. It's about the most exciting thing I've ever done!"

"He's going to get killed," I pronounced glumly. "All he ever wanted was a head start on his new profession, and he's going to die in a *game show*. I thought I was helping him!"

"You ought to be proud," Tanda said. "He's taking a chance. Most of your people never get the opportunity to really test themselves like this."

Bunny agreed.

"Everyone at the unicorn show was really impressed when I said they were all your students. The Geek is right. They're doing really well."

"*How?*" I demanded. "They're still as raw as steak tartare!"

"Oh, you wouldn't believe it," Tananda assured me. "You'd never know they're complete amateurs. I've never seen Pervects cooperate with any other race like that, well, since you and Aahz, really. The whole group operates like a well-oiled machine. They split up a task and tackle it. You'd think they had the details of every event planned out in advance."

"Knowing the Geek, someone might be tipping them off," I said worriedly. I scanned the other teams and groaned. Dragons! Trolls! Landsharks! Deveels! The opposition looked like the Who's Who Compendium of Tough Competitors. Next to them, my students looked like a field trip from a junior high school.

"But they all take an oath to play fair," Bunny insisted. "They wouldn't cheat."

"If they were told that being given the information was part of the game, they may not be aware it was cheating. Remember, they really are new at this. They won't know they're being manipulated," I said.

"Are you sure?" Bunny asked. "Melvine sounded pretty savvy."

"I think it's all window-dressing," I said. "He bluffed a lot. He'd say he knew how to cast a spell even when he had no idea."

"What about the Pervects?" Tanda asked.

"College students," I moaned. "They believed everything their professors told them. They would take anything an authority figure said at face value."

"Shh!" Bunny said. "The game is beginning."

Chapter Twenty-Two

"We're not dead yet."
M. PYTHON

The team pictures vanished in a dazzling array of colored lights. Schlein emerged in the center of the coruscation and smiled directly at us.

"And for our first task tonight, the Hot Potato contest! Yes, this is a very popular competition. All of the teams will send a representative to the Arena. This is a very special hot potato, as all of you know."

An irregular brown oblong appeared in Schlein's hand. He tossed it up and down a couple of times. "It gets hot then hotter then hottest! The player who handles it last is the winner! Of course, the one still holding onto it when it explodes loses. And occasionally we lose a couple of audience members, too, but it's all in good fun. So, who will win...*Hot Potato?*"

The invisible orchestra produced a deafening fanfare. The lights died away, leaving eight spotlights pointing down at the stage.

"Oh, who will the Sorcerer's Apprentices send?" Bunny asked, bouncing up and down in her seat clutching a handkerchief between her hands. "The Pervects can't handle fire. Tolk will burn his mouth! And Bee—"

In a moment we had our answer. On the floor of an arena with deeply raked sides, eight figures each took their places on a circle of light. A huge Troll, an Imp, a male Pervect, a female Jahk, a Gargoyle, a muscular man without a hair on his head, and a flying shark stomped, strode or wriggled into view. They were joined by a tiny figure wringing his hands together over his head in a sign of victory.

"Melvine?" I asked.

"Don't worry about him. We're pretty impervious to heat," Markie said, waving away my concern. "It's one of the first things you learn in fourth grade. That's the Fire Elemental class."

Schlein appeared on the center of the circle of contestants. He held up the brown potato, and tossed it to the Troll. The Troll caught it between thumb and forefinger and threw it to the next contestant in line, who passed it on at once. It didn't look like a challenging contest to start.

I was wrong. Before the vegetable had made a complete round it started glowing slightly. Sweat breaking out on the face of the Imp told me that it had grown almost too hot for him already. He tossed it away and rubbed his palms together. Disdainfully, the Pervect received the missile and sent it on. The Jahk threw it to the Gargoyle with a pained shriek.

"That hurts!" she cried.

"Come on, sweetie, suck it up!" Tanda advised the image. "You're a Jahk!"

The Gargoyle had no trouble holding onto the potato, but he wasn't very good at throwing. The bald male had to dive for the potato, and tossed it in his hands until he all but batted it toward the shark.

Faster and faster the glowing spud went around the ring. It burst into flames on the sixth round. The Troll yelped and started batting at the fur on his arms. Flames licked up and down his limbs. He had set himself on fire. While he was batting out the fire, the potato hit the ground.

"You're out!" Schlein's voice called.

"Aarrrggggghhh!" the Troll snarled. He stomped away. Gingerly, the Imp snatched up the potato and flicked it in the direction of the Pervect.

The Pervect held out his hands for it. I thought it was pretty brave of him, since fire is one of the few things that could harm his kind. At the last moment the flaming missile took a curve. Someone in the circle was trying to keep it away from him. The Pervect snarled and reached for it with his own magikal force. The missile did a right angle in mid air and headed for his palms. It looked like he had it in the bag, but at the moment before impact he winced, closing his eyes. The potato dropped straight down, hitting the ground. The Pervect opened his eyes, looked at his empty palms, and glared at the others.

"Who did that?" he demanded. The others all favored him with innocent expressions that changed to gleeful leers.

"All's fair in love and *Sink or Swim*," Schlein's cheerful voice said.

The Pervect gave his fellow contestants one killing glance, and stalked off to join the Troll on the sidelines.

The Jahk did better in the next circuit, speedily handing off the flickering potato to the Gargoyle. It looked like the Bald Guy with Muscles was going to make it one more round. His jaw was set. Bravely, he conveyed it to the shark then dropped to his knees. He held up his hands, and the crystal balls zoomed in to show them. The palms were blistered and swollen to twice their normal size. I cringed in sympathy.

"Medic!" shouted Schlein.

A couple of Sittacomedians in whites came racing onto the stage with a stretcher between them. The Bald Man waved them away, though perspiration ran down his face like a waterfall.

"It's just a scratch," he insisted.

In unison, Bunny, Tananda and Markie stated, "Men."

He was out. The Jahk joined him next, followed by the shark, who lost half a row of teeth three rounds later. Fortunately, he had several other rows of gleaming white fangs.

The Imp, still in the game, grinned madly at the departure of his fellow contestants. He underhanded the now incandescent potato to the Gargoyle. He made it look so easy I was suspicious. Imps were no more immune to heat than Klahds or Jahks. What was going on? It seemed as though I wasn't the only one who wondered about it. A green-skinned, tunic-clad official I hadn't noticed before came marching out onto the floor, and grabbed the Imp by the wrist. He examined the pink male's palms.

"He's wearing Burn Cream!" announced the Sittacomedian.

"No, never!" the Imp protested as he was hauled off the stage. "It wasn't me! They told me it was all right! I didn't do it! It's just magik!"

"Aw, pick a lie and stick with it," Tananda jeered him.

"Cheating!" Schlein said, clucking his tongue regretfully. "That means that Garonamus is disqualified!"

The Geek's bubble over the arena suddenly enlarged. We watched as he shook his head ruefully and scratched the team name off his slate. The bubble shrank to a pinpoint.

The official came marching on, picked up the white-gleaming potato and tossed to the Gargoyle. "Game on!"

The circle had shrunk just that quickly from eight to two contestants. Melvine seemed to be enjoying himself, returning the glowing potato almost the instant it hit his palms. He started pitching fancy throws, lobbing it overhand or pitching sliders in the direction of the slow-moving Gargoyle.

"Is that the best you can do?" he taunted the stone figure.

"Shut up, little man," the Gargoyle grunted, stooping for the potato just in time.

A humming arose.

"What's that?" I asked.

"Uh-oh, folks," Schlein said. "We're running into magik time! The potato is close to detonation. Will one of these brave competitors give it up before they're both blown into little pieces?"

"D'ja hear him?" Melvine said. "You can give up now!"

"No, you give up," the Gargoyle countered. "You're just flesh."

"No Cupy is just flesh, pal! We're Cupies!" Melvine heaved the flaming sphere into the air and hit it like a tennis ball. The Gargoyle caught it in one massive hand. The stone face seemed to contract for a moment.

Schlein leaned into his microphone. "These two just won't stop! I'm very impressed! This has got to change the odds for the Sorcerer's Apprentices. Odds-maker, what do you say?"

The Geek appeared again. He didn't seem impressed. He looked upset. "This moves the Apprentices up to four to one," he gritted out.

I twisted my lips. He assumed they were going to fail. Not MY apprentices!

The humming grew louder and more shrill.

Schlein yelled, "When will they stop?"

But Melvine and the Gargoyle still would not quit. The potato flicked back and forth between them so rapidly it looked like a solid line of flame. The two moved within a couple feet of one another, with the magicians covering the event picking up tight images of their faces and hands. Melvine was sweating now. The Gargoyle looked as though he was, too, until I realized it was the heat from the potato. It was actually melting the stone!

The huge, underslung jaw was set. He clapped his hands on the missile then batted it back. I could see that his palms were beginning to slag. In a moment they would melt off.

The Gargoyle knew it, too. He batted the potato one more time to Melvine then retired, flapping his hands to cool them. Melvine received the potato then floated it in the air over his head while he accepted the applause of the crowd.

Schlein's voice boomed over the noise.

"It looks like—yes, it is—Melvine of the Sorcerer's Apprentices is the winner! But what about the potato?"

Melvine looked up at it. The hum had risen to a scream. Red numerals appeared in the air. The audience chanted along as they counted down.

"Ten, nine, eight, seven..."

"It's going to blow," Schlein said, cheerfully. "Everybody duck! Bye-bye, Melvine!"

Melvine's face hardened into the stubborn expression I had learned to associate with his refusal to acknowledge what someone else had just said. He glanced upward then thrust his hand toward the blazing globe of fire. It shot upwards, with Melvine close behind.

One of the crystal balls following the match must have been operated by a wizard adept at flying, because it never lost sight of them. They flew up and out of the open arena, heading for the clouds. Melvine waited until he was well above the crowd then stuck his fingers in his ears.

High above him, the potato detonated deafeningly, sending flaming sparks off in a hundred directions.

"Wow, what a finish!" Schlein said. "Melvine, of the Sorcerer's Apprentices!"

I found myself cheering wildly along with the others. "That was amazing!"

"Very stylish," Markie said, applauding. "Did you teach him that, Skeeve?"

"Well, not really—" I began.

"He sure did," Bunny said proudly. "Melvine learned it from seeing him save us all from that explosion!"

Schlein appeared among us again, wiping his brow. "Well, that was dramatic, my friends. We've never come so close to having the potato blow in the head-to-head competition. I have to tell you, most of the first row was already heading for the door when—can you believe it?—that Cupy drove it right up into the stratosphere! Wait, I'm getting a message from the judges." He put a finger in one ear and seemed to be listening. "Yes, they are awarding an extra point for style to the Sorcerer's Apprentices. Way to go, guys!"

I cheered and stamped my feet. "Great job, Melvine!" I yelled.

This game show stuff wasn't that bad after all. I sat back to enjoy it. I had always felt that most of the sporting events Bunny viewed were kind of stupid. I felt no connection to images seen in a crystal ball, but this—these were my own students.

The next round was a challenge between paired teams. The Shock Jahks and Sharkbait went up first, chosen by small white feathers that floated out of the air and lit on the team captain's heads. One from each team had to walk on a tight-rope while the others passed items up that had to be assembled before the walker reached the other side. In deference to the shark's mode of locomotion, she was enclosed in a tube of magikal force.

"Touch any side, and it will be as if you fell off," Schlein warned. "The loser will get one penalty point. Once you reach the far platform, you must have a working Jack-in-the-box in your hands. Set it off to get a bonus point!"

We watched breathlessly as the 'walkers' moved forward. The shark assembled her items by magik as they floated in the air next to one of her lidless eyes.

The Shock Jahks didn't seem to have much in the way of magikal ability. If an item fell out of their uppermost member's hands, it fell down again. Still, teams appeared evenly matched. I was on the edge of my seat as they neared the second platform.

"It's the Jahks—no, the Sharks! No! The Jahks are pulling ahead! Hang in there, the shark just flicked her way through the last hoop—Ooh, no! She touched it! Too bad! Penalty!"

There was a loud HONK!

"With one moment left, the Jahk skips ahead and rings the bell! Wow, what an upset! Sharkbait, favored to win, drops out of this round. They'll be on the Wheel of Misfortune later today."

I peered at the flying shark's obstacle course. It seemed to me that the last ring of magik she had to swim through was just a little lower than the others, making it impossible for her to dodge. I shook my head. Maybe I was imagining the in-equality. The angle at which we were viewing the contest was an oblique one.

The rest of the teams played out the tightrope game. The feathers chose my students next.

"Have you ever been on a tightrope before?" the female commentator demanded as the Sorcerer's Apprentices made their way out onto the main floor of the Arena.

"Do we look like circus performers?" Pologne asked haughtily. "We're graduate students!"

The female beamed into the crystal balls tracking them. "And there you have it, ladies and gentlemen! They're graduate students! But who's going to walk the high wire? You?" she asked Bee.

"Well, personally, ma'am, I'm afraid of heights," Bee replied politely.

"Then, who?"

The Apprentices went into a huddle on the sidelines.

"And—break!" Freezia shouted perkily.

Jinetta withdrew from the circle, took a deep breath, squared her shoulders and marched to the narrow tower. Up, up went the former cheerleader, fifty, sixty, seventy feet. At last she reached the platform. I could see that she was trembling as she surveyed the narrow string before her. She breathed out a whisper.

"Is she praying?" Markie asked.

"No," I said, reading my former student's lips. "She just said 'spoo.'" I grinned. She couldn't fall now. To think that a haughty Pervect would rely in a moment of crisis on the discovery of a lowly Klahd—I was proud of both of them.

"The Sorcerer's Apprentices will face one of our most formidable teams," Schlein announced. "The Bald Guy with Muscles!"

The shiny-domed male hitched one arm through a rung of the ladder and waved to the cheering audience. He swung himself up effortlessly, and stepped out onto the wire.

"Come on!" he roared. "Let's get this over with!"

Naturally, a one-man team couldn't supply himself with the necessary components to build his Jack-in-the-box. A host of boiler-suited stagehands jogged out and assembled beneath his tower.

"Ready?" Schlein shouted. "Go!"

Jinetta tiptoed out onto the swaying wire. The others ran along underneath. Bee seemed to calculate the speed of the wind whistling down into the mountain bowl before throwing the components up to Jinetta. Tolk flicked his share of the pieces up to her with a toss of his head.

"Come on, come on, come on!" I could hear him calling as he ran. "You can do it! You can do it!"

Among the items Jinetta needed was a piece of string. It would be too light to throw without magikal aid, but Freezia had no trouble whisking it up to her sorority sister. Jinetta tottered along, keeping one eye on the wire and one on what she was doing as she wound the string around the spindle. She tucked the clown-faced doll under her arm, and lost her grip on a small brass box. It fell, but Tolk took a flying leap and caught it before it hit the ground. Pologne pointed her finger at him, and the box rose up within grabbing distance of Jinetta.

"Everyone levitate the pieces around her," Pologne said.

"I can't tell where to put this one!" Jinetta wailed.

"I think I see where it goes," Bee said. "Slide it underneath the black lever there!"

Pologne twisted her hands around, and the box followed the motions.

"Runners can't help with assembly," Schlein announced in disapproving tones.

"Drat!" Pologne said. "Jinny!"

"I see it!" Jinetta slotted the box into place and shoved the clown down onto a piece she had just attached.

They were only yards away from the other platform. The Bald Guy with Muscles had no magik, but he seemed to be working just as fast as Jinetta with magik and five helpers. Seeing his progress, the Pervect began to panic. Her hands shook, and small pieces rained down.

Her team, my students, were right there with her. Bee kept them organized, telling who to send up their next piece when. He had the last section, the wooden flap that formed the top of the box.

"And—one!" he cried. He hefted the piece upward. Freezia took it over and flew it to hover beside Jinetta.

Three feet. Jinetta tiptoed along. She began to crank the handle on the box's side. The Bald Guy was two notes behind her. With a grim look in her direction he started cranking faster. So did she. It was a race to see whose song would finish first. Jinetta all but leaped off the wire onto the platform just as the clown's head popped out of the box one heartbeat ahead of the Bald Guy's.

"We have a winner!" Schlein crowed. Graciously he escorted Jinetta down from her platform. "Too bad, Bald Guy! Next up, the Dragonettes face off against the Gargoyle Girls!"

The Geek's bubble inflated again to take center stage. The Deveel tried to look gracious about it, but I could tell he was taken aback that the group had prevailed against the muscular male. He clapped his hands, and the fiery letters rearranged themselves. My students were now at a respectable nine to five against.

I held up my glass of wine.

"To the Sorcerer's Apprentices," I said.

"To you," Bunny said. "Those kids could never have pulled it together without you."

"They did all the work," I said modestly.

"Oh, really? Who scoped out the sites ahead of time? Who sat up all night working on curricula so they would learn something?"

"C'mon," I said, embarrassed. "Let's talk about something else."

"Do you remember when that team from Crocodilia blew the Jack-in-the-box round?" Markie asked, adroitly changing the subject.

"Wait a minute—yes, I do," Tananda laughed. "That was hilarious."

"What happened?" I asked, curious.

"Oh, the whole thing was a mismatch," Tananda said. "Their feet aren't made for walking on something narrow. They should have given that poor female a tube like the shark's. Watching her scooting along the wire upright, going 'Ooch! Ooch! Ooch!' every step! I was on the floor!"

"And at the last minute she dropped it," Markie said. "It was a hoot. Her teammates dove for that box like dolphins after a fish. Too late. Crash!"

Since I was now passionately interested, the ladies shared their favorite *Sink or Swim* stories with me. I kept half an eye on the broadcast, waiting for the next moment when my students had another chance to shine. I was enjoying it all.

Chapter Twenty-Three

"I think the dragon's cheating."
BILGEWATER*

"And now," Schlein announced, gathering our attention once more, "today's third round! This is a free-for-all involving all of the groups still in the running. If one of the losers from the previous round wins, they get to give their penalty point to the team they triumph over! If they lose again, they're out of the game, so this is a crucial contest!"

All seven of the surviving teams assembled on the vast floor. Schlein settled to the floor in their midst, beaming with all of his shiny white teeth.

"You all have a designated area to which you must go. Your team name is on a sign overhead." Schlein gestured, and the names lit up around the perimeter of the huge room. "That's all. Or is it all?" he asked, with a witty look at the crystal ball which must have been next to his shoulder. "In order to get there, you have to get past your opponents, who must prevent you getting to your safe spot. Anything goes! And to make this REALLY interesting, we are bringing in some of our house champions! Welcome the She Spider!"

I gasped as a tremendous black arachnid lowered itself into the Arena. It was so big the hairs on the joints of its legs looked like marlinspikes. Its multiple eyes glinted. Schlein stepped up and pointed toward a complicated gizmo that the stagehands wheeled into place behind her.

"The way to get past the She Spider is very easy. All you have to do is shoot an arrow into the target over her head. That will dump this barrel of water on her head. She hates water!"

The invisible orchestra played WAAA waaa waa waaaaaaa!

---

* We'll give you this one—from the graphic novel DUNCAN AND MALLORY by Mel White and Robert Asprin.

The spider and her apparatus were at the center of the stage. I wondered how anyone would run afoul of her. There was plenty of room to avoid her reach.

"We also have Sergeant Pep-up's Mutileers!"

These were evidently famous and popular. As a host of purple-uniformed soldiers marched in to wild applause, the orchestra struck up a tune, and an unseen men's chorus sang, "We are the Merry Mutileers! We cut off noses, hands and ears! Hup two three four, you're going to die today! Here's to the Merry Mutileers!"

Tananda was singing along. She gave me a shy glance and fell silent.

"They're cute," she said. "I dated a few of them once."

"Do they really mutilate the contestants?" I asked.

"Oh, not most of the time!"

I gulped. The Mutileers were followed by a couple of Ogres in crash helmets, nine Imps with bludgeons on skateboards, and a barrelful of screeching monkeys. I'd thought the Arena stage huge, but it filled up pretty quickly with all the 'house champions.'

"A-one," Schlein began the count. All the players braced themselves, facing toward the haven they had to reach. "A-two. A-three. Go!"

Free-for-all was right. The chaos that ensued looked like Free Sample Day at the Bazaar. My students started out in the direction of their free space, only to be intercepted by the Gargoyle Girls. The stonefaced males and females matched every move the Apprentices made, dodging left and right, with big grins on their gray stone faces. Pologne's expression turned impatient, and she flung a hand upward. The Gargoyle nearest her went flying overhead. It landed on the back of the Dragonettes' dragon, who turned around with a roar, looking to see who had done that. The Apprentices scattered as the dragon charged them, followed by the Trolls.

My students didn't have the bulk or the strength, but they could move. Melvine took to the air and thumbed his nose in the dragon's face. It spewed out a hot jet of flame at him. Melvine easily ducked upward. The dragon spread its wings to follow him, and knocked half the Shock Jahks off their feet.

Sharkbait saw its opportunity. The whole school flitted neatly around the dragon's whipping tail and headed towards its glowing sign and freedom.

They had not reckoned with the Bald Guy with Muscles. Clambering up the She Spider's tower, he evaded her grasping legs easily, and leaped down on top of the two leading sharks. He rode them with one foot on each, punching at their sensitive gills. The rest of the school flew at him, mouths open to tear him to shreds. The Bald Guy merely smiled, as if this was what he had been waiting for all his life. He disappeared in a waving welter of tails and fins.

I caught sight of Melvine emerging in the middle of a circle of Pervects, their fangs gleaming as they moved in on him. He looked terrified. With a wild yell, Bee came swinging in on a rope and dropped into their midst, distracting the Pervects enough for Melvine to gather his wits.

BAMF! They vanished.

I just spotted the two of them as they appeared near the line separating the Sorcerer's Apprentices' free spot from the rest of the arena floor. Melvine staggered and shook his head.

"Oh, no, you don't," Schlein's voice chided him over the loud speaker. "No magiking your way to safety! Uh-oh, here come the Mutileers!"

Before Bee and Melvine could race over the line, several of the uniformed soldiers charged them. They retreated into the midst of the melee, where the Gargoyle Girls were duking it out with the Ogres. Freezia was in the middle, repelling blows with bursts of magik. She shrieked every time one of them got near her.

"Fresh meat!" a Gargoyle yelled.

Melvine turned and punched him in the face. The next moment he dropped to his knees, clutching his throbbing fist.

"Ooh," I groaned in sympathy.

"They always do that," the Geek observed.

"Haw, haw, haw," the Gargoyle laughed.

"Hey, ugly!" Bee taunted him. When the stone being turned to look at him, Bee stuck his thumbs in his ears and wiggled them. The Gargoyle lumbered after him. Bee ducked around the nearest Ogre. It seemed to shrink and become less hairy. I realized that Bee had thrown Datspell on both of them.

The Gargoyle grabbed the now disguised Ogre by the shoulder and spun it around. He landed one solid punch on the chin. "Bee" just staggered back half a pace then returned the roundhouse with interest. The two of them began to pound one another, to the delighted cheers from the audience, who had caught the whole transformation. Bee helped Freezia to her feet. Freezia tossed opponents out of their way as they ran to rejoin Melvine.

"Wheee-oop!"

On the other side of the She Spider, I spotted Jinetta running away from a trio of Imps on skateboards. She ducked around the stand of bows and arrows meant to disarm the spider, swung underneath the gigantic arachnid herself, and rolled. The spider noticed Jinetta and reached for her with one hefty claw. It just missed her ankle. The Imps swung their clubs at her. They whanged against the metal frame supporting the She Spider, making it ring. The spider whirled around on her silk thread and clawed at them.

Jinetta emerged from the other side, right into a mob of monkeys. They screamed and clambered up her body and perched on her head. She pulled one after another, throwing them at the irate spider. Distracted, she didn't see the Imps coming around the corner after her. They swung at her. Jinetta flung them back with a wave of magik. More Imps homed in on her. With a set jaw she started banging them into one another. They staggered and fell down. Within a moment, they were up again.

Pologne and Tolk had made it about halfway across the stage to the free space when a purple-clad Mutileer seemed to pop up right out of the stage. Tolk ducked underneath the soldier's sword, and grabbed the man's ankle in his teeth. Pologne ripped the soldier's helmet off his head and started belaboring him with it.

More Mutileers came out of the floor to the aid of their comrade. In no time Pologne and Tolk found themselves at bay, leaping back to avoid swinging swords and jabbing pikes. Pologne turned several of the weapons against their wielders, but she and Tolk were greatly outnumbered.

"Funny, it looks like the house champions are targeting my students," I said.

"No," Tananda reassured me. "They pick on everyone. Sergeant Pep-up likes to keep things moving."

"No, really," I said. "Look!"

The uniformed soldiers seemed to be everywhere. Several of them were in between Bee, Melvine and Freezia and the safe haven. Freezia was flagging, her arms no longer held as high as she fought to push the Mutileers out of their way. Bee looked tired, too. He was the weakest magikally, with only three really good spells at his command, none of which were much use in this onslaught. He had no other reserves than his muscular strength. Melvine helped keep both of them from getting hurt, but I saw sweat running off his little bald head. What's more, when one of my students did manage to score a hit on one of their opponents, it didn't seem to slow them down.

"Someone's protecting them magikally," I protested.

I heard a scream. Sergeant Pep-up himself had picked Pologne up in his arms. He dashed into the middle of the stage and heaved her into the waiting clutches of the She Spider. It bit her on the neck, and she went limp. The spider started wrapping her up in silk. I was furious.

A soldier raised his sword, and struck. Melvine went down with a bleeding gash on his head. The Mutileer threw the Cupy over his shoulder and headed toward the center dais.

Jinetta ran after them. She gasped as she saw her sorority sister in the spider's web, and dashed toward the rack of equipment.

"It's rigged," I announced as I saw a phalanx of uniforms surround the remaining Apprentices, now maneuvering them all toward the spider's lair. "They're all going to die. I have to get in there."

"You?" Markie asked. "You can't get involved. Those kids signed an agreement to participate."

"They didn't know it was going to be rigged," I argued. "Look!"

One after another bowstring broke as Jinetta tried to fit it onto a bow. She reached for another one. If she didn't manage to get the bow functional and shoot the arrow into the target, Pologne was going to be strangled by the giant spider.

"Maybe one," I said. "But I'll bet they are all frayed."

"They'll cope," Tananda said. "They have to."

Freezia grabbed a string out of Jinetta's hand and ran her hands along it.

"Attagirl," Bunny cheered. "She must be strengthening it."

Jinetta managed to get it onto the bow and notched an arrow. ZING! She hit the bull's eye over the spider, which ought to have released the deluge of water.

Nothing happened.

Jinetta looked around for an official. No one stopped the contest. Pologne's body was wound in nearly invisible threads from head to foot, and the spider was busily spinning more into the cocoon.

"I have to go," I said. I got up, but I couldn't take my eyes off the images. Tolk took a blow to the skull from an Imp sailing by on his wheeled board and went down howling. Bunny grabbed my arm.

"You can't," she said.

"Why not?"

"Because—because you've been banned from Perv. Remember?"

I groaned and sank back in my chair. It all came back to me now. The run-ins with the police, the long fruitless searches, the friend who turned questionable businessman and got me declared permanent persona non grata and blacklisted forever from a whole dimension.

There weren't too many people who could make a claim like that.

At the moment, I couldn't say I was grateful for the honor. I watched the fighting going, wishing that I could leap into the insubstantial images and take part in the action. The longer this mess went on, the greater the chance that one of my ill-prepared students was going to be pushed into a situation where he or she might be killed, and no lectures on teamwork or planning would make that any better.

"What can I do?" I demanded, stalking up and back. The more I watched, the more worried I became. "I've got to stop this *now*."

"Disguise spell," Tananda said promptly. "It's what you do best."

I waved away the suggestion. "A disguise spell is fine, but I can't pretend to be just anyone. I need to be impressive enough to step in on Perv and get people to do what I want them to. I need *credentials*. I can't just appear as a bystander and try to straighten things out."

"You have the perfect disguise," Tanda points out. "Aahz."

I stopped dead in my pacing. "I couldn't do that."

"Yes, you could," Tananda insisted. "Remember, I know more about him than you do. He's got an impressive record there. He was at the top of his class at MIP, and except for you, he's the most visible part of M.Y.T.H., Inc. What could be more perfect? Or Pervect?"

"He wouldn't go for it. I could really louse up his reputation."

Tananda came to put an arm around me. "Sure he would go for it, Tiger. Think about it—the story's gone around that he's lost his powers, but if you show up and toss a little magik around, they'll believe he's gotten them back. That won't harm his reputation, it'll enhance it. Let Aahz take it from there, if anyone is ever stupid enough to challenge him. But you need to get those kids out. They're out of their depth."

In the crystal, I watched Markie's nephew surrounded by a the entire contingent of Imps, raising their clubs to bludgeon him. Melvine started the elemental whirlwind, but they were prepared for him. A robed magician stepped in and waved his hands. Melvine stumbled to a halt, confusion turning to alarm as the Imps started swinging. Throwing his arms over his head, he began ducking and weaving between the wheeled menaces.

"Besides," Bunny said, "all this mess was Aahz's idea in the first place. He's the one who sent the Pervects to you."

"I'd better ask," I began weakly.

"*I'll* ask him, Tanda insisted, and BAMFed out before I could stop her. She was back in a twinkling.

"Go," she confirmed.

It took absolutely no time to assume my former mentor's face and form. The fact I was several inches taller than Aahz wouldn't make any difference in my carriage; Aahz's reputation for keeping strangers (and apprentices) at arm's length would help me maintain the subterfuge. I patted my cheeks, but I felt no difference, nor could I see any in the mirror.

"Perfect," Bunny said, walking around me to check the disguise. "Or, should I say, Pervect? Remember, don't smile. Aahz hardly ever smiles, unless he's really ticked off."

"I don't feel like smiling," I grunted.

"Gleep?" my pet asked plaintively. He sniffed me up and down, not able to reconcile my scent with Aahz's appearance. He and Aahz had never been fast friends.

"It's me," I confirmed, patting him on the head. "Don't worry, Gleep. This is for a good cause."

"I'd better go," I said impatiently.

"Not so fast, handsome," Tananda said, cuddling up close to me. "You don't think we're letting you go in there alone, do you?"

"I can't risk taking any of you with me," I said. "If they catch me, I could be locked up for years."

"They won't catch you," Tananda said. "But don't go in there without backup. It might take all of us to pull your students out of danger."

"What were you always telling those kids?" Bunny added, throwing a hand toward the image of the struggling team. "Team up and delegate?"

I groaned. "Don't throw my words back at me."

"Do you mean them, or don't you?" Bunny challenged me.

"Of course I do!"

"Then, it's settled." She nodded to Tananda and Markie. *BAMF!*

Chapter Twenty-Four

"I'm dealing myself in."
M. HALL

Thanks to Bytina, we were able to pinpoint exactly where we needed to appear on Perv. Though the Arena was supposedly in a "secret location concealed deep in the mountains above a lonely valley visited by no living creature since time began," the magik the place was giving off, not to mention the triangulation provided from thousands of crystal balls dimensions-wide, made it a beacon to the naked eye, let alone to a sophisticated piece of technology.

We arrived on the lip of a natural ampitheater. Winds whistled around us, nipping the tips of my ears. I ignored the discomfort as I stalked down the aisle past thousands of cheering spectators enjoying the brawl happening on the vast round stage below. The hollow stone bowl magnified the sounds so I could hear every grunt, every yell, every cry of pain. I jogged down the endless staircase with the three women behind me.

Every hundred steps or so there was a landing. About the fifth one, an adolescent Pervect in a vest and bow tie stepped out.

"Sir, may I see your ticket?"

"Out of my way," I snarled.

"I'm afraid you can't go into the lower sections without a ticket."

I was not in a mood to argue. I threw him out of the way, using my levitation skills instead of the Pervish strength I lacked. He landed on top of several spectators. Blurting out apologies, he crawled out and hurried after us.

"Stop, sir. You have to stop."

Tananda wriggled up and attached herself firmly to my elbow, playing the part of Trollish eye candy.

"Don't you know who he is?" she asked the usher.

"No, I don't. And if he doesn't show me a ticket, I'm going to have him thrown out!"

I ignored him, but by that time we had attracted the attention of several other ushers, not to mention hundreds of paying customers. I kept them at bay with magik, intent on reaching my destination. Any minute now one of them was going to call security.

"Wave to the nice people," she murmured. "Make them think you're a celebrity. Aahz would."

The next time I made eye contact with an audience member, I put on a big fake smile and waved to her. When she poked her neighbor and pointed, I waved to him, too. Pretty soon the whole march down the aisle, ushers and all, looked like the arrival of a star. I prevented them from following me up onto the stage. Even the ushers seemed to be having doubts.

"Thanks for the escort, guys," I called as my small party scaled the sheer steps to the stage.

My students were still in the center. Pologne was now wrapped up in spider silk. Jinetta and Bee were up on top of the framework, trying to dislodge the barrel of water with magik and brute strength. I applied my own power, but it wouldn't budge. It wasn't meant to move! More cheating.

I grabbed the first person I saw, a young Deveel woman in a tight pink skirt and white blouse who clutched a clipboard to her chest.

"Who's in charge here?" I demanded.

She looked at me and my three companions and put her nose in the air.

"I'm sorry, sir, but this is a closed set." She spoke into her lapel, and several large Pervect males in uniforms appeared at her back.

"I want to see the boss," I said.

"You're trespassing, bub. If you don't leave under your own power right now, we'll be happy to assist you," said the Pervect with the most gold braid on his sleeves.

"Power?" I asked, a slow smile twisting my lips.

Creating a band of magik around the entire group of guards, I squeezed them all together into a tight little knot. I was so angry that I channeled more energy than I ever could before. They started gasping, their faces turning interesting shades of green.

"Hey, Tiger, take it easy!" Tananda cautioned me. "Leave them some breath so they can answer your question!"

"Sir," the captain squeaked. "Sir, what can we do for you?"

"Who is in charge of this program?" I asked, very sweetly. "I want to see him. Pronto."

"The Executive Producer," the head security guard gasped out. "His name's The Geek!"

"Take us to him," I said. "The Geek knows me."

The knot of guards shuffled ahead of us as a single unit. Tananda and Bunny each held onto one arm, gauging whether or not I was going to fly off the handle. I tried to keep myself under control. I should have realized when I heard his name that he had to be more involved than just offering an analysis of the teams. He was responsible for all this! Markie toddled ahead of us, playing the part of my adorable little niece.

"Lookie there, Uncle Aahz!" she said in her cutest voice, pointing a tiny pink finger at a Deveel in a shiny suit. "There's Mr. The Geek right now!"

I thrust my way past more crew members, heading for that familiar face.

The Geek huddled under a scenery overhang with a collection of production personnel. There was a clutch of magicians in robes and holding huge, multifaceted crystal balls— members of several species but one union, to judge by the insignia prominently displayed on their right sleeves—and young women of various species holding clipboards. He turned at the sound of his name. First he saw the tightly clustered knot of guards. Then, over their heads, he saw me. He did a double-take then started running away.

"Hold it, Geek," I ordered. Releasing my hold on the guards, I threw out a loop of power, tightened it, and dragged him up and over the heads of his doorwardens. I landed him in front of me on his feet, nice and easy, but I kept a firm magikal grip on him.

"Aahz," he choked out. "You've—you've got your powers back. How—nice?"

"Yeah," I grunted, in my best imitation of my former mentor's voice. "And just in time to use them to right a major injustice. One YOU are causing."

"M—mmm—min—me? A mmm—major injustice?"

"You. You remember Markie, don'tcha? And Tananda? And Bunny?"

He certainly did remember Markie. She smiled sweetly up at him. In spite of the grip I had on him, the Geek tried to climb the sky.

"Aahz," the Geek squeaked. "Old buddy! Let's make this a nice, quiet talk."

"Let's," I said. "But first you stop that contest that's going on right now."

"Nnn—nn—now?" the Geek stammered.

I took a fistful of his collar and raised him over my head. It was part levitation spell and part genuine anger, but he ended up in the air, dangling from the end of my arm.

From out of nowhere, a second contingent of the usual kind of muscle came running towards us.

"Call them off," I said softly. "Call them all off."

The Geek, whose complexion began to darken as soon as I picked him up, waved his hands. The security guards backed away.

"Now, stop that contest. I insist." I shook the Deveel at every syllable.

Tananda came over and cuddled up against my right arm.

"Aahz, don't kill him," she said, in her most honeyed tones. "That gets so messy."

I shook the Geek again, who was doing a fair amount of vibrating all by himself. "Why not?" I growled.

"Well, if you do, they'll have to find another odds-maker."

"So what?" I asked. "This one's broken. They *need* a new one."

"Aahz, Aahz, *buddy*," the Geek pleaded. "What is it you want?"

"I've been watching this contest from K—from the Bazaar, and it just looks to me like you're shifting the odds to suit yourself.

"What do you care?" the Geek countered. "It's not like you've met any of these kids before." Enlightenment dawned on his peaky face. "You must have money riding on it. Put me down and let's talk insurance bets, Aahz. I promise you won't lose a single silver piece. How about it?"

"I don't have money riding on this," I snarled. I wasn't imitating Aahz; the fury emanated straight from me. "I wouldn't bet on anything you had a hand in."

"Er, I can see you might be a little reluctant—Could you put me down? I think people are starting to notice." He pointed over my shoulder.

I glanced back. Several Sittacomedians and a few Trolls wearing SOS insignia had started to move in on us. I flung back a hand, and the security staff went flying.

"Call off ALL of your security. And stop that contest! Now."

"I'll stop it, I'll stop it!" the Geek exclaimed. "Just put me down!"

I lowered him to the floor. "Do it."

The Geek gestured to another young female Deveel in a short, tight skirt. She scurried over, brandishing a pencil and a clipboard.

"Take this one down. Dip the lights. Go to commercial," the Geek ordered.

The young woman spoke into her collar.

Immediately, several flunkies in matte black clothing ran around to do her bidding. Sergeant Pep-up's men suddenly sprang to attention and jogged off the field, leaving their opponents looking confused. Teammates picked one another up from the floor, and limped to the side where white-coated Pervish medics waited with stretchers and little black bags to have their injuries seen to. The monsters all went back to the sidelines. Some of them paused to have makeup daubed onto their faces by Pervects in white smocks carrying palettes and brushes. The spider lowered herself to the ground, where her palps were shined by a couple of Deveels with buffing brushes. Tolk hovered around his fellow teammates, dispensing dogtor magik and sympathetic whines.

Schlein's resonant voice echoed over the darkened arena.

"And now, folks, a word from our sponsor, Caca Doodle Doo, the leading manufacturer on Perv of Realistic Doggie Doodle with Lifelike Odor that Sticks to Your Hands, a product of Edvik Enterprises…"

I didn't have time to remark upon the coincidence. I had more important things on my mind.

"Are you in charge of this entire enterprise?" I asked.

"Not so loud!" the Geek pleaded. "Come into my office." He urged me towards his bubble. I raised an eyebrow at the ladies. Tananda and Markie melted away into the crowd. Bunny attached herself to my elbow and accompanied me in.

I waited until the side sealed up, leaving us alone in the soundproofed sphere.

"Now," the Geek said, sitting down at his desk with his hands folded together on top. "What is troubling you, my friend?"

"It's very simple," I said. "I want you to halt this contest right now. It's off-balance, and people are going to get hurt!"

"I can't do that, old friend," the Geek said, regret written large on his ruddy face. "Danger is the name of the game. It spikes those ratings right through the roof. The sponsors love it."

"I'm going to spike YOU right through the roof," I growled. "Let me put it this way: I can handle the concept of danger. Sometimes it's fun, but only where there's a chance that I can win in the end—I prefer a good chance, but I'll take what I can get. But I have been observing this contest today, and I have seen good evidence that you are skewing the games to make sure certain teams are eliminated. That's bad, considering that your contestants come into this with the understanding that they have to play fair. That means they are expecting you to play fair, too. Right?"

"Er, I'm not really admitting anything, Aahz," the Geek said nervously. "You're not, not recording this, are you?"

I planted a hand on my chest. "Would I be as underhanded as you?"

"Frankly, yes," the Geek said. "I've known you for centuries, Aahz. You're doing some fine talking about fair play, but you haven't always been completely honest in your dealings."

"On Deva!" I bellowed. "On Deva, *anything* is fair if you can get away with it. If you want to play it by those rules, I can do that. You didn't get away with it. I saw you. These fine ladies saw you."

"A Trollop," the Geek scoffed. "A Klahd and a Cupy."

My voice dropped again. "You know who they are. And, I might point out, that the Klahd you are making fun of is a close relation to a very powerful man with important connections in the Bazaar and elsewhere. So, show some—respect."

I shoved him back in his chair with a thrust of magik, just to remind him I had it. "Now, I can go public with what I saw, and get your sponsors to yank their backing, or maybe you'll just have to stop interfering and tilting the odds the way you want them. I assume you have heavy bets standing on certain teams, and it would look very bad if those bets became public knowledge."

"I can fix everything!" the Geek said. My fist came up under his nose. He blanched to pink. "I mean, I won't *fix* it, I'll unfix it! I mean."

"You mean you're gonna make this a fair contest, don't you?" I asked, going from gravel-voiced to sweetness in mid-sentence.

"Yes! Yes! That's what I mean! It'll be even, I swear it! From now until the end, when the winner is declared, I swear, there won't be a single deliberate irregularity. Aahz, this is gonna cost me a lot of money. Can I count on you to keep it quiet, if I do what you want? Please?"

"All right," I said. I dropped him. The Geek scrambled up and beckoned to a third fetching Deveel in a very short skirt. She dashed into the bubble and put her pencil to her clipboard.

"Honey, here's what I want you to do…" He reeled off a long list of instructions. She scribbled notes. I folded my arms

as I had seen Aahz do so many times, and glared at the Geek
to make sure he didn't back out on any part of his promise.
"Oh, and get the lottery box, Honey. Bring it up here. I've got
to—take a look at it."

Honey gave us a toothy smile and vanished.

"Is that all right, Aahz?" the Geek asked, wringing his hands
together. "Is everything okay now?"

"Sure it is," I said. The Geek relaxed and headed for his
chair. Before he could sit down I beckoned with a finger, and
the chair came rolling over to me. I sat down in it and leaned
back with my arms behind my head.

"What are you doing?" he asked, aghast.

"Sticking around," I said. "I just want to make sure that
you keep your promises. I'll leave once this contest is over—
no matter who wins. It'll be a nice surprise for both of us."

"Yes, it will," he said weakly. He gestured to a stagehand
to bring him a chair for him and one for Bunny. I admit it was
rude of me to take a seat and not offer it to her, but I had to
make the point that I was in control. I glanced up at her to see
if she was angry, but she wore a very pleased grin.

The Geek noticed the expressions pass between us and
gulped loudly. "Er, may I offer you a drink? Miss Bunny?"

Music played to amuse the audience while the stage was
blacked out. The Geek lowered his bubble down to the Arena
floor to issue a few orders in person. Bunny sat drinking her
Pink Wyvern cocktail with a ladylike little finger stuck out
while I stumped up and back in the Geek's little office, trying
to look as much like Aahz as possible. I spotted the Sorcerer's
Apprentices a few yards from us then hastily glanced away. I
knew they couldn't possibly recognize me in this disguise, but
I was afraid one of my mannerisms might give me away.

Unfortunately, they had spotted us, too. Jinetta touched
her sorority sisters' shoulders and pointed in our direction. The
three of them came marching over.

"Hi, Bunny," they said.

"Hi, girls! I can't believe how well you're doing," Bunny said. "I didn't know you were going to be in this contest."

"Well," Freezia began, "we didn't want to say anything in case someone overheard us. Teams have been sabotaged in the past before they got to the contest. Skeeve isn't mad, is he?"

"Oh, no!" Bunny assured them, giving them a big hug. "He's very proud of you."

They all smiled with relief.

"Good," Jinetta breathed. "We all have a great deal of respect for him. We will always think of him as our real teacher."

I felt myself tearing up a little bit. I reached into my belt pouch for a handkerchief and blew my nose loudly to conceal dabbing at my eyes. That brought Jinetta's attention to me.

"Aahz. Are you connected with this game somehow?"

"N—no, I'm not," I said. "I'm just here to observe fair play."

"I see," she said. "Will you be here later? I want to talk with you when this is all over."

"Sure," I said. I didn't plan to be around to have my disguise penetrated, so I felt free to promise almost anything. She stalked back to the others. I could tell they were talking about us.

Bunny noticed. "You could eavesdrop," she reminded me.

"Somehow," I said, "I am not sure I really want to hear what they're saying."

The bustling ended, and the Geek returned to join us in the office.

"Up," he ordered it. Obediently, the silver bubble rose high over the great bowl.

Schlein appeared in the middle of the stage and held up a graceful hand.

"Let the brawl *recommence!*"

Chapter Twenty-Five

"My compliments to the chef."
S. TODD (THE BARBER)

"Well, we were sorry to say farewell to the Bald Guy with Muscles," Schlein confided to the audience at the start of the game the next day.

"Awwwww," the audience chorused.

I could see now that they were prompted on what to say by a gigantic cluster of fireflies that zipped around out of view of the crystal balls and spelled out words. At the moment they said, "Disappointment!"

"Yes, sir," Schlein continued, "it was a close one, but the Wheel of Misfortune stops where it will, when it will! And on this last day of *Sink or Swim: Peru,* we rejoin our celebrated odds-maker, the Geek, for his take on today's contests! Ladies and gentlemen, the Geek!"

The fireflies spelled out "You love him!" and the audience went wild.

Schlein appeared in the bubble. Dozens of magicians in robes appeared around it, all pointing their crystal balls at us. Bunny, wearing a very tight peach-colored dress that squeezed her natural attributes both up *and* down, perched on a stool next to the Geek's odds board, and twiddled her fingers at the handsome Sittacomedian. I stood near the wall with my arms crossed. Somewhere below, Tananda and Markie were keeping an eye on my students. One way or another, the Sorcerers Apprentices would be safe.

"And we have guests today!" Schlein announced, never missing a beat. "Who are these fine people, Geek?"

"Well, this lovely lady is Bunny," the Geek explained, nervously. "She's going to be pointing at numbers for me today. Show 'em a two, Bunny."

Beaming, Bunny obligingly stood up and indicated the nearest number two.

"Well done, lovely lady!" Schlein exclaimed. "And this gentleman?"

"He's a well-known businessman and magician who has interests in the Bazaar on Deva, but as you can see, he's a native of this wonderful dimension where we are having our game here today. His name's Aahz—"

"—Mandius," I finished, holding out a hand to shake with Schlein. "Aahzmandius is the name."

I squeezed hard so he wouldn't think about the lack of scales on my skin. He withdrew, shaking his fingers to restore circulation.

"Pleased to meet you," Schlein said. "Well, now, Geek, let's hear today's odds, ably assisted," he confided to the magicians hovering outside the sphere, "by the beautiful Bunny."

The Geek went into his talk. "Of course you know that Sharkbait took it in the teeth last night, and went out during the brawl. Not one single fishie was able to get to the haven before time was called. That leaves the Shock Jahks at eleven to one. The Gargoyle Girls moved up the list with an excellent showing, with only one of their teammates still out on the floor at the whistle. The Sorcerer's Apprentices are four to one. They suffered a setback when Tolk the Canidian lost all his teeth dragging that Gargoyle around the floor. They've been replaced in his jaw by our dentists, but he's a sore pup this morning. The Dragonettes are still at three to one, and the All-Pervects continue to be my favorites for the championship."

Bunny pointed to the relevant details. I caught her frowning at the second-to-last line, but she switched on the brilliant smile again in time to be captured from several angles by the magicians covering the interview.

"Do you hear that, folks?" Schlein asked, beaming for the crystals. "And we move along to the next in our eating contests. You've seen quantity eating in one of our earlier episodes. Now, we challenge the contestants to eat quality—or lack thereof. We've got five colored feathers to see who will take one in the guts for the team. Are you ready?"

While he had been talking, the globe drifted down so that we were once again in the midst of the contestants.

"Yeah!" the teams shouted. Tolk, a bandage wound around his jaws, leaped up and down. The dragon, under tight control by one of the Trolls on its team, bobbed its head.

Schlein stepped out of the bubble and pointed heavenward. "Here come the Feathers of Fate!"

Drifting lazily on the stray breezes that whisked around the huge stone bowl, the five feathers dropped toward each team. I watched them for a moment, and noticed a telltale jerk or two. The feathers were being guided by some unseen hand.

"Geek," I growled.

The Deveel turned to me apologetically. "Aahz, we've got to balance the rounds. What if we have the dragon up against the Cupy? It's no contest! The audience will hate it. I swear, there won't be anything in the food but food."

I had to settle for the compromise. At least it wasn't putting my students at a disadvantage. "All right."

Schlein was on the spot to announce the unlucky diners. "And the Feather of Fate has chosen—Grunt, for the Dragonettes!"

A hefty Troll with dark purple fur came forward, waving to the audience with both hands.

"He'll be joined by Meghan of the Shock Jahks. Here comes the red feather—Nita for the Gargoyle Girls! For the All-Pervects, Crasmer. And Bee, for the Sorcerer's Apprentices! Come on and sit down at the table, folks!"

"This one's for all the cookies, folks," Schlein announced. "Oops, sorry, kids, I shouldn't mention cookies. You don't want to think about cookies or anything you can toss. Here come our chefs! Now, remember the rules. This one's not for penalty points. You have to eat what's in the bowl AND finish it. No dinner, no dessert! The survivors—I mean, the *winners*—of this round go on to our final challenge, the Monster Monster Challenge, which will determine who will *Sink or Swim!*"

"Now, the servers have been blindfolded," Schlein continued smoothly as five white-coated Deveels carrying trays felt their way blindly into the room. "They don't know who they're giving each dish to. You've got to pray it's something you can stomach. If you don't hold it down through the end of the round, you lose, and your team goes home. No consolation prizes—but we will give you something for your tummy. Ready?"

"Ready!" chorused the contestants.

"This way, servers! Follow the sound of my voice."

"This is the best elimination round I've ever come up with," the Geek confided as the bubble rose out of reach of the contestants.

"Sucker bet," I growled.

"Not always," the Geek said. "You won't believe how some of the players manage! A little old lady in the Imper contest won this round. Turns out she just couldn't taste anything, so it didn't bother her."

Below, the white-coated waiters made it to the table. They deposited covered dishes in front of each contestant then pulled back as the covers lifted off all by themselves. The audience let out an "Ooooooh."

I winced. All of the dishes looked sickening, but to my horror Bee had received a bowl of purple pseudopods that were all too familiar. Pervish cooking! I glared at the Geek.

"I told you, the All-Pervects were favored to win," he admitted sheepishly. "If they happened to get some home cooking, well—"

"So you cheat."

"Balance, Aahz, balance! Anyway, it doesn't matter. Crasmer got, hmm, let's see: stone chips in sulphur gravy. Look, the Gargoyle's eyeing that. It's a delicacy where she comes from!"

Schlein appeared beside them holding an old fashioned dinner bell. He tinkled it.

"Soup's on!"

Bee looked as terrified as I felt. I was sorry for him. It shouldn't befall a decent Klahd like him to have to face Pervish food twice in a lifetime, let alone twice in a month. The animate goo writhing in the dish started to feel its way toward the rim. Bee halfheartedly shoved them back. His companions shouted encouragement from the sidelines.

I felt like adding my voice to theirs. I wanted to shout down to him that he'd done this successfully once before. He could do it again! But I also knew that he dreaded putting any of those things in his mouth. My own stomach heaved as I remembered the flavor and texture, not to mention the MOTION.

The Troll stared at his bowl full of live spiders and scorpions. Could that be fear on his face? I had never known a Troll to blanch at any physical contest, no matter how difficult. It took him a moment to overcome the revulsion. Resolutely, he reached out a hairy paw, seized a wriggling tarantula, put it in his mouth and crunched it.

In moments, his face began to swell up.

"What's the matter?" Schlein asked.

"I'b allerjhic to sbiders," the Troll said. "Gotta—"

He got up and staggered toward the wings. The medics followed him, clutching their black bags.

Schlein turned to the rest of the team, waiting anxiously in the wings. "Sorry about that, Dragonettes! You're out!"

"Come on, Bee! Come on!" the rest of the Sorcerer's Apprentices chanted. "Eat it eat it eat it eat it!"

Though his face was pale, Bee shot his comrades a hearty thumb's up. He took his spoon and resolutely thunked one of the pseudopods. It stiffened then went limp. With a visible gulp of nervousness, Bee scooped it into the spoon and brought it to his lips. The crowd fell silent.

Face wrinkled, he stuffed the mouthful in, and swallowed it.

The crowd went wild.

Next to him, Crasmer hunched over the plate of mashed stone, spooning it up as fast as he could, but each mouthful seemed to take an eternity to chew. I cringed at the cracking, crunching sounds, wondering if the teeth were grinding the rocks, or vice versa.

The Shock Jahk sat transfixed, staring at her entrée, which consisted of one single, round, white object twice the size of my fist that sat in the middle of her plate. The entrée stared back. It was an eyeball, garnished with a sprig of parsley.

"What about you, Meghan?" Schlein prompted.

"I—I—I can't do it!" The Jahk sprang up from her place and fled to the waiting arms of her teammates. The Shock Jahks all looked, well, shocked.

A Sittacomedian female with a microphone was in time to pick up the comment from the team captain, who was comforting his weeping teammate. "I didn't realize that when you said you were holding the contest *on* Perv that the contest would BE Perverted!"

The Gargoyle shoved away her empty bowl and rose to her feet with her hands clasped in victory.

The female commentator flew to her side and held out the microphone.

"Congratulations, Nita, and with five minutes to go!"

"Thanks," the Gargoyle said, winking at her companions. "And I just want to say—ulp."

"You want to say ulp?" the Sittacomedian asked, with a puzzled glance she shared with the audience.

"I mean—urp!"

"And what does that mean?"

The meaning became evident a moment later. Nita the Gargoyle dashed for the nearest receptacle and rejected the vile green and yellow mess that she had eaten.

"Too bad!" Schlein boomed, sympathetically. "Only two contestants left. Will they make it?"

I crossed my fingers. Bee was doing well. Except to stun his food long enough to eat it, he didn't look at it. Each bite went down very, very carefully, and he waited in between each to make sure it wasn't going to come up.

Crasmer was following a similar pattern. The Pervect challenger looked nauseated. There weren't many things one of his kind couldn't eat, in spite of the difficulty I'd had convincing my students of that, but unrefined minerals had to be on the short list. Scoop, crunch, gulp. Scoop, crunch, gulp.

Slam, scoop, gulp.

Scoop, crunch, gulp.

It was neck-and-neck to see who would finish first. Two more bites to go. One more—!

"That was it!" Schlein announced. "And here's the bell! We have two winners! Step up, kids. And how was it?"

"Awful," Bee said. "Worse than army food."

"Ha-ha," Schlein said. "How about you, Crasmer?"

"What he said," Crasmer agreed.

"Well, there you have it, folks! Going to the final round are the Sorcerer's Apprentices and the All-Pervects, your Perv home team!"

The audience didn't need the fireflies to go completely insane with joy. Bunny and I danced around the Geek's little office. On the ampitheater floor, the teams ran out to congratulate their champions. Both contestants waved bravely to the audiences.

"Stay tuned for the Monster Monster Challenge. And now, a word from our sponsor, Blix Restaurants. If you want the finest in Pervish cooking, or the best sausages, cabbage or stuffed peppers from any dimension, eat at Blix!"

At the very mention of food, Bee turned green. Crasmer turned greener. In unison, as if they had rehearsed it, they were violently sick. Stagehands rushed in with wands to clean up.

As soon as the lights went down, I saw Bee and Crasmer being sick. It didn't matter—the lights had already gone down. They had succeeded, and without any interference from the Geek's tweaking the odds.

"Who woulda known that the Troll was allergic to spiders?" he asked innocently.

Well, almost no interference.

"What happens now?" I demanded.

"Well," Bunny began animatedly, "the remaining teams have to make it through a maze. In the maze is a fearsome monster. The one you face is chosen at random depending on the color of the marble you pick out of the lottery box—Oh, I'm so sorry, Geek! You tell it."

The Geek sat back with a big smile on his face. "It's okay, honey. I don't mind a bit. You just proved you're a fan. Wouldja like to make a commercial for me? With those gorgeous looks of yours, I know I could get some more viewers."

"Well," Bunny was flattered, "I'll think about it."

"How about the Great Skeeve? Is he a fan, too?"

"He doesn't watch game shows," I said flatly.

"Too bad. An endorsement like his would be worth a fortune." The Geek sighed. "Let's go congratulate the winners."

Chapter Twenty-Six

"Follow the yellow brick road."
I. JONES, PH.D

"And now," Schlein boomed, "the final team elimination! And, folks, we've seen plenty of teams eliminated down to the last player, right here! Yes, indeed, it's the Monster Monster Challenge!"

"Congrats to both of you," the Geek said. We had landed on the main floor. Bee was still pale from his ordeal, but he looked okay. I didn't want to have to call for a doctor, not when the group was so close to achieving its goal. Incredible danger still lay ahead. On the way down, Bunny had regaled me with a list of monsters that the teams had faced in this contest before. It read like a Who's Who in Killing and Dismemberment. The Geek was pulled aside to review a list one of the Sittacomedian girls had on her clipboard.

"Hey, babe," Crasmer said, leering at Pologne. "Why are you hanging around with lowlifes like that Klahd? You ought to come over to our team. We're the winners. Not second-rate species like those."

Pologne snarled at him. "Are you insulting my friends, you ugly creature?" She raised a manicured set of talons and beckoned dangerously. "Come on over here and say that again!"

"Now, now," I said, getting in between them. "Nice job you did on the last round," I congratulated the Pervish champion. I gave him a hearty slap on the back with a solid magikal kicker. It knocked him stumbling. I grinned at my students, hoping none of them could penetrate my disguise. "Good luck to all of you in the final round."

"Thanks," Crasmer said.

I turned to the Sorcerer's Apprentices. "That was heroic of you, kid," I said, slapping Bee on the back in turn. "It ain't every demon who can face a bowl of Pervish food and live."

"Well, it wasn't the first time," Bee admitted. "Master S— my last teacher got me to try it."

"Like it?"

"Not a chance! No offense, sir!"

Apparently the name of Skeeve was not to be said out loud in this venue. I was amused.

Jinetta shot me a conspiratorial wink. "*His teacher* had us try a lot of things we would never have done before."

"Like teaming up," Melvine put in. "I'm not much for running with packs, but these kids have gotten to be my best friends."

"We put up with him," Pologne said. The two of them made faces at each other, but I could tell it was affectionate banter. I hoped Markie could see it from wherever she was watching. Maybe I *had* launched M.Y.T.H., Inc., Mark II.

Tolk leaned against Freezia, who was idly scratching his ears. The Canidian perked up suddenly, and came ambling over on all fours to sniff my wrist up and down.

"Hey, cut that out!" I roared.

"Sure sure sure," Tolk said, retreating. Instead of the suspicious expression he had worn before, he had a silly grin on his face.

"Oops," Bunny said.

"I better get out of here before Bee does Dispell on me," I whispered to her. I turned to the contestants. "Good luck to you all, and may the best team win."

We hurried back to the bubble.

The Geek did his round of handshakes then joined us.

"Now, we're gonna see some action," he said, rubbing his hands together. "We hire one of the local supermodels for this part."

A very slim, very tall Pervect female in a tight, pale yellow evening dress sashayed out of the darkness carrying a ceramic box that rattled as she walked. Wild whistling erupted.

"Now, calm down, gentlemen," Schlein instructed the audience, coming over to offer an elbow to the young lady. He escorted her to a fancy carved table. "It's time to draw lots then meet your monster!"

A hulking Pervect male came forward.

"Brucel will draw for the All-Pervects."

After a hasty conference, Tolk was urged up to the table.

"And Tolk for the Sorcerer's Apprentices."

I folded my arms to wait for the results. The Geek took my action as a criticism. He ran a finger around inside his collar.

"Aahz, I want you to know this is fair. It's entirely fair, I promise! I can't help it if the monsters are killers! It's all part of the game."

"Yeah, yeah." I steeled myself. This was my own doing. I had demanded a fair competition, and to make it fair, I had to stay out of it. This might be the hardest thing I had ever done. Whatever happened, I had prepared my students as well as I could, considering their inexperience, and I had ensured that they had an honest chance. They wanted to do this. They had come here willingly to be part of *Sink or Swim,* and they had earned the opportunity to go all the way. I couldn't do a thing without calling a halt to the entire proceedings. I looked down at my apprentices sadly. "I know."

Brucel stuck a hand into the box and came up with a marble.

"The All-Pervects have chosen orange!"

"Oooooh," breathed the audience.

Tolk planted one flat paw over his eyes and shoved the other into the lottery box. He handed the marble off to Schlein without looking at it.

"The Sorcerer's Apprentices have chosen purple!"

"Aaaaah," the audience responded.

"We'll be back in a moment, after this word from Duzzido, the detergent that can get any stain out of your finest clothing! Duzzido it? You bet it does!"

The stage went black for thirty very long seconds.

"Welcome our final two teams!" Schlein announced as the lights came up again. "First, the home team, those guys and gals in green—the All-Pervects! Yes, here they are, Pervect in every way! Welcome your home team!"

The All-Pervects, whittled down to five members by the preceding rounds, stepped into the spotlight from the right. They had on fresh jumpsuits of pale green that contrasted well with their complexions, but did not conceal the bandages around a wrist here, an ear there. They looked grimly determined.

"And the challengers!"

"Booo!"

I glanced down. The audience was actually cheering and waving its arms, but the sound that reached me was disapproval. The Geek shrugged.

"People like to have bad guys and good guys, Aahz. It's nothing personal. If, and it's a big if, they make it to the final round, we'll reverse the audience reaction. You'll see."

"Welcome the Sorcerer's Apprentices!"

I could see that my students were unnerved by the catcalls and hoots from the audience, but they stepped up bravely. They wore jumpsuits like the All-Pervects, but in a rainbow of different colors, none of which was green.

"Can't tell the players without distinguishing marks," the Geek explained.

"Except for the fact that one team is nothing but Pervects."

"Well, there's three on the other team. That made it okay with 29% of the focus group we're running if the Sorcerer's Apprentices should possibly manage to pull off a win. Honestly, Aahz, it's not likely."

"Yeah," I said shortly. "I knew that."

"You won't do anything rash to me if something goes wrong, will you?"

I looked at Bunny. She shook her head.

"No. Of course not."

"Well, it's never 'of course' with you, Aahz," the Geek said. "I just want your assurance, that's all. Can I offer you a side bet on the outcome?"

"NO!"

I turned my back on him.

There were two paths marked on the floor that led in opposite directions, one purple and one orange. From my vantage point, and from the views provided by a dozen crystal balls arrayed about the Geek's bubble, I had a view of a roofless, hatbox-shaped building. The paths led to diametrically opposing points that each led into a maze which took up half of the hatbox. Each maze was beautifully designed, with marble statues and pillars, tinkling fountains and potted plants for decoration. In the center, where the mazes met, was a set of double doors. Before them rose a pedamented pillar on which sat an ornate golden key, of the hefty variety chatelaines used to rap the knuckles of lazy servants.

"That's the door to the Chamber of Success," Bunny explained. "The team that gets there first has to go through to win. There are traps and deadfalls in the maze, and the walls move around to confuse the teams."

I nodded. I was much more concerned with a sealed chamber the shape of a drum in the center of each maze. Fire and smoke issued from carved openings in the walls of the drum in the orange sector. Cascades of hot sparks flew out of the sealed room in the purple sector. Both concealed monsters were roaring and banging around inside their prisons. The very walls shook.

The teams entered the maze. I could follow all of the action easily, in one or more of the crystal balls in the Geek's floating office. The All-Pervects went into their half like an army infiltrating enemy territory. One of them went first while the others covered him from the entrance. As soon as he signaled that he was safe, the others followed one at a time.

"Hup! Hup, hup, hup!" they chanted.

So, they'd practiced before they came on the show, too. No team was as inexperienced as the oath of amateur status would lead one to believe. They were simply unpaid. I grinned to myself.

The point man trotted down the first corridor. He reached the corner and paused, waiting for his companions. When they had all reached his location, he set out again, only to disappear from sight.

"Ayieeeee!"

"Deadfall," the Geek said. "You warn them and warn them and warn them, and they still all fall into the first one. I just won a thousand gold pieces on that. Sucker bet."

The Pervect's friends hauled him out. They felt their way along more cautiously, refusing to trust the floor unless they tested it first.

The Geek's engineers had a surprise around the next corner for those who used a toe instead of magik to try out the floor. A female Pervect, in her first turn on point, prodded a tile with a cautious foot. She looked up at the sudden whistling noise above her head. A gigantic weight flattened her to the ground. The others yanked her out from underneath it and propped her up against the wall. She looked winded and bruised. The team leader spoke to her in a low voice. She waved them away. They hup-hup-hupped onward.

I turned my attention to my students. They, too, had approached the maze with caution. Pologne, the research expert, was talking, probably giving them statistics on which way to turn at each crossroads. Bee kept track of the direction they were going, navigating by the stars overhead. Melvine was at the head of the group. The deadfall took him by surprise, but his reactions were quicker than the Pervect's had been. He only dropped a foot before he caught himself and hovered over the empty square.

"Nyah, nyah, nyah," he shouted, thumbing his nose at the sky. "Is that the best you can do?"

"Boy, that kid has attitude," the Geek said, looking pleased. "The crystals caught that. Great stuff!"

"Not that way," Bunny shrieked as the team turned right. That path led through a narrow gap in shrubbery to a dead end. As the students turned back, the plants reached out thorny tendrils to grab them.

"And the Sorcerer's Apprentices have found the Throttle Vines," Schlein announced. "Will they choke, or will they get past them?"

I was distracted at that moment by a loud roar. The All-Pervects had reached the big chamber in the middle of their maze where the monster waited. The huge container rocked wildly.

Bang!

The top flew off, and a twenty-foot-long red dragon crawled out of the box, hissing and tossing its head. It spotted the Pervects, and issued a stream of fire. The Pervects backed up into the nearest niche to confer. I saw them pretending to pound something, or throttling imaginary necks as they ran over their options.

A cloud of leaves blew upward from the left half of the building. My students jogged out of the dead end, unwinding pieces of vine from their limbs. They had escaped from the Throttle Vines, and were just a few paces behind their opponents in reaching the monster's chamber in their own maze. As soon as one of them set foot in the room, lightning began to shoot out through the container's walls, smashing the urns and statuary arrayed about the walls of the small enclosure. Melvine and Pologne flew upward. The rest retreated around the nearest wall.

"Make that louder," I said, pointing at the image. "I want to hear what they're saying!"

"Is that a weather elemental?" Pologne asked Melvine as they lit down near the others.

"How should I know?" he asked. "Do you want me to go and knock on the door?"

"That sounds like a really good idea," the Pervect snarled back. "There are only a thousand dimensions inhabited by lightning-spitters. Think you can get home town and date of birth, too?"

"You're the researcher—you ask it!"

"Now, stop it, you two," Jinetta said, pushing them apart. "We need to go through that room. We haven't much time."

"Jinetta, it's breaking out," Bee said. He had been keeping an eye on the room. They all peered around the edge of the doorway. A huge catlike backside reared up out of the ruins of the container, topped by a translucent, jointed tail with a stinger. The tail plunged down and stabbed the floor, then it reared up.

ZAP!

A lightning bolt shot out of the creature's backside. It went out the door, narrowly missing the team, and impacted on the far wall, destroying the bas relief of a shepherd and some kind of woolly ruminant native to Perv.

"A Manticore!" Freezia shouted. "It's a Manticore! Oh, no!"

"All right," Jinetta said, patting the air with her hands. "We know how to deal with one. We've done it before. Everyone calm down. Stay away from its tail. Don't let it grab you in those paws. The jaws are strong, too. Freezia, are you ready to levitate? Together we might be able to lift it."

Freezia felt the air.

"The lightning's sapped the magik!" she cried. "I've only got about half of what I stored when we started."

"I'm full," Bee said. "I used magik to Cantrip over that moving floor section, but I replenished my store as soon as I did it."

"So did I," Tolk said.

"I had to use some not to fall when the trapdoor opened up," Melvine said. "And flying takes up some energy."

"That's only three of us with enough magik," Jinetta said. "Well, then, perhaps we can capture it."

"Do you see a gum-gorse tree anywhere?" Melvine asked, baring his teeth. "We're toast!"

"We don't have to make it adhere to anything," Jinetta said, remaining amazingly calm. "All we have to do is get past it. We have proven that they are easy to confuse."

"When they're drunk," Bee reminded her. "This monster's sober as a judge."

"Even after Tolk cured Evad's headache he remained slower in the uptake than we are," Jinetta countered. "We will keep his senses busy until all of us, or at least one, can pass him and get through the rest of the maze. Only one of us needs to secure the key to win!"

"Good idea," Melvine said. "What do you want us to do?"

"Ready one of your tornadoes," Jinetta instructed. "It won't matter if you have any force left after that. Freezia, use your retrieval spell to pull its tail to one side. We don't want it aiming lightning at any of us. Tolk, you're good at dodging. Keep it busy."

"What about me?" Bee asked.

"I have an idea: can you reverse your Cantrip spell to make someone clumsy?"

Bee grinned. "I never needed it before," he said. "I was always clumsy enough on my own. But I'll try."

"Ready?" Jinetta asked, holding out her hand. The others piled theirs on hers, palms down. "Break!"

The team crept over the threshold. There must have been an alarm in the floor, because the Manticore, or rather its back half, redoubled its efforts, shooting lightning bolts and jabbing around with its spike. The students had to dash to get behind chunks of fallen marble. Melvine started twirling his finger in a circle. A tiny cyclone appeared on his palm. I was impressed how much the spell had been refined over the last several weeks. He tossed it up and down as if it was a coin, and sauntered out into the center of the room.

"Hey, Manticore," Melvine taunted. "Your mother stings her own butt! The city dump called. Your new face is ready. Hey, I hear your application for village idiot was accepted."

At the sound of his voice, the Manticore's head went up and his tail went down. He spun in a circle, his lion face the very picture of joy. I noted that he had pale whiskers, one of which was bent.

"Cupy!" shouted the Manticore.

"Evad?" Melvine exclaimed, breaking out in a huge grin. He threw the mini-tornado over his shoulder, where it sputtered into nothingness. "No way!"

The huge being came loping over to seize Melvine in a big hug and roll over with him in its paws. "Oh, Cupy, good see you!"

"Evad!" The rest of the Sorcerer's Apprentices recognized the Manticore that we had extracted from the town of Humulus. They rushed over to pet and hug him. I found myself grinning like a complete idiot. The contest was in the bag now.

"Evad?" the Geek echoed, rising to his feet in outrage. "They KNOW my Manticore? I'm going to call a halt to this contest. This isn't fair!" He started to lower the bubble. "We'll start over with new monsters."

I put my hand on his shoulder and shoved him down.

"Who says it isn't fair?" I demanded. "Do you think we live in a vacuum? The chances that a couple of demons might have met in the past is unlikely, sure, given the number of beings in the universe, but are you going to penalize them because it happened?

"And lose all that money? The audience wants a fight, Aahz, a fight! I'm going to throw a Minotaur in there. Maybe a Giant Squid, too. That'll up the ante for the outcome!"

"So, it's money, huh?" I snarled. "You do have bets against the Sorcerer's Apprentices."

The Geek backed away, his hands up in surrender. "Easy, easy, Aahz! If I didn't know better I'd think that *you're* the sorcerer they're talking about, except the last time I saw you you didn't have any magik."

"Things change," I gritted out, "but they never had Aahz for a teacher. That I guarantee. They'd have been a different group if they ever did."

"But what about the contest?" the Geek pleaded. "If the audience doesn't see a little blood, they'll riot!"

I glanced over at the Pervect side. There was plenty of blood. The team had managed to roll the dragon over on his back. Two of the All-Pervects were binding its legs with magik, but it kept kicking free. I blamed the Manticore's lightning for draining the force lines. They almost had it, though.

"They still have to get to the key first, right?"

"Right, Aahz," the Geek said, his face hopeful. "Is there any way you'll let me—slow them down a little?"

He didn't have to. The Manticore was so happy to meet his friends again that he kept pulling them back into the room as they tried to leave.

"...And when got back from shore leave, escort mission to tropics. Very nice! Hot! Perfumey! You would like! Ever want to come?"

"Maybe some day," Jinetta said, "but Evad, we have to get—" She sidled toward the opposite door, but he enveloped her with a friendly paw.

"And Klahd Skeeve give good idea, sell venom. Visiting wizard very interested! Start sideline with friends. Have money for drinks all around. So, last week, Captain says special mission. Good publicity for Navy! Volunteer? I say me! Here I am. And here is you!"

"That's great that you found a use for your talent," Bee assured him. "We're happy to see you, but we've got to go."

"No go! I buy drinks. Skeeve kind. Where Skeeve?"

"Skeeve's not here," Tolk assured him. "Just us. We're happy to see you, too!"

Doubtfully, Evad sniffed, his big furry nose twitching. "Smell Skeeve. Where Skeeve?"

"No, he's not here. Really really really."

"Let's get organized here," Jinetta said. "Evad, we're very glad you are safe, but we need to make it through this maze before the other team does!"

A frustrated roar from the other side of the wall made Evad raise his eyebrows. "What that?"

"Other team," Freezia said. She dropped into another language that consisted of growls and hisses. She must have gotten interested in Manticore after our previous encounter and taken the time to learn some. "We're in a competition. We have to get to the middle of this maze and secure a golden key before they do or we lose!"

"You not lose!" Evad declared. "I carry! Which way?"

It was going to be a close contest. The All-Pervects had succeeded in hog-tying the dragon, which lay on the floor, flaming everything within sight. With only a few injuries and no fatalities, the Pervects managed to flee the room and headed off into the second half of the maze.

The Pervects and Bee clung to the broad, furry back. Tolk led them out the door.

"Watch it watch it watch it!" the Canidian said over his shoulder. "Sometimes the floor falls out from under you!"

"That way," Pologne said, pointing right.

The All-Pervects turned left.

"Go left!" The Sorcerer's Apprentices reached a T-intersection. Melvine flew upward to look out at the top of the maze. At the lip, he flattened out like a bird smacking into a window.

"Magikal force field," the Geek explained. "They all try to do that."

"Can't get out to see!" Melvine yelled.

"Oh, I wish I had my detector," Pologne said. "I hate not being able to use technology! We'll go right again." The Manticore galloped forward, only to have to back out of a narrow spot that led to a blank wall. Pologne cried out in frustration.

"All right, it must be three rights and *two* lefts! Left again! Now!"

The All-Pervects cleared their last right turn and let out a cheer at the sight of the pillar. They were moving quickly. I could see victory written on their faces.

Suddenly, the Sorcerer's Apprentices burst into view, riding on the back of a full-grown Manticore. The furry beast galloped into the circular chamber just a pace ahead of the home team. The beast swung wide, depositing its passengers onto the floor near the wall.

Determined, the Pervects poured on extra speed, heading for the pillar. Crasmer, at the lead, was just about to take the key off the pillar when a canine head ducked under his hand, seized the golden object in his mouth and gave them a friendly smile.

"Sorry sorry sorry," Tolk said. "I believe that's ours."

Chapter Twenty-Seven

"Only one will remain."
D. TRUMP

"No, for the last time, it's not illegal to use the monster from the Monster Monster Challenge as a steed," the Geek said as the All-Pervects surrounded him, shouting for justice. "There's nothing in the rule books. You can do anything you want to the monster as long as you get past it to the Final Chamber. Didn't Schlein say anything goes? Well, it does!"

"I heard them talking to that Manticore," Grunt argued. "That's collusion."

"They picked a marble at random out of the box, same as you," the Geek said, passing his hand over his horned head wearily. "It was a one-in-a-billion chance that they had met the guy before. Look, you might have known the dragon. There was one on the Troll team—you saw him. I'm sorry, fellows. The decision is final. The Sorcerer's Apprentices won. Come on, let's go back and smile for the audience. You don't want the rest of the universe to see Pervects as sore losers, do you?"

"Why the hell not?" Crasmer asked.

Bunny and I stood by as the All-Pervects let themselves be bandaged and daubed with makeup by the Geek's numerous assistants. I didn't want any trouble. I wore my most fearsome expression, which Bunny assured me looked just like Aahz with a hangover. Inside I was beaming with joy. My students had won!

Tananda and Markie seemed to shimmer into existence beside us. "Congratulations, Hero," Tananda crowed. "That was fantastic! I was all set for a big fight, but this was better! You should have seen the confusion in the ranks, there. No one knew what to do about it."

"They were all set to mop up blood," Markie pouted, still in character, "but no one liked them being friends. That's *mean*."

"What's next?" I asked.

Bunny held up one finger. "Only the final ordeal, to see who wins the grand prize."

"Ordeal?" I swallowed nervously. "What kind of ordeal?"

"Well, it varies," Tananda said. "On Zurik it was whoever could dodge the most bullets. That got a little messy, even for Gnomes. Mmm, I can't remember what *Sink or Swim: Mantico* did."

"That was the great Lightning Battle," Markie giggled.

"These all sound kinda fatal," I said.

It came back to my friends that they were dealing this time with people that they knew. That put a different face on the subject.

"All we can do is hope for the best," Bunny said.

"I think we can do better than that," I said. "I'll just remind him that for every one of those kids who gets hurt, I'll pull off one of his limbs."

A drum roll came from the invisible orchestra. Schlein stepped forward.

"And, now, for the final contest, for the all-over winner, the being who will be awarded a once-in-a-lifetime job with Mistress Monestruc, we present The Final Ordeal! As always, the fairness of this contest will be decided by Frankenmuth, Spalanade and Rockrose, our accountants." Three Sittacomedians in blue suits and striped ties stepped forward.

"Does anyone know what we're going to be doing?" Freezia asked. "I'm still tired from the last couple of stunts."

"Will it be like any of those?" Bee asked.

"It could be worse," Melvine said grimly. "I remember one on Trollia where the players threw knives at each other."

Tananda scoffed. "That one was nothing. Bronze knives that didn't go even two inches into the contestants' fur."

"Well, maybe that's so," Bee said. "So the contest might be geared to the team itself?"

"But we're not the home team," Freezia pointed out. "We might get through it, but you're not Pervects."

"I won't hurt any of you," Jinetta insisted. "You're my friends!"

"Whatever happens," Pologne said stolidly, "if I win and any of you survive, I'll give you all jobs—if I have any hiring authority."

"If I make it, I'll heal everyone," Tolk swore.

Emotions were having a battle royal on Melvine's face. "I really want to win this, guys. But I'll do it fairly, I promise."

"I'll throw it, if I have to," Bee said. "I can't hurt my team. What would Sergeant Swatter say?"

I cleared my throat and turned it into a growl. "He'd say do your best, and play fair."

"Gosh, you're right, sir. You must know Swatter pretty well."

"I do," I said, clearing my throat uncomfortably. "And I know the kind of people he'd pick for a squad. Do what you think he would do."

Bee grinned unexpectedly. "He'd figure out some way everybody could come out of it alive, sir. And Master Skeeve would figure out a way we could all win."

"I—He sure would. Good luck, kid. Good luck to all of you."

"Thanks, Aahz," they chorused.

Schlein struck a pose. "Step forward the Sorcerer's Apprentices!"

The team appeared in a spotlight. They were holding one another's hands and looking young and scared.

We all went up to sit in the bubble with the Geek. The Sorcerer's Apprentices were a team. I was proud of them. In fact, I was sort of proud of me. They had absorbed what I'd been trying to hammer into them about teamwork and delegation and finding their own strengths. I guess I'd done it right. Whatever happened from now on was all their own. I wished them victory.

Schlein swooped in upon the cluster of students and peered at the audience over their shoulders.

"The Sorcerer's Apprentices will decide The Final Question with a killer round of *Rock Paper Scissors!*"

I gawked.

"Rock-Paper-Scissors?" I looked at the Geek. "After all those brutal rounds?"

The Deveel laughed at me. "You must not watch the show much," he said, leaning back and snapping his fingers. A crystal decanter rose out of a drawer and poured him a dram. "If it looks like the home team is favored, we *always* have a nonlethal competition set up. The ratings drop pretty badly if we kill off the locals."

"Yeah, but that's a kiddie game. You're insulting your audience."

"S—Aahz!" Bunny said. "You *want* something more dangerous?"

I waved away her protest. My businessman instincts had kicked in.

"Won't this be the opposite of what they expect?"

The Geek sat up. "You think this won't get lively? Watch how we do it. Special effects! Music! Lighting! And there's Schlein giving the live commentary. The man's worth his weight—er, a LOT in gold."

The audience was already chanting. "We want the champion! We want the champion!"

"You all know the rules," the Sittacomedian instructed the group. "As soon as the count is complete, present your hand. We're playing this for—sudden death!"

I gulped.

The Geek snorted. "That just means it's not a round-robin contest, Aahz."

"Oh," I said in a small voice.

"Ready—play!"

Spotlights chased around the floor, and sweeping orchestral music boomed up.

"One two three!" the Sorcerer's Apprentices chanted. Pinpoint spots lit their hands individually. Two were holding paper. Three of the others were holding rocks. One had a scissors. Images of parchment scrolls, glittering gemstones, and one pair of gleaming shears overlay the students' hands. The shears attacked one scroll. The remaining parchment covered one gem. The other two gems moved to smash the scissors.

"Tolk, out! Freezia, out! Bee, out!"

BOOM boom *boom*, came from the drums.

"Three at once," the Geek crowed. "This is *great*."

I groaned with disappointment for the three students who walked, shoulders hunched, away into the darkness. The music struck up again, more tense than before. The Geek was right: it was thrilling.

The remaining three—Pologne, Jinetta and Melvine—eyed one another suspiciously. Melvine tried to fake out the others.

"One two—not ready," he said, drawing his hand back.

"Stop that!" Pologne snapped.

"We will go on three," Jinetta said firmly. "No hesitation. Ready?"

"Oh, all right," Melvine said sulkily.

"One two three!"

"Paper!" Schlein announced. "Identical choices!" Three rolls of parchment hovered in between the group.

"One two three!"

"Scissors!" Three pairs of scissors.

"Paper!" Three scrolls.

"This is remarkable," Bunny said. "The odds of all of them choosing the same item three times running is—"

"Nine hundred seventy-two to one," the Geek said, rubbing his hands together. "Hold on, I've got to get some action going on this."

He leaned over one of the crystal balls on his desk and started talking to the Deveel who popped up in it. I ignored the complicated negotiations as I watched my students eying one another.

"Rock!" Three gemstones twirled and threw colored lights on their faces.

"Paper!"

"Paper!"

"Scissors!"

"Incredible," Tananda said. "How long can they go on like that?"

"I want to assure you, ladies and gentlemen," the smooth voice of Schlein said, "that there is no collusion between these three individuals. What you are seeing here is unique in the history of *Sink or Swim.*"

"Paper!"

"Rock!"

But even phenomena had to end sooner or later. Pologne stuck her hand out with two fingers parted.

"Scissors!" she cried.

"Rock!" chorused Melvine and Jinetta.

"Ooooh," said the audience.

The music rose chillingly. Pologne stared at her hand with an expression of utter betrayal just before the spotlight cut off, leaving her in darkness.

Melvine hunched over and faced Jinetta. "Just you and me now, doll," he said.

"Go," Jinetta said. "One two three."

"Rock!" Once again, they chose the same item. The audience was cheering wildly. The fireflies were drawing hearts, flowers and fireworks.

"Paper!"

"Scissors!"

"Scissors!"

"Rock!" Melvine shouted, shoving a fist into the light.

"Sciss—" Jinetta realized even before she finished the word that she had chosen a loser. "Scissors."

The orchestra rose into a triumphant fanfare. Schlein rushed over to grab Melvine around the shoulders.

"Congratulations, Melvine! You are the winner of *Sink or Swim: Perv!*"

"Me?" he asked, in a voice that rose to a squeak.

He looked dazed.

"Snap out of it, kid," Schlein hissed at him.

Melvine looked up at him in astonishment. Schlein beamed.

"Come on over here, Cupy. You're setting out on a whole new life. Tell all of us how you feel!"

For the first time since I had met him, the Cupy guy was lost for words.

"Well, sir, I promise I will do my best, uh, especially if I have my friends around me."

He glanced over at the team as the lights came up on the rest of the Sorcerer's Apprentices. Pologne and Freezia were sulking a little, but offered sickly smiles when the spotlights hit them.

"I'm sure you will," Schlein said.

Suddenly the two of them were surrounded by magicians wielding crystal balls to catch every angle.

"And, now, I want to bring out the woman who is the unseen presence behind *Sink or Swim*. Will you welcome the elusive, the marvelous, the very rich Mistress Montestruc!"

A narrow way opened to admit a tall and formidable-looking woman with thick auburn hair.

"Congratulations, Melvine," she said, patting him on the head. "You are a very interesting person. I have been watching you since the contest began. Your audacity and confidence interest me. I don't like yes-men, and I don't like people who can't think for themselves. Therefore, I am giving you an assignment that will be a challenge. I'm making you the Chief Executive Officer of one of my favorite business enterprises, Brandex!"

I joined the audience in a general gasp. Who hadn't heard of Brandex? It manufactured a little of everything you could find in almost every store in every dimension I'd ever been. Most small magikal goods probably had "Brandex" imprinted somewhere. They weren't necessarily the top of the line, but they were fairly sound and usually cheap to buy.

"I'm putting you into a position of authority with full hiring and firing power. You'll have some tough decisions to make. You're expected to make a profit, of course. What do you say?"

"Can I hire my own executive staff?" Melvine asked at once.

The great lady laughed, and the audience joined in, urged by Schlein and the fireflies.

"Of course," she said. "Why do you ask?"

Melvine looked uncharacteristically modest. "Well, maybe you didn't notice, but I'm not the natural leader of my team. Jinetta is. I only won by a stroke of luck. I'm not the best researcher like Pologne, or the best magician in the group like Freezia. I'll never be as courageous or organized as Bee or as compassionate as Tolk. In fact, if you rolled them together, you'd have a much better CEO than you'd get out of me. That's the truth. I want them on my team. I'd never have gotten here if not for all of them. If I can't have them," his face screwed up as if he was about to start crying, "I don't want the job."

"Of course you may hire them," Mistress Montestruc said. "I will be pleased to have such talented people on my payroll."

Melvine sighed, and his shoulders slumped. "That's a relief."

The shoulders, and his head, continued to drop downward.

"What is happening to him?" the lady cried. "He is shrinking!"

Markie burst through the crowd to hug her nephew.

"You did it!" She hugged him. "You must have broken the mental block that was keeping you a big baby. You're normal size again!"

Melvine looked down at himself. He stood about two and a half feet tall, much more in proportion to his looks than he had at four feet. His new, tiny body swam in the jumpsuit.

"Yeah!" he cheered, jumping up to punch the sky. "I'm the Cupy! I'm the Cupy!"

Reporters crowded in to interview the winner. Melvine floated up to hover over their heads in the oversized garment, cracking jokes and generally basking in the attention. Markie stayed nearby to keep an eye on him.

The magicians stepped back to view the Geek as he came over to shake hands with the All-Pervects. We followed him out onto the arena floor.

"Sorry you didn't manage to achieve a victory on home soil," he told them. His face was full of genuine regret. I was willing to bet it was for the lost bets, not the disappointed Pervects. "But you know, there's only one prize on *Sink or Swim*. Thanks for playing."

"Yeah, thanks a lot," Crasmer said shortly. "Come on, guys. Let's go get drunk."

"Yeah."

"And there they go, your home team!" Schlein announced, as a spotlight hit them.

Not bothering to turn around to acknowledge the cheers and applause, the All-Pervects stamped off the stage.

Chapter Twenty-Eight

"I think it's time to leave."
LOUIS XIV

The Sorcerer's Apprentices came over to where Bunny, Markie, Tananda and I stood. Jinetta stood on tiptoe to give me a big kiss on the cheek.

"Gosh, thanks for everything, Mr. Aahz. You're fantastic. And your partner is the best. *I wish we could tell him how grateful we are,*" she added.

"Uh-huh." I couldn't miss the meaning. "I, uh, I see that Tolk told you."

Jinetta grinned down at the Canidian, who was leaning against my leg. "He did. We all hope you aren't upset that we didn't tell you why we needed your help."

"Not any longer. I have to admit, when I found out you had come here, I was a little upset that you didn't tell me about the contest."

"Well, with all the ordeals you were putting us through, we all thought you knew," Jinetta said, surprised. "I thought you were totally savvy. Was it all by accident?"

"Er—yes," I admitted, a little unhappily. "I didn't connect the time frame with the beginning of the new SOS contest. I just thought you really wanted some practical experience before you went into the business world. Using ideas I scooped from some of the Crystal Ether network was pure coincidence."

Jinetta and the others looked more admiring than ever.

"It takes a big soul to admit that," she said. "You could have lied and told us you did know. I like your honesty. No wonder Aunt Vergetta thinks you're the spink's left nostril. Wait until I tell her! You're a terrific teacher, Skeeve." She crushed me in an enormous hug. The others followed suit, leaving me gasping.

"Gee, that's really nice of you," I said, embarrassed.

"How come you didn't tell us you were coming?" Tolk asked.

"I didn't want to interfere with your style. If you knew I was here, you might not have relied on your own skills to get through."

"And he's been tossed off Perv," Melvine put in, returning from his interview. He was still floating on air. "He's not supposed to be here at all. That's what the disguise is for." He smiled down at me sweetly.

"How much more did you hear while eavesdropping?" I demanded.

"Enough," Melvine said with satisfaction. "No good blackmail stuff, though. Hey, watch who you're talking to! I'm the new CEO of Brandex Enterprises. These are my executive vice presidents in charge of—the things they're good at." He waved a vague hand. "Do you want a job? I'd be honored to have you. Mistress Montestruc's giving me a humongous budget to find talent."

"No, thanks," I said. "I've still got a lot of—research to do."

"Too bad. We're gonna do big things!"

"I'm happy to do little things for the moment," I said. "I think I can be content with having launched a whole new generation of magicians on their way, and I'm glad to have gotten through this without having been detected."

"Hear, hear," Bunny agreed.

"Listen," Melvine said, confidentially. "I've gotta apologize. I took the money out of your strongbox and put it in Jinetta's briefcase. I thought if I could get the three little maids from school disqualified as pros I'd have a better chance of winning." He made a face. "Who knew I'd *need* them all so I could win?"

"Teamwork pays off every time," I said. "You know that now. But who set off Massha's ring?"

"That was me," Tolk said, in a very small voice. "Sorry sorry sorry. It was a joke, just like you said. Then I couldn't turn it off. I'm a doctor, not a munitions expert! Forgive me? The others have."

"You bet," I said, ruffling his ears. "I'm proud of all of you."

Bee blushed. The Pervects giggled. "Thank you, Skeeve!"

"Aahz! Aahzmandius!" a voice boomed out.

I turned in the direction of the voice. It was familiar, but I couldn't place it. Then I saw her.

Waddling towards me, dressed in what could have been the same faded, tentlike house dress she had been wearing when I visited her a couple of years back, was Aahz's mother, the Duchess. The elderly Pervect glared through her little glasses.

"Where is he? My little boy! My ungrateful son! Holding back on his mother's millions! No, he thinks that I can get by on air! And there he is!"

Suddenly, I found myself under a spotlight. All the magicians who had been interviewing the Geek turned to cover me. I saw my face multiplied a thousand times, each image wearing the same gudgeonlike expression of horrified astonishment.

"He comes to play in this fancy game, but he doesn't come to see his own mother! Just when I'm waiting to make another investment. I can't wait for the capital, you stingy boy! What will the neighbors think? There you are!"

"Duchess," I said, weakly, backing away from her. My escape was blocked by the dozens of people crowding in to see what all the shouting was about. "How nice to see you."

"My son!" She threw herself at me. "You've lost weight!"

No one, especially not a dozen, multi-focus crystal balls could possibly have missed when her arms sank right through the meaty sides of "Aahz" and wrapped around my much slimmer body.

"It's a disguise spell!" someone shouted.

The Geek went wide-eyed. "If you're not Aahz, there's only one other person who knows everything he does—Skeeve!"

"Skeeve!"

The guards on the side of the stage looked at one another, and started heading in my direction. I fought loose from the Duchess's embrace. I had to make a quick getaway. I concentrated on my comfortable little study on Klah, and squeezed my eyes shut.

"Not so fast, buddy," a harsh voice said.

I opened my eyes. No BAMF. My transportation spell had not worked. The arena guards had been supplemented by the Perv police force. I stopped counting after the first twenty uniformed officer. The most decorated, whom I assumed had been the one who spoke, held up a short silver wand.

"Trying to escape," he said, one eyebrow raised. "Just what we'd have thought from someone with your record."

"Isn't that the Great Skeeve?" one of the magicians asked.

"Yeah! Get a good angle. We can get this on the evening news!"

"Just a minute, sergeant," Jinetta said, stepping in between us. "What's the problem here?"

"This Klahd has been exiled from Perv, lady," the officer said. "Having broken the terms of his parole, he's going to spend a couple of years in jail thinking about why he ever bothered to come back."

"Sir, I believe you might be mistaken," Pologne said, adding her slight frame to help shield me from view. "This is a game show. There have been a lot of illusions employed during the course of this contest. Why would you think this is the real Skeeve? This is a Klahdish wizard Mr. Geek hired to impersonate him. He's one of the monsters for the Monster Monster Challenge. Wouldn't you be afraid to face a wizard of his caliber?"

"Frankly, no," the sergeant said, looking me up and down. "He looks like the real thing to me."

"A lot of Klahds look alike," Freezia said. "Are you sure it's really him? It could be that one over there?"

Bee caught the hint and promptly Datspelled himself into a duplicate of me.

"Or one of those two over here?"

Pologne and Jinetta became Skeeves and started moving around me. I took one step back and to the right. Tananda grinned and nodded toward the half dozen people on my left, now all wearing my face.

"Stop that!" the officer barked. "This isn't funny, lady. All of you back away from the perpetrator."

"Which one do you mean?" Jinetta asked, innocently.

"I'll show you which one." The officer pointed the wand at us. Just then, Tolk gathered himself and leaped into the air, grabbing the wand out of his hand. He galloped about ten feet away and lowered his forequarters, wagging his tail with glee.

"Come here, Canidian. Give me that!"

"Come and get it!" Tolk shouted. "Let's play keepaway!" He dashed away into the darkness, pursued by ten policemen and two magicians with crystal balls. I backed into the crowd with the other Skeeve-faces. Something hit me on the shoulder. It was Melvine.

"Go on," he whispered in my ear. "Get out of here while the going's good! See you around! I owe you. We all do."

I didn't hesitate a second.

BAMF!

Safely back in the inn on Klah, I threw myself into my easy chair. Tananda slid into the cushioned recess with me. There wasn't really room for both of us, but I didn't mind. Markie served us all a glass of wine. I took a grateful sip and let out a long breath.

Bunny opened Bytina and reestablished the connection to the thread of ether displaying the *Sink or Swim* arena. There was no sign of the police or any other disturbance. Melvine was in the center of the stage wearing a gold medal and waving to the people as the rest of my students stood behind him and smiled. The Geek came out and gave Mistress Montestruc a huge bouquet of flowers. Names and titles appeared over the faces, and the orchestra struck up once again with farewell music. Schlein's voice boomed out.

"This has been a Deveelishly Handsome Production."

"You did a good job," Bunny said, snapping Bytina shut. "If you weren't sure before that they are going to be all right, you should be now."

I dropped my eyes modestly. "I have to admit, I think I did all right for my first big teaching job."

"Your first?" Tananda asked. "You're going to do it again?"

"No!" I protested. "I mean—that's not what I mean—well, maybe," I added wistfully. "It was kind of fun. And I'd know more of what to do and what not to do in the future."

"That reminds me," Bunny said, tapping her toe impatiently on the floor. "What are you going to do about getting a piece of the fees Aahz collected from YOUR apprentices."

All three women looked at me expectantly.

Sheepishly, I took a sip from my glass. "That's one of the things I haven't really learned how to do yet."

Robert Lynn Asprin

Robert (Lynn) Asprin was born in 1946. While he has written some stand alone novels such as *Cold Cash War*, *Tambu*, *The Bug Wars* and also the Duncan and Mallory Illustrated stories, Bob is best known for his series: The *Myth Adventures of Aahz and Skeeve*; the *Phule's Company* novels; and, more recently, the *Time Scout* novels written with Linda Evans. He also edited the groundbreaking *Thieves' World* anthologies with Lynn Abbey. His most recent collaboration is *License Invoked* written with Jody Lynn Nye. It is set in the French Quarter, New Orleans where he currently lives.

Jody Lynn Nye

Jody Lynn Nye lists her main career activity as "spoiling cats." She has published 25 books, such as *Advanced Mythology*, fourth and most recent in her *Mythology* fantasy series (no relation), three SF novels, four novels in collaboration with Anne McCaffrey, including *The Ship Who Won*, edited a humorous anthology about mothers, *Don't Forget Your Spacesuit, Dear!*, and written over eighty short stories. Her latest books are *The Lady and The Tiger*, third in her Taylor's Ark series, and *Strong Arm Tactic*, first in the Wolfe Pack series. She lives northwest of Chicago with two cats and her husband, author and packager, Bill Fawcett.

Phil Foglio

Besides working on the Myth Series, Phil Foglio has been drifting through existence these last two decades, pretty much doing what ever he felt like, as long as he could make money at it. Currently, that would include *Girl Genius*, the comic to which he currently devotes his penciling and co-writing skills. He has done comics for DC, Marvel, Comico, First Comics, Dark Horse and WARP. He created *What's New* for Dragon magazine, and was even able to resell it thirteen years later to The Duelist magazine. They never noticed.

Phil has published a novel (*Illegal Aliens*, with Nick Pollotta), as well as a short story or two, and has scripted several comic series about battleships in space, super heros, giant robots, talking gorillas and five-year-old children. (Though not all at once).